THE THINGS W

Lisa Appignanesi has been a university lecturer in European Studies and was Deputy Director of London's Institute of Contemporary Arts. Her works of non-fiction include *Freud's Women* (with John Forrester), a biographical portrait of Simone de Beauvoir, and a history of cabaret. She has edited *The Rushdie File* and a number of books on contemporary culture. *The Things We Do For Love* is her fourth novel. Lisa Appignanesi lives in London with her two children.

By the same author

LISA APPIGNANESI

The Things We Do For Love

HarperCollins*Publishers*

HarperCollins*Publishers*
77–85 Fulham Palace Road,
Hammersmith, London W6 8JB

This paperback edition 1998
1 3 5 7 9 8 6 4 2

First published in Great Britain by
HarperCollins*Publishers* 1997

ISBN 0 00 649670 9

Set in Sabon by
Rowland Phototypesetting Ltd,
Bury St Edmunds, Suffolk

Printed and bound in Great Britain by
Caledonian International Book Manufacturing Ltd, Glasgow

For my son, Josh
Who does a great many things

As a man of desires, I go forth in disguise

PAUL RICOEUR

Without the possibility of a double life, there is no morality

ADAM PHILLIPS

ACKNOWLEDGEMENTS

I have received considerable help with the scientific aspects of this novel, in particular from Steven Rose, who welcomed me into his Open University laboratory and helped along the way to align science and story. I am also indebted to Daniela Rhodes, who kindly invited me into the MRC Laboratory of Molecular Biology in Cambridge, and to Kiyoshi Nagai, who talked to me about inventions and patents and led me to the patent lawyer, Claire Irving. In Prague, Jan Bures of the Institute of Physiology at the Academy of Sciences was both hospitable and helpful. In the United States, Monica and Douglas Holmes kindly provided me with essential information about the field of biotechnology.

Any mistakes are my very own.

I also owe debts of gratitude to my first readers and editors: my agent, Caradoc King; Nick Sayers and Susan Opie at HarperCollins; Suzette Macedo, who offers encouragement and perspicacity in equal measure. I am, as always, deeply indebted to my partner, John Forrester, who fills me with scientific lore, mans the temperamental machines, gives me a patience greater than my own and imbues our daughter Katrina with just a little of it. Thank you.

PART ONE

1

———✻———

From all appearances, Stephen Caldwell was not a man cut out for love.

He was neither tall nor small, old nor young, but depending on how he stood somewhere in between. His hair was an indeterminate brown and fell over his pale skin in the cropped lines that unrepentant barbers and preoccupied mothers inflict on fidgeting schoolboys. Behind the square specs, his eyes were as vague as the shape of his worn cords.

None of this might have mattered except that Stephen Caldwell moved as if his skin weren't his own. Perhaps he had yet to set up home in it.

On this wintry Friday in the last decade of our tired century, he was making his way up carpeted stairs to the deck of the cross-channel ferry which linked Dover to Calais. A fierce gust of wind greeted him as he pushed open the outer door. He gripped his large shoulder bag more firmly to his side and patted it once as if to reassure both himself and its contents. Then he propelled himself towards the precarious rail and watched the chalky cliffs, the avid swoop of the gulls.

He liked this palpable sense of England receding into the distance. First it dwindled into a picture postcard. Then the postcard became pattern, a series of lines and bumps, a contour on the horizon. And then, nothing. Just sky and sea and a trace in his memory which he could colour into being or not, as he chose.

He didn't need to take the ferry, of course. He could afford to fly or use the shuttle, but he preferred that last glimpse of the cliffs, symbol and substance of his island home. Then, the slow, unruffled going and the equally slow arrival. And in between an interim time made up only of buffeting winds and rocking sea and anonymity.

The slowness augmented the taste of his secrets.

Sometimes he thought that for him the ferry was really a way of walking to the Continent. As he was doing now. Fore and aft, upper deck, lower deck, quickly through the bars and restaurants smelling of tepid hamburger and massed bodies, more happily in the open air on the all but empty decks, wet from the light drizzle.

When he gauged they were over halfway there, he stopped in the men's room. He took some time to come out and when he did there was a difference about him. It wasn't only in the dark, flowing coat and Homburg he had donned or in the freshly shaven face. There was a new set to his shoulders, a conviction to his step which seemed also to have deepened the colour of his eyes. Only the way he patted his bag was instantly recognizable.

On the train at Calais, the woman opposite looked up at him once and then a second time and a third. He didn't return her glance.

Anglais, she thought. Englishman. And she craned her neck to look at the print of his book and check her assumption. The open pages showed diagrams and clusters of letters she couldn't interpret.

Aware of her prying eyes, Stephen at last gave her a quick, oblique smile. As if by rote, he tapped his bag again and drew it a little closer, before returning to his book.

The bag, the woman noted, was large and new and good, with a sturdy lock dangling from its side and an intriguing number of zippered compartments. A man who had something worth carrying, she speculated, and peered to make out the title of a silvery paperback tucked in a side pocket.

'*A Perfect . . .*' she read upside down, and strained to see the rest.

'Do you read English?' Stephen suddenly asked, in a very good approximation of French.

'Sometimes.' The woman smiled.

With a direct gaze and a hint of a grin, Stephen handed her the book. 'You might like it. It's all about spies.'

The woman laughed, cloaking embarrassment. Decidedly, she thought, these English were deceptive, full of surprises beneath their impassivity.

Maybe, after all, the man had as many compartments as his bag.

2

---*---

The post, as it always did on a Saturday, arrived with her second cup of coffee. The fact that she had barely slept and was feeling out of sorts could hardly be expected to make a difference.

Tessa Hughes pulled back the striped kitchen curtains to reveal a stretch of wintry garden. Bare branches of weigela and honeysuckle jostled against the murky brown of a shaky fence and a matching kennel. Even the startling red of the single remaining rose looked muted in the grey drizzle. And the corner rubbish bin had taken on a disproportionate prominence.

She rubbed her eyes and overlaid the scene with the brochure image of the sundrenched beach where she would soon be travelling for a holiday. Carefully, she inserted herself in her new black swimsuit against a stretch of silver sand and turquoise sea. She watched herself shake her hair out to give herself a sense of freedom, rub creams and oils into her skin. She could almost smell their sweet, heavy scent. But even they did nothing to lift her spirits. The dull patch of Cambridge garden was still there waiting for her like a tired skin, too tight to shed.

With a sigh, she padded over to the front door to pick up what the postman had left. A couple of bills, an invitation to win £100,000 if only she could be bothered to read through, scratch out, fill in pages of junk, a letter for Stephen, his name neatly handwritten, the 'Dr' prominent.

Irritation pricked at her. Yes, Stephen was distinctly one of its major components. She stared at the letter, had a savage desire to rip it in two, then in four, then in eight, until there was nothing left but a little heap of shreds. Instead, she walked up the stairs to his attic study. Out of habit, she raised her hand to knock, though she knew perfectly well he wasn't there, had left yesterday, had given her his abstracted goodbye nod and peck on the cheek before averting his face. As if he couldn't bear to touch her. As if he were going off to the office rather than abroad.

Tessa grimaced at her raised hand, at the tug of habit, at the empty courtesies that framed their life together, then prodded open the door with a jerk.

There it was. Stephen's study. The best room in the house really. Certainly the largest. Sky poured in through the high window, over the neatly ranked books, the soft wing-backed chair, the childhood microscope on a corner table, the polished mahogany desk which she had given him. It was a suitable setting for the man one of her ingratiating junior colleagues had recently dubbed, when she introduced them at a gathering, 'one of our foremost scientists'. The woman's voice had been lowered in awe as she'd said it and Tessa hadn't been certain if her preceding murmur of 'So that's Stephen Caldwell. Stephen Caldwell is your husband,' had signified surprise at Tessa being married to a man of such note or the man of such note being the man who had just turned away from them. If she had still been a person who laughed readily, Tessa would have done so then and dashed to recount the incident to Stephen. But she didn't laugh much any more and when she did, the sound had a hollowness to it.

Stephen's desk was bare today, devoid of papers and books and laptop. Its pristine bareness gave her a start. The thought sidled towards her that perhaps Stephen had not simply gone off yet again to one of his numerous conferences or meetings, but had gone for good.

Tessa tasted the thought. Wondered if it was a wish. Turned it over in her mouth. It gave off a slow excitement. Stephen gone. Why not? It might be for the best. She moved towards the desk to check her first impression. No, nothing. Bare. Then, in the far corner tucked between the three fossil rocks which Stephen used as paperweights, she saw his plastic security pass and key ring. Odd, that. Stephen usually carried his keys.

Tessa placed the letter she was carrying in the middle of the desk and picked up the keys. She dangled them in front of her as if they were some tempting bauble, put them down again, was about to pick them up for a second time when the telephone startled her with its ring. Stephen's phone. His own line. Before she could decide to pick up the receiver, she heard the click of the answering machine and then a voice. A woman. Soft, measured tones, speaking French.

'Tu ne m'oublieras pas. J'insiste.'

That was all she caught before the whirring and click of the machine took over. Tessa stared at it, hesitated. She wanted to hear that voice again, knew at the same time that there hadn't been much more to the message than that reminder: 'You won't forget me. I insist.' No name. Just the intimacy of a voice that knew it would be recognized.

Funny. She had never considered the possibility of another woman. Even now, with those intimate tones replaying themselves in her ear and a quick calculation of Stephen's numerous trips over the last years, let alone over the lifetime of their marriage, she couldn't quite believe it. After all, there was the joint project with a French laboratory, indeed a whole host of collaborative projects. But what if work was not the only lure across the Channel? And he had been more than usually distracted of late. She had assumed it was to do with a breakthrough at the lab, had thought he had intimated as much. Yet that voice suggested otherwise.

Yes, another woman. That would explain a great deal: his shiftiness when she suggested they talk, his elusiveness. Provide a ready reason for the distance that had fallen between them – a swamp of infested waters over which neither of them seemed to be able to build even a rickety, makeshift bridge.

Tessa tested her feelings. She felt something that wasn't quite anger, but wasn't quite not anger either. Beneath it, that excitement she had tasted a few moments ago took on a sharper edge.

With the covert gestures of a self-acknowledged trespasser, she tried the drawers of Stephen's desk. There wasn't much here – except a reminder of the orderliness which was Stephen. Stationery in one drawer, an assortment of pens and pencils, paperclips, stamps in another. A drawer with guarantees for appliances and instruction manuals. Next there was a stack of computer disks, backups numbered according to a system which for Tessa was as intricate as their imagined content. She couldn't bother with those now, even if she could overcome the additional difficulty of incompatible systems. Then came a drawer full of bills. She picked up the telephone batch and glanced through the itemized list, was about to jot down two Paris numbers when a card tumbled to the floor.

There was a name printed at the top: Simone Lalande Debray. Beneath it, a Paris address and a formal invitation, followed by a slur of handwriting she couldn't quite make out, except for the opening words: 'Mon très cher Stephen . . .'

Very dear, was he? With a little shiver, Tessa put the card into the pocket of her dressing gown and dropped Stephen's keys in after it. For good measure, she noted the two Paris numbers, then brazenly pushed the rewind button on the answering machine and listened once more to that seductive voice. As she went downstairs, a smile began to tug at the corner of her lips. With it came the rudiments of a plan. It matured as she smoothed the sitting-room sofa, tidied away newspapers, stray magazines, a lone glass. In the lacquered vase on the corner table, the roses Stephen had offered her the day after her birthday drooped their last. She bundled them into newspaper and took them out to the bin.

There had been a book, too, as if what she needed were yet another book, she who spent her life surrounded by them, reading, editing, publishing. But what could he give her since he wouldn't give her the one thing she really wanted? A child.

Tessa looked round the room she had taken such pains over when they had first moved here in the third year of what was now a decade-old marriage. Everything was in place. The round dining table with its mellow gleam, its bowl of sculpted fruit, the arched lamps, the tiled fireplace, the watercolours and prints vivid on the walls. The two sofas facing each other across the divide of a low coffee table, waiting for easy laughter, conversation, the clink of glasses.

A setting for a life that had never quite taken place. And now the sofas were frayed and the walls had lost their brightness.

It had been well over three years since they had stopped talking of anything but the routine matters of daily life. Just before that there had been a brief phase when she thought Stephen was trying to speak to her, really speak, but only through print. He would leave articles lying around the house, where she would be sure to find them, indirect messages coded in the language of his trade. At least she assumed they were for her, these cold tracts, perhaps intended as consolation, though they only left her increasingly discouraged.

She had read how eight out of ten fertilized eggs in women attempting to become pregnant were spontaneously aborted because they carried lethal mutations. So it could only be to the good that she had miscarried her one and only certain conception, way back when, before the turn of the decade. She remembered another article telling her that chromosomal mutations were thirty times more common amongst women of thirty-five and over than in teenagers. And that the rate of spontaneous abortion went up five times between the ages of thirty-five and forty-five. So all was for the best in the best of all possible thirty-five-and-over childless worlds.

Sexless too. Soon after the spate of articles, they had all but stopped making love. No point to it, really – she had put herself in Stephen's well-worn shoes. After all, if the gene's mission was to reproduce itself and reproduction wasn't in the offing, why bother with all that business?

Age, she had read in one of those scattered DNA articles, was the antithesis of sex.

And now she was thirty-nine, half a year older than Stephen, and she could count the occasions she had been to bed with him in the last three years on her fingers. Not that she cared all that much about the sex any more, but the lack of it hardly left much hope for those two out of ten eggs which didn't carry lethal mutations. Nor for much else. The stigma of her childlessness seemed to accompany her wherever she went, even latterly to the office. She would find herself searching for something she thought she had lost and then realize she hadn't lost anything specific. Only that. She felt bereft, in mourning for something she had never had, somehow not even any longer a woman.

Oh, she and Stephen trundled along, of course, talking of the weather or the latest book she was editing, dining out with friends or round the mellow walnut table, remembering birthdays and anniversaries – if a little late. They were amicable, polite, busy, coupled. Sometimes, Tessa thought, they were perhaps already dead.

Not that bed with Stephen had ever been a matter of lightning and thunder and pounding horses' hooves, Tessa reflected as she washed the grounds out of the cafetière. When she had met him, she had been in the last throes of a once-passionate, now painful, affair with an older married don, whom she had at last realized would never leave his wife. She had gone to see Dr Stephen Caldwell on recommendation. She was editing a history of Cambridge science and she needed some expert advice on the final period the book would cover.

She could still remember the details of that first meeting as vividly as if they had been stored on some ineradicable videotape. Perhaps the weather accounted for that, she now thought with a touch of cynicism. A freezing fog had covered the city overnight and the morning had dawned with icy whiteness in thrall to some snow queen's glacial magic. Every roof, every branch of every shrub and tree, sparkled with myriad needles of crystalline brilliance. In response to the gusts of wind which whipped her cheeks as she walked along the Backs, the trees tinkled softly. Rapt by their music, she took a detour to peer into the Clare College gardens, to watch the ducks scuffle along a thin crust at the edge of the Cam and fluff their wings into downy shields as they tipped into the waters.

She arrived at Stephen Caldwell's rooms in Trinity a little late and full of smiling apologies.

'Oh, no. I quite understand.' He smiled straight back and turned her towards his windows which gave onto the Backs. 'I've been doing nothing but standing here myself.' They had continued to stand there and stare out in companionable silence for some moments before he at last gestured her towards a chair. It was only then that Tessa finally took in the man.

He had regular features in a narrow face topped by a sandy mop of hair, which fell over his brow and occasionally got entangled with his specs. These he removed and put on again at random intervals as he talked in response to her questions. The gesture seemed to punctuate his conversation. He wasn't as attractive as Jonathan, her don. He had none of those little niceties of charm, those well-practised flourishes of smile and rhetoric. But when he warmed to his subject, she began to see a surprising force in him, an intensity which belied the surface diffidence.

In the heat of discussion, his glasses moved on and off more frequently. Without them, his eyes were a little bewildered, sad, and she wondered at the cause of their sadness. At one point he pulled off the bulk of his slightly tatty pullover to reveal a slenderness that bordered on gauntness. She really ought to invite him out to lunch, she thought. He needed the food. Unlike her don, who needed a diet.

The pullover was thrown carelessly onto a threadbare sofa which had witnessed too many student supervisions. But the desk was good and of an impeccable neatness. There was a ranked series of trays bearing typed labels: Students, College, Lab, Research. Apart from that, there was only a pad in the centre and a number of sharpened pencils. Occasionally Stephen would make a note with one of these. Tessa took the opportunity to glance at the bookshelves. These sported a predictable assortment of scientific tomes, but she saw other things as well, a range of histories, books whose spines looked decidedly old and foreign, a bottom row of paperbacks, Le Carré, Deighton – a slew of spy and brightly jacketed cyber fiction. The variety surprised her. A friend had warned her that as brilliant as Stephen Caldwell was meant to be, he would resemble all other scientists of his generation and know nothing about anything except his immediate field, and certainly nothing about the history of science.

She tested him by asking him a question about Cavendish and drew a blank, but on Max Perutz and X-ray crystallography and John Kendrew and his proteins, he was effusive, if critical. She smelled the hunger of ambition and was not altogether displeased. She was also pleased when she turned round to find that the wall behind her was covered in old maps. Her little brother had collected maps, though his were all of the old Empire, and he had duly taken himself off to its furthest point, from which the annual letter still reached her. Stephen's maps were of Europe, though it took her several moments to determine this since they seemed at first glance to bear so little relationship to each other.

When she mentioned her confusion at the flux of borders in his maps, mentioned her brother's collection, too, he smiled a little shyly. And before she quite knew who had asked whom they were sitting in the Mill and digging into shepherd's pie. The appetite with which he consumed his made her think he had probably forgotten to eat properly for some time. She had a sudden vision of herself cooking him nightly and wholesome dinners.

With her second glass of cinnamony mulled wine she found herself asking him why he looked so sad.

'Do I?' He had flushed a little, fumbled with his glasses, stared into the middle distance. 'I'm not. Not really. Not now. Today.'

'That's good.' Tessa had sipped her wine and kept her eyes on him, a part of her relishing his embarrassment at her personal question.

Over coffee, Stephen had come back to it. 'I have been a little sad,' he said with a slight tremor in his voice. 'A friend of mine died, you see. Some months back. I . . .'

'A girlfriend?' Tessa had pried uncharacteristically.

'Sort of. Yes, I suppose so. Still . . .' He had waved the subject away and given her a smile of such sweetness that she realized she felt altogether happy for the first time in weeks, if not years.

They had met again the following evening and the one after that. Stephen, she soon came to understand, for all his verbal passion when it came to the romance of science, stammered when it came to intimate matters. He didn't like to delve. She took it as a sign of delicacy. He was tactful and gentle and yes, the word struck her as an odd one, good. He asked her about her work at the Press, about her family, but he didn't question her about her own past loves, which relieved her since the subject would have made her uneasy. She didn't want to replay the adolescent involvements of her student years. Nor did she want to lie. And it would have mortified her to evoke the tawdry details of what had increasingly become a seamy affair. The last thing she wanted was to infect this fresh friendship with its rot.

Stephen made her feel young and new and yes, like herself. She wasn't made for scurrying round corridors, living secretly and in fear, whatever the compensations of weekends in grand foreign hotels or what at least initially had been the heated thrills of passion. Everything with Stephen could be open and public. She didn't have to look over her shoulder or be afraid to pick up the telephone. She could introduce him to her friends, take him to parties or home to her family. For the first time in years she felt wonderfully, blissfully, free. In love, too, she decided, but since the expression had been tainted by her affair with Jonathan, she preferred simply to think that she loved Stephen.

About Stephen's dead friend, she was consumed with a curiosity she couldn't quite voice. Prying would have entailed revealing. Tit for tat. But when, now and again, she saw that pensiveness tinge his features, she vowed to herself that she would overlay it with brightness.

For the rest, Stephen had an incisive intelligence and was good company. He was also sane and sensible and provided a wonderful contrast to her harried, lying don. Beyond all that, he intrigued her, for Stephen was at one and the same time boyish and antediluvian. Instead of passes, there was the aura of romance, a kind of chivalric and considerate politeness in which she blossomed. They didn't make love until their wedding night.

Tessa smoothed the quilt and plumped the pillows on

her half of the conjugal bed. She gazed at its arid neatness, felt melancholy as thick as the winter quilt shroud her spirits. On occasion over these last sterile years it had occurred to her that perhaps she had made a terrible mistake, that Stephen had really always preferred men.

There was no one she could share such fears with – none of her friends, not even her sister. It was too shaming. Her friends saw her as a successful professional woman, successfully married too, to a man of undeniable stature. Her residue of pride robbed her of the comforts and laughter of female complicity.

The second problem with her condition, Tessa thought as she pulled trousers and shirt from the wardrobe and forced her gaze to the mirror, was that she felt herself robbed of presence. Of late, when she looked at herself, all she saw was a negative: a woman who couldn't seem to have children, a woman who was undesirable. Not a woman at all, really. No one.

With a shiver, Tessa curled her fingers round the card in her dressing-gown pocket. The keys next to it set up a nervous jangle. She straightened her shoulders and looked at the card again. Simone Lalande Debray. At least the voice on the telephone had been a woman's. That was a start. Tessa laughed, suddenly alert to the humour of her thoughts. It was not every wife who could extract a blessing from the notion of a mistress. A mixed blessing. She was angry, too. But anger was a fuel, one that could propel her out of the grey limbo of suffering and into action. She would find proof of Stephen's transgressions.

And then what?

One step at a time, Tessa counselled herself. A step out of an impasse was already a change. It was a great deal.

Midsummer Common was a misty wash of green, but above the spire of Jesus College Chapel the sky showed a streak of pale lemon light. By the children's playground on the banks of the Cam, the brown and white and polka-dot cows munched away, oblivious to weather.

Tessa pulled her cloche of a hat down over her ears and clipped the lead into the golden retriever's collar.

'Quick walk to the river and then it's off to the kennels, Paws.'

The dog gave her a single beseeching look, as if he had already accepted his fate, then matched his pace to hers.

No sooner had they reached the last of the row of houses that gave onto the Common, than the first of Paws' infant admirers was upon him, tickling his ears, rubbing against him, making lop-sided faces. Tessa smiled and waited patiently.

Had Stephen known, when he had brought the dog home one day soon after her miscarriage, that Paws would have every child under ten on the Common scurrying towards her? Probably. Paws was a sop, a sweet, bounding creature on which to fasten the runaway emotions of those sad and bitter days. But a dog wasn't a child and it was a child she wanted.

Why? Tessa asked herself for the thousandth time. She didn't really know the answer. It wasn't only to do with a contrariness which made the most difficult the most desirable, nor with her mother's callous harping nor her perennial jealousy of her older sister with her two children. Nor was it that she was particularly avid for the battle scars of child-bearing which she had had recounted to her in rigorous detail on any number of occasions. Nor, she told herself, was she especially romantic and gooey-eyed about babies. She knew about the dangers of post-partum depression. She could list the upheavals that a child would bring into one's life – the inattention of husbands, the boredom and sheer tedium of mothering, the desire for a world which wasn't all nappies and mindless babble and endless chores and responsibility and not a moment of one's own.

She had enumerated all this often enough to herself as she tried to come to terms with her childless condition. Yet, for all that, she couldn't get rid of the desire. And she had only to be with her niece and nephew for five minutes or with the children of her friends to find the want engulfing her.

Sometimes, when her niece and nephew came to stay for the weekend, she felt she was close to an answer. The empty, cloistered silence of the house filled up. There were no more shadowy corners. Life and bustle reigned everywhere.

Her own childhood home had always been crowded with ringing voices and stray socks and bickering. It was hard for her to admit, since she wasn't particularly close to her parents now, but she missed that – the busyness, the clutter, the noisy sense of casual chaos, out of which one carved a momentary order.

Stephen's home hadn't been like that. But they had had so much in common in those early days that Tessa had assumed they had this, too. Nor was Stephen particularly uncomfortable when her niece and nephew came to visit. It was true that he talked to them in his usual tone, as if they were already grown up. But they didn't seem to mind. And on their last visit, when Tom had fallen over and gouged his forehead on the corner railing, it was Stephen who had calmed him down, even made him laugh on the way to the hospital, held him as the doctor administered the single stitch.

Tessa shook herself. They had reached the car. This was no time for her customary reveries. It was time to face realities, write new scripts, ones which might take Stephen out of her life altogether.

As if in recognition of that, she gave Paws a fierce hug and urged him towards the back seat. 'It won't be so bad, old thing. You'll make new friends while I'm away. You'll see.'

She edged into the Saturday-morning traffic, saw a cyclist overtake her with omnipotent glee and race away. Perhaps that was the trouble with living in Cambridge. Once the realization that you were no longer a student suddenly came upon you – far too late – you were confronted at every juncture by the signs of your ageing. While the students renewed themselves, ever young, ever fresh.

The journey round the outer edges of the town centre, past the botanical gardens and into the flat countryside was slow, but it gave her thoughts time to consolidate. That seductive foreign voice in her ear had grown a body, lush, dark hair, a hotel room, a bed on which scenes of rapturous love were played out. They acted as a spur. She was faced with the fact that she had allowed herself to sink into a habit of waiting – waiting for Stephen to make love to her, waiting for a child, waiting for change. It was more than time to lift that shroud of depression which had covered their marriage and all but obliterated her.

Tessa dropped Paws off at the kennels, didn't permit herself to be dragged into conversation with the keeper and retraced her route. Halfway back, she turned into a side road and stopped at a car park marked 'Staff' next to a sleek, modern building. The sign announcing Camgene to the right of the glass-fronted door with its bronze double helix was as discreet as she remembered it and in the same place.

She slid the plastic card into the identity slot beneath it, heard the answering click and made her way into a deserted reception room where a vast wall chart in bold plastic colours paraded as a work of abstract art. Lines of apple green and blood red, some with additional purples and blues and oranges, strained towards the ceiling. A code at the bottom announced 'Products in Development', and cited strings of letters and numbers designating particular pharmaceuticals and the stages they had reached: green for research and discovery, red for preclinical development, all the way up to the orange sky of large-scale trials and product registration. Stephen, she knew, was at the head of the green stage.

And there was his picture, suitably serious, staring out at her from the more smiling faces of Chairman and Chief Executives and Finance Directors. Tessa grimaced. When Stephen had first had the offer of a part-time link with the then nascent Camgene in the third year of their marriage, she had joined in his excitement. Until then, they had made do with a shared arrangement between his college rooms and her old flat. Now there would be far more money, a new home, the children she had taken for granted. Not only that. There would be far more resources for research, a sparkling new lab. She was thrilled for him.

Then, it must have been at the turn of the decade, soon after she had lost the baby, Camgene with its race for patents and products had taken Stephen over. The romance of science hid a world whose competitiveness she had only remotely glimpsed at the outset. And it had gradually swallowed Stephen up. He had become a man of import and a certain fame, but all of it, work, travel, excluded her.

Not that he hadn't been immersed in his work or travelled before. But now, for long weeks she would hardly see him except over morning coffee or at dinner parties which had too quickly lost their gloss. Stephen inevitably went off to discuss incomprehensible matters with colleagues while she tried to make conversation with wives who shared few of her interests and talked of little but their children's schools.

And there was the rub again. Her persistent childlessness made her desire for a child somehow shameful, as if it were a perverse wish which could only be aired when it was satisfied.

In the meantime, Stephen had become as grey a presence

for her as the muted tones of his photograph. When she thought of him, it was as the man who wouldn't give her a baby. And of this she thought obsessively. Sometimes at night she would wake in such murderous fury at his softly snoring limpness that in the morning she couldn't find the requisite voice to ask him to pass the butter.

With a sigh, Tessa made her way up to the second floor, slipped the plastic card through a second identity slot. The laboratories were too quiet. She felt she could hear the rodents scuttling in their basement cages while her heels clacked out her presence as an interloper. She stilled her feet and her nerves. She had never been here at a weekend before, had indeed not been here at all for some time. She moved briskly down the corridor with its lining of labelled refrigerators and averted her eyes from the doors where she might spy some hard-working technician who would spy her.

Stephen's lab was at the end of the corridor, past the room with the vast electron microscope encased in glass. He had taken her in there one day to show her the structure of a protein and she had been stupidly astonished to see that the microscope required no looking through apertures, but automatically reproduced its findings on a computer screen. It made pictures of the invisible.

Stephen was good at some forms of the invisible. Not her forms. Once, in the early days of their marriage when they still looked into each other's eyes while talking, she had charged him with blindness, with refusing to see beneath the surface of things. It had been a very mild charge, really just a tease. But he had balked.

He had asked her what she thought water looked like and Tessa had answered, like a child being tested, that it was a transparent liquid, clear and wet, and she had laughed. He had marched her to his old microscope, left her for a moment, and then come back with a slide. 'Look,' he had ordered her. 'Coloured water.' She had put her eye to the lens and seen a mass of shapes engaged in erratic movement. The vision had both delighted and distressed her.

Yes, Stephen knew that things were not always what they seemed. Yes, Stephen was good at some forms of the invisible. Too bad she couldn't isolate a molecule for humiliation or longing or fear and offer it to him on a slide.

She had arrived at the door of his lab and nervously she searched for the appropriate key. The first one wouldn't fit, nor the second. She hesitated, unsure now of the necessity which had driven her this far. She steeled herself, tried a third key, heard the awaited click. She opened the door to find a young, broad-shouldered man barring her way. Startled, she stepped back, tried to prise an apology from dry lips. But something about the man's bullish demeanour made her stand her ground.

'What, may I ask, are you doing here?' Tessa used the clipped tones of authority.

'Surely that's for me to ask.' Dark eyes focused on her with a hint of menace.

Tessa pulled the cloche hat from her head, shook out blonde strands of hair.

'I'm Dr Caldwell's wife.'

'And how do I know that?'

'You don't.' Tessa's momentary confidence began to dwindle. 'Look, Dr Caldwell asked me to fetch something for him.'

The man examined her with scrupulous slowness. Was there a particular way one looked if one was Stephen Caldwell's wife, Tessa wondered.

'Do you have any ID?'

Feeling like a criminal, Tessa dug out her driver's licence and handed it to him.

'I know. You must be Pavel. Pavel Kat . . .'

'Katuretsky,' he finished for her with a sheepish

expression. 'And you are Tessa Hughes. I am so sorry. But these days we cannot be too careful.'

'Yes, of course. Animal rights,' Tessa mumbled, hoping he wouldn't press her any further.

'Not only that . . .' He hesitated.

'You're from Brno, is that right?'

'Yes. Good to meet you.' The man suddenly stretched out his hand and gave her a smile which reminded her she was a woman. 'My apologies again. I was working and you took me by surprise.' He waved at a lit computer screen. 'Dr Caldwell has warned me about security.'

They looked at each other, at a loss for the next conversational gambit.

'I'll only be a few moments. Don't let me disturb you.'

She walked past him, between the counters laden with beakers and test tubes and trays of blue-tinted jelly-like substance – a casual chaos which she had never quite learned to reconcile with her media myth of pristine laboratories. More like the kitchen of a large restaurant.

'No, no. It's not a problem. You have the key to Dr Caldwell's office?'

Tessa turned back as much to look at the young life of him as to murmur, 'Yes, thank you.'

No wonder Stephen preferred to work late in the lab than make his way home, if the lab provided him with a stream of loyal assistants like this. She felt colour warm her cheeks and she turned away, edged carefully past microscopes and a centrifuge, to take refuge behind the door of Stephen's office.

For a moment, she couldn't remember why she had come. Then she realized she didn't exactly know what she was looking for. Proof of duplicity? Hard evidence of an affair? A hoard of letters, a diary? A key to Stephen's inner life. Something, someone, to blame for the dissatisfactions, the impasse at which they had arrived.

She sat down with a thump in the swivel-back chair and

let her eyes rove round the office. The only inner life it gave evidence of was that contained in the letters CGAT and their endless permutations. There they were on a print-out in his letter tray. Indecipherable sequences of symbols. A set of biological basics as closed to her as Stephen himself now was. As mysterious as the prints on the wall with their ribbon-like strands and floating blobs of X-rayed matter.

In the centre of one of the bookshelves there was a more familiar image, though she didn't instantly recognize it. Herself. Six year ago, seven perhaps. She was standing in the gardens of Trinity College. She was already too thin, though her tightly belted raincoat belied the fact, and her hair blew softly round her face hiding the angles. She wore a smile, slightly wistful. Not unattractive.

Tessa turned away and began to sift through the papers in the letter tray. Not a single one of them was handwritten, except for a PS from an Edward S. Knight which said, 'See you in Paris.' In a second tray, there was a series of printed papers in unrecognizable languages, Russian, she thought, amongst them. What on earth was Stephen doing with Russian papers? She shivered despite herself, then spotted at the top of one of the papers a note in Stephen's writing. 'Copy to Simone', it read. Her pulse quickened. Simone again. Her instincts had been right. She only wished she could understand the language of the text. Perhaps Simone was a translator. That would make sense.

Quickly, Tessa shuffled through more papers, found a number of conference schedules, including one for a Paris conference on *La Nouvelle Génétique*. This was one she had hoped to find and this too had a 'copy to Simone' handwritten on it. So he would be meeting her there. For a moment, anger at Stephen's duplicity engulfed her. She forced herself through it, tucked the papers into her bag, then tried the top drawer of the desk. It was locked. Of course it would be. Everything here was locked, secret, kept remote from intrusive eyes.

She took a deep breath and was about to reach for the key ring when a knock made her leap from the chair.

'A coffee?' Pavel Katuretsky peeked round the door. 'I can bring you one from the machine. Plastic coffee.' He made a face. 'But drinkable.'

'No. No, thank you. I've found what I came for.'

'Are you sure? I want one myself.'

'All right, then. Black, one sugar.'

He flashed her a happy look, as if she had just answered an earnest desire, and ambled off.

Tessa smiled to herself. Perhaps her life wasn't over yet. Perhaps she could once again be a woman, even if not for Stephen. She flicked a comb quickly through her hair, and was about to try the desk again when she heard Pavel's footsteps.

He beckoned her towards a small windowside table, brought out a packet of chocolate biscuits, proffered them. 'They make the taste better.'

'Yes.' Tessa bit in. A chocolate digestive hadn't tasted this good in a long time.

'So, you will be joining Dr Caldwell?'

Tessa flushed. 'Perhaps,' she mumbled.

'You are busy with your work.'

'And you? Will you be going to the conference?'

'No, no. There is too much to do here.' He waved his arm round the room. 'This is an exciting moment. Dr Caldwell's new research . . .' He gave her a complicit grin she didn't know what to do with, so she simply nodded.

There was that smile again. She basked in it, only to have a computer beep rupture the moment.

'There's my call – the program's finished running.' Pavel didn't move for a moment, as if he were waiting for a sign from her.

'I had better let you get back to it, then.' Tessa drained her paper cup. 'Good luck.'

'It was a pleasure to meet you,' he said with emphasis.

'And you.'

As she left the lab, Tessa reflected that it had indeed been a pleasure. The long-lived mists of depression seemed to have dispersed a little. She felt buoyant, prepared to embark on that journey which had only become imperative a few hours ago. She didn't imagine that spying on Stephen, let alone confronting him, would continue to prove quite so heady a business. But she was ready.

3

———✳———

Things started to go awry for Tessa the moment she emerged from the cocoon of the gleaming high-speed train. Maybe she simply wasn't meant to be a creature with wings in this Paris where the powdery markings of beauty were so important.

On the train she had been warmly pleased with herself, proud that she had cancelled her island holiday and decided at last to take active charge of a life that had run away from her. She had imagined herself as a cool investigator. She had seen herself phoning the intimate-voiced Simone, going to see her, confronting Stephen with frosty aplomb, making him take note of her, forcing change. All this was also somehow entangled with once again feeling like a woman.

She had said as much, though perhaps a little more obliquely, to her older sister, Pen, at whose house she had spent Sunday night. Pen now lived in London, conveniently not so very far from Waterloo.

'Good, I'm glad,' Pen had said firmly when Tessa had told her about her change of destination. 'He neglects you. He thinks he can get away with anything. You've been coddling him for too long.'

'Have I?' Tessa hadn't been certain of that, but she had been glad to have her plan approved.

Nonetheless as soon as she stepped out into the Gare du Nord, her courage dwindled. First there was the station crowd, so determined in its hurry that it was hard to pause and read signs. Then there was the smell of Paris which she had quite forgotten: a smell composed of urine and petrol and something else which she couldn't quite name until she found herself standing in front of a butcher's display and gazing upon rows of innards, hearts and kidneys and lungs, gutted rabbits still wearing their fur, birds hanging from wrung necks – all laid out like some exotic garden. So she decided the final component of the smell was slaughtered flesh, and she fled.

After that she was turned away from three hotels with a laconic murmur of '*complet*'. In the final one, when she picked up her case to leave, a woman started to shriek at her, and it took Tessa a few moments to realize that she had picked up the wrong bag and was being treated as a thief.

To regain her composure, she sat in a café and ordered coffee and a sandwich from a self-important waiter, who looked at her askance because she was at a table laid with white mat and knife and fork – the signal for a substantial lunch. So she moved outdoors to a poky round table with a plasticized marble top, took one bite of her baguette and found that she was up to neither the forceful chewing it required, nor the crumbs.

When she called the waiter over to pay her bill, he gave her an odd look.

'*Terminez déjà?*'

'*Oui,*' Tessa said, and thought that she was probably already finished in more ways than one. But that was no reason for him to look at her as if she were some mad old bat.

She found herself in front of the butcher's window again and she suddenly remembered how Stephen, a few years back, after a Christmas visit to her parents', had abruptly announced that no nation which cared so much for animals would ever know the meaning of cuisine, let alone how to eat. She hadn't paid much attention to the remark at the time, had thought it was just Stephen's way of letting off steam after yet another of her father's frontal attacks on scientists and their use of laboratory animals.

Her parents, in their retirement, had moved to Gloucestershire, where they lived with three dogs, a neatly tended vegetable garden and a great many of her father's newly found passions, which he vented splenetically whenever he had a chance. One of these was animal rights. Another was Europhobia. Given even half an audience he would deliver a lecture on how all of Britain's ills were due to an influx of corrupt European ideas. Stephen would sit silently through these lectures, staring at his gravy-covered plate with its untouched mound of sprouts, his face a mask of politeness. Only that once, as far as she could recall, had Stephen made a critical comment.

On impulse last year Tessa had sent her father a book she had edited. It contended that Britishness was an eighteenth-century invention, not some primordial essence. The invention had taken shape over what could be seen as a hundred years' war with the French. It was a useful invention, since it kept England and Scotland and Wales united against the enemy. One of its wheels was the Bank of England. Another was the propaganda, which became assumed fact, labelling the nasty, foppish French everything that the brave and manly, sincere and innocent British were not: Catholic, superstitious, militaristic, wasteful, corrupt, oppressed, badly paid and self-flaunting, garlic-eating hypocrites to boot. So being British had only taken on meaning when set against the French, our closest and preferred enemy. The problem was that now that we were all supposed to be friends in one not altogether comfortable union, the very idea of Britishness teetered precariously, no longer able to gloss over a spectrum of internal differences.

But her father was impervious to rational argument. He clung to his prejudices, as much a part of him as his digestive tract. And maybe, Tessa thought as she continued to be transfixed by the butcher's display, she was more her father's daughter than she acknowledged. Whereas Stephen had moved on. Yes.

With a shrug, Tessa hailed a taxi and asked to be taken to Saint-Germain. She would treat herself, go up-market. After all, she hadn't been to Paris for some eight years. She found a little hotel in the Rue du Dragon, amidst antique shops and boutiques which wafted perfume, and women like iridescent butterflies. She sat in her hotel room and gazed at the telephone next to which she had placed the card with Simone Lalande Debray's number, and felt like a faded moth waiting for light. At last she forced herself to pick up the receiver and dial.

A clear, self-sufficient voice replied, eliciting messages with seductive charm. Tessa hung up promptly, her resolution vanishing as quickly as it had come. She couldn't face the owner of that voice. Not yet. In any event, what would she say?

'Hello. You don't know me, but I think you've been sleeping with my husband. Oh, it's all right. I don't mind. Not really. Not today. It's just that I need to know. So that I have a reason to leave him, you understand.'

What could the woman say in response? Would she offer her coffee to assuage her ruffled English dignity? Would she protest in utter incomprehension? Would she hang up?

No, a little more preparation was necessary. Tessa had to see the woman first, get a feel for her. And before she could even do that, she had to do something about herself. This different mirror, which she forced herself to look into, reflected a woman who was all but invisible, too pale, too thin, insignificant. All her fears were written large within its gilded frame. And it shouted at her, told her how much she had let herself go these last years, had become merely the woman who couldn't have a baby, not a sexed creature at all, really, just a shadow.

In the beauty salon, all chrome and mirrors and outsize posters of androgynous youth, a graceful and tanned young man who might well have stepped down from one of the images except that he was smaller, flashed her a bright smile and showed her to a chair. She smiled back weakly and told him she wanted a change, anything he might suggest, within reason of course. With a serious air, he studied her face in the mirror, held it this way and that, brushed her hair up and let it fall. Good hair, he commented and the comment made Tessa disproportionately happy.

She relaxed in his hands, let him apply a lightening rinse, to bring out the gold he said, listened to his chat as he washed and cut and styled. He surprised her by telling her, now in his lilting, accented English, how much he loved London, how the best fashions came from there, how English women were always nicer, easier to please, less pernickety.

When she looked at herself, Tessa had to admit that she was pleased. He hadn't done anything radical but her hair had a glowing, sculpted look to it, freed only by the swoop of a wave at her right temple. And her face looked less drawn.

'You have a special occasion tonight?' he asked, smiling at her pleasure.

'Sort of.'

'May I suggest a little colour here and here?' He pointed to a space above her cheekbones, to her lips.

Tessa tipped him generously. She also followed his orders and promptly found a *parfumerie* where a woman advised her on blushers and bases and shadows and lipstick. She went further than that. At a boutique near the salon, she bought herself a beautifully tailored jacket in a rich charcoal-brown, a matching skirt, shorter than anything she had worn for years, striped trousers with loose pleats at the top and pencil slim at the base, and two jerseys recommended by the assistant, who was as quick to point out what didn't suit her as what did. Tessa appreciated the help. She wanted nothing more than to be made over. When she finally got back to the hotel with her numerous purchases, she fell soundly asleep and dreamt of a woman called Simone who looked remarkably like her re-made self.

In the morning the courage of make-up almost failed her, but she chivvied herself into the masquerade and set out along the Boulevard Saint-Germain into the narrow streets of the fifth arrondissement. She found the stretch of embankment easily enough. In another mood she would have gasped at the almost flagrant beauty of the view, the airy stone haunches of Notre Dame spread astride the sinuous river. Now, she was too nervously intent on locating a house to match the number indicated on the card. When at last she spied it atop heavy wooden doors at the corner of a tiny side street, she realized she had already passed in front of it three times. The doors seemed barred to casual entry, but an unpretentious café on the pavement opposite provided a convenient spot for a little harmless spying. Tessa positioned herself beneath a striped awning, ordered an orange pressé, unfolded a newspaper and waited.

The first person to emerge from the heavy doors was a man carrying a ladder. Obviously not a candidate for the name Simone, Tessa mocked herself. He returned a few minutes later without the ladder, but with a roll of wallpaper, and disappeared into the house. Then for a good half-hour there was nothing.

Tessa consoled herself with the notion that she was soaking up atmosphere. She tried to imagine Stephen walking up the street. She gave him a box of chocolates, one of those expensive ones full of truffles and exotic creams, all hand-made and hand-picked and wrapped in metres of gold ribbon by a coy woman in a choice *confiserie*. She saw him punch out a door code, step over the threshold, slam the door in her face.

She poured more water into her orange pressé and remembered a conversation she had had with her sister, in the early days of her marriage with Stephen. Pen was miserable at the time. The sisters were out of step. Pen's marriage to Robert was on the rocks and she had come to stay with Tessa and brought Tom, then two, along with her. They had talked late into the night and Pen had said she suspected Robert was having an affair and she had to find out about it. She talked wildly of hiring a private detective.

'Why don't you just ask him?' Tessa had queried.

'Because he'll lie.'

'How do you know?'

Pen had shrugged and taken on that newly bitter voice of hers. 'Because men want everything they can get away with.'

'I don't think Stephen would lie. Not to my face.'

'Ha!' Pen had sneered. 'Not yet.'

As it turned out, there had been an affair, but Robert and Pen hadn't split up. They had had another child instead.

And that, Tessa thought, was the difference.

Just before she and Stephen had stopped talking and more or less stopped doing it, they had both gone off individually for fertility tests – at her insistence. The doctor had told her there was nothing wrong with her. She must just be patient. Sometimes, when one had reached one's mid-thirties, he had smiled at her kindly, it took time.

Stephen, too, it seemed was all right, though he had done no more than grunt in response to her questions. She had wondered then what he thought about when he had to do it into a bottle. Did he look at pornographic magazines, think of her, of other women? She hadn't dared to ask, of course. Sex was not something one could talk about with Stephen. He would shuffle his feet and grow remote and awkward, like a schoolboy. He had been like that in the early days too. But then it hadn't mattered, since their bodies had taken their own course. She had liked this darkness of passion, speech through another medium. She was a romantic at heart and sex talk reminded her too much of her don and his embarrassing worldliness. But if romance went awry, as it had done after her miscarriage, talk, with all its difficulties, seemed necessary.

When she had dared to say to Stephen that perhaps they should seek more specialist advice, get treatment, he had lost his temper for perhaps the one and only time in their marriage. Did she know what all that involved, he had railed, the time, the expense, the anxiety, the obsessiveness of it? Did she realize how many failures there were for every success? Did she really want to have months of repeated hormone injections? Undergo lengthy courses of antibiotics? Lie supine for weeks? Be able to think of nothing else?

Tessa had railed straight back, told him he was a funny kind of scientist if he didn't even believe in his own science. Then she had gone off and immediately found out what it did involve. She had written away for leaflets, brochures, scoured the press and specialist magazines. She had learned about cervical mucus defects and endometriosis. She had discovered that the first could be overcome by sperm being placed directly into the uterus or with in vitro fertilization, which could also overcome the second. She had imagined a fine, hollow needle guided by ultrasound finding its way through her insides, harvesting eggs like some skilled truffle digger. She had imagined the eggs making their way into an incubator then out again to be mixed with sperm. She had considered first Stephen's sperm, then that of an unknown donor in the little dish.

She had rather liked the idea of an unknown – some young, unruffled medical student earning his fifteen pounds a throw. So as not to have to bother Stephen with it, of course. Stephen, she secretly thought, was probably against the whole idea because he couldn't face doing it into a dish, let alone doing it. She had imagined sperm and egg meeting in the dish, making a love match, then the slender tube containing the embryo slipping its way into her womb. And then she had stopped imagining.

After that, after the interventions of medical science, the real magic began.

She had left some of the leaflets and brochures lying around for Stephen. Her response to the articles he had left for her. She had specially selected the ones with statistics and graphs in bright primary colours showing that the success rate of IVF was around twelve per cent. Given that the average monthly chance of conception for an ordinarily fertile couple was only twenty to twenty-five per cent, this was hardly terrible.

But Stephen had never commented, had pretended not to notice, had perhaps not noticed. She had grown angry then, had escalated what she had begun to call in her own mind the battle of the articles. Right in the centre of his desk, she had placed a piece about the decline in quality and quantity of human sperm from average levels of about one hundred million sperm per millilitre of semen in the 1970s to about forty-eight million in the 1990s. Not only that, but a much higher concentration of the sperm had lower motility, lacked tails or had two heads, were as misshapen as those of endangered species.

When Stephen didn't respond, she had goaded him with more articles on the same theme, panicking features describing the disastrous effects on sperm of pollutants, of clingfilm, of heat, of oestrogen remains from contraceptive pills in drinking water. At last he had met her provocation. He had placed two tedious, carefully photocopied essays on her desk. At first glance, they seemed to have nothing to do with the subject at hand. One dealt with statistical noise and showed how similar experiments could be used to provide wholly different statistics, depending on the model used. The second was a more general piece about millen-arian anxieties, the growth in end-of-the-world scenarios as the year 2000 approached. A footnote cited Anglo–Danish studies in sperm decline as an instance of this anxiety.

The articles arrived with a box of chocolates. Insult piled on injury, Tessa thought. As if chocolates might put her fears and longing to rest. After that, there was silence. Maybe Stephen's mind and other vital parts were already in Paris.

Abruptly, Tessa got up and dropped some coins on the café table. She would go to Stephen now, straight away, find out the truth without all this duplicitous spying, scream her anger which was suddenly as vibrant as the hissing tongue of a snake. She would make an end of it then and there. He would probably be relieved.

As she crossed the street, the door of the house opened again. Tessa paused. A child's buggy appeared, closely fol-lowed by a svelte, dark woman and a toddler in a sweater of many colours. Tessa's heart skipped a beat. Could this be Stephen's Simone? Somehow she hadn't considered the possibility of a child. His child? Her palms felt clammy. That would explain everything, explain why Stephen wouldn't even try, why he had rejected the fertility clinics, turned a deaf ear to her recent talk of adoption.

Her fury evaporated as quickly as it had come, leaving only a dense sludge behind it, thick with the odour of her own failure.

A large black and yellow ball rolled towards Tessa's feet. She stooped to pick it up and found the toddler lurching against her. His face beneath the mop of sandy hair was gleeful with naughtiness. Could she see Stephen in it? She put out a hand to help him regain his balance and held soft, pudgy fingers. A desire to embrace him gripped her. She wanted that warm, powdery smell close to her.

'Jacob!' Tessa heard the woman's voice and leapt away.

'*Dis merci à la dame, Jacob.*' The woman who could be Simone was right behind the child. She gave Tessa a hint of a smile and strapped the boy emphatically into the buggy. Meanwhile Jacob made a sound vaguely akin to a thank you.

Tessa's lips strained into a curl. The woman was pretty, all high colour and fine bones. She tried to imagine Stephen with her, but her imagination wasn't good enough. Her mouth opened of its own will as if it were about to speak something she would later regret. Tessa closed it, nodded, darted away. She stopped herself from running, but she walked quickly in the opposite direction and hailed a taxi. She didn't have the strength for the streets.

Inside, before she could change her mind, she leafed through her address book and said, '*Rue des Beaux Arts, s'il vous plaît.*'

The hotel was tucked away on a small street south of the river. One had to look hard for any identifying sign, as if it wanted to hide its function from passers-by. But inside it was far grander than Tessa had expected, all polished wood and brass and a tiny library into which she walked, thinking it might contain a reception desk. When she came out again, she found herself at the base of an utterly circular staircase, like some great hollow column surrounded by a frieze. She carried on, discovered a small bar and then a restaurant with a wondrous geometrically moulded ceiling. From its far end came the soft tinkle of water plashing into a fountain.

It was not at all what she would have expected of Stephen. And then she thought again and decided that perhaps she had misjudged him and this place was like the him she had never managed to follow – like walking into a microscope replete with hidden, invisible life. The thought excited her, dispelled her gloom.

A waiter appeared from behind a door, guided her back

to a reception room she had somehow missed by going into the library. An elegant young woman sat behind the desk.

Tessa decided against French. 'I'm looking for Dr Stephen Caldwell. Is he in, by any chance? Otherwise I'll leave a message.'

The woman passed a manicured nail down the register. 'No one is here by that name, madame.' She looked up at Tessa expectantly.

'But he always stays here.' Tessa felt her voice rise, too shrill. 'I mean, he told me he was staying here.' She lowered her pitch. 'At least I think he did.'

The woman turned the register towards her so that she could look for herself.

'I shall check the advance bookings. Perhaps he has not arrived yet.'

'No. No, that won't be necessary.'

Tessa turned away. Stupid tears stung at her eyes. In the street, she hid them behind sunglasses. If she had wanted proof, she told herself, she now had it. Stephen wasn't where he was meant to be, where she had assumed he would be. Hadn't he once told her he always stayed in the Rue des Beaux Arts? How long ago was that? It was a concrete measure of how far apart they had grown that she had no idea where he stopped while in Paris.

And if Stephen wasn't where he was meant to be, it almost certainly followed that he wasn't who he was meant to be. Now that she thought about it, it wasn't only that Stephen found talking about personal matters difficult, he was downright secretive. She had read of men with double lives – lives which ran on parallel courses and never met, separate wives, separate families, separate identities.

Tessa walked blindly in she didn't know what direction, stumbled upon a cinema, went in and watched a film play itself out in her mind which had nothing to do with the one on the screen. At some point in its unfolding of tawdry adultery, secret lives and B-movie melodrama, she told herself in a bitter little voice that she really ought to have found a less hackneyed script. But who was to help her with that?

The Maison de la Chimie was at the end of the Rue Saint-Dominique, a narrow street of tricolour flags and policeman's glass cubicles and self-important government buildings. It had its own stately courtyard, but no flag or uniformed guard, though it did sport a large board announcing the '*Congrès de la Nouvelle Génétique*'.

Keeping her eyes down, Tessa made her way through clusters of people up to the indicated first floor and slipped into the back of a large, well-appointed auditorium. She had timed her entrance precisely. If the schedule was being kept to, Stephen should be some ten minutes into his presentation, his attention riveted on his text.

The lights were dimmed and on the distant screen there rose one of those globular structures which meant as little to her as a Martian calculus. Over the microphone, a voice was speaking French. They were running late, Tessa thought and considered going out again, then, spotting a seat at the end of a row, decided against it. She sat down just as the lights went up.

When she looked at the stage, she saw a man standing casually to one side of an oak lectern. She blinked, tried to refocus eyes that seemed to be failing her. The man was definitely Stephen, though on the platform he looked taller, far more prepossessing than he did across the breakfast table. It was the voice that had deceived her, a certain, unstammering voice, well-modulated, a voice she barely remembered from their early days together and speaking a language she had no idea Stephen had so firm a grasp of.

The toll of deceptions her husband was capable of seemed to mount exponentially with each passing moment, Tessa reflected. But, of course, it all made sense. He had to speak something to this Simone – and didn't they say that the only way to learn a language properly was in bed? She searched the room, tried unsuccessfully to detect the woman she had seen on the street. Tried to find another likely candidate for Stephen's Simone, though she hadn't a clue to a possible appearance.

With a grimace, she gave up and forced herself to try to follow Stephen's words, but the double barrier of language and content made her dizzy. She comforted herself with the thought that at least he was here and soon she would confront him. But all she could really think of was that the man standing there at the front of this large and evidently respectful gathering, this man who had been her husband for nigh on ten years, was a stranger.

She waited for an opportune moment when Stephen was looking down at his notes and stole from the room. Not that she seriously imagined he would spot her. At the best of times, he hardly looked at her, and here, in this unexpected context, she would probably have to walk straight up to him and pronounce her name before recognition took place. Tit for tat, Tessa told herself, with a touch of what had once been customary wryness. One stranger deserved another.

The lounge area next to the auditorium was deserted, the bar closed. Tessa perched on a window seat and looked desultorily into the courtyard, then at her watch. With luck, Stephen and this Simone of his might walk out together and at least she would have the pleasure of causing him a momentary embarrassment.

On the seat beside her, she spotted some glossy brochures. She picked up a few and flicked. They were multilingual, English – no, American perhaps, French, German, and advertised the present and future wonders of biotechnology.

In no particular order, she read about strange genetic crossovers – pigs that were goats, potatoes that contained pea genes, rape that was also radish. She read about human organ factories which could supply new synthetic 'replacement parts' for defective ones, protein drug treatments to break up blood clots, a gene to combat cystic fibrosis. As she read, she didn't know whether she wanted to applaud or to cry. It wasn't that she had strong feelings about natural purity. Nothing was pure, after all. In time, everything got chopped and changed. Even the English were way back part French. And her garden was filled with hybrids. On the other hand, pigs and goats, laboratory created animals, genetic tamperings. With a shiver, Tessa realized that one way or another this was what her husband – that same husband who wouldn't consider an assisted birth – was involved in. She shrugged this aside, imagined a new millennium peopled by strange creatures out of a Bosch inferno, twisted the kaleidoscope and saw children so much more perfect than their parents that they turned on parental imperfections in a rush to stamp them out. She suddenly felt tired, spent, as if the confrontations of the day, the child and then this different Stephen, had robbed her altogether of purpose.

'Hello, *bonjour, guten Tag, buon giorno*.' A gusty voice startled her from her doom-laden reverie.

She looked up to see a tall, lean man with spiky white hair above a startlingly youthful, bronzed face. Bright mischievous eyes grinned down at her.

'Hello,' she murmured.

'Phew, that's a relief. For a moment I thought you might be Finnish, which would put a rapid end to my repartee. Not Finnish, then, but bored?' He raised a shaggy inquiring eyebrow.

'And you?' Tessa was cautious.

'Not bored. Never bored. It's just that I already know Stephen Caldwell's work pretty well. So I thought I could skip question time. And you looked more interesting.' He gave her that grin again. 'I saw you walking out.'

'You're American.'

'Is that a crime?'

Tessa was surprised to hear herself laughing. 'No. Possibly a misdemeanour.'

'That's honest.'

'I'm not. Honest, I mean. Only sometimes.'

'Well, that might make a refreshing change.' He eyed her with the kind of overt relish she no longer thought she was capable of eliciting. 'Speaking of which, I could use some coffee. There's one of those French things they call a café just a block away. Could I induce you to join me?'

'You could,' she said, but didn't move for a moment.

'Well then, what are we waiting for?'

Tessa hesitated.

'It's your teatime, isn't it? You could have tea.'

'You might tell me your name.'

'Easy. Ted. Ted Knight, as in the ones on horseback. Though I always leave mine back at the ranch,' he chuckled, surveying her as she rose. 'And you're ... no, don't tell me, Lauren, as in slim Bacall, she of the glossy hair and martini-dry wit.'

'Hardly,' Tessa murmured, though she liked the image, liked even more the sense of being swept up by a whirlwind of energy when she felt sapped of her own. And now that she saw people beginning to stream out of the conference room, it came to her that challenging Stephen here in front of colleagues, in front of this attractive man, was not something she was capable of. Then, too, this Ted Knight might be able to tell her things. Ted Knight. The name meant something to her though she couldn't quite place it.

'So? Are you going to tell me?'

'Tessa. Tessa Hughes.'

He paused for a moment. Reflected. 'Like it.' He stretched out his hand, clasped hers firmly.

In the café on the corner of the Rue Bourgogne, they sat on red plush and ate strawberry tarts.

'You're a scientist?' Tessa asked as she watched him tuck in greedily.

'No. Not really. Studied it. Even worked in a lab once.' He shrugged. 'But I'm unhampered by patience, so I didn't fit the bill.'

'Yes, I can see that.'

'Can you? I hope you don't mind, 'cause I think I'm going to like you.'

Tessa felt warmth rising up her neck. 'So what do you do?'

'That's not a very English question. Too direct.'

'We're not in England.'

'Right.' He considered her for a moment, then bent forward conspiratorially. 'I'm a headhunter.'

'Sounds nasty. Do you take the bodies along as well?'

'Usually.' He chortled, looked at her like that again so that she realized what she had intimated.

'And what do you hunt?'

'Geneticists, molecular biologists, technologists. You perhaps . . .'

She deflected him. 'And is France one of your preferred hunting grounds?'

'France is good.' His expression grew more serious. 'Lots of talent. And they love the adventure of the new. They embrace it. But on the whole, they prefer to stay in France. Can't say I blame them.' He waved a hand round effusively. 'And life apart, the government is pretty good to them. Nor are the investors half bad. Now the British, that's a different story. Riven by ambivalence. They can never make up their minds whether they'd prefer to go back to leeches, thatched cottages and morally sound hot water bottles or leap into the twenty-first century.'

He looked at her to see if she was offended by his words.

'If you mean, do I want my pigs to be half goat, then I don't. And I'm rather partial to hot water bottles. You can't snuggle up to a radiator. On the other hand . . .'

He caught her tone, crinkled his nose at her, rushed on. 'Wasn't always like that, needless to say. A lost time ago, technology used to be a god for you English, a veritable good. Now the country is hardly kind to its scientists, gives them little respect, less money. Yet you somehow manage to produce these brilliant guys and gals – unhampered by impatience . . .' He shook his leonine head in evident perplexity. 'Like this Stephen Caldwell we just walked out on.'

Tessa all but choked on a strawberry. Now was the time to say it. Yet the words wouldn't form themselves on her lips and he carried on.

'And he knows how to go into hiding too.'

'Go into hiding?'

'Yeah. You know, doesn't answer his post, the telephone, even e-mail. I haven't touched base with him for ages until this week.'

'I see.' Tessa began distinctly to sympathize.

'And you? Are you one of these brilliant gals?'

'I'm afraid not. I work in publishing. Academic publishing.'

'So you're headhunting too?'

He had provided her with an alibi. 'In a manner of speaking.' She faltered, grappled for a little truth. 'I'm about to start a holiday.'

'Oh? Well, what do you say you start it right now? Forget about the rest of the conference for today. We can take a little stroll towards my hotel. Give me a moment to check messages. And then the president of the Edward S. Knight Agency will offer you the dinner of your choice.' He winked at her roguishly. 'Maybe even dancing.'

Edward S. Knight, Tessa thought. That was it. The name on the letter she had seen in Stephen's office.

'The S by the way stands for Samuel. What do you say?'

'I'm not sure,' Tessa demurred.

'I am. That's always a start.' He glanced down at her

46

hand and she was suddenly aware of her wedding band. 'Unless you're otherwise and irretrievably engaged?'

'No. Yes. No.' Tessa was no longer sure which of his series of questions she was answering.

Ted Knight leaned back into the banquette and smiled lingeringly at the woman opposite him. He was back in Europe, he thought, and he liked it. A part of the globe where there were an infinite number of subtle gradations between yes and no and where the arts of flirtation he had imbibed with his French mother's milk so long ago did not constitute a felony. He had missed it. Lord knew, he had missed it. And this Tessa Hughes was interesting. She looked as if she wore very clean, very white underwear and had forgotten how attractive she was. He would remind her. He liked her. He liked women. They had nearly always been good to him. And useful.

4

—————*—————

Stephen Caldwell stepped out of the train into the small station which despite its proximity to Paris retained an air of countryside quiet. Outside, along the strip of track, birds swooped from mountain ash to bramble in search of late berries. Their chirping followed him across the narrow bridge. At its end, he paused at a flower stall and after a moment's reflection, he bought the entire contents of a tub of white tulips at the vendor's urging. Cut rate for closing time. Ariane had a predilection for white flowers. Only white, he had learned.

He hadn't intended to see her. But when he had arrived at the flat in the Marais, there were no fewer than three messages from her. She was in some kind of trouble, she intimated.

That was the single disadvantage of using Marco's flat in Paris, as he mostly had over these last two years. People knew where to get hold of him.

When he had returned Ariane's call, she had insisted he come out to the house. For dinner, like in the old days. She needed to talk. He couldn't really say no, even though the pressure of work was more than usually acute. Stephen grinned to himself. He had never been able to say no to Ariane.

The last time he had walked up this slight incline and turned into the street of small, steeply roofed stone houses, they had been all but hidden by a thick canopy of chestnut

48

trees. Summer. Over a year ago now. The months had sped by, eaten up by work. And in these last months, hard, utterly absorbing work in the relative tranquillity of the lab.

Stephen felt excitement tingle through him. He had come up with something singularly important this time. A veritable coup. A ground-breaking discovery. He could barely restrain himself from talking about it, had almost found himself doing so to a French colleague today. And in Lille, where he had stopped over on his way to Paris to take a look at the bioengineering plant with which Camgene had recently set up an affiliation. But Jan had to come first. Until then and after that for the time it took to file the patent application, the discovery had to be kept secret.

Stephen had bumped into Ted Knight in Lille. What Ted Knight was doing there he had no idea. But the man was everywhere, sniffing out his contacts, plying his trade, looking out for investments.

Still, the meeting had had its use. He had taken the opportunity of telling Ted about Jan, built him up. And Ted was a good catalyst. He always knew where the action and the money were. Scared him a little, though. The man had a way of entering a room or a life and pouncing with such vigour on whatever it was that he wanted, that one had to have one's immune system in full working order.

Stephen chuckled out loud. His immune system must be all right. He had managed to stop himself from burbling his findings to Ted.

The wooden steps to the porch creaked a little beneath Stephen's weight. From the basement flat, the old landlady's dog barked once hoarsely. Stephen turned to see whether Ariane was poised behind the white of her curtains as she had sometimes been in the past at his arrival. But there was no dark-eyed face peering through the intricacies of lace. She was probably in the kitchen preparing one of her sumptuous dinners, all sweetened cream and dill and roasts surrounded by black cherries.

She had chosen this suburban house, she had once told him, because it was like the dacha she would never have. And she had reinvented it in that spirit, covering every surface with embroidered cloths and gutting candles, draping shawls over sofas, painting old furniture with bright motifs, filling the open fire with pine cones. So that when he crossed the threshold, he lost his bearings and was no longer quite sure what country he had travelled to.

Stephen smiled, suddenly pleased that he had made the journey, instead of seeing Ariane in town as he had mostly done of late. After all, he had cause for celebration.

He pressed the doorbell and waited for the sound of answering footsteps. There were none. He tried again and glanced at his watch. Trust Ariane to be late, after all her insistence.

He paced a little, shifted his computer bag onto the opposite shoulder, and then with a grunt of impatience began to retrace his steps along the street. It really was time he stopped standing to attention every time someone shouted, 'Help'.

A car screeched to a halt behind him.

'Stephen, wait. Forgive me.' Ariane's throaty voice hailed him.

She was out of the low, sleek car in an instant. Thigh-high boots like a second skin on long slender legs, soft clinging jacket, a broad-brimmed hat half-hiding a vivid face. The stark drama of her beauty always startled him anew.

She caught his appraising glance and, with a smile that was both rueful and teasing, she placed a gloved hand on his shoulder. 'You should know not to be so admirably punctual.'

'I should.' He laughed, a little embarrassed. 'But you were so urgent.'

'It's hard to get you here these days.' She took the flowers from his hands and nestled her nose in them. 'Perfect,' she purred and led him into the house. As she took off her hat, dark, abundant hair cascaded over her shoulders.

'So. Now I can greet you properly.'

Stephen met the proffered embrace, smelled a scent both delicate and tangy.

'I'll begin to think you're trying to seduce me all over again.'

'Maybe.' She gave him an arch look. 'But not until after dinner. And only if you're very good.' She took his computer bag from him and with long strides walked into the living room and placed it carefully on the small desk beneath the front window.

'Have I ever been very bad?'

'You neglect me,' she sighed, though the face she turned back to him was impish. 'But never mind. Now you are here. And you may light the fire and I will bring you something to warm you up even better.'

Within moments she was back with a tray, a bottle of vodka and two tiny crystal glasses. She poured.

Na s'drovie.' She emptied her glass while Stephen lingered a little over the sharp, peppery taste. 'You have been well? Yes, I can see. You are tired. Very tired but very well.' She appraised him as frankly as a doctor performing a check-up. 'And if you are very well that means your work is very well. Am I right?'

'You are right. As always.' He laughed.

'Good. That has a good sound. You will tell me about it. And I will tell you my problems. But first, I must see to the dinner. You relax now.'

'Can I help?' Stephen called after her.

'Never. I do not allow men, as you know, into my kitchen. Especially Englishmen, my Stephen.'

Stephen eased himself into the deep fireside chair and gazed into the flames. It was true he was tired. He was always tired of late, except when it came to work. Though he had thought he had left the tiredness at home with Tessa, had hoped the crossing would eradicate it. But he could still see her gazing at him with that abject disappointment he could do nothing to rescue her from, since what she wanted was not in his power to give. Tessa's suffering, that waiting and wanting and silent accusation, annihilated him. It reduced all his accomplishments to nothing.

He had always assumed that time would do its work and heal the scars and sadness the miscarriage had left. But it hadn't. Time had simply made the problems more intractable.

It was too bad about the lack of children. Really too bad. For her sake. He didn't mind one way or the other. They had got into a knot about it. The more she tried to untie it, the tighter it got. And the more she asked of him, the less he seemed to be able to give. All tangled up.

Stephen shifted uneasily in the comfortable chair and prodded at a log in the fire. Though he was no expert at such things, didn't really like to think about them much, it was clear to him that Tessa wasn't interested in him any more, nor really in the sexual act. Only in its possible product. Her single-minded purposefulness made him utterly weary. Impotent, too. Yes. He might as well put a word to it, though it went against the grain, as if the naming fixed in stony permanence what he hoped was a passing difficulty.

Nor did he want them to go through the endless haul of an assisted pregnancy. Like Sisyphus, pushing his rock up the mountain, only to find next month that one had to start all over again. Tessa didn't really understand how potentially long and difficult and obsessive and too often unsuccessful the process could be. He didn't think she, let alone their marriage, could take it.

Tessa and he had started out so well, too. He liked her so much, respected her. He liked the mixture of sunniness and coolness in her, her dry humour, her incessant curiosity which had nothing invasive about it, her ability to be silent, to immerse herself with intense concentration in her own projects, her self-containment which obviated any need for those kinds of confessionals he felt intensely uncomfortable with, her patience with his own lacks. He had felt safe with her. And lucky. So very lucky that she would have him.

He had never told her that he knew about her and Jonathan Faulks. He had waited for her to tell him herself, and when she hadn't he had felt strangely pleased. Tessa had discretion and integrity, an inner honesty that didn't ask for public confirmation. She had no need to spill or spell things out. A woman after his own heart.

He had learned about Jonathan Faulks in the way one always learned things in that small world which was Cambridge – by chance or grapevine. It was after a guest lecture he had given at King's. His host had taken him to the Combination Room for a drink and introduced him to a gaggle of Fellows, amongst whom there was one who prodded and sparred with him, not unintelligently, about certain points in his talk. Jonathan Faulks. Later, when he had already picked up his coat and bag in the hall and had wanted to ring Tessa, he had seen Faulks in the telephone box ahead of him. He had stood by idly, but he couldn't help noticing the sequence of numbers Faulks had tapped out. He spent most of his life, after all, with sequences. And this one was Tessa's number. He had heard Faulks quite clearly, could only not have heard if he had left the corridor. And he was too interested to do that.

Funny, how he could still quite clearly recapture Faulks's words and tone. First a little bark, a surprised yelp, 'What do you mean, you've fallen in love with someone else?' And then after a pause, in a voice that was all smiles: 'But, my dear Tessa, you and I have been going on for some four years now. It's a little late to complain about secrets.

You're being childish. When you grow up a little more, you'll realize secrets are amongst the best things in life.'

He couldn't, of course, hear Tessa's response, but Faulks had looked thoroughly disgruntled as he left the cabin and had given Stephen only the most cursory of nods.

Stephen had been privately proud of Tessa then. Altogether thrilled when she answered the phone to him and in a blithe voice told him he must come over straight away. She was cooking a special dinner for him. He felt not only chosen, but as if he had helped to save her from a fate she didn't want. That night he had given her the locket he had purchased for her from a jeweller's in King's Parade a few days back. It had seemed so right for her with its delicate leafy tracery and pale amethyst flowers, its subtle clasps and tiny partitions. The rightness had been confirmed by the glow in her eyes as she lifted her hair and asked him to fasten it round her neck. A smooth, graceful neck, which he had touched with shy lips.

Yes, it had all started so well, Stephen thought. Within a few months of their marriage, Tessa had been promoted to commissioning editor and his own work had flourished. He had published a series of papers in quick succession, the fruit of long research, and he had been toppled into something approaching scientific fame. They were happy, settled, productive, fed off the warm certainty of each other.

And after the fiasco of the miscarriage, it had all come to nought. Sometimes he thought that his life with Tessa now had become an endless circling round a windowless, airless tower. At times, she was barricaded inside and there was no height he could scale to get her out. At other times, he was on the inside, his cries silenced by the sheer thickness of the walls. In or out, his helplessness stifled him.

Stephen sank more deeply into his chair. Yes, he was tired. But this room of Ariane's did him good. It hadn't changed. The baby grand was still there with its candelabrum; the vase with its surfeit of white flowers, brought, he had no doubt, by some ardent admirer; the table in the alcove, covered by a starched embroidered cloth and carefully set for two, the sofa with the bright shawls draped over it. They had had good times here. On and off over that first year, before guilt had taken him over. Wonderful times. At home he was about as adept as a fumbling schoolboy. But Ariane had turned him into someone else.

'So. You must start with these that you like so much.' Ariane was back, carrying a platter of canapés: dark bread covered with herring and caviar. 'I have been to Moscow, so the caviar is the real thing.' She ruffled his hair. 'You are already beginning to look more relaxed. Another five minutes and I am with you.'

Yes. Ariane, this house, there was a genie in them which knew how to make him relax. How to take pleasure.

Even after they had stopped going to bed together, he had kept coming back, sporadically, in nostalgia, in friendship. Ariane would tell him stories. Stories which entranced him, literally put him into a trance. In that rare state ideas, connections popped into his mind, more readily and boldly than at work, which too often – particularly in those early years when he had first gone full-time at Camgene – had meant too much time away from the lab.

It didn't matter whether the stories were about her family, her friends old and new, the run of everyday events. Or whether they were wilder, more fanciful childhood tales about the witch Babayaga. Tales that always included three sons, the youngest of whom, the innocent fool, inevitably embarked on a quest which always lasted three times a year-and-a-month-and-a-day. And somewhere on that tripling quest for a princess spellbound in a frog's skin, or imprisoned in a distant tower, or for a golden apple as bright as the sun, or a fiery bird with lavish plumage, he would meet Babayaga. Babayaga, who lived in a little cottage surrounded by a fence made of bone and skull deep in a dark forest.

Like his own witch, Stephen reflected. He remembered distinctly how during one of Ariane's Babayaga stories, he had seen models for the interactions between calcium binding proteins and neurotoxins spring up before his eyes.

This house was part of the magic too. A small, secret place, concealed from the rest of his world, to escape to now and again. Yes, it was the secrecy he had been hooked on, as much as anything else. Had thrived on it, like some spy made superfluous by the end of a war, hot or cold, who still needed his fix.

Perhaps he hadn't got over it yet, he thought as he watched Ariane wheel her serving trolley into the room. She had piled her hair up and the mysterious symmetry of high cheekbones, deep-set eyes and a neck, languidly long, played over him.

She met his gaze with a knowing smile. 'Come. You're hungry. I can see. And you need another glass of vodka.' She poured without waiting for his answer, cut into a duck stuffed with kasha, heaped his plate. 'The vodka is good. My mother made it. Better than my big brother's wine. Ha!'

She sat down opposite him. 'I saw Sacha. He has grown fat.' That deep, luxuriant laugh tumbled out of her and tickled Stephen's skin. 'He has a new business venture. He is importing wine. Wine from Texas. Texas! Do you believe it? It is the first time I have drunk wine from Texas. Texas in Moscow. Sacha has been watching Dallas. Watching with all the seriousness he once gave to medieval icons. And he has been inspired.' She rolled her dark eyes at him. 'I think he wishes to be like JR. I have no doubt he will succeed.' She hoisted up her shoulders, puffed out her stomach comically and was suddenly walking round the room with stiff, heavy steps, making the parquet rebound.

Stephen laughed. 'And your mother?'

'My mother is not so good. It is not good for old people in Moscow. Even with the money I give her.'

He searched her face. 'Have you lost your job with the computer firm? Is that the problem?'

'Not so fast, my Stephen.' She chewed a piece of duck carefully. 'And no. You are out of touch. I had a new job months ago.'

'So? What is the problem?'

'Okay. You don't want to enjoy my food in peace. I will tell you then.' She folded her napkin abruptly, lowered her voice. 'It is my little brother, Dmitri, the one who lives in Petersburg. I saw him too. He has got himself into serious trouble.'

'What kind of trouble?'

'It is a long story. Some years ago, he had a brilliant idea. He set up as a middleman, a kind of travel agent. He contracted boats to take foreigners up the Volga. For cruises, you know. Vodka and culture cruises, with lectures and everything. The shipping companies had nothing to ship so this was a good deal for them too. And Russia is popular with tourists. I even got him some French ones.' She paused.

'It sounds good. You never told me.'

'I have not seen you so much lately.' She poured some more vodka.

'And then?'

'Well, in September his offices were burgled while he was with the last of the summer's boats. Everything was taken. Computers, furniture. And his accountant, a young man who had been working with him for months, was shot. Wounded slightly in the arm.'

'God!'

'No, no, Stephen. That is only the beginning. The accountant was apparently so scared that he ran away and my brother could not track him down through mutual acquaintances or anywhere when he returned. Anyhow, then my brother started to receive threatening letters from the shipping company. They claimed they had received no payment for that summer's boats. When my brother put his nose into the accounts, he found that not only had they not been paid, but the accountant had run off with all the income from the tourists as well.'

'Awful!'

'I told you it was just the beginning.' She plied him with more food. Ate a forkful herself. 'Then Dmitri hired a private detective.' She laughed. 'We have a lot of them in Russia now. Redundant KGB men. With soft shoes and big guns. So this detective went in search of the accountant. And after a while, he comes back to my brother with a bill and a mournful expression and he tells him it would be better to drop the whole thing. Much better. My brother doesn't. He thinks he is brave. He gets an address from the detective and goes to it. He is met by three mafiosi who beat him up and tell him that if they ever so much as see him again or if he breathes a word to the police or anyone else, they will not only do more than beat him up, but they will get his sister in Paris as well.'

'You're not serious?'

'I am very serious.' She sighed, took their plates and piled them on the trolley. 'Then, while I am in Russia, my brother is visited by the police. Or he thinks they were the police. By now he is a little bit crazy. They tell him that if he doesn't pay the shipping companies quick, he will be arrested. So he tells them the story he isn't supposed to tell. And now my brother is living in fear from all sides and is beginning to think Siberia would be better than the mafia. And he worries for me. I worry too.'

She gave him her dark gaze and shrugged. 'I'll bring the fruit and the cake and you think what we should do.'

Stephen paced and stopped to stare out of the window, which gave out onto the small back garden. It sloped darkly beneath the shadow of a spreading magnolia. That first autumn he and Ariane had planted a host of daffodil bulbs beneath it and in the spring the garden was a dazzle of yellow.

'The daffodils were wonderful this year.' She had come up softly behind him and seemed to read his mind. She draped her arm round his waist and nestled into his shoulder. 'So. What does my Stephen say?'

'I don't know. I really don't know. It all seems so improbable.'

'But it is true. Or so my brother tells me. You have not been to my country for some time. Things are not good.'

Stephen drew her towards the sofa, took her hands. 'The first thing is that I don't think you need to be frightened. This is France. Nothing will happen to you here. Those little gangsters won't extend themselves so far.'

She shivered. 'I don't know. I have had these strange phone calls. People hang up. I'm afraid to be alone at night. Natalya comes to stay with me – if there is no one else.' She gave him her slow smile. 'Tonight you will stay. You can sleep on the divan upstairs.'

He looked away. 'We'll see. The second thing is the shipping company needs to be paid.'

'Ha! You don't know the money that's involved. Not in twenty years could my brother . . .' She stood up abruptly, her back erect, a haughty look on her face. 'No, Stephen. I am not asking you for money. I do not want anything from you, except . . . except clarity. When I talk to you, things become clear. All my Russian friends, bah, melo-drama. And the French . . . my colleagues, I don't like to tell them. They will think I am mad. But you, you under-stand and you are cool-headed. A cool-headed Eng-lishman.'

'Have you spoken to Simone?'

'You have not seen her for some months. I do not think she is very well. She doesn't need my problems.'

'So. Let's think. You find out exactly how much your

brother owes. You go to the bank, ask for a loan. I might be able to stand you security. Some others too, depending on the amount. Your brother clears his debts, gets a visa and leaves the country.'

Ariane laughed. 'You make it so easy. But, Stephen, I cannot be indebted to you for my whole life. It is not so easy.'

'One step at a time. You find out first.' Stephen leapt to his feet, paced the width and length of the room. 'Your brother writes to the shipping company and says he is raising the money. He will pay them slowly, if needs be. In instalments. Better something than nothing as far as they're concerned. He can say he'll raise the price for the tourists for next summer and pay them more. At least they stay in business that way, keep their ships working. And meanwhile, with any luck, your little gangsters will kill each other off in their next escapade.'

She clapped her hands. 'Yes. You are right. Of course. Of course. Keep the business going.' She threw her arms round him and held him tight. 'You help me breathe.'

Stephen looked into her eyes and stroked her hair softly. Strands had fallen round her cheeks. As she pressed herself against him, his body suddenly tingled with the memory of her. He drew away.

She laughed. 'You know what. I have this great desire to beat you at chess. Like in the old days. A lightning game. Fifteen seconds a move. Do you still have that computer program with the little hourglass and the dings?'

The telephone rang as he nodded.

Ariane shivered, let it ring and ring. Finally, with a determined set to her shoulders, she marched over to the small desk and picked up the receiver. After a moment, her features relaxed. She broke into Russian, smiled and gestured him towards her. She covered the receiver with her hand. 'It's Natalya. Start the program while I listen to her.'

Stephen switched on the machine, punched in his code,

waited for the chessboard to flicker onto the screen. Ariane edged beside him and with deft fingers tapped her king pawn forward. He replied with a pawn to queen bishop three.

Moments later, she surprised him by playing a sharp reply to his Caro-Kann defence, enticing his queen into the centre of the board with the bait of a central pawn. She followed up with a series of forced exchanges which left his king exposed to a mating attack. He didn't know whether she was giggling to Natalya or over his queen stranded out of play. In another few moves her queen and knight had bulldozed their way through the centre, trapping his king in an embarrassingly simple checkmate.

She put down the phone with an air of triumph.

'You haven't lost your touch. All those years trouncing your brothers have paid off.'

'And you look so tired that I think I shall have to put you to bed and not offer you a return match.' She grinned. 'I have exhausted you with my problems.'

'No, no,' Stephen demurred.

'I insist. You must take a nice hot bath now and I will prepare your bed. You will sleep the sleep of angels.' She winked at him. 'Sometimes without one's wife, one sleeps better, eh, Stephen.'

Stephen lay in the vast old tub amidst a mountain of bubbles and once more acknowledged his weariness. It had come over him again at Ariane's mention of Tessa. Her hopeless, accusing face hovered over him and with it came that sense of helplessness. There was an irony in having arrived at the summit of his scientific achievement and feeling that nullity at his core, as if the inevitable mid-life crisis had caught him out too soon, his organism sniffing its end, the junk DNA piling up and snuffing out any vitality. Not that he had ever been much good at sex and all that. Hated talking about it, too, particularly in the way that Tessa had latterly attempted – with a kind of tortuous banality, full of clichéd magazine solutions.

He was too inhibited, he supposed. Except with Ariane, who had enough desire and wit for two.

Maybe it was because he had spent too much of his life in and around schools, in the constant shadow of their discipline. A host of rules that he couldn't even begin to rebel against since any act implicated his father, whom he loved but was afraid of. His father had been a Classics master, large and stern and too dignified in the black graduate's gown which always covered ordinary clothes. Because of his father, the other boys had left him pretty much alone, apart from the occasional run of teasing.

There had been that one summer, though, when he was fifteen and they had all gone off to the West Country to spend a few weeks with a cousin of his mother's. It had been his first real taste of freedom. Of girls, too.

He could still see Jennifer, with her wild tangle of hair and skimpy summer frocks, leading him a mad chase across fields and fern-strewn woods. She was thirteen, but she might as well have been twenty to his studious timidity. She always made him take off his glasses before they went into the barn. There she would let him touch her. Tiny breasts, downy legs. She would touch him too, examine him all over and laugh. He could still hear that peal of a laugh. One day, towards the end of their enchanted stay, she had given him her knickers, and her white slip of a bra with the daisies embroidered on it. To keep under his pillow, she said, and to take home with him, so that he would remember her. For weeks he had slept with them clutched in his hands, then grown more adventurous and wrapped them round his quivering penis.

Soon after they returned to the cottage that bordered the school grounds, his mother had died. Even though he knew by then it was cancer, he felt responsible. He hadn't been kind to her that summer, had wanted to act the man for

Jennifer and so had refused her attempted embraces. He was miserable after her death, guilty. She had always been so gentle with him, had always attempted to counteract his father's distance and severity. The only soft presence in the male world of school.

The day of his mother's funeral, he buried Jennifer's things at the bottom of the garden. It was raining. The ground was sodden and even before he had thrown earth over them, the garments turned a muddy brown.

His father became sterner after his mother's death, but seemed to crumble internally. Conversation was reduced to a series of Latin quotations, as if his father could now only speak through the voice of others and by repetition. Stephen hadn't realized this Spartan, self-sufficient man depended so much on his mother. She had been the quiet one, filling her time with amateur ornithology, embroidering lavish birds on teacloths and cushions. Perhaps she had simply wanted to fly away.

He could still remember some of his father's quotations. '*Voluptatem sapiens minimi facit.*' The wise man makes little of pleasure. Or '*ne libeat tibi quod non licet*' – let not that please you which is not lawful. Or '*virtus plurimae exercitationis indiget*' – virtue needs very much practice.

When he had gone up to Cambridge, his father had shaken him firmly by the hand and intoned, '*Solent diu cogitare qui magna volunt gerere*' – they are wont to reflect long who wish to do great things. And in his father's last letter to him, though Stephen hadn't known at the time it was to be his last, he had once again had recourse to Cicero and written, '*Ad bene vivendum breve tempus satis est longum*' – for living well a short time is long enough – the very words he had uttered at his wife's death. The stroke which killed him occurred a matter of days after Stephen had received this letter, as if his father had had a premonition of it.

It was towards the middle of his first year at Trinity. A

chemistry graduate who had befriended him had offered to lend him his car, so that he could drive to the funeral, bring back what he needed. Stephen didn't have his licence yet, so they had set off together and returned with a boot-load of his father's books and his mother's cushions.

He had lived under their aegis for the next few years, only breathing freely when he was distant from them – either cocooned in the microscopic world of the lab or, yes, here, on the Continent, shielded by the expanse of the Channel.

Stephen opened his eyes. Above him, hanging from a ceiling rail, was a silk slip of a nightie. It glowed softly peach like Ariane's skin. An image of Tessa padding up the Cambridge stairs in her old robe and slippers suddenly came to him and with it a tangle of emotions he didn't want to face. He whipped them away, focused instead on that peach garment which bore a trace of Ariane's shape.

Ariane. He remembered precisely the occasion of their first meeting. Moscow in the February of 1990. He remembered so precisely because it was the first Soviet scientific congress he had managed to get his friend Jan invited to. Remembered too, because it was only a few months after Tessa's miscarriage and he had intended to tell her before going off about Jan and all the parts of his life he hadn't been able to make her privy to before. But Tessa was unapproachable, inhospitable to any confidences. It wasn't the moment to burden her with his past. Then the moment had slipped away. And after that, she seemed to have lost interest in him altogether.

It was Jan who had introduced him with a rakish wink to Ariane Mikhailova.

'The best interpreter I've ever met. It's too bad I don't need her,' Jan had laughed and in that laugh Stephen had heard the sound of yet another of what he supposed to be Jan's innumerable conquests. Jan was good with women.

He had confidence and an enviable charm. Waitresses, nurses, lab technicians, everyone responded. Even those hatchet-faced women who collected all tickets and monitored all exhibitions in the Eastern bloc. He could see the effects of that charm in the look Ariane thrust at his friend from beneath the thick curtain of her lashes.

She was a tall, slender young woman, a girl really, if one focused beyond the requisite garb of sternly grey suit, white shirt and graceless shoes. Her face was a perfect oval. Her skin flawless, rendered even creamier by the contrast of dark hair and eyes. But it was her neck which captivated Stephen, its movements as languid and graceful as rushes in a breeze. Lucky Jan, he had thought to himself, happy in a vicarious game of identification.

But Jan had been effusive in his introduction of Stephen, noted him as certainly the most important scientist at the congress, and the next day Ariane had approached him during the lunch break. She had asked him if he mightn't like a little air. It was nice down by the river. She could show him the sights, perhaps.

He knew the sights well enough, but he didn't like to say no, so they walked together in the brightness of a day which obliterated the grime of the city. On the way, she plied him with questions, about London, about Cambridge, about the West, eating his words so greedily that he wasn't sure his supply would be adequate. He didn't mind her hunger. He understood it. It was a hunger born of closed borders and big skies. When they were as blue as today they stretched the imagination as extensively as frontier guards patrolled the country's limits.

'I should so like to travel,' she had said to him when they paused briefly on the banks of the Moskva. With a little tremor, she had squeezed his hand. Then she had taken out a compact from her purse and with a gesture he only knew from old black and white movies, held a mirror to her face and carefully applied bright lipstick. He was standing behind her and he could see his lips above hers in the glass, the quick flicker of her moistening tongue, the trace of a languid smile. The moment captured a transgressive intimacy.

Nonetheless, when he returned to the stolid grandeur of his room later that evening, he was shocked to find her stretched on his bed. He wasn't even certain he recognized her. She had exchanged the severity of her daytime garb for a bohemian blackness of pencil-slim trousers and roll-top sweater. But it was her hair that threw him. He hadn't imagined its lush length, nor a face transformed in the soft lamplight into a series of mysterious planes.

She had leapt up at the sight of him and put a stilling finger dramatically to her lips. Then she had proceeded to make love to him. Stephen still flushed at the ardour of it. Even had he tried, he wouldn't have been able to resist the silent secrecy, the risk of her lips and limbs.

The next day in the bustle of the Congress Hall she had put a note stealthily into his hands. He had kept it there until the next session, when the cover of his papers made an unobserved reading possible.

'Take me to the West,' the note said. 'Invite me to a conference. Anything. Please.'

That night he had hoped he would find her again in his room. He had brought back a bottle of wine for the occasion. But the room had been miserably empty. Not his dreams though. She had filled them with traces of herself as luminous and vibrant as her presence.

The following morning, he saw her talking to a French delegate and he wondered whether she had spent the night with another man, sowing her chances liberally. Jealousy nudged at him, but he couldn't attribute blame. He knew enough about the ways of the East, the nature of her particular desire, to recognize that any man must for her simply be the means to an end. Before he realized he had moved, he found himself at her side. At lunchtime, they were walking together again, this time along the Arbat, with its new tourist boutiques.

He had stumbled over his words. 'I'll try. Though England may be difficult.'

She had looked at him, her face a bright gem above the swathe of heavy fur, like a younger Simone, he had thought for a moment. She had taken his hand, fingered the wedding band gently. 'Paris, then. I would love to see Paris. Stay there for a while, if it is possible. You will be my saviour. Please.'

That night she was in his room again. And a few months later, at the first opportunity, he had had her invited to a conference in Paris. It hadn't been so difficult. Borders were crumbling. The world was taking on a different configuration. His world too.

One taste of Paris and Ariane was certain she didn't want to go back. He had prodded Simone into helping. She had come through as she always did. Favours had been called in, papers arranged. And on a wintry day, Ariane had urged him out of the city to see this house, the house of her dreams she had called it. He had paid her rent for a while. But soon enough, she was earning her own keep. She had been well-educated, scientifically educated, as Jan had told him from the start. Her father had been a chemist. Her mother at that time was still teaching in a school on the outskirts of Moscow. And Ariane had languages, French as well as English and her native Russian.

No doubt, in these last years, there had been a slew of other saviours. He had no illusions on that score. She was too beautiful and avid a woman for any single man. But she had kept up with him. Made time for him. And he was more than grateful for that.

Stephen stretched out his hand to touch the silk of the nightie. It fell towards him, floated on the water, caressing his skin. He stood to hang it back on the rail. In the wall mirror he could see his torso straining. Could see something else as well. He stared down at the erection in disbelief. That hadn't been there for some time. And through the opaque shimmer of the fabric it looked huge. Too big. He didn't want to touch it, didn't quite know what to do with it.

'Stephen?' He heard a knock at the door and Ariane's voice. 'Have you fallen asleep?' The door opened and she gazed at him with a little smile. 'I see you have missed me after all, my friend.' She put out her hand to him.

Later, in bed, after the repeated tussle and greed of their mingled bodies, he felt oddly buoyant, as if some bright, multi-coloured balloon had lifted him out of the mire into a stratosphere of blue, traversed only by the most limpid of clouds.

As sleep tugged at him, he thought of Tessa again. He hoped she was having a good holiday, basking in the sun, that she would come back renewed. He asked her to forgive him.

5

—— * ——

Tessa woke up in a hotel room that wasn't her own. The walls were covered in pale yellow brocade. A walnut escritoire on spindly legs stood in one corner. Sunlight peeked through shutters and fell in mellow stripes on a deeply piled carpet. She stretched languorously, touched the pillow next to hers. There was a note. From him.

She looked at the flowing scrawl of the writing, so like the man.

'*Bonjour, ma belle Anglaise.* Don't forget. Lunch at one at the Brasserie Lipp.'

Tessa smiled. She lay back on the pillows and remembered. Remembered everything.

They had walked past the Assemblée Nationale with its great stone figures, along the Boulevard Saint-Germain, then down boutique-lined streets and across the Pont du Carrousel. They had paused to look at a view which only that morning had left her devoid of emotion and now filled her with excitement. Then they had strolled through the grand square of the Louvre and stopped for a drink in a café tucked inside its ornate columns. As if by some juggler's magic, one side of it gave onto interior sculpture gardens while the other flanked the Pyramid.

On the way Ted had told her about some of his favourite bits of the city – the ones they weren't passing; the ones he had a special feeling for because they marked a childhood year here with his mother, way, way back in the late

69

forties: the steep and raucous market in the narrow Rue Mouffetard; the menageries on the right bank of the Seine, with their doves and strange fish and hens and kittens, all overlooked by the turrets of what could have been his knightly castle; the street smell of plump round apple doughnuts, which still made him salivate.

She had liked his evocation of his childhood. She could see him as a small boy in neat short trousers and bruised knees, his head a tousle of blond locks, his eyes a mischievous blue as he looked up at the woman who was his mother. Stephen never talked about his childhood. Maybe that was why he wouldn't talk about children of his own. She had a sudden happy memory of all those articles she had read on sperm and the comparable superabundance of those of men born in the forties.

After that they had walked along the softly illuminated paths of the Tuileries Gardens, where the earth was starkly white and pebbly beneath their feet. It was growing chill and when she had shivered, he had put his arm around her as if it were the most natural thing in the world to do. When he had stopped under a tree and turned to kiss her lightly, that too felt good, right, a little affectionate step on the road to something. Or not. Somehow, it was easy. It didn't matter. He made her feel, she didn't know quite how, and maybe it was later, that they were both old enough to know there was no necessary destination. Journeys were there for their own sake. Little snatches of a different life, intense with their own sounds and smells and sense.

It had been so long since she felt like that – at once desired and protected and adventurous – that the tears had suddenly bitten at her eyes and she had insisted on waiting in the lobby while he collected his messages and made phone calls. Then there had been dinner. He had spent a good quarter of an hour considering the restaurant. He wanted something to suit his wry and secretly romantic

Englishwoman, as he had then named her, who obviously didn't like this city as much as he did.

'I'm getting to like it better every minute,' Tessa had noted and he had parried, 'So the evening won't have been wasted.' And they had looked into each other's eyes then and both smiled in a shared expectation which wasn't yet knowledge.

The restaurant was airy and white and had thick, priestly candles on each of its tables. There were windows overlooking the river and every time a boat went by, they were floodlit, so that Tessa had begun to feel she was on a film set, which was fine now, since someone else seemed to be handling the script. He had, he told her, gone for atmosphere rather than food, though the food seemed more than adequate and the wine delicious, if not quite so delicious, for her, as the quality of his attention.

They exchanged few facts and more stories. She learned, in passing, that he had been twice married and now long divorced, probably to the relief of all parties since good relations on the whole prevailed. Names of children and stepchildren dotted his conversation as erratically as they seemed to drop in and out of the Malibu beach house, the ranch (yes, he said, there really was one and with horses) and the apartment in San Diego.

She had the sense that he spent his life whizzing from place to place. And the intimation that he probably kept his women happy enough because there was so much of him to go around. What he told her was that he was impossible to live with because he was never there and somehow wives expected you to be, which was fair enough, but didn't work for him. Not now, not any more in any case. He was getting on and there was too little time left not to fill it as best as one could.

Tessa had told him that, in comparison, she was the world's most boring person, that she had lived in two English towns in the whole of her life, but that she liked her work and was good at it. And that was always new. She had talked about the current crop of books she was editing and they had exchanged anecdotes about authors and about Cambridge, which he knew a little, particularly the Laboratory of Molecular Biology where he had once visited Stephen, amongst others. She hadn't wanted to talk about Stephen then, hadn't prodded him.

Nor did he question her directly about anything more personal than she was prepared to reveal. She was pleased at that, decided he was a man of tact.

Later, they had walked along the river and he had asked her if she would like to come back with him. She had liked. She liked it even more afterwards. She had forgotten what it was like to be with a man. A new man who seemed to know more about her than she knew herself. A man with rippling limbs and deft hands, who made her feel desired, desiring, alive.

She didn't think of betrayal. She wasn't giving him anything that Stephen wanted. Morality was such a tedious and barren schoolmistress and she was too old for school. She felt, too, that though she was now launched on an adventure rather different from the one she had first intended, this one was somehow fitting, an adequate counterpart to Stephen's.

But on the whole, she didn't think very much. She simply let vitality course through her.

He had undressed her slowly and smiled. 'White, I knew it.'

'Don't you like white?' She had felt shy, feared that she would fail him.

'I love white,' he had whispered and kissed her. 'And I'm going to make you love you too.'

He had.

Tessa rolled out of bed, a hum on her lips. She turned on the bath tap and watched water stream onto glistening porcelain. There had only been one moment when she had wanted to stop him. When he had expertly and automatically tugged on a condom, she had wanted to stay his hand, say, 'No. I don't mind. Please.'

Ted's child.

She hadn't, of course. Couldn't find the words.

Gone were the days, Tessa thought as she washed and dressed and didn't for once check for new creases in the knees she now hated, when she might have been accidentally impregnated. Now one had to speak out, make an issue of it. Raise the spectre of decisions. And the future. Yet he would never have to know if it happened. And it could happen. Why not? It was possible. She suddenly felt anything was possible.

She wondered if she could say it to him, tell him she was clean, healthy, and if he was, then why not? But no, she couldn't. It was only really because she didn't know him well enough. Not yet.

When she left the hotel to tackle the streets, they felt far less romantic than her recent memories. She decided to go to the Musée d'Orsay as Ted had recommended. It was a way of keeping up a link with him in his absence. She imagined him striding through the gates, stopping to smile at an attendant, then greedily absorbing the pictures.

But when she reached the first room off the main concourse she forgot him. All her attention was taken up by a man escorting two small girls who held on tightly to his hands. They were twins, blonde and ringleted and bewitching, each one wearing a different brightly coloured toque and each one listening raptly as their father spoke. Tessa could barely turn her eyes away to look at the pictures. It was not only the children: it was the look on the father's face as if his little girls had descended from a special place to be put in his care and he had somehow to preserve that specialness lest they vanish.

She scolded herself for her sentimentality, sensed it was

part of the cloud she was walking on which might at any instant brew storms. But she felt it all nonetheless. She also felt, as she absently followed them from room to room, that she was in danger of becoming one of those mad women who impulsively kidnap infants only in order to smell the talcum powder on their bottoms.

When she finally focused on canvases, all she saw was peach-tinted women holding babies, a mass of plump and luminous flesh. Mary Cassatt. Had Ted guessed, she suddenly wondered? Was that why he had sent her here rather than the Louvre?

She lingered in the room and considered for the hundredth time the different ways there were of having babies. You could have them with men, which seemed to be the simplest, most efficient way, but could also prove the most difficult. You could have them with science, which posed, as Stephen had so emphatically told her, some risks. But then everything in life had a risk attached. Or you could have them in a way that was also socially useful – a kind of redistribution of wealth: you could adopt. But for that in England, she needed her husband's cooperation, so she was back to point one. A vicious circle.

She had read of bold single women who had travelled to distant countries – India, China – and after years of preparation, come home with a child. Perhaps that would have to be her way. Yet again, though, she would have to confront Stephen, charge him with his double life. Whichever way she turned, this husband who had become a stranger stood in her path.

He was probably at the conference now, Tessa thought. Maybe he would see Ted and they would face each other, not knowing one particular item they had in common. For some reason, the notion made her vengefully happy. But she didn't want to search Stephen out now. Not yet. She felt a little like someone who was slowly beginning to recover from a long illness and is suddenly newly awake to colours and scents and sensations. She wanted Ted's strength to flow into her, make her vigorous. Then she would face what had to be faced.

After the exhibition, she went shopping. She hadn't shopped so much in years. A displacement activity, the women's magazines said, while the ads opposite offered sumptuous titbits for consumption. Displacement of what? Would she shop more and more the less and less possible it became for her to have a child? Would she become a menopausal shop-lifter as she crossed over from one age into the next, stealing to fill the void of hormones and love?

Tessa put it out of her mind. For today, for now, she was shopping because she was in Paris and soon she would see a man who noticed what she was wearing. That was certainly reason enough.

Punctually at one, after a rapid change in her own hotel room, she was sitting in the Brasserie Lipp decked out in a new dress, the smoky colour of Paris rooftops, and with a hint of raindrops in its clinging texture. A moment later, she saw Ted fling open the door and dash in. Once again she was filled with an impression of boundless energy. It seemed to flow into her, shore her up.

'Hello, there.' He brushed her lips, surveyed her. 'Grand. Is it new?'

She nodded, flushed a little.

'For me, I hope.'

'Especially for you.'

'Good. And this is for you.' With a teasing smile he handed her a small packet wrapped in glittering paper.

She opened it quickly. 'Ysatis. How lovely!' She sprayed a little on her wrist.

He drew her hand to his nose and sniffed. 'Mmm ... Guess it's for me too. We'll have to find something which is just for you.'

'This will do just fine.' She considered him, slightly at a loss as to what to say next. So she babbled. 'Do you know, I once edited a book on smell.'

He chuckled.

'Yes, really. If I remember correctly, it claimed that smells influence us biologically. Musk, ambergris, civet, I think it was – all those glandular secretions from animals – are apparently incredibly close to human testosterone. In one experiment by some perfume consortium, they found that women who sniffed musk developed shorter menstrual cycles, ovulated more often and found it easier to . . .' She clamped her hand to her mouth, realizing where her chat had led her.

'Conceive,' Ted finished for her.

There was silence for a moment. Tessa stared at the table in mortification. Now he would recognize the failure that haunted her.

'You don't have any children.'

She heard the flatness in his voice. It wasn't a question. 'Is it that easy to tell?'

He cleared his throat. 'I've been with a number of women, Tessa. I'm not exactly a stripling.'

'Of course.' She couldn't bring herself to meet his eyes.

'And you want a child?'

She nodded, was about to flee from the table when he put a staying hand on her wrist.

'It's hardly a perverse desire, you know. Nothing to be ashamed of. Altogether natural.'

Tessa stared at the consoling bluntness of the long fingers on her arm.

'Though these days, it gets a little hard to locate the natural – particularly in my line of work. What with test tubes and donor eggs and donor sperm and surrogacy . . . there are miracles everywhere. Virgin births by divine medical intercession. What will you have?'

Tessa looked up in disbelief, only to see a suited waiter at their table. She stifled a giggle.

'A glass of white wine would be nice.'

'Bubbly?'

'Why not?'

She watched him as he conferred with the waiter, liking his garrulous ease, liking the way he discussed the menu, suggested dishes to her. So unlike Stephen, she thought, and put the thought away.

Ted turned back to consider her. 'You know, when I was a boy, my mother used to tell me a whole lot of fairy tales. I think she made them up, because I never managed to read them anywhere later. There was one particular one I never forgot, all about a brave knight and his lady in some great fortified castle in a remote French region. They were desperate to have a child, a boy, of course, though a girl would have done. But the years came and went and never brought a child. So the king consulted the wise man of the court, an old chaplain, all clad in black I guess, and the chaplain suggested fervent prayer, offerings and above all that the knight and his men join a crusade and make their way to the holy city.

'And though he was loath to leave his lady and his castle and his dogs, the knight went.

'The very evening of the knight's departure, the chaplain brought a young man, a troubadour, or perhaps he was a wandering scholar, to his lady's quarters and told her that she was to entertain the young man until the moon was again full and to do everything that he bade her. It was God's will. So the lady, noting that the young man's locks were as dark and rich as her husband's had once been, did as she was told.'

The waiter brought their food, salad, large slabs of buttery sole. But Tessa was more intent on Ted's narrative. She urged him on. 'And what next?'

Ted grinned. 'And after a year or so, when it was

rumoured in the castle that the knight and his remaining men had been seen in the region, the chaplain rode out to welcome them and announced to the knight that the Lord had chosen to smile on his deeds and answer his dearest wish. A son had been born to his lady some three moons back and his hair was already as fiercely dark as his father's. Needless to say, there was great jubilation in the court and they all lived happily ever after. Though of the wandering troubadour nothing was ever heard again. Even the good lady rarely thought of him.'

Tessa looked sceptically at Ted who gave her a broad grin. 'Your mother told you this?'

'In a much, much longer version over many nights and with many deviations and variations over the years. But that was it, in essence. I told you she was special.' He raised his glass to Tessa and winked. 'I think she was trying to tell me something about paternity. My own, maybe. My father was a lot older than her and much absent. I used to think about it over the years, though I never confronted her.'

Outside a cloud had burst. They could hear the rain splattering on pavement and awning. A couple came excitedly through the doors, chose the table next to theirs and sprinkled them with wetness as they removed jackets.

'Some dessert while we sit it out?'

Tessa nodded. 'And the moral of your tale?' she asked a little breathlessly, wondering whether he was offering to act the troubadour to her lady.

'Just what I was getting to. Long way round.'

Irony played over his features.

'Well, when I grew into the age of reason, I used to think it was that women are our touchstones for nature. To witness a birth is to know by the evidence of our senses, to know with certainty that the child is the mother's child. Hers by nature. Biologically hers. As for the father, well ... they say that one per cent of males are responsible for partnering sixteen per cent of females.'

He flashed her a rueful smile that she didn't know what to do with. She cleared her throat but he rushed on before she could speak.

'All of which means that paternity has to be authorized, confirmed by law or by belief, an act of faith. Like Mary and the Holy Spirit. Or the Public Record Office. And our entire civilization has been built on this difference between men and women. The entire apparatus of law and property came about because we can only be certain about maternity. Nature doesn't like the male, so he has had to defend himself from it, shore himself up. Now we're a little more even.'

This was not the moral Tessa had expected. Or wanted.

'So that's why you're a biotech enthusiast,' she said with more bitterness in her voice than she had intended. 'Get rid of women, get rid of the natural altogether. Mix goats and pigs in a test tube.'

'No. No. You're jumping to conclusions.' He eyed her shrewdly. 'Though you see what a topsy-turvy world we're moving into. We're in the midst of a revolution and half the time we don't know it, can't bring ourselves to know it. It's too distressing. And too exciting. I suspect that's why we're in such a mess about sex roles. Technoscience has ruptured the link between mother and nature. You can no longer know for certain, by the evidence of your senses, whether the mother you see giving birth to a child is really that child's biological mother. And presto.' He snapped his fingers like some cabaret magician. 'Everything, all identity, is up for grabs. Brilliant.'

'And only you scientists, by administering your little DNA fingerprint tests, can tell us for certain.'

'You don't like this conversation.'

'I'm not sure.'

'You're an old-fashioned girl who'd like her hot water bottle.'

Tessa shrugged.

'And a child.' He said it softly. 'Presumably your own?'

She met his eyes for a fierce second, then looked away. 'The rain's stopped.'

'Good. Let's go. Though I don't know if you're gonna enjoy where I'm gonna take you.'

Moments later they were standing in a small boutique on the Rue Jacob. On folds of muted blue velvet, chains of thickly coiled silver, intricately linked bracelets, earrings roped and thonged, pendants with cryptic fetishes rested like so many miniature items of bondage laid out for a secret rite.

Tessa suppressed a shiver. She looked up at Ted without knowing quite what to say.

'Like it? Come and meet the artist. She's an old friend.'

The woman he introduced her to looked neither old, nor like the kind of woman who could ever be a friend. She was tall and blonde with a blondness that smelled of diamonds and villas on the Riviera and with lips that looked as if they had been stung by a whole hive of bees carrying paintbrushes.

'Sylvie dos Santos. Tessa Hughes.'

Stung lips curved into the glimmer of a smile. Fringed hair swished gracefully and Sylvie dos Santos put long cool fingers into Tessa's unwilling hand.

'*Enchantée.*' She dangled a pair of keys towards Ted. 'Enjoy.'

With a glimmer of apprehension, Tessa wondered what it was that was to be enjoyed. Wondered, too, as Ted led her through vast double doors into a courtyard, whether she had made a serious mistake.

'There. Seemed to me it would be more fun to drive out to the fair.' He ushered her into a white, soft-top Mercedes. 'And quicker.'

'A fair. I see.' Tessa slid into the soft leather of the passenger seat and mocked her own dark fears. 'Your Sylvie dos Santos is a very fetching woman with a very fetching car,' she murmured as he manoeuvred through the narrow streets with the dexterity of a native.

'Mmm . . .' Ted wove his way between cars, shifted gears with pleasurable aplomb, came to a sudden halt at a red light as they crossed the Pont des Invalides. 'Quite often the boys make the most gorgeous women.'

'What?' Tessa knew she hadn't heard him correctly.

He revved along the opposite quay, swung down a ramp so that they were level with the river. He laughed. 'I know it's hard to believe, but Sylvie used to be a boy.'

'What?' Tessa repeated inanely.

Ted threw her a comical look. 'Don't tell me you're going to go all puritanical on me.'

'I think I am. Puritanical, I mean. You're not serious. About that woman. Sylvie?'

He took her hand and placed it on his thigh. 'You weren't so very puritanical last night,' he said softly, then laughed. 'And I'm perfectly serious. I told you identity was up for grabs these days. Sylvie was a very unhappy young man whom one of my sons befriended in Rio. And then she became a woman. I helped her find a clinic, all that medical side. And then she moved to Paris. She's talented, beautiful. She's okay.'

By the time they had whizzed along a stretch of motorway then slowed into a suburb and arrived at the vast stony expanse of the Château de Vincennes, Tessa thought she was probably just about okay, too. She stole a glance at the man at her side. She liked the decisive ruggedness of his profile, the sprawling size of him. She liked the feel of his thigh too, beneath the soft wool of his trousers. His enthusiasm. For everything. She hadn't thought of Stephen or felt resentful for at least an hour. She cleared her throat. 'And what is this fair you're taking me to?'

'Pharmaceuticals. Instruments. I've got a meeting at

Stand G in twenty minutes or so. It shouldn't take too long.'

He swung into a road which cut through graceful woods, then into a car park surrounded by trees. A path led them to a large exhibition hall. Inside everything was shrill voices, a dazzle of light leaping off shiny surfaces, a bevy of computer screens.

Ted was evidently in his element. 'If we lose each other, or you feel like wandering, we can meet back at the main door at about five. Okay?'

Tessa nodded. But she didn't stray from his side as he whizzed round from stand to stand, pouring information in her ear. About new drugs and magically constituted hormones. About nerve growth and diagnostic techniques and probe assays and lasers and Ciba and Roche. He paused to pick up leaflets here and there, stopped for a moment to talk to one white-coated man and then another and another. She had no idea whether he knew any of them or whether the friendly manner was simply Ted Knight.

Stand G bore the name Pharmacor. Behind its polished counter stood a striking, long-legged woman in a black suit, which showed no trace of blouse beneath its severe jacket. Her dark upswept hair left her ears free to display heavy thonged rings. These bore a distinct resemblance to the jewellery Tessa had seen earlier.

The woman moved towards Ted and smiled at him from sultry eyes. Tessa stood aside. She had no doubt, this time, that here indeed was an old friend.

'Give me a few minutes.' Ted left her to follow the woman through a door at the back of the stand.

Tessa waited. She sat on a chair at the stand's side and glanced nervously through a stack of glossy company reports. Pictures of women and men in laboratories, white-masked and capped and goggled. Vials and bottles and syringes. Children of all colours and sizes benefiting from drugs, offering testimonials.

As she flicked the pages and looked round her, Tessa realized that she felt like some fish that had strayed from its familiar school and blundered into an alien sea. Headier, more brightly coloured waters, filled with vivid objects, exuding danger. Stephen had never taken her into these waters, though presumably they were his as well.

The minutes passed and with them came a glimmer of jealousy of the woman who was holding Ted in that back room. Unreasonable, she told herself. She had only known the man for a little over a day. But it told her she cared, though she didn't quite yet know, sensibly, what it was she cared about.

To prove to herself that she didn't care any more than she ought, she got up and started to walk around. She scanned incomprehensible video diagrams, watched miniature films with commentary in both French and English. At one stand where she paused for a film on HIV research, she was approached by a sweet-faced young woman who barraged her with information. Tessa thanked her in her clumsy French, then, with a quick glance at her watch, pleaded an appointment and darted away. Ted would already be by the doors.

But he wasn't. She waited with a sinking heart. That woman had kept him. By the time six o'clock had come and gone, she began to chastise herself for her own stupidity. She was chasing daydreams, like a schoolgirl, instead of taking her life in hand. Though Ted had seemed to be giving her exactly the confidence she needed to confront it. Gone now. Evaporated into a mist. Not that she could blame Ted. She couldn't compete with the woman she had seen. She was too conventional. It was too long since she had engaged in passionate games. Stephen's fault. Her own, too, if she was honest. The honesty didn't taste good.

She started towards the taxi rank, joined a queue, had almost reached its front when she felt a hand on her shoulder. Ted.

'I thought I'd missed you,' Tessa murmured.

He muttered a brief apology, barely looked at her. There was an angry set to his shoulders. The scowl on his face transformed his features into something she hadn't imagined. He looked hard, cruel.

He swung the car abruptly into gear and raced them along the wooded road, dusky with shadows now that evening had set in. When they met a snarl of traffic, she heard him curse beneath his breath.

'Has something gone wrong? Would you like to drop me off somewhere?' she finally forced herself to ask.

He gave her a blank stare, then focused on her with evident difficulty. 'No, no. Just a hiccup. But I have to get back to the hotel. Check some things out. Do a little work. Rearrange a meeting.'

He didn't speak again until they had reached Notre Dame where, with an abrupt change of direction, he veered into a small semi-circular street and stopped short.

'Can you wait here? It'll save me a ticket.' He suddenly smiled his charming smile and raised her fingers to his lips. 'Okay?'

'Okay,' Tessa echoed.

She turned round to watch him go. With a start she realized they were next to the street where she had sat yesterday morning staring so vigilantly at a door. Ted now seemed to be heading straight for it. She got out of the car and stared after him. But she couldn't see beyond the corner and, with a shrug, she sat down again.

He was back within a few minutes, visibly more cheerful.

'Sorry about all that. Business sometimes has to come before pleasure. And there's just a little more of it.' He stroked her hair. 'Nice. I prefer blondes.'

Tessa wondered whether he was comparing her to the woman at the Pharmacor stand. She wanted to ask him whom he had just been to see, whether it might be a certain Simone Lalande Debray and whether she was a brunette too. But before she could phrase the question, he was chuckling, veering them into traffic with brash carelessness.

'You remember your Raymond Chandler? There are blondes and blondes . . . That wonderful catalogue?'

Tessa didn't like to admit she had no idea what he was talking about. She made a sound which was neither yes nor no.

'Well, I suspect, though I'm not quite sure yet, you're the perky, companionable sort, full of good old common sense. And you can toss a truck driver over your shoulder without missing a sentence out of the editorial in whatever highbrow paper it is that you read. Not the metallic one who has a disposition as soft as a sidewalk. Nor the shimmering, hanging on your arm sort, who develops that god-damned headache as soon as you take her home. No, the first.'

Tessa wasn't sure about the description, but she was pleased he was smiling. 'Speaking of editorials, did you find me any prospective authors at the conference this morning?'

'Not sure. You can always try me.'

'Do you write?'

'No. But fifty's as good a time to start as any. Don't you think?'

She raised mocking eyes to him, 'You'll do me a history of headhunting, no doubt. Blonde heads, maybe. I'm not sure that's quite in the Press's line . . .'

'Maybe not,' he said a little ruefully. 'But there are other subjects I can think of.'

Tessa laughed. 'Like the provenance of babies. *Children and the Ethics of Origin*. Something like that.'

'Now there's an idea. Might even surprise you and do it.'

They had pulled into an underground car park and were making their way towards the gilded glass doors of his hotel. In the lift, Ted rubbed his face with a grin. 'But first

85

I could use a shave. What do you think?' He drew her fingers over his cheeks.

Inexplicably an image of the garden of her childhood home in Sussex came into her mind. The children were the weeders. Every summer Saturday, they went out into the garden and pulled and dug and cut creepers and twiners and lush moss and clover and dandelions. By the next day, as if by magic, there was a whole new crop. 'Fertile soil,' her father said. 'Grows everything. Won't stop.'

'Mmmm,' Tessa murmured, then suddenly laughed. 'Look.' She pointed to a small engraved notice beneath the mirrors of the lift. 'A perfect rendition of French into English.'

She read aloud. ' "Please leave your values at the front desk".'

'I'd be happy to oblige, ma'am.' He grinned and kissed her.

The next morning dawned as bright and crisply clear as Ted's eyes when he waved her off at the door of her own hotel.

'I'll be back at eleven thirty. Only got one meeting and a trip to American Express. So I'll be punctual this time.' His gaze was rueful. 'And don't forget to check out.'

Tessa went up to her barely used room and packed and wondered what the surprise Ted had promised would be. He had first mentioned it last night. She had left him to work in quiet and gone back to her own hotel to change and have a leisurely bath before dinner. Lord knew she needed the bath after what they had got up to. It made her realize that Stephen and she had never really had sexual passion, not that she could remember any more, in any case. She prodded her thoughts away from Stephen.

When Ted had come to pick her up last night, he had been as gleeful as a child to whom Santa had delivered a long-desired present. When Tessa had mentioned it, he simply said he had missed her. He liked having her around. No one, she realized, had said that to her in a long time.

As she folded her clothes into a case grown too small, it passed through Tessa's mind that she had carried out none of her intentions in coming to Paris. She really ought to go back to that conference, which should be ending about now, and hunt down Stephen and have it out with him. There was just about enough time for it. And she would relish the look of astonishment on his face as she flounced off and said she had a date with a better man. With the emphasis on man.

But she really didn't want Stephen invading the dream she was living. There was a danger that he would confront her with his blurry, uncomprehending eyes and reduce her to nonentity. To silence, too. No. The confrontation could wait.

In the midst of that previous night of endless loving, a fantasy had pounced on her. It still caressed her with its soft paws. Another few days and she would cajole Ted into leaving those condoms aside. He had already asked her whether she wanted to accompany him on the next leg of his journey. East to Prague. The idea enticed her. Even more did the distant prospect of a softly rounded belly, a child, the occasional visit from a loving father.

As punctually as he had promised, Ted was waiting for her in front of the hotel on the Rue du Dragon. They wove their way through Paris traffic onto the Périphérique, and then past Fontainebleau onto the A10 towards the south-west. The vibrant rhythms of a tango filled the car and punctuated the flat expanse of fields.

'I used to come mushroom-picking around here,' Ted boomed over the music, then turned it down. 'If it were the right season, I'd take you off on one of these side roads and into a little wood.'

Tessa shot him a glance and thought she had a pretty good idea what he got up to in little woods. 'You'd have to watch out. I'm an expert on mushrooms. I could feed you some meaty chunks of *Amanita muscaria* and send you off into twitches and wild hallucinations. And you'd wake feeling elated. Or dead, of course.'

'Dangerous woman.' Ted overtook a car with swift precision.

'Dangerous, common little fungi. Pretty, though.'

'I'll have to watch you carefully.'

'You do that,' Tessa laughed.

'And where'd you pick up all your lore? No, don't tell me. You edited a book on mushrooms.'

'I had a world expert for a teacher.'

'No kidding.' He shot a glance at her. 'A lover, I imagine. You have that murderous look in your eye.'

'I didn't know it showed.'

Tessa gazed out of the window at a landscape blurred by speed. It was true. She had wanted to murder Jonathan once. It was towards the end of their long-drawn-out affair and she had imagined serving up a plateful of his beloved fungi, tossing in a little death cap masked by plenty of garlic, and waiting for the ghastly and inevitable symptoms to set in. A fitting end, since they had met on a mushroom hunt organized by the college.

She could still remember the way Jonathan had ploughed his little fork into the ground, had pulled out base and earth and fungus, sniffed and peered at stem and flesh and gills and ring. Occasionally tasted and spat, his lips pursed like those of a triumphant child engaged on something naughty. He had talked too, conjured up a darkly fertile world, a vast thread-like undergrowth which spread for miles beneath their feet and of which the visible mushrooms were only the reproductive organs waiting to spill their spores. When they had first made love in the woods, she had imagined she was lying on the crest of buried trees as thick beneath as they were above, a bed as abundantly fruitful as its canopy of oak and chestnut.

But, of course, she had been on the pill, Tessa reflected. So all that fertility had done her little good. Perhaps she should have taken more note of the lethal bombers overhead, darkly ominous birds which took off from the sprawling Lakenheath airbase and regularly punctuated the tawdry idyll of their lovemaking with their ear-shattering noise.

Stephen had saved her from all that. She had loved him then.

Tessa shook her head and avoided his image.

'Where are you taking me?' she turned to Ted.

'Vendôme. Another forty-five minutes or so and we'll be there. Why don't you choose your favourite music and put your hand just where I like it.'

The first she saw of the town was a curling river, followed by a steep hillock topped by clustered gables and slate roofs. A towered gate complete with sculpted dolphins led them into its centre.

'Fourteenth century,' Ted offered. 'The abbey and the church are even older. Flamboyant Gothic, I'm told. Apparently old Geoffroy Martel, while he was in Constantinople, picked up the tear Christ shed at Lazarus's resurrection and brought it back here. It used to be a great pilgrimage centre.'

'Can we visit?' Tessa gazed up at ancient stone spires and a wonderfully slender bell tower.

'Sure. But I have to tell you, just in case you're feeling in need of resurrection, that the Revolution put an end to all that. A little blunt reason in place of Christ's tear.'

'You approve, of course?' Tessa had rather fancied a touch of salutary magic.

'That's hardly up to me. The Lazarus motif is still everywhere, though.'

They parked, and walked through a pretty, perfectly

89

symmetrical square where the market was just shutting down.

'Which reminds me. If we don't eat now, we won't get any lunch. We're in the provinces. And lunch is as sacred an affair as any church visit. How about it?'

Tessa laughed. 'I suspect you didn't bring me here for sight-seeing in any event.'

'Maybe just a very little. After lunch.'

They ate tucked away in an arched alcove of a small restaurant, had a peek into the cold, silent church, then strode rapidly through the town.

'It's time for your surprise.' Ted urged her back into the car.

They drove over narrow roads which cut straight lines through bare, wintry fields, a flatness indented only by small stone hamlets. Ruffled clouds scudded across a vast sky. Their destination, when it emerged, bulked large on the landscape, a turreted stone building at the end of a row of sentinel-like cypresses. The open iron gate bore a plaque.

Tessa read: 'Centre de Procréation Médicalement Assistée'. She hesitated, felt the aura of romance she had created for herself plummet as surely as a wounded bird. 'Is this what I think it is?'

'Yeah. It's one of the best IVF places. Professor Marriot has a high success rate. And he's discovered this apparently brilliant technique for testing frozen embryos which I need to check out. Meanwhile, I've arranged a tour for you. Thought you'd be interested after our conversation yesterday. I want to introduce you to the excitements of the twenty-first century.'

Tessa found a brittle laugh. 'I suppose I should be relieved you haven't brought me to a cryogenics centre.'

They walked into an airy waiting room, leafy with fern and ficus and dotted with armchairs in bright primary colours. The chairs were discreetly distant from one another, perhaps so that the waiting patients couldn't see the expressions on each other's faces. Tessa stared.

The couple in the far corner were leafing unseeingly through magazines. Their faces had a dogged patience about them, as if they had been here many times before and were clinging to hope against the odds. Another woman beneath a vast potted palm sat very still, all her nervousness displaced into her gloves which she wound and rewound into tight, thin strips with quivering fingers.

In the window seat, a man was clutching his wife's hand. There was a look of entreaty on his face. His eyes had a vagueness about them, a poignant, unfocused air of loss. Perhaps he was at fault, Tessa thought, his sperm unequal to the task. She glanced at the woman's haughty face and wondered about their rows – bitter, accusing.

She shivered and turned away, met the eyes of a small, dark woman, who beamed a confident reassurance, as if she wanted to tell Tessa that it could be all right. It could work. Her hands, Tessa noticed, were clasped protectively round her stomach, signalling a tell-tale bulge which wasn't yet visible. Tessa returned her smile.

With a deep, uncertain breath, she positioned herself and Stephen in a more distant, shadowy corner. Stephen would have that blank look on his face, the one that denied his surroundings, denied her, refused to face their plight. Unless she kidnapped him, she would never even be able to get him near a place like this. That was clear. He had never actually said so, but she sometimes thought that he didn't really want a child at all, that the notion of a baby's eventual reality had less existence for him than any of those gooey substances in test tubes. He left all that to her. And now he had left it to her absolutely.

Tessa forced a brightness onto the face she turned towards Ted, who had just finished talking to the receptionist. Moments later a man and a woman emerged from separate doors and Tessa found herself shepherded off by the woman, efficient in a white uniform and sensible shoes. Her English was only slightly accented as she explained the various kinds of fertility treatment the clinic offered. Tessa listened with half an ear. She was more intent on seeing what she had only read about: banks of donated eggs and sperm, dishes where the two met for fertilization, ranks of instruments and hormones her mind wouldn't focus on.

Yes, Tessa thought. Everything would be so much easier with Ted. Sex. Simple. Infertility treatment. No problem. He would ring and fix up the dates. Quieten her fears. Happily do it into a bottle. Might even twinkle and ask the nurse for a helping hand.

Yet, as she tuned into a ream of statistics about the relative successes of intra-uterine insemination and in vitro fertilization, the wonders of the newest technique of intra-cytoplasmic sperm injection – which culled a single recalcitrant sperm and introduced it directly into an egg – she had to acknowledge to herself that, for all the romance of science, she would far prefer the human romance.

Averting her eyes from her guide's, she hid her hands behind her back, crossed her fingers, thought of Ted and made a wish.

6

————— * —————

Stephen Caldwell cast a covert glance at his watch and waited impatiently for old Lefort to get through the rhetorical flourishes which were *de rigueur* in his quarterly progress reports. No sooner had the man finished speaking than he sprang up, muttered apologies for his haste, and stole, a little guiltily, from the meeting. To delay would mean to be caught up in the inevitable drinks and chit chat. He had two pressing reasons for avoiding these. The first was pardonable: he didn't want to have to avoid Lefort's eyes as he grilled him about his own research. The second was less so.

Stephen rushed down the boulevard, squeezed between the homeward-bound commuters on the RER and found a few centimetres of space at the rear of the train.

When he had left her yesterday morning, Ariane had told him she finished early on Thursday, so he could be as early and as punctual as he liked. She had said it with her teasing smile, straightened his tie flirtatiously. Wednesday evening wouldn't do though. She was busy then.

He hadn't liked to ask whom she was busy with. What did it matter in any case? He would have one more glorious night with her before leaving Paris. The knowledge of that had floated over these last hours like the promise of brilliant sunshine. It was odd how the excitement of her had returned to him, as potent as in those first days. He wondered for a moment why that should be. Maybe the success of a long bout of scientific work really could have an effect on his private parts.

As her station approached, he ceased wondering and raced over the bridge towards the house. No need to stop for flowers today. He leapt up the stairs of the porch and pressed the bell into prolonged shrillness. He hoped Ariane would like his little present for her. He hadn't been able to resist it when he had spied it in a shop on the Rue du Bac. A translucent perfume flask, bell-shaped and ripely yellow, at once opaque and vivid, as lovely and mysterious as one of Morandi's bottles. Or Ariane herself.

He peeked round the banister of the porch to see if he could spot her through the window and suddenly noticed that her lace curtains were down. She must have embarked on one of her cleaning expeditions.

Stephen rang again, impatient now. Ariane couldn't be late today.

From somewhere he heard a dog's bark, the sound of a door. A moment later a voice called out to him, *'Il n'y a personne.'*

Stephen turned and saw the tiny figure of Ariane's landlady, making her way slowly from the side of the house.

'Ah, Monsieur Caldwell. C'est vous. Venez, venez.'

Pebble-dark eyes beamed at him from beneath a wisp of white curl. *'Entrez,'* the woman repeated. She stilled her yapping terrier and ushered Stephen towards the door of the basement flat.

'Mademoiselle Ariane has gone. Didn't she let you know?'

Stephen stared at the woman in incomprehension. 'Gone?' he mumbled. 'When will she be back?'

'No, really gone.' She gave him a sympathetic smile. 'Left yesterday. Gave me two months' rent to complete her lease. And this morning the removal men came. They didn't take everything though. I'm to keep the rest. *Un petit verre?*'

she queried as he followed her into her overheated front room. 'I was just going to serve myself one.'

Stephen shook his head, then changed his mind and nodded. 'But I don't understand, Madame Sorel. You mean Ariane has moved out.'

'Yes. All of a sudden.' She handed him a glass.

'Do you know why?' Stephen felt a shiver of apprehension.

'No. She didn't say. I shall miss her.'

'Did she leave a message for me? A letter perhaps?'

'*Ah non*, Monsieur Caldwell. I would have given it to you straight away.'

'Of course, of course.' Stephen downed the sweet apéritif.

'And the movers? Did you speak to them? Do you have a forwarding address?'

'Mademoiselle told me she would send me one in due course.' She peered up at him curiously. 'I think she was putting her things in storage.'

'I see.'

'If you know any other charming young women like Mademoiselle Ariane, you will tell them about my house, yes?'

'Yes, of course. Thank you.'

Stephen let himself out before he was drawn into further conversation. His pulse raced more quickly than his feet on the pavement. He should have paid more attention to Ariane's fears instead of behaving like a man made complacent by too many years in a country where the rule of law largely prevailed. There must have been a new threat. Or worse. He didn't want to think of that.

His mind sped over the list of friends and contacts they had in common. Then he hastened his pace, burst into a run as he heard the sound of a train approaching.

* * *

At the flat, there was no blinking light to signal the hoped-for message. Quickly, he disburdened himself of computer and conference materials and Ariane's present in its careful boutique wrapping. He hunted through the Minitel to see if he could locate her friend Natalya Yurasovska's number. He searched under various spellings to no avail. Just to check he wasn't dreaming, he tried Ariane's number and got only a high-pitched tone. Disconnected. He chased away the image of a hand brutally yanking a cord from a wall.

He was about to leave the flat when he remembered the igloos. Better to check those out now, just in case he was detained. He couldn't take any chances, even if the freezer had proved reliable so far. Deftly, he pulled the styrofoam cages from the compartment, extracted the small tubes from the dry ice and examined the tiny quantity of sludge at the bottom of each. No change. Elation shot through him and disappeared as quickly.

After that, he took the metro to Pyrénées. He walked along darkened streets dotted with homely restaurants, Chinese, Yugoslav, Portuguese, Armenian. This old working-class quarter with its tiny, hidden work-and-sweatshops had paid host to immigrants and refugees for centuries. Here they lived side by side, whatever it was that divided them in their own countries.

Stephen turned into a deserted square where regularly placed iron poles and heaps of rubbish signalled a daytime market. A woman appeared from nowhere, dragging a squalling toddler behind her. The child gulped down his whines at the sight of two patrolling policemen, gazed up at them with frightened eyes before he was yanked away with a '*Ça va pas, non!*'

Stephen crossed the street, stopped in front of a door which had needed a coat of paint some years back, and pressed a buzzer.

'*Da?*' A muffled voice eventually emerged from the intercom.

'*Boris est là?*' Stephen didn't dare try his few rusty phrases of Russian.

The door opened into a hallway cloudy with smoke, which grew thicker as Stephen walked into the main room. Even at this early hour the place was crowded. Couples and groups sat huddled over small, square wooden tables dense with bottles and glasses. Ashtrays disappeared beneath their baggage of ash and old stubs. Muted voices occasionally burst into argument or spilled over in laughter. In the distance there was the sound of a wailing violin.

Half club, half dive, Stephen had told himself when he had first come here with Ariane some years back. He had always liked the place.

A balding man with a snub nose and moistly dark eyes came towards him. His shirt was rolled up to the elbows. His baggy trousers were loosely gathered with an old belt which flopped as he walked. He stretched his arms out to Stephen and hugged him hard.

'Long time no see, Stephen. Welcome. Welcome.' He spoke in heavily accented English.

'Good to see you too, Boris. Can we have a chat?'

'And some dinner, yes. Come, come. In the back.'

Boris led him up some stairs into a smaller room where tables were set for dinner. The violinist, as lean and pale as if he had been starved of food and daylight for years, sat in the centre of the room on a creaking wooden chair. A cigarette hung from his lips as he played.

'In a moment you will hear something fabulous.' Boris urged Stephen into a chair, came back with a bottle. 'That one, he is very good. And that one, he is at the Conservatory and almost as good.'

A younger man bearing a cello sat down beside the violinist. They gave each other a single look and burst into a duet, staccato rhythms gathering momentum as they played, challenging each other with virtuosity.

Stephen listened, fascinated by the cigarette between the

violinist's lips. Its ash grew and grew, defying gravity, beating it as the duet reached its climax and the room erupted in applause. Only then did it spill over the violinist's knees, a prisoner of music released.

Boris hastened to put a glass of vodka in the men's hands, patted each on the shoulder in turn.

'With these two, we shall soon rival the Salle Pleyel,' he grinned at Stephen. 'So what brings you to us? You want some best piroshki? Anya will fetch them.' He gestured at his plump wife, held up two fingers.

'I was wondering whether you'd heard anything from Ariane. I'm worried about her.'

'Our Arianouchka? Ha!' He slapped his head in evident exasperation. 'She's been behaving like a bear who has danced for too long and wants to breathe the fresh air of the forests. Always in a bad temper.' He lowered his voice. 'My Anya thinks she maybe is . . .' His hands drew a circle around his stomach and he winked at Stephen. 'Maybe it is yours?'

Stephen flushed. 'No, no. I don't know . . .' He pictured Ariane's slender curves, then forced himself back to Boris. 'She's left her house.'

'Really? This I did not know. The last time we saw her, three weeks ago, four maybe, when she came back from Russia, she mentioned nothing. Only said she had to work too hard. Then made the piano tired.' He gestured towards an old upright in the corner of the room as his wife set a plate of piroshki and sour cream in front of Stephen and smiled.

Stephen shook her warmly by the hand, waited while Boris spoke to her in Russian for a few moments.

'No. Anya knows nothing of this move.'

'Did she mention anything about her brother to you?'

'The one who imports wine from Texas?' Boris guffawed.

'No, the other one, the younger one.'

The man shook his head. 'Natalya. You should speak to Natalya. She knows everything. Even that Frenchman, what's his name, François something, who was courting our Ariane. A conductor or a banker. I don't remember.'

'Do you have Natalya's number?'

'Sure, Anya will bring it for you.'

Stephen made himself swallow the food, chatted for a few moments more with Boris, tried to draw him out on any Russian racketeers plying their trade in Paris. On the last score he met only with deviations and finally a stubborn silence.

When he went into the narrow corridor to telephone, there was no response from Natalya's number. A sense of dejection hovered over him. He stifled it in movement.

Half an hour later, he emerged from the metro into the Place Saint-Michel and walked through busy nighttime streets bursting with youth towards the Quai de la Tournelle. When in need, what did one do but turn to Simone? Grand and wonderful Simone. He had to see her in any case, apologize in advance for not being able to accept her invitation. She wouldn't like that. But she would understand. Simone always understood.

Ariane had once reminded him of Simone. They shared a vivid beauty, an aura of enigma. But Simone wasn't replicable.

He allowed himself a moment's pleasurable reminiscence to keep his fears at bay.

When he had first met Simone, years before he met Tessa, he had still been a student – green and quivering behind the ears, as unworldly as they could come.

It was late in the summer of '78. He had just completed his first degree and his supervisor had taken him aside and suggested that a complete break, a genuine holiday, would do him no harm before he immersed himself in research. Even scientists, he had added with a wryness which had only later become apparent to Stephen, needed to know something about the world outside the laboratory. If he wanted to travel, a grant might be found, and there were always contacts, former students or researchers who had returned to their native countries, places to stay, people to visit.

It was Stephen's first introduction to the international community which was science.

He had cycled round the north of France and Brittany with a friend, slept in youth hostels or a tent and gradually in August made his way to Paris. The city overwhelmed him with its beauty. He was not, by experience or nature, a city person. The schoolboy trips, once to Hamburg, and once with his parents to Rome to visit classical sites, had left him untouched. London, he was a little afraid of. But Paris, in the quiet of August, wooed him with its formal splendour. The geometry of squares and boulevards and hidden courtyards fascinated him. He explored the city's structure with all the fervour he normally gave to cellular forms of organization and he ended up by staying far longer than he had planned.

When Pierre, the biochemist and absent host of the spare two-room flat behind the Panthéon, returned from summer beaches, he invited Stephen to camp out on the sofa for a few more days so that he could introduce him to an insider's Paris. One of the points on that insider's map was Simone, the mother of Pierre's girlfriend.

Stephen had never met anyone like Simone before, never would again in fact. Nor had he ever been in an *hôtel particulier* with its own courtyard and fountain, its own stone nymphs above the threshold, its own unfolding series of rooms with pictures on the wall, which looked as if they might have come from one of the museums he had visited. He felt like some clumsy feudal peasant who had been thrust from the cowshed into the queen's presence with no adequate preparation.

The queen, contrary to expectation, wore no gilt or royal

robes. She sat on a capacious white sofa in a room washed by early evening light, and she too was all in white, but for the gleaming darkness of hair, the flash of eyes and the curl of a ruby smile with which she welcomed them.

Stephen, who was usually tongue-tied with women, didn't know how it happened, yet by the end of the evening round that dinner table where he sat at her right, it was clear he had told her more of his life history than he realized he knew or cared about. He had also told her he was planning to visit Prague and she had asked him whether he might consider taking something along for a friend of hers.

Of course he had said yes. If she had asked him then and there to walk across hot coals or dive a hundred feet, he would have done it. The wonder of it would have been that he would probably somehow have emerged alive. Simone gave him a kind of courage, an importance, an interest – in himself as well – which he had never before tasted.

Later, but that was a good deal later, he also realized she had the invaluable talent of making him think he had arrived at ideas or perceptions himself, when in fact she had helped him to them.

Stephen saw her three times before he left that summer, and after each visit his fascination grew. He dreamt of her, dreamt of the mobility of her face and the intensity of her eyes, dreamt of witty, rambling conversations about the state of the world and the state of the self, dreamt of a room where the curtains blew light and airy and candles gutted in an ornate candelabrum.

He also dreamt her as the city, a series of brightly illuminated parallel boulevards and intricate, densely inhabited side streets which abutted on splendour or mystery at every turn.

The fascination had remained despite the closeness of their bond. He would have liked to introduce Simone to

Tessa, Stephen reflected, but the timing of that, too, had been wrong. And then, after Ariane, it didn't seem right to bring Tessa to a woman who knew far more about him than she did.

Stephen tapped out the door code and made his way into the courtyard where the fountain still stood, as unageing as Simone herself. He had begun to suspect that Simone lied upwards about her age, if only to produce a greater effect. Only the last time he had seen her, had she begun to show her years. There was a certain fluttering in her movements, a shortness of breath. But he wouldn't lecture her about her cigarettes again. They were as much a part of her as her unerring instincts.

He pressed the inner doorbell and was met by Yvette, the housekeeper, in her perennially neat black dress.

'*Ah, Monsieur Stephen. Madame vient juste de terminer son dîner. Elle est un peu fatiguée. Mais . . .*'

'*C'est qui, Yvette?*' Simone's husky voice emerged from a side room.

'It's me, Simone. I hope I'm not too late. I needed to see you.'

'Stephen. A welcome surprise. I was wondering this very afternoon when I would hear from you. I was too busy to drop in on your conference.'

Simone stood before him, offering her cheek. She was regal, as always. Dark, elegantly cut hair, eyes that flashed brighter than her rings. A soft, deep blue dress moulding slenderness in impeccably restrained lines and broken only by the knotted flair of a teasing silk scarf.

'Come in. I was just having some coffee in front of the fire. My latest grandchild paid me a visit today and now I'm only good for staring into the flames. But you're troubled by something.' Simone surveyed him with practised eyes and noted that Stephen was at last losing the boyish air which had been his for so long. She was pleased about that. It was time he made his true stature known.

'I'm worried about Ariane.'

'Oh?' Simone hesitated for a fraction of a second in her pouring of coffee. That wasn't what she had been expecting. 'A cognac, Stephen?'

He nodded absently. 'I was meant to see her this evening at her house. And she's vanished.'

'Vanished?'

'Yes. Moved. Moved suddenly, according to her landlady.'

Simone bent to stoke the fire. 'And you think this is more than her dislike of saying goodbye?' she asked softly.

Stephen stiffened. 'When I saw her on Tuesday, she told me she was scared, living under a threat. She didn't like to bother you with it.' Quickly he outlined Ariane's brother's plight.

Simone listened carefully, her face unmoving. When he had finished she took a cigarette from a gold box and lit it slowly. 'As far as I know, Stephen, Ariane's younger brother went to America some months back.'

'Went to America?' he repeated inanely. He started to pace the room, stopped in front of an abstract oil to gaze at golds and russets blending into each other.

'Yes.' Simone came up behind him. She placed a hand gently on his shoulder. 'Ariane talked about going to join him when I last saw her. She said she was tired of Paris . . . Come and drink your cognac, Stephen.'

He sat down opposite her and emptied his glass in a single gulp. 'In other words, you think I've been fed a line. Given the brush off?' Stephen tasted humiliation.

Simone shrugged. 'I don't know.' She paused. 'I thought the two of you . . .' She waved elegant fingers in the air, smiled. 'I thought you were simply friends now. Had been simply that for some time.'

'I thought so, too, until this week.' Stephen struggled to erase the note of self-pity which had crept into his voice.

'Someone mentioned to me that she might be pregnant. Do you think . . . ?'

Simone gave him one of her inscrutable looks. 'That, of course, is possible. I have no certain knowledge. But we must talk of more significant things, now.' She threw up her hands. 'We cannot let a pretty girl interfere too much with the progress of science.'

Her laugh tinkled in his ear, compelling a sense of proportion. With effort he shifted his thoughts onto another track and told her in broad terms of what were indeed more important things. She listened with her usual total attention. Her face, beautiful with the trace of its years, mirrored his narrative.

'But that's wonderful, Stephen. Congratulations are due.' She hugged him, refilled his glass, then studied him in silence for a moment. 'And your wife, Stephen, this wife you keep so wonderfully to yourself, whom you promised to introduce to me some time ago, have you been remembering her in the midst of all this? For some years now, I have been hoping for a little godchild from you. It's perhaps what I am best at now. Soon it will be too late.'

Stephen started to pace again, randomly picked up a book that lay on a corner table, flicked through its pages: *The New Economies of Eastern Europe.* He turned abruptly back to Simone.

'I shan't be able to come to your gathering, Simone. I'm sorry.'

'*Bonsoir, grandmaman!*' A young woman who was all long limbs and pert bosom strode into the room and placed airy kisses on Simone's cheeks. With a coltish toss of honey-gold locks, she glanced up flirtatiously at Stephen and stretched out a hand. '*Bonsoir.*'

Stephen stared at a wide, pouting mouth, limpid eyes, didn't allow himself to stare at the tight crop top and tighter jeans.

Simone laughed. 'I can see you don't remember Antoinette, Stephen. Paule's daughter. She's become quite a beauty, hasn't she?' She turned to her granddaughter. 'You're refreshingly early tonight. Jean-Michel is away, I take it.'

Antoinette sank into the sofa, tossed off her shoes and curled her legs under her. With a little moue, she complained to Stephen. 'Grandmaman doesn't approve of my boyfriend. That's because she refuses to read her Aristotle. I showed her the passage.' She shot her grandmother a look of pure provocation. 'The best, the most fruitful unions are made between women of eighteen and men of thirty-seven. While both sexes are in their prime. That can't be wrong, can it?'

Stephen looked uncomfortably away. It was hard to believe this young woman was Paule's daughter. God, he was getting old.

Simone noted his unease and smiled at them both benignly. 'Aristotle also says if you're too young or too old, you only make girl babies. Which I think, Stephen will back me up, is hardly the wisdom of science.' Humour lit up her face. 'Antoinette has taken to quoting the greats at me to support her view of the world. It keeps me on my toes, which aren't as nimble as they used to be.'

'Yvette didn't by any chance leave me any dinner?' Antoinette dropped the argument as abruptly as she had started it. 'The late shift at the hostel makes me ravenous. All those Italians and Americans munching their sandwiches as they come in.'

'Off you go.' Simone shooed her away. 'Into the kitchen and leave us to talk.'

They watched her go.

'Antoinette is the bane and joy of my life these days. Paule sent her to me because she wants to study acting. And Paris has more possibilities than Geneva. But until her course starts, despite her job, she seems to spend all her time with this wholly unsuitable boyfriend of hers.' She shook her head with a sudden air of exhaustion. 'But you were telling me that you couldn't come to my gathering, Stephen. I'm sad about that.'

'Yes, I am too. I have to be in Prague for a few days. And then I'll have to get back to Cambridge and immerse myself in interminable form-filling. I've already left it for too long.'

Simone slowly reached for her coffee cup. She looked suddenly frail, her arms too thin.

'Very sad. It was to be an occasion for me. An important one. I had hoped all of you, everyone, would come. The whole network.'

Stephen sat down beside her and took her hand. 'I'll try. Perhaps just for the night.'

'You see, I'll tell you now, it's a kind of farewell. I am giving over this house, funds, everything,' she gestured around her majestically, 'to create a centre for Eastern European studies. And then I shall move to the sea and live very, very quietly. And privately. No more committees or boards or lectures or articles or pretences at an expertise I do not feel.'

'Simone!'

'Ah, yes. My time is done. Has been for some years now. I have delayed, too long really. And one must mark the end of an era.' She waved away his protests. 'So tell me, what will you do in Prague?'

Beyond the bright smile, he suddenly detected the abyss of her melancholy. 'Why don't you come with me?' he found himself saying. 'A change. It will do you good. Revisit old haunts. And we can have some time together. You can see Jan. He often asks about you.'

She rose abruptly, searched for a second cigarette, then put the pack down again and laughed. 'Perhaps. Why not? I can take your mind off Ariane. I'll sleep on it. But now you must leave me. I have a few things to do before that sleep.'

*　　*　　*

As he walked east along the river, Stephen could not quite take his mind off Ariane. He replayed their last evening together, that night with its reborn passion. He felt a sudden, stupid stirring of it in his newly kindled body, felt the brush of her limbs, the secret movement of her tongue.

Had there been any indication that it was all a deliberately staged goodbye? The thought depressed him. He remembered how, in that first of her years in Paris, Ariane had fallen in love with a song which she played over and over for him, almost like a tease. Fifty ways to leave a lover. Was that what she had done? Get out the back, Jack. But why entice him, only to leave him?

Rain had started to fall, thick, cold, slushy drops. They beat down on his hat. He secured it more firmly as a gust of wind blew across the river. But he didn't want a cab now. He turned onto the narrow bridge which led past the memorial to the deportations of the Second World War. Dark now. Everything dark and hushed in the shadow of the cathedral.

No. He wasn't altogether convinced by what Simone had intimated. Ariane had told him that she hadn't confided in her. He couldn't shake off the sense of danger Ariane had conveyed.

Suddenly, from the other side of the bridge, he heard a shout, the sound of feet scuttling on wet pavement, a wail.

A figure was running at breakneck speed in the direction of Notre Dame. Another bulkier form set off in pursuit, then stopped in visible hopelessness and shouted, 'Stop, please.'

As Stephen crossed over, the shout became a whimper.

'Can I help?' he asked, having just registered the bulky, hooded form spoke English.

'He grabbed my purse, my bag, my camera. Everything.' A woman turned towards him. A girl, really. She was sobbing. 'My first day. My very first day.'

'Bad luck,' Stephen murmured. He peered in the

direction he had seen the man running, looked down along the bank of the river. There was no one to be seen, except a shape huddled on a bench. 'I think you had better go and report it to the police.'

'The police?' the girl wailed.

'Yes. There's a Commissariat not too far from here. Come on, I'll show you.'

She sobbed once, then trotted along beside him, wiping her tears on her sleeve.

After a moment, she said, 'You're English?'

Stephen nodded.

'That's good. I'm American. Though today they've made me feel I might as well be from Mars. I hate it here already. The jostle and the stench and the bitter coffee and all those supercilious French guys ogling you. And the muggers . . .' She stifled a sob, added plaintively, 'I was just trying out some nighttime photography.'

In front of the imposing stone of the Commissariat, she looked up at him. 'I . . . I don't have much French. Could you come in with me?'

'Of course.'

One policeman guided them to another who sat behind a battered typewriter in a shabby room too large for its few occupants. Stephen explained, waited as the man wound a form into the machine, and proceeded to translate. He found out that her name was Cary Wilkinson, that she was twenty-two and came from Lexington, Mass; that her camera was a Pentax and her bag contained her passport, airplane tickets, a credit card, traveller's cheques and all her money, as well as a hairbrush, a diary, a pen and other bits and pieces. That she had that very morning left her suitcase at a youth hostel behind the République, though she couldn't remember the exact address. It was in her bag. She sobbed again at that, then took off the bulk of her hooded coat. Beneath it she was surprisingly pretty, all curling copper hair and blue eyes and a smattering of freckles.

The policeman advised her to come back in the morning with an address and a telephone number. Stephen, once they were outside again, suggested she ring home to have some funds transferred and set off for the American Embassy straight after breakfast.

She stared up at him with a bleak face, stained by silent tears, murmured a 'Thank you', then gazed round at a loss.

'Look, my flat's not far from here,' Stephen heard himself saying. 'Why don't you phone home from there. I know that can prove difficult at a hostel. Then I'll give you some money. For a taxi and whatever.'

She beamed a smile at him. 'That would be great. What's your name, by the way?'

'Stephen. Stephen Caldwell.'

She stretched out her hand to him. 'Hi.'

Stephen reflected, as they walked through the wet cobbled streets of the Marais, that he had always ended up bringing home strays – cats, dogs, the misfits in the classroom. And now this girl. Guilt, he guessed. They hadn't located the gene for that yet, his recklessly reductionist and irresponsible fellows. There had been a few at the conference. Sometimes he was ashamed to find himself tarred with the same brush. He could almost hear the bowdlerized media version of it already. Gene located for disposition to guilt. Treatment soon available.

'It's just in here.' He punched out his code and led her into the dim courtyard. 'Top floor, I'm afraid, and no lift.'

Cary giggled suddenly. 'I've only ever met two English people before. At college.'

She was sweet, Stephen thought. Sweet and innocent and very young, like Simone's granddaughter. Sometimes, now, he missed having students. A sign of age, he suspected, as he watched the girl rush up the stairs ahead of him while he trailed wearily behind. Ariane leapt into his mind. He would ring Natalya again. Despite the hour.

'The phone's just over there.' Stephen led the girl into

the one big room. 'It's six hours earlier on the East Coast. You dial 19–1 and then your area code and number.'

'Thanks. This is really very nice of you.' She handed him her coat, displayed long jean-clad legs he didn't like to look at, perched on the telephone stool.

'I'll make you some non-bitter coffee.'

'Great.'

He stooped to light the fire, then went off into the kitchen and automatically checked the freezer again.

When he came back, balancing two cups and a plateful of slightly stale madeleines, she was staring up at the nude on the wall with a mixture of nervousness and disapproval.

'There was no one at home. My mother doesn't usually get back till seven. I left this number on the answering machine. Is that okay? I can let myself out if you want to go to bed.'

'That's all right. I still need to get a few things done.'

'Where's your washroom?'

Stephen pointed her through the bedroom, then hastily dialled Natalya's number. Still no one there. He could try tomorrow morning. Could Natalya be with Ariane, he asked himself? Maybe Simone was right. Maybe Anya, too, had been right about the pregnancy. He hadn't liked that. It had made him think miserably of Tessa.

In any event, he was probably fretting for no reason. Refusing to recognize Ariane simply wanted nothing more to do with him. He ought to go to bed and lick his wounds quietly.

'It's nice here, spare.' The girl had come back. Her boots and socks were off and she stretched out on the floor, her toes by the fire. They were very pink. 'Do you live here all the time?'

'No. It belongs to an Italian friend. I use it when I'm in town. Look, maybe you should try ringing someone else. Your father at his office? Or a friend? Your mother might be late tonight.'

'My father's in California. We don't speak to him. And my mother will be home all right. She's got a new boyfriend. Whole lot younger. She needs to go home and spend a few hours prettying herself up for him. That's why I've been sent here.' She tossed her head angrily, her eyes flaring.

Stephen was at a loss. He looked at her in silence, watched her toes wriggling towards the flame.

'So that's not your picture?' She gestured at the nude.

'No. But I quite like it.'

'I don't. It's degrading. It humiliates women.' She got up, strode past him, brushing his legs, pointed at the picture, arms flying. 'Do you think the model wanted to pose like that? Do you think any woman would like to be seen like that, all fat thighs and pink, exhibited flesh? Circumstances forced her. Some man.'

Stephen felt his penis lurch absurdly. He tried to still himself.

With an abrupt movement, she sat down opposite him, crossed her long legs and looked at him boldly. 'You want to fuck me, don't you?'

Stephen swallowed hard, coughed. 'Is it that obvious?' he mumbled.

'Well, I don't. Do it with men, I mean. I prefer women.'

A smile tugged at his lips. Sitting there barefoot in her jeans and floppy jumper, her small, pert nose twitching, she looked very young for such a big preference.

'That's all right. You're quite safe with me. I'm not always sure I like women that much either.'

She gazed at him with something like surprise.

'How old are you?' she asked.

His throat made an odd sound which could have been a laugh. 'Almost old enough to be your father.'

'And you're still not sure about whether you like women?'

'There are a great many things I'm not sure about. Most

things, in fact.' He looked at the serious set of the features in that heart-shaped face. 'Whereas you seem to have quite decided views.'

'Yes.'

The phone rang and, without waiting, she leapt up to answer it.

After a moment, Stephen left her. He went into the bathroom and saw her boots standing there. Not like Ariane's boots. More solid. Somehow innocent. Gaily patterned socks hung from the radiator. Again his erection strained. He was definitely in a bizarre state, Stephen reflected, and tried to ignore his ridiculous body.

When he went back to her, she was sitting listlessly on the telephone stool.

'I guess I'd better go. That was the boyfriend. They're going to wire money to American Express tomorrow. I have to have a code word. "Serendipity". 'Cause I haven't got a passport.' Her voice faltered. 'Look, I . . . could I just bed down here for the night? I'm kinda tired. And, like, I'm not sure the hostel will let me in this late.'

'I suppose so.' Stephen hesitated. 'But there's only the one bed and . . .'

'That's okay. It's huge. I saw it. And you say you're not too sure about women. Anyhow, I won't get undressed.' The girl beamed a smile at him and marched into the bedroom.

With a shrug, Stephen sat in the armchair and waited. He glanced at his watch. Over fifteen minutes of silence had passed. She must have fallen asleep by now, he decided. And he needed to get some rest too. He tiptoed into the bedroom, took off only his trousers and slipped into the far corner of the bed. He felt absurdly like a student, forced by penury and circumstance into strange sleeping arrangements.

Streetlights glowed faintly through the thin curtains. In their muted beam, he could see the outlines of her face, a downy, rounded arm poised above the bedclothes.

'Hi.' She turned towards him. 'Shall we have a little cuddle? I won't shout. Promise.'

Stephen leaned on his elbow, gazed down at her in surprise. 'Look, Cary. I may seem old to you, but it happens that these days I'm not altogether extinct. And if you throw yourself into strange men's beds, you may find yourself in something of a pickle.'

She stroked his cheek lightly. 'I want to see if you really don't like women.'

'I never said quite that. It was you who said you didn't like men.'

'Well, I don't. Not usually.' She sat up and he noticed that she had taken off her sweater. 'But you're nice. I think I like you. And you look better without your glasses. Like an out-of-shape Harrison Ford.'

'Thanks.'

She was still for a moment. 'You can touch me if you want. Tell me what turns you on.'

'That's a secret.' Stephen stopped her straying fingers and grunted with too much pleasure. He brought her hand to his lips.

'Does that mean you want me to shut up or tell you mine?' When he didn't answer, she went on. 'I bet you really do prefer men. Or think of a man when you're with a woman. Is that it? That's almost the same thing.'

Stephen shuttered his ears. He didn't like talking about sex. But the girl was oddly prescient in her way. When he had first made love to Tessa, he had found himself imagining he was Jan with her. That had somehow made it doubly exciting. Jan was good with women. And Stephen, as Jan, had been good enough with Tessa too. Did that need the label of homosexual? He didn't think so. It was more complicated than that. And simpler. Fantasies were not the same thing as reality. And, in any case, fantasies were private. That's what made them exciting. Simone knew that. Wise Simone, who made him aware of the world beyond the laboratory.

He had had dinner with her once when she had just come back from the States and was complaining about all the clamour about sex: exhortations, prescriptions, preaching, psychobabble. He could still hear the humour in her voice.

'Sex may have started this century as a religion, but some of us were secularists even then and really didn't need to hear the message all the time.' She had sighed, a little ruefully. 'Anyhow, if it's going to be a religion, it should be as personal as a religion. I don't really mind what people's orientation or faith is, how often or not they go to church, whether they prefer to pray with men or women, I just get tired of hearing about it non-stop, so that it shapes everything. What about pronouncing a moratorium? A ten-year silence, so that sex can become personal again, a language of intimacy, of flirtation, of imagination, hidden in the pages of books or between sheets. What do you say, Stephen?' She had laughed in the way that she liked to when she said something startling.

The girl was staring into his eyes, caressing him with more curiosity than passion. It stirred him nonetheless and he was about to clasp her closer when she pulled away abruptly.

'You're not positive, are you?'

Stephen shook his head. 'Not that unlucky.'

She relaxed for a moment, then bolted up again, held his eyes. 'And you won't put it inside me?'

'Not unless you want me to . . . Look, perhaps we should just go to sleep.' He rolled over on his stomach. 'Forget about all this. I have to get up early.'

'Okay. If that's what you want. I'm tired too.' She sounded hurt, but she snuggled up against him, then got up before he had a chance to touch her. He peeked out from between his arms and saw that she was taking off her jeans. She flung them towards a chair and stood there for a moment, all small, high breasts in some clinging garment and long legs and copper hair. She seemed to be debating whether to take any more clothes off and evidently decided against it, for she lay down next to him as she was.

'G'night,' she said softly.

'Goodnight.'

After a moment, her hand came towards him, fingers found his chest.

'You have soft skin,' she whispered. He turned towards her and she started to lick him, little lapping movements like a cat but with a more delicate tongue. She took his hand and placed it on her breast. He rubbed gently, firm, taut flesh as muscular as a boy's, encased in some elastic fabric arching against him.

'There.' She moved his hand lower and pressed her mound against him. He heard the gasp of her breath in his ear and then in the hurried tumble of things he stopped noticing, only remembered that at some point in the play of bodies and tongues and limbs, her leg had brushed against him and he had come tumultuously somewhere amidst the bedclothes.

Afterwards, he held her and she said in a small, polite voice, 'Thank you, that was very nice of you. And I was only a teeny bit scared. Once . . . It's not really very scary, is it? Not like this.' She put her hand on his limp penis.

Stephen found himself laughing. 'Probably scarier for me. You never know whether it's going to work.'

She laughed too. Then she said, 'Have you ever thought you might be part woman?'

He cleared his throat. 'There's only one wobbly little leg of a chromosome between us.'

'And a whole lot of culture,' she reminded him, as if she knew.

'Yes, a whole lot of that.'

In the morning, when he dropped her off at the youth hostel, he felt decidedly odd. He gave her enough money to get through the week.

'I'll pay you back,' she said to him from the midst of her bulky coat.

'Only if you think it's necessary.' He smiled at her. 'Enjoy Paris. But be careful, won't you.'

The words had a strangely paternal sound and he found himself flushing. He kissed her lightly on the cheek, watched her make her way with long strides up the stairs.

At the top, she met another jeaned woman, with blonde hair and a black leather jacket. Antoinette. Simone had told him her granddaughter worked here. Both girls were suddenly waving at him. Stephen waved back and to hide his confusion made a great show of digging out his flight ticket and directing the driver to the airport.

To remind himself that he was after all a serious person and not an embarrassed adolescent, Stephen tapped his bag and felt for the presence of the precious igloos.

7

———— * ————

After Stephen had left, Simone leaned back into her chair and gazed at the intricate pattern in the Persian carpet at her feet. Scrolls and arabesques and entrelacs chasing each other across a pale rose ground. Recurring. Merging. Like so many figures in her life.

She closed her eyes, reimagining the progress of the pattern, her fingers tapping out a repetitive rhythm on the heavy fabric of her chair. Abruptly they stopped. Those threats had come into her mind again on the curve of an arabesque, their ugliness veiled by the casually seductive voice that had uttered them. With a swift movement, Simone dislodged the plump marmalade cat who had settled himself on her lap. He gave her a haughty look of disgruntled surprise.

'Yes, Peluche.' Simone's laugh had a grim undertow. 'You are right. I am a fool. An old fool. The worst kind. And a coward as well. I fear I may have done something very bad.'

With sudden resolve, she went to the telephone, searched through a thick address book and punched out a number. In a steely voice, she uttered a few sentences in Russian, waited for a moment, then scribbled a note and put down the receiver.

Wearily she made her way up the curving staircase to the first floor and opened the door to the library. Once, it had been her favourite room. Four large rectangular windows looked out on the splendid rump of Notre Dame. While she sat at the central table and wrote her articles or speeches, she could take sustenance from the way in which heavy, unyielding stone had defied its own nature to rise and curve in an airy grace.

But now, neither the view nor the book-lined walls comforted her. She made for the far corner of the room, beyond the leather chesterfield and the old escritoire. With surprising ease, she slid back two seemingly solid panels of books. After a moment's reflection, she pulled out a large leather-bound tome, placed it on the central table and went back to fetch two similar volumes. She rifled through pages of tiny script which resolved itself into no recognizable language. Some thirty minutes of intense concentration passed before a smile creased her lips. She made some notes on a pad, replaced the volumes and slid the book-lined panel back into place.

A moment later, she was arguing into the telephone, her voice vehement and persuasive by turn. Just before she hung up, she switched from Russian to English. 'Never mind about all that. Just find her and follow her. Don't let her out of your sight.'

In the oval mirror on the landing, she stopped to scowl at herself. She noted the spray of wrinkles round her mouth, the vein at her temple, the transparency of skin round bone. As if age were a paring away, a revelation of depths better hidden.

She twisted her lips into a mockery of a smile. Time was such a consummate artist. She couldn't compete with the range of his palette, the ingenious dabs and scratches. It was better not to study his work too closely, lest one despair.

She had decided that over the years in any case and had made it into something of a general philosophy. In most instances it was better not to look too closely. Better to believe in the best, the mask, the face put on to meet other faces. If you thought the best of them, people sometimes lived up to it. Were seduced into good. That usually worked better than flagellation. The whip only resulted in more whipping or festering wounds which eventually polluted the atmosphere for everyone.

The trouble was, the whip was sometimes necessary. She would have to use it now. On herself as well. She had left too many things undone. And now, one last act of courage was necessary.

She undressed with quick efficiency then stretched out on a bed that had grown too big. Yes, it was time. It was almost too late. She hadn't foreseen this particular damage.

Restlessly, she got up again and looked at the door on the other side of the room. It beckoned to her as seductively as a siren. Why not? Her nights had grown so long and so wakeful. A little trip in her time machine would shore her up for what needed to be done. She smiled to herself. Time machines might come in all shapes and sizes, Simone thought, grand streamlined crafts with supersonic gadgetry, intricate watches moulded to the curve of a wrist, the redolent pages of a favourite book. For her, her wardrobe served the purpose.

It was a closet, as capacious as a middle-sized room, filled with shelves and racks several layers deep between which one could stroll at one's leisure. At its uppermost level hatboxes were stacked and dated; at its nethermost, shoes. In between were the dresses and gowns, sweaters and blouses and suits and coats and scarfs that had clothed a lifetime. It wasn't that Simone didn't give things away. Every season she sorted and sifted and gave and donated. And every season, she kept back one or two or three items from which she couldn't bear to be parted because of a fineness of line or texture or because they evoked a particular moment.

As a result, she now thought of her wardrobe as a vast

archaeological site replete with splinters and shards, worn coins and half-obliterated runes – a forgotten civilization whose traces only she could decipher.

Of late she had taken to browsing through the furthest recesses of the site, burrowing into forgotten boxes, lifting sheets of cotton to reveal the gossamer silks, the slippery satins or tufted wools of memory.

She had fingered the ivory softness of her wedding gown and thought of the moment when she had said 'yes' to Michel in front of the mayor, proud in his tricolour sash, and promised herself in that word no longer to think of the past and to embrace the present. She had followed the dress home to this very house, decked in flowers. Had felt herself tremble as the maid helped her undo its myriad clasps and buttons. Had sniffed the hint of cologne on Michel's face as he moved to kiss her on that first night, his lips more serious than the droll light in his eyes, as if he wanted her to acknowledge that the whimsy of pageantry and parties aside, there was something abiding between them.

On another night, she had stumbled upon the dress which had cloaked her first pregnancy, its ample pleats expanding with the months, its little white collar above the darkness of wool already a premonition of the schoolgirl ways which were soon to inhabit the house. She had been happy then, full of the vigour of new life, which seemed also to quieten her dead.

One morning, as she was burrowing about to find a half-remembered scarf, she had come across the grey tweed sheath she had worn to give her first seminar. Its clean, skilfully cut lines, the subtle detail of darts at waist and neck and cuffs, reminded her that she had said to Michel as she tried thoughts out on him, that she wanted her talk to be as well constructed as this garment. She remembered acutely then how their years together, even when everything else was at a low ebb, had been marked by a passionate exchange of ideas and she tasted again the tart and sometimes acid sharpness of his mind.

Not far from the sheath hung the wine-dark gown she had worn for her first dinner at the Elysée Palace. It was on that night that she had whispered her desires and plans in the President's ear and had been rewarded with official sanction, as well as the site for the first of several congresses which brought Eastern European writers and poets and thinkers to the West.

Seeing the gown had given her an idea and she had brought it out and tried it on. She worried whether the décolletage was too low for the piano scale of bones which these days worked its way down from her neck, but on a whim she had rung her dressmaker and the dress now hung in anticipation at the front of the wardrobe, waiting for the event Stephen had told her he would most probably miss.

Simone glanced at it now as she opened the door of the closet and approved of her commemorative act. She scolded herself a little nonetheless. She knew that her prolonged visits here bore the distinctive seal of an old woman's silliness. But she didn't care. Increasingly she delighted in her treasure trove, the flutter of silk which brought back light-hearted affairs – the Russian poet pouring his soul out to her knees, the stiff-necked politician she had taught to laugh, a stream of friends she remembered with nothing but affection.

She moved slowly round the racks, pushing back hangers, letting her fingers caress materials. She had almost reached the very back of the room when she saw it, half-hidden by a thick coat. A single-breasted woollen suit in deepest brick. Michel had chosen it for her because of the colour and she had loved it because of the ample cuffed pockets and the long centre-back kick pleat made to match her strides. It was the suit she had worn on her first return visit to Prague. She shuddered at the acts the garment brought to the fore. But it was right that she should stumble upon it tonight. She stared at it for a moment, then carried it to the front of the room, as if its visible presence would ensure a resolve which threatened to disappear by morning.

It was odd that from those earlier days of her first marriage, her marriage to Staszek, she had kept nothing. Perhaps because he was as irretrievably lost as her first youth. Or, more accurately, she scoffed at herself, because she had once wanted emphatically to obliterate that past. She had come to Michel from her father's house with little more than a single valise.

Simone rummaged through racks, shifted garments. Could she have given away the particular dress she was looking for in another fit of deliberate effacement?

From beneath a black coat, a beam of colour caught her eye. There it was, a yellow so ripe she should never have considered it. But she had wanted to be bright that spring, deliberately cheerful, so as to wake from her year-long mourning for Michel. It had been a good marriage, a solid partnership in every respect. And suddenly, it was over. She was alone. More so with each passing day as her teenage daughters leapt into the galloping intensity of a decade earmarked for youth.

Simone released the dress from the sombre coat which cloaked it and stared at it. A geometric A-line in woollen gabardine, fashionably short and pert in the style of the time, and with a striped jacket; too youthful, she had thought even then, for what were her forty-two years. But the girls had encouraged her, declared she could now pass as their older sister.

A dreamy expression on her face, Simone carried the dress back to her bed and lay down beside it.

Prague in the spring of 1968. That was where the dress had gone. And she inside it. Pauline, a journalist friend, had insisted Simone accompany her. She needed someone beside her who understood the language, who understood the ways. Simone's protests that she hadn't been back to Prague for some fifteen years, that she would probably understand little more than the language, had been half-hearted. In truth, she now wanted to go, though she couldn't altogether understand the desire. Perhaps it was simply because a sufficient number of years had passed. Perhaps it had something to do with Michel's death. Whatever the case, she was curious: about her own reactions as well as about the new political openings that year had brought.

As a child, she had adored Prague, where her diplomat father had been stationed before the war. She had loved the steep, twisting streets which lost themselves as they groped towards the fairy-tale castle; the candy-floss pink of the French Embassy, the snow-clad roofs, the mist which rose from the curving river and shrouded the city in magic.

She had loved Cook with his floppy pudding of a hat, who conjured up sprites and goblins and wizards with the same ease as he stuffed dumplings and transformed left-overs into tangy sauces and surprising pies. She had loved his avid piggy gleam and his shiny, perspiring cheeks; the way his mouth would form into an intent, silent circle as he had her taste a smidgen of soup or sniff a sour apple tart. The rest of the time it was always moving. It was Cook who stood like an icon over that golden period of her childhood, he who had really taught her Czech and, with it, embued her with his own version of history.

It was from Cook that she first heard of the great and mad Rudolf II, his humour as black as his garb, who had moved the centre of the Empire from Vienna to Prague in the sixteenth century. And with Rudolf came natural scientists and unnatural alchemists, makers of tricky mirrors and makers of devilish homunculi, astronomers and astrologers, Tycho Brahe with his astrolabes and measurements and artificial golden nose, and earless

English sorcerers who could turn base metal into the life-giving elixirs Rudolf desired above all else.

As Cook chopped onions and carrots and threw them into a vat of a pot, he would list the contents of Rudolf's cabinet of curiosities: shells of topaz and jasper and agate, rhinoceros horns, the head of Polyphemus, musical clocks and grandfather clocks and trumpeting clocks, spectacles of all sizes and shapes, nails from Noah's Ark, crocodile and lizard casts, chalices for boiling poisons and potions, stuffed ostriches, mandrake roots reclining like little men on velvet cushions. The list grew, was added on to, repeated from day to day, until the pots were full. And always and ever as the lid went on, Cook would say, 'Oh, yes, I almost forgot the most important of all: a lump of earth from the Hebron Valley, the very lump of earth from which Yahweh, that's God to you, formed Adam.'

Yes, Cook had given her his version of history. Not so very different from his version of magic.

'See,' he had said to her one day as he kneaded dough with fat, deft fingers. 'This is how you make a golem.' He had cackled merrily, poked and prodded until the dough produced the rotund shape of a man with an imbecile's grin and hands as large as shovels. 'We can all be gods.'

'A golem?' Simone had queried.

'You don't know what the golem is? And you a nice little dark-eyed girl with a Jewish mother! Why, Rabbi Jehuda Loew, King Rudolf's friend, made the first golem, right down there in the Josefov. He took some mud, some earth and, just like his god, created a man.'

With a high-pitched cackle, Cook had poised a floppy hat on his creation's head. 'Now comes the difficult part. We're meant to walk our little man round in a circle four hundred and sixty-two times while we recite the letters of the tetragram, backwards, forwards, inside out. That's Jehovah in four letters to you.'

But instead of walking, Cook had simply tweaked her

cheek and popped his little man into the oven. 'Short cut,' he had said. 'I'm too lazy for all that walking. And anyhow, it's probably better to eat our golem before he eats us.'

So they had eaten Cook's golem, all rotund and golden brown with raisin-dark eyes. And while they had eaten Cook had told her ever more and wilder stories. About an ugly, clumsy golem who was a good servant to the rabbi until he cast eyes on his daughter and fell madly in love with her and stole her away. The rabbi had then to track him, come upon him secretly in the night and whip the name of God from his mouth so that the golem went limp and reverted to his muddy state.

He told her how another golem, an envious clod, had organized a rebellion against his master, and could only be put down when the E of *emet*, the Hebrew for 'truth', was wiped from his brow, leaving only *met*, which means 'death'.

Simone turned over on her bed and sighed. Yes, she had swallowed Cook's magical history as readily as she had swallowed his thick slabs of yeasty bread with their coating of plum jam. Until Staszek had come along and opened her eyes to a grimmer version of the world. One where another kind of golem, with a small moustache on his face and hatred in his heart, was running rampant.

Staszek. She didn't want to think of him. Not now. She fingered the heavy texture of the yellow dress and forced her mind forward to the spring of '68.

The city had appeared to her in all its golden beauty during those weeks, as if Cook's aegis had been restored. Everything was bright with the vivacity of a dawning freedom, the bad days as lost to her as they seemed to be to the Czechs she encountered.

Pauline and she had stayed in the shabby splendour of the Europa Hotel. From her window, she could see the euphoric crowds gathering in Wenceslas Square. Their jubilation had infected her. The world was changing, none too soon.

They spent their days in interviews with politicians and playwrights and members of the Writers Union and students. In the evenings, they crowded into theatres or steamy, smoke-filled bars rife with the odours of excitement and sour beer and herby *becherovka*.

It was in one of these that she had met him on her third evening in Prague. He had squeezed in beside her on the long, narrow bench and given her a look of such pure delight that she had assumed they might know each other. They didn't. It was Pauline he had met that morning in the course of a series of student interviews. But everyone behaved like old friends during those weeks, all conventions of correct behaviour forgotten. And he was beautiful. He had a vivid freshness of face, a gleam of hair, a newly laundered look about him. Except for his mouth, which curled with wry intelligence. In the heat of the evening's discussion, she had learned little more about him than that he was a student. And had had confirmation of that humorous intelligence.

Later, in her hotel room there was more. Much more.

As he had brought her fingers to the taut stretch of his skin, a shiny newness of stomach and chest which glowed in its obliviousness to time, he had woken a long-forgotten passion in her. An ache composed of greed and longing. It had grown over that long night and the subsequent days, so that in the midst of meetings or dinners she had to reach out and touch him. And when he wasn't there, she could smell him on her skin, feel the brush of his thigh on hers as she stepped off the pavement or pulled on her stockings. She wanted to press her fingers against his groin, to sniff the sweat of him, rub herself against his moistness.

An older woman's mad passion, as unreasonable and inconsolable as an infant's tantrum.

As the days grew into weeks and Pauline had long gone,

the inappropriateness of it filled her with terror. He was eighteen. A Himalaya of time separated them. Yet she would have done anything to seduce him into coming home with her. As, years ago, she had tried to do with Staszek.

And then, one night, as they lay on the bed in the shabby grandeur of that hotel room, he had started, as lovers do, to reminisce about his childhood. What he had told her had made her blood run cold.

She couldn't convey the burden of it to him. She had invented a story, a telegram from Paris, she had to go back. They would meet again, perhaps. She had attempted kindness, but been deliberately vague.

The next day, she had fled, never to return to Prague.

During those first aching months back in Paris, she had been haunted by a story an African friend had told her. She thought of it as the clay sister story. It told of a peculiar rite of passage. In the southern African tribe that was its home, boys and girls were reared separately in the years leading to puberty. During those years they were taught the secrets of love and the intricate pleasures of their bodies. Then, at an appointed date, boy met girl for a single night of love. In preparation for the tryst, the girl was wrapped in clay – became a hardened doll to be cracked open by her lover. Released, she could share with him all the stored knowledge and desire of the separate years. But only for that one night.

Simone had felt like that clay-wrapped figure, but one whose age-hardened carapace had been cracked open to release too much yearning. She had miraculously been allowed to extend the single night of love into several. But, like the clay sister, she had to retreat, never to share more than words with her youthful lover again. Or the order of the known universe would crumble.

So with a struggle she had wrapped her carapace round her again. And, like a good clay sister, she had done her best for her now untouchable young lover. She had tried to look after him in whatever little ways were open to her. She had sent representatives. Eventually, when the pain had abated. But she had never had the courage of honesty. That had cost her dearly in more ways than she liked to think of.

And now honesty was long overdue.

With a little shiver, Simone returned the yellow dress to her wardrobe. It was not, she consoled herself, that she hadn't taken up the strings of her life again after that. She had worked harder than ever. There had been other affairs too. She did not have the instincts of a puritan. And her bones had served her well, had allowed her to pass for many years as an attractive woman of uncertain age. But the ache those weeks in Prague had woken in her, that longing, those hidden recesses of the romantic she had forgotten she had once been, had never surfaced again.

The guilt had, though, so hot and shaming that she had allowed herself to fall prey to the menace of revelation. No longer, she vowed.

When dawn edged its way round the heavy curtains of her bedroom, Simone rose. She granted herself the pleasure of a cup of coffee. Then she positioned herself at her desk and began a series of phone calls. After the third, she rang Stephen.

'I will take you up on your invitation, Stephen. Book me a room. At the Europa. For next week. It will do me good.'

She said it with a forced cheerfulness, but perhaps he didn't notice the strain. He sounded subdued.

For good measure, she added, 'And don't worry too much about Ariane. I imagine she's all right.'

PART TWO

8

———✳———

The Prague airport terminal stood white and functional against a slate sky. Wind whipped unhitched baggage trolleys and stray scraps of litter into erratic motion. Signs clattered on rusty hinges. Tourists, hats and bags awry, gazed round, veiled suspicion or bemusement on their faces. Oblivious to weather, the new kind of Czech businessman poured orders into mobile phones.

As the airport shuttle wheezed slowly into motion, Stephen Caldwell steadied the case on his lap and breathed the covert sigh of relief which over the years had become habitual. A driving, icy rain spread in rivulets against the window. In the past he had welcomed the rain, which cloaked his movements. Now that the iron curtain had been replaced by the more permeable one of bank notes, he would perhaps have preferred a little sun.

It had taken him a mere fifteen minutes to get from plane to coach. Customs officials, if existent, were invisible. Police presence took the form of a single young man in uniform standing at flagrant ease. The woman at passport control had smiled at him and said thank you. Of such small absences and pleasantries was democracy made.

Not so very long ago he would have spent far longer in the airport building, calling on all his reserves of diffidence and patience to see him through. Bringing to bear, too, as he had discovered after his first few journeys, a certain flair for dissimulation. It had become clear to him that he revelled in both the danger and the masquerade of it. He was the young scientist travelling to consult with colleagues, to take part in a seminar or conference in Budapest or Moscow or Prague or Warsaw. He was also more. He was a courier, a carrier of illicit information, an agent of openness in an over-policed world where the State considered ideas to be as explosive as bombs.

The more was what he had loved. The rush of adrenalin at border crossings, the fear, the transgressive schoolboy secrecy of it. Perhaps he had simply not committed enough trespasses as a child.

It occurred to him, as the coach clattered over the tram lines and cobblestones of the first of the Prague suburbs, that he still missed the excitement of it all.

How many years ago was it that he had first made the journey? By train, in those days, from Paris to Vienna and finally a coach to Prague. It must have been in 1978, the summer of his twenty-second birthday, the year he had met Simone. It was she who had set him up to it.

When he had arrived at her house to collect the parcel she had asked him to deliver to a friend in Prague, he had quickly realized that this was no ordinary favour. She had handed him a large envelope and, with something of a challenge in her voice, had told him to look through it.

The envelope contained a number of photocopied chapters of books and articles. Material he knew: on the isolation and characterization of globin genes; on hybrid plasmids; on Bill Rutter and William Goodman's work on cloning the insulin gene. And material that was unfamiliar: a few pages of Hayek, some essays on civil society and governmentality. She told him it would be a good idea if he familiarized himself with what was in these pages, since if anyone with a uniform asked, he should say that the articles were part of his studies. But the likelihood was, and she examined him carefully as she said this, that no one would bother to ask.

Since Stephen was then as ignorant about recent history as he was adept in the lab, it had taken him a little time to grasp the full sense of her words. She had gestured him closer to her on the white sofa as if an intimacy were about to be revealed and asked him to imagine what it would be like to live in a country where basic rights didn't exist, where all information was monitored by a policing state, where censorship was rampant, where access to books and ideas and foreign newspapers and travel was severely curtailed – so that the individual was ground down into thinking that such an existence was the only one possible. The norm of human life.

As she talked, he had begun to feel trapped in a dark and dizzying maze where the exits were all barred and the signs spoke only lies. He had sensed the relief of a window, glimpsed the hope that even a small ray of light might bring. He had understood that as those windows and lights multiplied, the walls of the maze must crumble.

It came to him that what he was about to take on, however small, was important.

The following morning before boarding his train, as he shaved and studied himself in the mirror, he concluded that Simone had been right to say no one would bother to stop him. He was in that sense a perfect courier. With his round National Health specs, his slightly pink though no longer spotty skin, his tumbled hair and unremarkable features, he looked utterly innocuous, a nondescript young man, an overgrown English schoolboy. But Simone had done something remarkable. She had given his very innocuousness, his social invisibility, a meaning.

It was a meaning he came to take pride in. It straightened his shoulders, gave an added bounce to his step. And it remained a secret between himself and Simone, all the more precious for that.

Over the years, after that first successful mission, he gradually realized that he was hardly alone, that Simone, apart from her more public role as the head of an international relations think tank, managed a whole network of carriers – academics, scientists, businessmen, musicians, tourists – messengers who covertly brought the West to the East and occasionally the dissident East to the West, and allowed for some uncontrolled flow of information and ideas. It was a loose network and Stephen hadn't knowingly met any of its Western links. In the East, as he grew in stature and reputation and was invited to seminars and conferences, he increasingly made his own.

His profession helped. Simone must have spotted that it would early on, had probably singled him out for that very reason. As a scientist, he was for many of the countries of the Eastern bloc a man almost beyond suspicion, a respected and prized member of society, a carrier of progress. Even during the iciest days of the cold war, Academies of Science in the East kept up some links with Western counterparts, and if their directors were not always the first people Stephen wanted to speak to, there were usually others lower in the ranks with whom conversation and exchange were fruitful. These he would mention to Simone. In due course he would find that by some complex network of diplomacy and funds a travel grant had been arranged for them, a visit to a Western institute or university, a chance to taste a different world.

He had grown adept at the work which lay beneath the surface of his official business. He knew how to bind and rebind volumes so that articles of a quite different nature could be slipped into scientific treatises with titles impenetrable to the English- or French- or German-speaking layperson, let alone a Czech or Polish policeman. He knew how to crumple letters amongst old chits in his pocket or strap documents beneath his shirt and sweater and jacket. He knew how to read cues, how to spot which conference delegates or seminar members were Party hacks or spies. He knew how to put an impassive mask on his face, control the twitch of eyebrow and lip, so as not to betray contacts met in inappropriate settings. He knew scores of safe dropping points in any number of countries – loose floorboards, gaps between wall and blackboard in seminar rooms, empty churches. He knew how to look bored or impatient when a customs official searched his luggage, how to explain at tedious length and with excruciating attention to detail what each supposed chapter of a book contained. And on the two precarious occasions when he had been stopped, once in Czechoslovakia early on and then more dangerously in Romania, he had handled himself well enough so as not to implicate any of his contacts.

Sometimes Stephen thought that his research, as much as the spy fiction he had always loved, had formed him for this new task. The language of molecular genetics with its bits of information, its regulator genes and promoters and operators, its translational control sites and switch sites and terminators, had made him into a carrier of the code, a useful bit of messenger RNA moving deftly through the system, helping to produce those proteins necessary to the continuation of life.

If he had started off with no particular idea of why he was doing what he was doing – except that Simone had asked him – he quickly learned the reason. It wasn't that he had any particular politics. He didn't believe in Capitalism or Socialism or Communism or any ideologically enforced 'ism'. What he did gradually realize he believed, more from seeing its negation than from any abstract standpoint, was that openness of borders, of information, was crucial. Otherwise policing of its citizens became the State's primary function.

Simone had put it for him once in her inimitable way. 'What we need, Stephen,' she had said, 'is to respect personal secrets and for the State not to have any. The State must be open and the individual must be allowed privacy.'

Yes. He concurred with that.

*　　*　　*

The rain was still falling, heavier now as they crossed the windy sweep of the river. In the distance, domes and spires wavered like shadows of themselves against the cloud. Closer to, a new hotel spread brash opulence along the borders of the Vltava. There was scaffolding everywhere. The city was in a frenzy of renewal, shedding recent history with builders' dust, reasserting its place in the centre of Europe with each freshly treated stone.

Despite the rain, the double row of taxis waited along Revolučni Street, their voluble drivers urging tourists towards open doors. Stephen took a shallow breath. The air raked his nostrils and throat with familiar toxicity. It was still heavy with the particles of years of uncaring Soviet pollution, gritty with rubble, topped with a reek of sewerage. After a day or two, only his eyes would cry their alertness to it.

He leapt into the first cab without haggling over a fare. Whatever he did, it was inevitable that he would be charged at least double the metered rate. He told himself he didn't mind these frontier tactics, these signals of the deregulation which also brought freedom in its train. But they rankled a little, as did the McDonald's sign poised at the entrance of the Old Town Square like a symbol of liberty.

What was it that Jan had said to him on his last visit? 'Instead of the Politburo, we now have governors of banks to determine our future. Instead of bosses, promoted not on merit, but on grounds of loyalty to the Party, we have management consultants who have just as little experience of running things. But never mind. Money is better than ideology. It is more neutral.'

Stephen could see its supposed neutrality everywhere. In the bright new coats of pastel paint, in the litter of shops which sold everything from Czech glass to artificial Polynesian flowers to English porcelain to German appliances, in the multi-lingual signs which beckoned tourists to bars and cafés and museums. He wondered whether that generous neutrality had begun to extend to hospitals and schools, or to the causes of that terrifying level of pollution which foreshortened lives. To Academies of Science. But that took far longer, as everyone knew. And that in part was why he was here. To help the extension.

The taxi turned away from the river and up past the dilapidated greenhouses which bordered the botanical gardens. He had rarely seen anyone in these gardens, but today, despite the rain, he spied an old woman with an umbrella poised over herself and a shaggy-haired mongrel who walked sedately to heel. He smiled. People walking in gardens and parks somehow reassured him, if nothing else at least of the fact that he was English.

As he neared his destination, excitement gripped him.

'*Tu, doleva.* Go left here.' He pointed the driver to the colonnaded doors of the stately, if dilapidated, edifice. With only a briefly admonishing 'How much?', Stephen paid him and raced into the shelter of the building.

A blast of disinfectant mingled with the subtler scent of mouldering plaster greeted him as soon as he swung open the heavy door. The Institute shared its premises with a sprawling hospital. Somehow the splendour of the baroque frame which housed them acted as a constant and mournful rebuke to their present crumbling state.

He nodded briefly to the dour receptionist who had earned her face in a previous regime, and walked hurriedly up to the third floor which housed the Institute. The Gothic-faced clock at the end of the long, musty corridor told him it was only eleven o'clock. He slowed his pace so that his footsteps didn't echo with quite so much resonance. The place seemed eerily empty.

Jan had written to him about that. Told him jokingly that he didn't think it was merely a matter of his directorship, but everyone, all the best people, were leaving. It was hardly surprising, given that a senior researcher now earned less than a cashier in a shop. It would change,

Jan had reassured him, perhaps trying to reassure himself. Periods of transition were difficult. Always difficult. And it was not a time for despair.

Stephen circled round a uniformed cleaning woman who was mopping the floor with the unhurried precision of a somnambulist. She turned a disapproving face on him as he tracked through wet to knock on the door of the lab.

'Dr Caldwell.' The assistant he knew from previous visits gave his name the particular lilt of a V and smiled with an edge of fluster. 'I'm afraid Dr Martin is in a meeting. We were not expecting you until twelve.'

'I know. I just want to deposit these.' Stephen pulled the two styrofoam cages from his case and opened a freezer. 'In here, if I may?'

'I don't know.' She looked at him doubtfully. 'Perhaps better I just ask.'

'There won't be a problem,' Stephen said with that definitive edge he had heard Jan use to such effect. Hesitation, diffidence, entreaty, had no place in a world that had learned its social relations from authoritarian masters. 'None at all,' he emphasized. 'It's all arranged. Don't let anyone touch. I'll see you later.'

He walked out of the lab before she could ask anything more and paused halfway down the corridor at a door marked WC. Locked. He had momentarily forgotten the protocol of keys. Keys for cabinets which held dishes or paper or instruments or files. Keys for everything, including the loo.

The door opened suddenly, almost toppling him.

'Stephen!' Jan Martin embraced him warmly. 'Welcome. Welcome. It's been too long.'

At arm's length, they inspected each other for a moment. As always, Stephen was filled with an impression of fierce nervous energy, austerely contained. Jan was all taut wiry movement and hawk-nosed intensity, like a conductor poised to spring into action at the pulse of some wild internal beat. The smile, when it came, was a contradiction, a continual surprise. It was boyishly mischievous.

'You've caught me out. I was taking a break. From boredom. But I'm afraid I have to return to it. For a few minutes at least. Boredom with big planning words is a necessary part of our week. Even though everything has changed.' He tapped his forehead in self-derision. 'I will be with you as soon as I can. Here, take the keys to my office.'

He pulled a heavy ring from his pocket and passed it to Stephen. 'Or perhaps you would rather wait in the restaurant. The one round the second corner, where that pretty young woman from the provinces tried to make an assignation with you last time. You remember? The Czerny Pivovar?'

Stephen flushed. 'Your office. I have some work to get on with. Has the new computer arrived?'

Jan shook his head wryly. 'Soon. I'm told soon. Now, very soon. Something important on your neurotransmitters to show me?'

'No. Something else.'

'What . . . ?'

'After your meeting.'

'A mystery. I'll have to make it quick.'

Jan's directorial office was an airy, imposing room with windows on two sides, high ceilings from which the paint peeled in great strips, pale greenish walls on which the grimy rectangular outlines of a former occupant's professional diplomas were still evident and a dearth of furniture. There was a utility desk and a table arranged together to form a 'T', three plastic chairs of varying shades of orange and grey and a filing cabinet of pre-computer age proportions. Beside the bookcase in the far corner of the room, there was also incongruously a chaise longue with elegant lines covered in a tatty blue fabric.

When Jan had first moved into this office after the Velvet

Revolution of '89, Stephen had thought his wife, Hanka, must have placed it there. For just above it, on the bookshelf, stood a portrait of Hanka in a pretty, curving ironwork frame. The two objects appeared to belong together and with nothing else in the room. But now the photo of Hanka seemed to have disappeared.

Through the window, he could see a child playing in the courtyard, skipping forlornly in the drizzle as if someone had forgotten her existence. Beneath her toque of a hat, her hair shone. She looked up at him and curled her lips into a shy smile. The shyness reminded him of Cary. He found himself waving vigorously and wondered for a moment whether the girl in the courtyard could be Jan's daughter. But, no, she was far too young. Jan's daughter was a teenager now. She had been a baby when he first met Jan way back in 1981.

That spring, Stephen had bought his first car, an ancient Mini that rattled mercilessly when it reached sixty miles per hour. But he had decided to drive in any case. For the adventure of it. He was bound for a conference in Vienna and would then make his way across Moravia to Prague, where, through the head of his lab at Cambridge, he had wangled an invitation from a group of geneticists at the Academy of Sciences. And from there, all being well, he would go on to Poland. He was eager to see unknown countryside and Simone had armed him with a list of contacts at possible stopover points along the way. These he memorized carefully.

He left Vienna early and by mid-morning had reached the border near Brno. Armed uniformed guards patrolled barbed wire and barrier in the midst of empty fields that looked too innocent to merit such vigilance. At a brusque gesture, Stephen handed over his passport. It was studied with slow precision. A gruff command motioned him towards the side of the road and a small cabin-like building. Stephen parked, aware that his passport had been carried off, aware too that a second guard was watching him with tense menace.

He waited in the car for some thirty anxious minutes, before he determined to stretch his legs. But when he opened the door of the Mini, a rifle butt urged him back into his seat. He calmed himself by running through his mind a series of molecular structures linked to his current research. By the time the first guard returned to lead him unceremoniously from car to cabin, he was relatively composed.

It was as he walked up the wooden steps that Stephen noticed the doors and boot of the Mini being flung open, his luggage being hauled out, scattered. He tried a protest which met with no response. The man had no English. No expression either in the square, narrow-eyed face beneath the cap. He looked about forty, a sullen, slightly paunchy, broad-shouldered, but unreadable forty.

He led Stephen through a bare office into a tiny, windowless room and locked him in. A single light-bulb hung from brown wire over a rickety chair. The heat was suffocating. Sweat gathered in Stephen's armpits, trickled from his forehead. Minutes turned into hours. His captors had little to keep them busy. Only a single lorry had made the border crossing while he sat in his car. They could decide to use Stephen for entertainment. Or perhaps, after they had pondered the books and papers in his case, they would send for an English-speaking official. That was the optimistic guess.

He didn't like to consider the pessimistic one.

He sat in the hard-backed chair, examined the wall, paced out the cell-like dimensions of the room. He plotted his chances for making a quick escape back across the border, once they moved him from this cubicle. He reached into his jacket pocket for a pen and a piece of paper so that he could reconstruct the lie of the land. It was then he came across the letter. Of course. The letter. He banged loudly on the door, carried on with increased emphasis until the guard appeared.

Waving the letter in the man's unblinking face, Stephen pointed to the address. He insisted with his few words of German that the number at the Academy of Sciences in Prague had to be tried. They were expecting him.

The guard stared at the letter with animal dumbness. Stephen heightened his protest, evoked the British Embassy, recited Professor Klima's number in a stentorian voice. At last, the man went off with the letter, not before once again locking Stephen's door.

As the hours passed, with nothing to signal their passage except the hands on his watch, Stephen wondered whether his guards would return only to find him dissolved in a mixture of urine and perspiration. At least it wasn't blood. He banged on the door again, was faced by the same sullen guard. He demanded a WC, was relieved to find himself being led to one, decided that this could only be a good sign, that something in his favour had occurred.

At about five o'clock, he was roused from he didn't know what gloomy reverie by the sound of voices. His door opened and his guard led him out of his cubicle into the main office, where a youngish man was sifting through the texts which had once lain in Stephen's case. Clear, coldly sombre eyes examined him. Overly precise English landed in his ears. He was being grilled about his reasons for coming to Czechoslovakia, the contents of his documents, his motive for having a Polish visa in his passport. Stephen matched his impassivity to his interrogator's.

The questioning went on and on. A longer discussion in Czech followed amongst his jailers. At the end of it, without meeting his eyes, the uniformed guard brusquely returned his passport. For good measure, he confiscated two of the scientific papers Stephen had picked up in Vienna.

What came next startled Stephen more than any question during his interrogation.

'The officer has asked whether you might be so kind as to give me a lift into Brno,' his interrogator said politely. 'They cannot spare anyone at the moment to take me back.'

Stephen had no choice but nervously to acquiesce.

When they had driven for a mile or two in silence, Stephen was surprised by a burst of gleeful laughter. The sound was so unexpected that he veered the car dangerously towards a ditch.

'I must apologize for the way I treated you back there. But it was necessary. You will forgive me, no? I did my best not to concentrate on your less scientific material.'

Stephen shot his companion a swift glance. The charming, mischievous face that met it bore little relationship to that of his stern interrogator.

'I'm not sure I understand.'

'No, our manners are a little curious at the moment. Our habits, too. You see, we live under an army of semantic occupation. We have got used to saying one thing while thinking another.'

Stephen waited in silence, afraid that this show of congeniality might be a ruse.

'I suspect it was the Polish visa that made them stop you. We are not intended to know about Solidarity, the Polish troubles.'

'I see.'

'Still, you will want to understand what I was doing in that frontier post. Well, I was passing my Chief's office at the hospital just after he had received a call from Professor Klima in Prague. I have English. And I am menial enough to be sent on tedious errands. So I proposed myself as an emissary. I like to propose myself for such duties.'

He winked at Stephen. 'And the grapevine had already alerted me to your possible arrival. I was hoping we might meet.'

Stephen joined him in laughter.

'By the way, my name is Jan Martin.'

It was one of several names on the list from Simone that Stephen had memorized.

When they arrived in Brno, it was already evening and Jan urged Stephen to come home with him and accept his hospitality, if he didn't mind the occasional interruption of a squalling baby. It was not a bad house, he told him, on the outskirts of town, close to the hospital and slightly ramshackle, but they had the advantage of sharing it only with his sister and stepmother, and a reliable couple upstairs.

By that time, Jan had also told him that he had once been to Cambridge with his father, many years back now, when he was still a high-school student. On the cusp of that spring which had given them so much hope only too quickly to dash it.

A few queries had led Stephen to suspect that he might already know Jan by reputation. As a student, he had heard the head of his lab at Cambridge sing the praises of some mythical youth who had briefly worked there in the late '60s. The story had the form of a trope. It was one of those tales that circulated like legendary material round every laboratory, told of great scientists, who had innate tacit skills, who saw things in slides no one had seen before, or who could grow giant crystals or tumble upon Nobel prizes. This particular tale had it that this youth, a mere stripling of seventeen who had accompanied his father on an exchange visit to the Cambridge lab, had had skills so remarkable that the professor constantly invoked them in order to chastise his current clumsier or slower researchers.

The years that separated the thirty-year-old Jan from the seventeen-year-old who had grown into a Cambridge legend had not been kind ones. Those who had worked abroad during the brief efflorescence of the Prague Spring had too often returned to Czechoslovakia to find themselves under suspicion, demoted, sent into oblivion or ordered into menial jobs far from their area of expertise.

Scientists on the whole had fared less badly than intellectuals or writers whose forms of communication were easier of access. Jan's father had been sent off to work in a pathology laboratory in provincial Brno and had died soon afterwards. Jan himself was eventually allowed to continue his studies but, despite his evident brilliance, he was shunted into practical medicine rather than research and had spent long years as a lowly hospital doctor, assigned to the terminal wards which were equally terminal in the matter of research prospects.

It was through Jan that Stephen began to have an intimate insight of what an accident of geography could do to a life.

Only a few years older than him, Jan shared his interest in molecular research and his passion for experiment, yet none of Stephen's opportunities had been his. In the course of their sporadic late-night conversations over the years – about work being done by scientists in Stanford and LA and Cambridge, of new discoveries in microbiology, of gene sequencing and the potential of monoclonal antibodies – Stephen also grew shamefully aware that Jan was indeed the potentially legendary figure of his professor's narrative. But that legend had been nipped in the bud by a politics which had little to do with science.

He began to see Jan as his double, the person he could all too easily have been had chance cut the historical deck differently.

Superstitiously, he began to feel that he owed a debt not only to Jan, but to Eastern Europe as a whole. Began to think that because the East had lived out all the ills of occupation and fractured borders and political passions and centralized authority, the West had been spared.

Each time he came to Czechoslovakia and particularly after Jan had moved back to Prague, he brought him as many scientific journals as he could manage, as if they were not only the tools of their mutual trade, but talismanic objects which would somehow placate the goddess of fortune. Gradually, too, in the latter part of the '80s, he had been able to put in a word here and there and help to ensure Jan a place at the Institute.

And now that everything had changed and East and West were no longer markers of political difference but had supposedly returned to being points on the compass, Stephen still had the sense of outstanding debts that had to be paid if new evils – of poverty and retribution and ethnic conflict – were to be kept at bay.

The latest and grandest instalment in that debt was in part the reason for this visit.

Stephen lifted his Powerbook onto Jan's desk, flicked the switch just as the phone began to ring with monotonous insistence. He picked it up.

'Jan?' a woman's voice at the other end queried.

'No, sorry. He's not here. May I take a message?'

There was a pause. 'Is that Stephen Caldwell?' the voice asked hesitantly in English.

'Yes.'

'Stephen. It's Hanka. Hello.'

'Hello. Good to hear you, Hanka. Are you well? And Eva?'

Another pause. 'Has Jan told you?'

'Told me what?'

'No. I see. That we do not live together any more.'

'No.' Stephen put the phone in his other hand. His palm was moist. 'I'm sorry,' he said lamely.

'It is not for you to be sorry. It is for him to be sorry. But that is neither here nor there. Please remind him that he must go to Eva's school tonight to meet her teachers. At seven o'clock. Goodbye.'

'Hanka. Wait. I . . .'

Stephen heard the signal crackling in his ear. Slowly he put the telephone down. He felt . . . well, he didn't know exactly how he felt. Distressed, embarrassed, at odds, disappointed, surprised, sad, uncomfortable. He wasn't good at dealing with emotion. He had heard Hanka's. And he liked Hanka. Had always liked her. He had always thought she was like Tessa, a Czech version of her perhaps, blonde and cool and self-sufficient. And flirtatious where Tessa was wry. He had always thought Jan would like Tessa too if he met her. Though Stephen hadn't introduced them on the one occasion when Jan had come to Cambridge some three years back. He didn't quite know why. It just hadn't happened.

He played with his tie for a moment, loosened the knot, and went to stand by the window. The little girl with the skipping rope was gone and in her place there was a puddle of rainbows where a pale sun now glimmered on wet pavement.

It had something to do with Sonya, a kind of tact perhaps, that didn't want to introduce another woman where Jan's sister, Sonya, should have been. Stephen had felt that, but had preferred not to probe the feeling. He didn't like to unlock that room in himself. Within it, he was paralysed, useless, a stunted being, barely capable of deep breath.

Yet the door to the room was ajar now and Sonya stood at its threshold, shy, silent, with that beautiful downturned gaze, which spoke to him more loudly than bold looks and a quantity of words. Just as she had stood at the door of that house in Brno.

Jan's half-sister, Sonya, whom he had met the evening after that incident at the border crossing. She was a slim waif of a girl, with angel-pale hair and a musing expression, as if she were wandering in some airy, remote sphere far removed from the overcrowded rooms with their heavy, scratched furniture. When she had turned her slow, gentle gaze on Stephen, he had felt like some uniquely precious creature beckoned towards that distant place. He had followed her movements round the house that first night without quite knowing he was mesmerized by them. And by the soft, lilting cadences of her voice.

He had discovered that she was older than he had estimated, older than him in fact, and already a practising chemist who worked in a plant where chromite ore was converted into ferrochromium. He had stayed on in Brno for another day. Sonya had an afternoon off and she had offered to show him the sights. She was the only sight he had taken in. Her voice, her long, slender fingers, her musing eyes drew him as surely as a siren song.

The following morning while he was making his way, already behind schedule, to Prague, it came to him that he was in love. Sonya's presence trailed him. Her voice with its charming broken English sang in his ears. He postponed his trip to Poland and returned to Brno. But he didn't know how to speak his emotions. His experience with women was hardly extensive. And they had always been the ones to make the first move. Indeed, the second. Sonya just smiled her sweet, slightly melancholy smile at him and he remained speechless on all the points where it might have counted.

At Christmas, he went back to Brno, determined to make an overture. But Sonya was unwell, had a racking cough which he could hear at night through the thin partitions of the house. Her mother wouldn't allow her out into the icy cold of that winter. And under her mother's watchful gaze, Stephen found himself unable to broach anything intimate. Only on his last night had he managed to see her alone for a moment and ask her whether, if it could be arranged, she might like to visit England.

She had looked at him with a golden expectancy in her features and nodded a breathless 'yes'. He had kissed her then, first her smooth cheek and then, unable to stop himself, her lips. They were warm and dry and fluttered with hesitancy, like the fingers she raised to his neck. He had held her then, felt a fragility he wanted to shield with his life. When he finally released her, her eyes glowed, their melancholy extinguished and he had whispered the words of love he had never before uttered.

Back in England, he had embarked on inquiries. The process was even more complicated than he had presumed and there was no guarantee that the Czech authorities, with their arbitrariness, would sanction a visa. He started to write to Sonya, soaring letters where he began to say some of the things he couldn't bring himself to utter out loud. He didn't know whether she received all of them. Her answers were sporadic, friendly, but matter-of-fact and never to the point. When he applied for a new visa to visit Czechoslovakia the following summer, it was refused. He wrote to her to suggest they meet in Budapest.

A few weeks after the visa application, a telephone call from the Foreign Office beckoned him to London to lunch at a club in Pall Mall. He went with alacrity, seeing a chance here of a plea for Sonya. The man who met him had a pudding of a face beneath wispy blond hair and a thin pin-striped suit which crumpled round his girth in comfortable dishevelment. He poured and downed claret at a startling rate. Yet his watery eyes when they fixed on Stephen had an uncanny shrewdness. And about Stephen's history, he seemed to be better informed than Stephen himself. He knew the exact trajectory of his parents' lives as well as the timing of their deaths. He knew about Simone and about Stephen's trips to the East. He knew about his work. The only thing it seemed he didn't know were Stephen's political opinions and, since these hardly had much shape, Stephen, his discomfort growing, found himself reduced to rather fewer words than the solemn waiter who brought their steak and kidney pie.

When, towards the end of that lunch, Stephen enunciated the words he had barely dared to utter to himself – that he wanted to marry a Czech woman – the man looked at him oddly and murmured, 'No, no, dear boy, that wouldn't do. That would pose problems.'

It was only in the train on the way back to Cambridge, as he ran through the lunchtime conversation in his mind, that Stephen realized he was being recruited by MI6. He felt at once uneasy and strangely flattered. When a second call came, this time to lunch in a room at King's College, he made it clear amidst the innuendos that he was not a political animal, that he was primarily interested in his laboratory pursuits.

'Of course, of course.' The man had given him a faint smile and settled his tie primly on his ample stomach. 'But if you hear of anything in that domain, anything that may be useful to us, research into interesting chemicals, you know the kind of thing, you will naturally get in touch with me.'

'Naturally,' Stephen had murmured, hoping that the word would magically result in a new visa to Czechoslovakia. He had never found out whether it eventually had. Nor had he ever contacted the man again. When it came to the bottom line, he preferred to be a free agent. He had other priorities.

When he mentioned the incident to Simone, just before heading off to a Budapest where Sonya wouldn't be, she had smiled her enigmatic smile and told him that now, there was an inevitability to it, he would find himself asked to contribute an article to some Moscow journal. He must be a little wary. This was the way the KGB liked to begin their recruitment.

He had gone on then to tell her about what he hadn't previously been able to bring himself to report: the misadventure of the tricky border crossing. How that had led him to Jan and then to his sister, Sonya, whom he was in love with, wanted to marry.

Simone had looked at him in troubled astonishment. 'Sonya Martin, you say?' She had turned away, as if she didn't like to chastise him face to face for the folly of his innocence. 'But, Stephen. This is impossible. It is also dangerous. Not so much for you, but for them. I hope you have covered your tracks.' His look must have revealed his stubbornness, so she had thrown up her arms dramatically. 'It would be far wiser for you to form a partnership closer to home, Stephen. And soon. You should leave Czechoslovakia alone for a while.'

He hadn't listened. At Easter, he returned to Brno. The buds were just beginning to be visible on the tips of the chestnuts. As they strayed for a weekend walk into what was almost countryside under a sky dotted with a pale fluff of clouds, Sonya had looked so ethereally beautiful that he had poured out his love, his hopes, in one great ungainly splutter. She had smiled and curled her hand into his. He had taken it for a yes.

Two days later, when he could tear himself away from her, he had spoken to Jan. It was already late. Jan was on night duty and Stephen had accompanied him on the short trek to the hospital. He had put his arm round Stephen's shoulder. 'I would not deny you anything, my friend. You must know that. And I have wanted Sonya to be happy. But it is not so easy.'

He had said nothing more for a block and Stephen had grown nervous with apprehension.

'You see, Sonya is ill. Very ill. She does not know herself how ill.' From the tense grip on his shoulder, Stephen had realized how ill. He had stopped in the middle of the pavement as if an abyss had opened before him. Jan had had to urge him on.

'In the best of all possible worlds, even in an only slightly better one, I would say to you, go. Take her to England. Make her happy even for a short time. But we do not live in that world. Already the neighbours have begun to notice your repeated presence here. They are suspicious. And my mother and Hanka, they are worried. Your letters were not such a good idea. If now you marry Sonya, manage to take her away, given that she has the strength and the will for it, it will almost certainly rebound on us. Badly, I fear. Jobs, you know. All that.' Jan had shrugged his misery.

Stephen had been mute, unable to take in the full weight of what was being said to him. Only in the long hours of that night on the narrow sofa with its prodding springs had he begun to experience the acrid taste of despair.

The next evening Jan had visibly chased everyone from the house so that Stephen and Sonya could be alone. They had sat on that same sofa, stroked each other's hair, kissed, touched with a longing which held more passion than the room seemed to be able to contain. Only the imminent return of Sonya's mother had prevented them from stumbling towards the bedroom. Instead, they made promises of a sweetness so poignant that Stephen began to feel the world could be changed in their image.

He stayed in Brno until his visa allowed him only a single day for that sanctioned visit to the Academy in Prague. He told Sonya that by summer he would arrange all the necessary papers with which to whisk her away. As he said it, he believed it. And in the intervening months, he moved heaven and earth and Simone to make his fantasy fact. Simone, despite her counsel to the contrary, came through. Perhaps she had determined that things had already gone so far that there could be no return. Sonya was granted the ten-day visa which would take her to Paris in August.

But by the time August arrived, she was bed-ridden, unable to move. Stephen only saw her one more time, for the aching length of an afternoon. The frailty of her, the wide, gentle eyes she had turned on him, had rent him in two, as certainly as if a scalpel had sliced through the thin armour of skin and tissue. He had wept for the first time since childhood. Wept at his own helplessness, too.

Then Tessa had walked into his life. Her vigour, her good sense, her flashes of wry humour, had steered him towards less rocky shores. He had buried Sonya in the recesses of his mind. Only in his work did she sometimes surface in the recurring compulsion to find a cure.

Jan and his family had moved to Prague after Sonya's death. Jan had lost his post at the Brno hospital. His new job was as a hospital orderly and that had only come through the good graces of an old friend of his father's.

He never blamed Stephen for it, though Stephen knew the worst. He had allowed himself to forget the omnipresence of informers, the thousand eyes of the secret police. He had been careless and Jan and his family had paid the consequences. He vowed to himself that somehow he would make up for it.

When he had met Jan in Prague for a walk along the dusky paths of the Petřín Hill, Jan had told him that the particular kind of lung cancer Sonya had died of was chromium-induced. There was a high incidence of it in Czechoslovakia. If nothing else, his country had a genius for producing lethal industrial pollutants. Jan had laughed a short, bitter laugh.

'If only we could find some substance that killed those dangerous cells, eh, Stephen, a magic injection. Or an inhalant. Since we can't expect my countrymen to stop meeting their production quotas.'

Stephen's eyes focused on the drab furniture in Jan's office. Shrugging away memories, he returned his attention to his computer and tapped in his code. He half-watched the data protection program come up on the screen, tapped again, and saw the wondrous forms take shape, the coils and folds of the protein he would present to Jan. He breathed a sigh of quiet satisfaction.

It had all been one of those miraculous accidents. He had been testing his then current work on calcium when something in a particular sequence of amino acid chains and peptide bonds, a pattern of encapsulation, had given him an idea. He had dropped everything and started the business of fashioning. A few days and sleepless nights later, the chromium binding protein had emerged. Tense with excitement, he had called the DNA sequence up from a bank and placed the plasmid into the *E. coli*. And waited. The worst part of it was the waiting. But the miracle had occurred. The *E. coli* hadn't been killed off.

Then came the first testing stage. Into the Petri dishes with their jelly mixture of healthy and chromium-infected cells, they had placed a small quantity of the protein bacteria. The infected cells had granulated, had literally curled up and died. The healthy cells were unaffected: they retained their pretty freshness. Stephen had stared at the dishes for a long time. A wonder, akin to that he had felt as a child when he had first looked into a microscope, had filled him, and with it came a sense of jubilation. This was not just a breakthrough. It was a major discovery. With a little gulp of awe, he had named the protein: Chrombindin.

A small quantity of the separated-out protein and the plasmid were sitting in the igloos in Jan's lab right now. Jan would share his jubilation in Chrombindin.

Stephen had kept the discovery from the directors at Camgene. A few more weeks would make no difference. First he needed to speak to Jan. It was Jan who had been his point of inspiration and he owed it to him. The patent application would name them jointly as inventors. And then Camgene would see the reason for a collaboration with Prague. The trials would be carried out here. First animal, then clinical – under the aegis of Jan's Institute. Trials were far cheaper and simpler to run in the Czech Republic, in any event. Then, too, Stephen thought with an edge of grimness, there was no lack of potential patients here.

It would be a proper inter-European cooperation, the very kind they had long envisioned. The very kind the meeting he and Jan were jointly hosting this week was aimed to promote. Jan's Institute would become one to be reckoned with on the scientific map. Sorely needed funds would come pouring in.

Stephen slowed the pace of his plans. These were still early days. There were a great many hurdles yet to leap before a discovery became a tried and tested pharmaceutical. Nonetheless, he was as certain of the importance of Chrombindin as he had ever been of anything in his life.

He gazed down at the computer screen and started to run through the material. Something jarred. Some difference of detail. What was it? He scrolled back and started again. No, nothing. It was all exactly as it should be. But the nibbling at the edge of his consciousness persisted. He called up a previous screen, started again from scratch.

The diary of entries, that was it. That odd date next to the Chrombindin program and his lab files. He couldn't remember having accessed them in the last week. His day files, yes. Some random notes from meetings. He searched his mind. Perhaps he had looked at Chrombindin just for reassurance, or checked some laboratory record for the conference. Or simply pressed the wrong keys.

A prickle of fear edged up his spine. He had been so vigilant during the journey, but his vigilance had been directed at the styrofoam cages. Not at his Powerbook, secured, he assumed, so long as it was with him, by his password. He gazed at that date again, the time code still ticking to a British clock. He took out his pocket diary as an aide-memoire. But in a flash, without looking at it, he knew exactly where he had been at that time on that day.

Ariane. She had been so nonchalant in her suggestion of a game of chess. She had stood at his side talking on the telephone as he tapped in his password. And then he had gone off and lain in her bath, like a sentimental fool.

But what possible interest could she have in calling up his work?

Stephen ran his hands nervously through his hair.

'You are not happy, my friend.' Jan's voice reached him from the door.

Stephen turned a grim face towards him. 'No, no. I have some very good news. Though it may not be undiluted.'

9

---*---

'Glad that you accepted my invitation?' Ted Knight looped an arm round Tessa's shoulder and followed the direction of her gaze.

Below them the river curled as lazy as a well-fed boa in the gleam of the early-morning sun. In the distance a dense tracery of trees clustered against a fairy-tale castle.

'Ecstatic.' Tessa looked up at him. 'I don't know why I waited so long to come here.'

'Waited for me. Waited for an American to show you Europe.' His face was suddenly impish beneath the spiky bristle of his hair. 'A reluctant European. Very English of you.'

'Is that what it is? Well, then, you had better get on with it. There's an awful lot out there to see. And I still haven't had a cup of tea. And we've already wasted a whole hour.'

'Wasted?' He pulled her a little closer.

'Wasted beautifully,' she acknowledged, sniffing in the fresh morning smell of him. She ruffled his hair and for some reason she thought of Winnie the Pooh and his honey pots as she snuggled closer to this handsome, unlikely man who had swept her up and might yet deposit her exactly where she wanted to be. 'What I like best about you . . .'

The phone rang before she could finish and she watched the quick stride with which he crossed the hotel room, the instant concentration as the voice at the other end engaged him. She shivered with pleasure.

It was odd how easily they got on, playing to each other like the two hands of a counterpoint, well-rehearsed yet full of surprises for all that. And yet she had never rehearsed it, had never had an affair which had little to do with the heart and less with tomorrow. As long as one didn't break the unspoken rules – which were all, she sensed, to do with introducing the heart and its future – it was as delicious as a soufflé – a lemon soufflé, all light and sugary but with a bracing tang of tartness. And as evanescent.

Her impressions of the last few days were fleeting too. There were so many of them. They had covered so much ground. From Vendôme, back to Paris, then in a hired car to Strasbourg, then a flight to Prague. She hadn't moved around so much and with such speed in years. Not ever, really. And she found she loved the breathlessness of it all. It didn't leave time for dark musings.

Tessa smiled, then flushed a little at her own thoughts. Sexually, too, she had never experienced anything quite like it. As if with Ted she were someone else, someone freer, more daring. She had been ripped out of the quotidian, out of time as well as place. No longer the sensible, responsible Tessa Hughes of Cambridge, who hurt and couldn't get her husband into bed and worried about tomorrow and herself; but a woman, any woman really, desired and desiring, immersed in touch. She liked whoever that woman was, wished she could somehow package her and bring her home with her. Not to Stephen, though. Funny how she had hardly given Stephen a thought since they had left Paris. There would be time enough for that, Tessa reflected, forcing the shadow away.

'A couple of faxes waiting for me downstairs.' Ted was by her side. 'Tomorrow I'll have it installed up here. More convenient.' He kissed her delicately on the forehead, left a lingering touch on her hip. 'Meet you in the dining room. Okay?'

'Very okay.' She waited for him to go, then turned back

to the magical view. From the street she heard the clip-clop of horse's hooves. She imagined the two of them as they had been yesterday just after they had arrived, in the streets swept clean by rain and a watery sun glimmering on the cobbles, as the carriage they had hired drove them through the city. She had insisted on the carriage, because of the sign she had seen in the agency. 'Take one of the horse-driven city tours,' it had exhorted in that new Euro-English which leaked with wondrous inadvertent puns. 'We guarantee no miscarriages.'

Tessa giggled, then grew more serious. Tonight she would ask him. Yes. With Ted, she felt certain it would work.

The dining room had an air of such newness that Tessa wouldn't have been surprised to find the last dabs of paint still wet and the furniture bearing price tags. She spotted Ted at a buffet table. He was heaping cereal into bowls, fruit and rolls onto plates, as if he thought she too might be some famished Californian jogger in need of high-voltage vitamins.

He gestured her towards a windowside table and followed a moment later, bearing the overloaded tray.

'I've ordered tea. And coffee. Just in case.'

'Wonderful. You're spoiling me, you know. You'll never get rid of me.'

He looked at her a little reflectively, then chuckled. 'But I have a favour to ask of you.'

'Oh?' She sat up, suddenly nervous.

'Nothing that terrible. It's just that something's come up back home. And I'm going to have to sit tight by fax and phone and try and sort it out. That, plus a few more meetings to set up. There are some interesting heads gathering here. It'll take me a good few hours. At least.'

'I'm sorry. But that's all right. Really. I'm quite good at keeping myself busy. Was expecting to.'

'I had no doubts on that score. There's still the favour, though.'

'You want me to type some documents for you. Is that it?'

'Heh ... I'm just about your new man. An old hand with the keyboard. No, not that. I'd like you to keep an appointment for me. I can't seem to reach this person on the phone and it would be rude not to turn up.'

'And what do I do? Pretend I'm a junior headhunter with loads of bucks to squander?'

'Sure, why not. My temporary assistant.'

'But I know absolutely nothing about science. Nor about Centocor or Chiron or Genentech or any of those other appealing little names of firms you drop that sound as if they've fallen out of some primer on mythology.'

'You've been paying attention.' He wagged a mocking finger at her. 'You could, of course, simply tell him the truth and have a pleasant lunch.'

'You mean that I've come along for the bed and breakfast.'

Ted's coffee cup met its saucer with a spill and clatter. 'Now, now, Tess, we don't want to give the man ideas. How about you just say I've got a crisis on and I'll catch up with him later.'

'Okay. I'll be a proper little English Miss. Mrs, I mean.'

'Not too proper.' He grinned suddenly, brought her hand to his lips. 'You can come back and tell me all about him – what he plans to do with the rest of his life, what he thinks of the dear old US of A, how many dependants he's got ... That kind of thing.' He pulled a map from his case and a guide book.

'Start to build up a dossier, in other words.'

'Call it what you will,' he said as he carefully circled the name of a restaurant and marked an X on the map. 'But make sure you're back by three or I'll begin to wonder what kind of truths you're telling him.'

Ted Knight watched her go, the swing of bag on hip, the hint of shyness in the smile and wave as she turned back to him. She was proving a treat, this Tessa he had found for himself, avid in bed and cool out of it. With touches of acerbity. He liked that. It kept him on his toes. Perfect. She was making this trip a pleasure.

She was clever, too. Had a magpie mind, full of the jewels and trinkets she had picked up here, there, and everywhere. Too clever, perhaps. He would have to watch that. He didn't want anything interfering with what was proving so successful a journey. No doubt about it. Luck was on his side.

The streets of the old town, with their golden domes and red roofs and amber stucco, formed a labyrinth so full of architectural marvels that Tessa wasn't sure she would want to find her way out even if a minotaur lurked. But when she realized that her sparse map bore little relation to the density of the city and it was almost half past twelve, she made a concerted effort to locate the restaurant.

She found it just a little late at the crossroads of a named and unnamed street. The promised wooden fish flapped above its doorway, like some wingless prehistoric bird trapped in an inbetween state. She made her way quickly past ornate oak tables and ballooning paper lanterns towards a desk with an old-fashioned till at its centre.

'Mr Knight's table?' A young woman looked at her curiously. 'But you are not Mr Knight? You would like another place, yes? Your guest has already arrived.'

'Oh. No.' Tessa explained hurriedly and peered beyond the woman to a table where a man sat staring out of the window with evident impatience. His face was thin, slightly forbidding, the chin marked by an indentation, and the eyes he turned on her were of so startling a clarity that she stumbled over his name.

'Dr Martin.'

'Mar*tin*.' He emphasized the last syllable. 'But you are not Edward Knight – unless he has had one of those operations the tabloids in Romania were recently so proud of.' He grinned a little crookedly. The expression so transformed his face that Tessa forgot to let go of his hand as she introduced herself.

'Dr Knight asked me to convey his apologies. He couldn't reach you in time to do so himself and he asked me to stand in for him.'

'Sit down. Please.' He pulled out a chair for her with old-world courtesy.

'So, you work with Dr Knight?'

'Temporarily. In a manner of speaking.'

He examined her intently.

'We're travelling together,' Tessa burbled.

'I see. A fortunate man.'

She couldn't tell from his face whether that was another instance of flattering courtesy or whether it meant something else, so she studied the menu that had just been handed to her and which was inordinately long.

'Don't waste your time. The only edible food is on the board.' He gestured towards the wall. 'But you are not American?'

'No. No. English. From Cambridge.'

'Oh.' He smiled that miraculous smile again. 'I have a very good friend in Cambridge who also knows Edward Knight. Perhaps you have met him. Dr Stephen Caldwell.'

Tessa gazed into the middle distance. She would have to come out with it now, though her mind was having distinct trouble shaping itself around the concept, let alone the word, 'husband'.

'No, well, Cambridge is larger than one suspects. You are not at the university.'

Tessa held her breath, shook her head. Then plunged, 'And you . . . you would like to go and work in the States.'

'No. No. Not really. Or perhaps just for a year at some

time. To see how money can organize things.' He leaned closer to her as if he were about to reveal a confidence. 'It is really my friend Stephen's idea that I meet Edward Knight. Stephen has decided to become my career adviser. No, my place is here. Here, is what I wish to speak to Mr Knight about.' He gestured emphatically with quick graceful hands.

'So I've been wrongly briefed. There's really no need for this meeting,' Tessa gabbled, laughing to still her nervousness.

He joined her. 'Perhaps not. But you are here. So we shall eat. And talk. And when you go back you can communicate to Dr Knight that when we finally do meet, what I am interested in are funds to be invested here, cooperation with American companies.'

He proceeded to chat to her with great charm about the parlous condition of research in a country where it had once thrived. He talked to her about Prague, about its theatres where illusion and revolution were made, about Kafka's secret and forbidding castle and its transformation by Václav Havel.

By the time dessert arrived, Tessa felt herself so utterly in Jan's thrall that she was sorry she had lied to him and had listened under false pretences. For he told her not only about Prague, but also a great deal about Stephen, perhaps courting her through the English association, but also, she felt, because he meant it. He had hailed Stephen as a genius and also a generous man, a true believer in scientific community, a man who had helped him enormously, a brother who had seen him through dark times.

At one point in this eulogy, which had something of an obsessional edge, Tessa began to wonder if there was more to this scientific brotherhood than met the eye. She studied the man's gestures, watched his expression. She wondered how one ever knew what men were to each other unless they came out openly and told you. And even then.

She also wondered why Stephen had never said anything to her about Jan Martin. The fact that he hadn't incensed her. It also made her glad that she was now being as duplicitous as he was. A gleeful tingle of vengeance went through her.

Just then she heard Jan Martin say, 'And, of course, one cannot bury the recent past and all the grudges and bitter memories that come with it. But to be mired in vengeance is destructive for a nation. After all, so many are implicated. No, we have to strike a balance between the past and the present. It is delicate and difficult.'

Tessa coloured at her own paltry version of vengeance and nodded. 'Very difficult. Perhaps more difficult than anything else.'

'For our children's sake.'

'Yes,' Tessa burbled.

'The generations succeed each other so quickly. You see our waitress, over there, with the three rings in her ear. For her 1968, so important to our historians, is as boring and uninteresting as her parents. But you must be all too aware of that, coming from a university town.'

'Too aware,' she echoed.

Just before they got up, Tessa asked him, 'And when did you meet Dr Caldwell?'

'Oh, many years ago. When we were both still young men. But you shall perhaps meet him. He was called away but he will return to Prague soon. Unfortunately he will miss the opening of our congress.'

Tessa hid her confusion. Stephen in Prague. Something else he had omitted to tell her. She must make sure she didn't bump into him. Not now. Not when she had plans for Ted. Though the thought of Stephen's surprise should Ted or Jan let her name drop in conversation rather thrilled her. Bumping into him, face to face, was another story. She had the sudden sensation that they were circling round each other like hawks, but that at any moment, one of them might become the other's prey. It was better to keep circling.

'No, no, that's mine. I insist. Ted Knight insists.' She took the bill the waitress had handed to Jan and busied herself with the paying of it.

'If you are going in my direction, I shall be happy to show you some sights on my way to the Institute.'

Tessa accepted gladly. As they walked, she found herself thinking how different this man's quick, light gait was from Ted's energetic stride. Then she found herself wondering what he might be like in bed and she called herself a heartless whore and asked him, 'Do you have a family?'

He made a sound that was not quite a laugh. 'A lovely daughter and an estranged wife.'

'Oh. I'm sorry.'

'No, no. Don't be sorry.' He took her arm to lead her round a noisy group of tourists and down a little cobbled side street. He pointed to twin Gothic towers capped by what looked like nothing so much as sorcerer's hats. 'You can visit Tycho Brahe's tombstone in there. Perhaps not now. Or I shall have to leave you.'

Tessa matched her pace to his.

'You know,' he said in a voice so low she wasn't sure she was meant to hear, 'sometimes, only when things get a little better,' he gestured expansively around them, 'do you realize how bad they have really become. Or maybe, it's just that when life becomes about more than blunt surviving, you learn about wanting. This is what happened to my wife and me. Or perhaps it is simpler still. We had grown tired of each other and loyalty became less important than truth.' He laughed with soft irony. 'Like the story of my country in recent years. Truth won out over Party loyalty.'

They paused on the kerb to let a large cement mixer inch its way into a narrow corner. 'But my friend Stephen is disappointed in me.'

'Oh? He's fond of your wife?'

'That too.' He glanced at her oddly. 'You know. I feel I already know you quite well.'

'The Cambridge connection,' Tessa mumbled, extricated her arm. They had come out on a market square crowded with stalls. There were heaps of grotesque puppets, apples, potatoes, scarfs and amulets and hippy gear from India. 'This isn't actually so different either.'

'Except to us it's new. A shopping revolution. You don't approve?'

'I approve, though it's hardly for me to do so.'

'But you English are so good at morality.'

'Are we?'

'Yes.' He met her eyes for a moment with the intensity of his. 'You can help me with a problem I have. If a friend were to offer you something very precious which he shouldn't be offering you, but which he wanted to give you and wanted you to accept and which you wanted, but couldn't really accept, would you accept or refuse?'

'First I'd have to have the proposition repeated,' Tessa smiled. 'Several times. I'm not sure my morality is subtle enough.'

'But only then does it becomes interesting.'

'Are you going to fill in the blanks?'

Jan looked perplexed.

'I mean, give me a for instance. Tell me about the friend, about the you, about the gift?'

'Would that make a big difference?'

'I think so.'

'But there isn't the time now. We'll meet again, yes?' He pulled a card from his jacket pocket and handed it to her. 'And there on the second street to the left, you have a very interesting church. St Cyril's. You will see. It is a surprise.' He stretched out his hand to her, bowed slightly. 'Give my best regards to Edward Knight.'

She watched him walk hurriedly up the street, his

shoulders tensed, his head bent in concentration. An interesting man, she thought. Decidedly an interesting man.

It came to her as she walked in the direction Jan Martin had indicated that the world from which Stephen had so secretively excluded her grew richer daily. The anger lay heavy in her stomach, but it was overlaid by something else – a wonder, perhaps a fascination. What else would she find in this shifting world in which he seemed to appear in a different guise behind every tree?

Tessa glanced at her watch. It was two forty. She would just have time to inspect the church before going back, a little late, to Ted. Her pulse raced ahead of her footsteps. Tonight. Tonight she would ask him. He had already given her so much. A new confidence. A new sense of herself. And now there was only a tiny transparent sheath of a border to cross. He couldn't refuse her.

She clenched her hands into fists and stared up at the unprepossessing wall of the church towards a plump dome. Halfway up, fresh flowers graced the wall, above them photographs, a plaque, like a small shrine. She climbed up the stairs and read the inscription, then turned to her guidebook.

St Cyril's was the church in which the British-trained Czech paratroopers who had assassinated Heydrich, the author of the Final Solution, had holed up, only to bring upon themselves the full wrath of the Gestapo. It was the site of a bloody battle. The two men had killed themselves with their last bullets, after having held out against three hundred and fifty Germans for the length of a night. In retribution, the Nazis had killed some five thousand people, including, in June 1942, the entire village of Lidice. The barbarity marked a turning point, stirred, as Anthony Eden had proclaimed, the conscience of the civilized world. After that, the British at last repudiated the Munich Agreement.

Tessa stared at the blurred photographs of two fresh-faced young men and shuddered at a history she had been lucky enough to escape. It made her own little drama negligible, a mere question of unfulfilled desires, of mundane frustrations and reproofs.

Chastened, she made her way into the church. The heavy doors opened on a space that was oddly intimate, informal, like someone's sitting room. Yet her heels echoed on stone, invading silence. There was a man standing in the midst of the room, gazing towards where an altar should have been. He was very thin, haggard, an old tramp she thought until he turned towards her and she realized he was very young, with jutting features, skin tautly stretched over bone. Furtively, he walked past her.

She penetrated deeper into the church. She was all alone now amidst the lingering smell of incense and she deduced from the screen which stood in the altar's usual position that she was in an Orthodox church, the sanctuary separated from the nave by what should have been an icon-covered wall punctuated by three doors. She remembered reading about that somewhere. An iconostasis, that's what it was called. Yet here there were very few icons on the stasis.

Tessa perched on a rickety wooden chair and looked up into the dome. She wondered about those blurred youths in the photographs, how they had felt as the guns began their fire and their own deaths came closer. A dizziness took hold of her.

Suddenly a cry pierced the stillness. Tessa leapt up. Behind her, half-hidden by shadows, she saw a woman with streaming dark hair, a shapeless dress. Clutched to her bared breast was an infant. She looked like some savage madonna for whom beatitude was not even a dream. Tessa stared, then turned away guiltily, as if she had interrupted a secret rite.

She edged towards the front of the church, pretended to examine stone and sculpture on the way. At her back she heard the woman's footsteps, then her voice, insistent, incomprehensible. She felt a tug on her arm. She turned, to be confronted by a barrage of sound. The woman seemed to be pleading. Her eyes were very black, her face thin where it might once have been voluptuous. She was holding the baby, a tiny bundle in a worn blanket, out to her.

Tessa reached into her bag, took out bills as meaningless as the verbal currency, handed them to the woman who looked and smiled and, holding up five fingers, stretched the baby towards her.

Tessa took the child, cradled it, while the woman put the money into a skier's shiny purse belt which sat oddly on her stained cotton frock. She kept talking all the while. Tessa gazed into the infant's face. It was all big staring eyes and tiny, slightly chapped lips in a grubby blanket. A minute hand flew at her, tugged at her beads, randomly touched her face. She folded her little finger into its grasp and made a gurgling sound at it.

'Pretty baby,' she said more coherently to the woman, but when she looked up there was no woman. She was gone. Tessa peered into the shadowy corners of the church.

'Your mama will be back in a moment,' she crooned, suddenly understanding the woman's gestures. She sat down and held the baby close, rocking it. 'Just a few more minutes.'

But when the few minutes had passed and then a few more and the church took on the hollow silence of unpeopled stone, an odd feeling came over her. Tessa sat very still. Her mind was playing tricks on her. The woman *would* be back soon. She sang the baby a song, then another. It was sleeping now, its little face all soft, dark lashes shadowing pale cheeks. It didn't smell very good, not like the infants she knew, with their powders and milky lotions. More like musty old socks left for too long in Wellies in some back cupboard. Poor little mite. She held it closer. It was cold in the church and the rough chequered blanket had begun to feel distinctly damp. Perhaps the mother had gone off to buy provisions.

Tessa glanced at her watch. An hour. She couldn't have been sitting here for an hour already. Panic pricked at her with icy fingers. She forced it away. The woman would be back soon. Should she leave the child here for her? No, she couldn't do that. It would wake in terror. She rocked the baby with simulated calm and stared at where the altar should have been.

The door of the church creaked open and she saw an old man come in, cross himself. She walked swiftly towards him and tried to ask about the baby, its mother, but he looked at her with the same incomprehension she had felt when the child's mother had spoken to her. And now the child woke up and started to whimper, then cry, and the man shooed her towards the door with impatient gestures.

Tessa went out and looked up and down the road. There was no woman with streaming dark hair and shapeless dress. She had known there wouldn't be. There were only two men, their thin, jagged faces half-hidden beneath coat collars, lurking at the bottom of the stairs. She didn't like the dark eyes they turned on her with a glint of malevolence.

Tessa walked blindly down the stairs. The full force of her predicament suddenly hit her. The woman had gone, gone deliberately. Had she taken Tessa's money in exchange for the child? She looked at the little mite, quiet now in the fresh air. What should she do? It was a nice baby and she felt a stir of temptation as it waved its little hand at her face. But one couldn't just run away with someone else's baby.

She tried to see whether any side doors might lead to priests or wardens, but the structure of the church was as solid and unyielding as a barricade.

Police. She would have to find a police station. She spotted a woman further down the street and chased after her.

'Police station. I'm looking for a police station.'

The woman gave her a blank stare.

'*Polizei.*' She tried German. '*Bitte,*' she managed to add and then, for good measure, '*s'il vous plaît, la police.*'

A tentative response crossed the woman's square face, but when she started to speak, Tessa understood nothing, tried instead to follow her gestures.

'*A gauche,*' the woman finally said, pointing to a street on the left. '*A droit et à gauche.*' She traced a complicated map in the air, then held up five fingers.

'Five minutes away,' Tessa interpreted, thanked her, set off in what she hoped was the right direction, downhill and then along to the left, balancing the baby on her hip. She prayed it wouldn't start to wail, draw attention to them. This street was a busier one and she kept her eyes open in case the mother turned up. Perhaps she would. Perhaps she would accuse Tessa of kidnapping, demand more money.

Tessa felt she would gladly give her everything she had, but whether to keep her quiet, avoid embarrassment, or to keep the baby, she wasn't sure. It snuggled against her now, warm and damp and helpless, its little face against her breast. She tried to keep panic at bay. There was still no police station in sight. She stopped someone else on the street, a youth this time, and repeated her query, but he shrugged, gave her an odd look, then pointed vaguely in the direction of another church.

Her guide book, Tessa thought. It might help. As she unearthed it clumsily from her bag, she heard footsteps coming up on her from behind and she veered round half in fear, half in expectation. The man passed right by, his face averted. She tried to read her guide book round the baby's bulk, but whether there was simply no listing for police or whether she was too nervous to see properly, she found nothing.

She walked on past the designated church which sat

astride a little mound banked by high walls. The street had grown quiet again, graceful with the tracery of trees and newly stuccoed houses. It didn't feel like the route to a police station. She pushed back the tears that bit at her eyes, found herself babbling nonsense at the infant, which had grown heavier in her arms.

When she looked up, she saw in the middle distance a man in hat and coat standing by a wrought-iron grill and bending towards a gate. Stephen, she thought to herself in wonder, only to realize with a dejected shiver that she was conjuring him up out of distress and a decade-old habit.

She walked on, more quickly now, almost running. It had started to drizzle, sleet really. She tried to shield the child with her coat. She would have to get it some food soon, a bottle. How did one say 'bottle' in Czech? Had she passed any chemists? She looked around for a green cross. And then she saw it, right there in front of her, on the corner of the street, a shabby nondescript building with the letters P O L I C I E half-obscured above its door.

She slowed her steps, passed a hand through her hair. Hoping she didn't look as unhinged as she felt, she took a deep breath and, with a last cooing sound at the infant, pushed open the door.

The large, shabby room was all but deserted. A solitary policeman with grey indoor skin and skimpy hair sat behind a desk with an antique portable typewriter at its centre. He looked up at her with singular uninterest.

Tessa started to explain and as she spoke she realized that he understood hardly a word.

'French, *français?*' she asked.

He shook his head, motioned for her to sit down. He disappeared into a back room and came back with an older man in plain clothes who proceeded to address her in German.

'English or French,' Tessa insisted.

The baby began to wail. The two men looked at them

in sullen displeasure and for a moment she thought they were about to show her to the door. She hushed the child, grappled in her pocket for some tissues with which to wipe its face. A card came out with the tissues. Jan Martin. She stared at it and then pointed towards the telephone.

'*Dolmetscher,*' she said. 'Interpreter.'

The uniformed policeman passed her the telephone.

What had her sister told her about hungry, crying babies, Tessa tried to remember as she dialled and prayed that Jan Martin would be in.

A man's voice answered on the third ring.

'Dr Martin?' she asked. Simultaneously, she put her little finger into the infant's mouth, felt the suck, the relief of quiet. The double relief of the 'Yes' at the other end of the line.

'Dr Martin, I'm so very sorry to trouble you, but I'm in a police station and no one understands me. I need someone to translate. Do you think you might?'

Tessa explained as succinctly as she could and passed the telephone over to the officers, who looked at her and the grizzling child with growing disquiet as they listened, then handed the phone back to her.

'I shall be with you in a few minutes. I'm not far away. Would you wish me to ring Mr Knight?'

'Please, that would be kind. Just say I'll be late.'

Tessa sat down on the single wooden bench and tried to calm the fretful child. The officers stared at her as if she were some troublesome leper who had come to ruin their afternoon. With sudden decision, she thrust the baby into the older one's arms, and said loudly, 'Pharmacy. Chemist.' She made a sucking gesture with her lips and held an invisible bottle to her mouth.

The young one suddenly beamed a smile at her and pointed her across the street. '*Lékárna.*'

'Thanks.'

She bought Pampers and tissues and talc and a bottle

and some German formula milk and, for good measure, some cereal and a striped blue stretch suit that was buried behind some stockings. When she returned to the police station, a buxom woman had been found from somewhere and was holding the baby and playing cootchy-coo games with it. Typical, Tessa thought, not without a little tinge of – what was it? – jealousy perhaps.

Together they went off to a slightly grimy bathroom and washed and changed the child. 'It's a girl,' Tessa said aloud as they unwound a swaddling of rags. 'A sweet little girl.' And she really was sweet, Tessa thought, with her dark, feathery hair and watchful expression and her new powdery smell and thin, fragile limbs covered in fresh clothes. She cupped the small head and hugged her and thought she might cry right there in front of the other woman.

When they came out, Jan Martin had arrived and he strode quickly towards her. 'I am so sorry. You will remember St Cyril's as a place of great misadventures.'

Tessa tried to smile, but it didn't come out quite right.

'You will have to answer some questions and then I will take you back to the hotel.'

Tessa nodded, felt the child being lifted from her arms.

As she sat there being grilled, she watched the buxom woman prepare milk with practised efficiency and feed the child. Sadness engulfed her. If she had been a little more daring, the baby girl could have been hers. She had paid in a way, after all.

The policeman were particularly interested in that, in whether the exchange of monies was a payment or an act of charity. Their suspicion cloyed, stuck to her like a dirty garment. She told them over and over again that she didn't know how the woman had interpreted the money. She had meant it as an act of charity.

When they were at last free to go, she lifted the child to her, kissed her sleepy face. The eyes grew round and wide and clung at her, so that she could barely bring herself to return her to the other woman.

In the taxi she asked Jan in a shaky voice what would happen to the child.

He shrugged. 'They will take her to an orphanage and if they find the mother, they will reunite them. But, of course, they won't find the mother.'

'No, of course not,' Tessa said dismally, aware as she hadn't altogether been before of that truth.

'If she was in St Cyril's, then she was probably Bulgarian. So she came to Prague to make money – perhaps worked as a prostitute – and the child was an unwanted accident. Maybe wanted, you never know. There are many stories which circulate that say rich women from the West will pay vast sums for babies.' He looked grim. 'You know, we have many new ways now of generating foreign exchange. And women have proved to be excellent entrepreneurs.'

'But I didn't give her vast sums. I didn't have very much on me.'

'Perhaps it was very much for her. It's not legal, of course. We have signed all these agreements.'

'Which is why the police had misgivings about me.' Tessa tried a laugh but it didn't ease the great stone of sadness that weighed on her. 'Did they think I'd got cold feet at the last minute?'

'My dear Miss Hughes, our police are experts at suspicion. They do not need many grounds for it. It is a habit. Everyone is guilty. Occasionally, rarely, they may be proved innocent.'

She could feel him studying her. She stared out of the window into drizzle to avoid his gaze.

'But you are melancholy,' he said softly. 'You worry about the fate of this poor baby.'

The taxi was pulling up by the hotel and Tessa took a deep breath.

'Thank you. You've been very kind. I'm sorry to have wasted so much of your time.'

'Nothing. But I will see you at the reception, yes? After you have had a little rest, perhaps.'

'Reception?' Her mind had gone blank. Suddenly she gripped his arm. 'Please, don't talk about all this to anyone. I'd rather ... well ... explain for myself.'

'Of course.'

The heartwarming look he gave her made her think he was wasted on centrifuges and chromatography columns and whatever else they had in labs these days. A look like that could revive a dying patient. When he saw it, Ted would probably try to clone and package it as a new wonder drug. In fact she might suggest it to him herself.

Tessa tried to smile in return, but as she disappeared into the lift, all she could think of was the puckered face of a little motherless girl who would suddenly find herself in the dismal world of orphans. For a moment, stupidly, she found herself considering what Stephen would make of that tiny solemn presence. She gripped her bag to her chest. When the lift stopped at her floor, she realized that she had clenched her hand so tightly that her nails had left welts in her skin.

10

—— * ——

London was a frenzy of snarled, impatient traffic and burdened Christmas shoppers.

Stephen signalled his taxi to a complete halt and joined the heave of pedestrians along Regent Street. It would be quicker to walk the few remaining blocks. Time pressed on him, as surely as if he could hear the sand slithering through the hourglass, threatening to cover him in its grains.

Katherine Williams had unwillingly agreed to give him an hour. An hour wouldn't be enough, but she was due in court the next day and could barely manage even that. Still, it was Katherine he needed. She did the majority of Camgene's work and with her background in molecular biology was quick to appreciate the scores of details other patent lawyers would take weeks to understand.

The building in the square behind Regent Street had a muted stateliness. After the blare of the streets, its marbled lobby seemed as quiet as some church to industry. Impatient of lifts, Stephen raced up to the third floor, where a receptionist waved him on.

'Third door to the right.'

Katherine sat behind a desk bulging with dossiers. She was a small woman with neat, unemphatic features which only sharpened into foxiness when a problem presented itself. Her voice had a staccato dryness.

'I hope this is going to be good. I've got a mountain of work I'd rather not be deflected from right now.'

'It's good,' Stephen assured her.

'And you want to file for a priority date which passed yesterday, or maybe weeks ago, if I understood you correctly on the phone.' She grinned. 'You know these things take time, Stephen. Patent applications are not made in a couple of months. Let alone an hour.'

'I've tried to get it right. Worked on it all weekend. Pared it down to three pages. So it should be nearly there. But I've come straight from the airport and we'll have to print out. In colour for the designs.'

She sighed and gestured him towards the print room. 'Tell me about it.'

He gave her the gist of his Chrombindin work and she listened carefully, let out a low whistle.

'This is going to make Camgene a mint, Stephen. But what's the hurry? I can't believe someone else is going to beat you to the punch. We'd have heard rumours.' She gave him a sudden glare. 'You haven't been blabbing, have you? You scientists never know when to keep quiet. I've lectured you before. No chit chat, no conferencing, no publishing, until after you've filed.'

'It's not that.' Stephen watched the pages coming out of the printer and felt depression tug at him again. He waited until they were back in Katherine's office with the door safely closed behind them.

'I suspect someone else has been in here.' He tapped his computer.

'Someone who shouldn't have been?'

Stephen shrugged. 'I don't know. That's just it. I haven't got any certain proof. But I don't want to take any chances. It's safer to file as quickly as we can.'

'What do you mean, you don't know?'

Stephen considered. 'Well, it could have been an accident. A mistake.'

He replayed the story he had tried to tell himself. Ariane sitting down to play another game of chess while he was in the bath, getting into the wrong documents. Eventually finding the chess program. The trouble was that every time he put this innocent light on it, the fact of her disappearance hit him in the face. And then he was confronted by the next problem. If she had read through the material, even perhaps copied it once she had sniffed its importance, what would she do with it? He didn't like to think of that.

'Shall we get on with this, or you'll tell me my hour's up.'

Katherine gave him a questioning glance. He deflected it, took her through his discovery point by point: the design of the protein, the laboratory process, the trials that would still need to be done, the eventual uses.

'Okay,' she said when he had finished. 'I'll have to go through the specification again on my own. Get all the legal bumf in order. Maybe, just maybe, I'll get some time today. I can't promise. It may have to wait till the end of the week. I'll fax through any queries. You'll be at the office?'

'Most of tomorrow. Then you can reach me here.' He scribbled a number from his diary.

'Prague?' She looked aghast.

'It can't be helped. I'm meant to be hosting a big conference. I'm already late.'

'You don't make my life exactly easy,' she grumbled.

'No. Mine neither.'

'Hey. Don't look so grim.' A smile lightened her face. 'You should be drinking champagne. Save the bleakness for when we send you our bill.'

Stephen was in no mood for celebration. He took the tube to King's Cross and arrived in time for the next Cambridge train. As he watched the endless suburbs of London roll past, he forced himself to think of the worst possible scenario.

If Ariane had stopped to read the Chrombindin program, she was knowledgeable enough to grasp its implications. Would she then have copied the program onto a disk? She had said she needed money. That would mean selling his discovery on to someone. Japan would be a ready market. So would America. Neither country fell into European patent agreements and the buyer could always invent a case for first discovery, alter some tiny points in the process or in the making of the compound. That could lead to a costly court case he would rather not face. And if it was the Americans who got hold of it, they would gear up to aggressive clinical trials at twice the speed of anything that Stephen could organize.

France or any country in Europe was a possibility too. It would take a year before an application could be made to the European Patent Office. They would then initiate a thorough search of publications and other research in the field. His prior claim to discovery could be contested.

Over the weekend, he had tried repeatedly to trace Ariane through Natalya, through the few mutual friends they had. He had even managed to contact her brother in Moscow. But all inquiries abutted at a dead end. He considered hiring a detective and chasing up the lead Simone had suggested in the US. But he felt uneasy about that. Even if Ariane were located, she wouldn't have to admit anything to a stranger. The trace on his computer could all too easily be denied. Her word against his. And Ariane could act her way through anything. He was dismally aware of that. Then, too, if it came to court, he would have to explain the situation publicly. Tessa would find out. He didn't like to think of her distress.

Shame engulfed him. And with it a looming depression. If only he had gone to see Katherine before he had left for

France. But he had wanted the time to double-check. And to share Chrombindin with Jan.

Jan had refused his gift. After the congratulations and enthusiasm, when he had at last understood that Stephen wanted the work to be patented with both their names listed as inventors, he had stared at Stephen in astonished silence for a long time before at last saying, 'But, my friend, that would be a lie. We have lived with lies for too long in this country. Now we need a solid diet of truth.'

Stephen had tried to convince him that it didn't constitute a lie, that Jan had been at the genesis of the idea; that if Jan had been in his shoes, he would have been capable of far more. But Jan would have none of it.

'I know you want to help us in some way, Stephen,' he had said. 'But it will be enough if by some miracle we can arrange to have some of the trials done here. Perhaps even establish a scale-up manufacturing unit to produce the quantities of Chrombindin needed for the trials.' He had laughed then. 'What did you tell me that would cost? Half a million. Maybe the investors will trust us with that. The Czechs are good at breweries and the process is not so different.'

At some point in their discussion, he had put his arm round Stephen's shoulders and murmured, 'You know, Stephen. We should have no more secrets now. Only open relations. We need that.'

The rebuff was mild. Effusive thanks followed it. But Stephen had understood that Jan was hinting at something deeper. It came to him now, as the train rattled over weary tracks, that Jan might have been suggesting that Stephen was attempting to prolong what had once been the necessarily covert flavour of their relationship. That secrecy was no longer appropriate. There was nothing to be secret about.

As the train pulled into Cambridge station, Stephen let out a snort of self-derision. Yes, indeed. If his intimacies hadn't been based on concealment, then the fix he was in because of Ariane would never have occurred. But how did one rid oneself of a habit that had become second nature?

Outside it was already dark. Wet and dark. A cold wind whipped round him and covered him with the dankness of the Fens. Cambridge at its least inviting: a small town with a few good buildings shrouded in bad weather. And nowhere to hide. If he went straight to the lab, he would have to explain why he was back before schedule. He didn't feel up to that right now. He directed the taxi homewards instead, and wondered why he had so emphatically refused Ted Knight's offer last year of a post in California.

The house was cold and hollow. His shoes trailed mud from the meadow and he cast them off in the middle of the hall. Their clatter echoed up the stairwell. No Tessa. She was off sunning herself on some island. He should be relieved at that. But he wasn't. Everything felt oddly empty. As he started to brew some coffee, he realized he missed her. It was her house, really. Had no sense without her.

Exhausted, he switched off the kettle and left the beans unground. He would go to the office after all. Most people would have left by now. And he should leave a note together with a copy of all the patent application materials for his chief, arrange for a meeting to talk through at least some of the preliminary implications of the discovery. He hated being forced into haste like this, but there was no help for it now.

It was only when he reached the Camgene building that he remembered he had left his keys at home. He prodded the bell in exasperation. All he needed now was some new security guard who failed to recognize him.

'Ah, Dr Caldwell. It's you.'

He was grateful for the small mercy of the familiar portly face that greeted him.

'Forgotten your key?'

'I'm afraid so.'

'I'll see you up.'

'Thanks, Tom.' The man's name came back to him as they trudged up the stairs.

'Pretty quiet tonight. But your assistant's still in. The foreign chap. So I can leave you right here.'

Pavel. He had forgotten Pavel, who put in even more hours here than he did. Stephen took a deep breath and pushed open the laboratory door.

'Stephen!' Pavel pulled back from his computer with a start.

'Sorry to take you by surprise like this.'

'No, no. No matter. But I didn't expect you until at least next week.'

'Had to come back to . . .' Stephen fumbled with his coat, averted his eyes. 'Look, Pavel. I think we've had a leak. On the Chrombindin program. You haven't talked to anyone you shouldn't have about it, have you? Has there been anyone in here? Anyone asking questions?'

Pavel frowned. 'No. Just Mira and me, as usual. Dr Franklin dropped in, but he was looking for you and didn't stop. And your wife, just after you left.'

'My wife?' Stephen stared at him.

'Yes. Your wife. Pretty woman . . .' He stopped, gestured confusion. 'She said she was your wife. Like the picture in your office. She said you forgot something. She had the key.'

'Of course. Of course. Thanks. Any messages?'

Pavel gestured towards the inner office. 'On your desk.'

'You'll have to let me in. I've left my keys.'

Pavel turned a worried face to him. 'So we have a problem. A big problem?'

Stephen shrugged. 'We'll see. I'm not sure.' He waved Pavel away. 'But we may have to work more quickly than I'd bargained for.'

As he walked into his office, a peculiar sensation made

its way up his spine. He hadn't asked Tessa to pick any-thing up for him. What had brought her here?

He stared at the photograph of her, as if it might provide some clue. He hadn't really looked at it for some time. There had been something different about her then. What was it? That smile. She looked happy. Not that abject, reproachful face she now turned on him at every occasion. With a shiver, Stephen faced the thought that had bounded into his mind. Was Tessa planning to disappear too? First Ariane. Now Tessa.

A wave of panic clutched at him. As he tried to ride its crest, he scanned the office to see if she had left any sign of herself, a note perhaps. There was nothing. He rifled through the sheaf of messages and faxes, thrust them into his bag and hastened towards the car, barely remembering to say a 'see you in the morning' to Pavel. He could check his e-mail then.

At home, he scoured the rooms for messages. Finding none, he hesitantly opened the door to Tessa's closet. Her cases were gone, of course. That was as it should be. But he had so little inkling of her clothes, he couldn't tell whether what she had taken was all that was necessary for a holiday. He held the panic at bay, reiterated to himself that everything was as it should be. He would phone her. Somewhere he had made a note of the hotel she was staying at on St Kitts. The travel agent would have the number. He would try them first thing in the morning.

Without noticing he had undressed, he found himself on the bed, his eyes latched to the ceiling. Tessa wasn't like that, he told himself. She wouldn't vanish without making a sign. But the more he thought about her, the less he suddenly felt he knew what she was like. Everything about her had coalesced into a single unscalable mountain: the desire for a child. They lived in its silent shadow, couldn't see each other for its looming bulk.

A child. Why should that obsessive desire tie him up in

knots, render him impotent? It wasn't like that with Ariane. Hadn't been like that with that girl, Cary, almost a child herself. A sweet girl, he thought wistfully. He must write her a note. Make sure she was all right. Had found friends.

The panic gripped him again. He closed his eyes and forced himself to breathe. Deep, slow breaths.

He was coming out of some large building, a church perhaps, no, a train station with fat Mussolini columns and the pomp of a steep, broad staircase, a temple to technology. Halfway down the stairs he stopped and waited. For a friend. Yes, he was waiting for a friend. Where was the friend? He couldn't see him. Or was it a her? Not even down there amidst the file of waiting taxis. Old taxis. Yellow and quite old. Where was he? Anxiety filled him. Because of the waiting.

He looked towards the taxi rank again. He saw his cases and his laptop on a small, old-fashioned wooden trailer, like those one used to attach to cars when there was too much baggage to move. On top of the heap, a baby sprawled. A large baby, too big for the nappies it wore. But it shouldn't have been there, so naked in the cold. He pulled his coat more closely round himself.

His friend must have brought his cases there. But he didn't know that child. Yet it was winking at him, its face like an old man's. For a moment the face was familiar. Then the familiarity vanished and the strange baby started to wave.

Stephen looked round for his friend once more. Afraid now, he started to walk towards the taxi and his luggage. It was precious. But just as he neared it, the taxi pulled away. He shouted, hailed. No one paid any attention. He ran, ran and stumbled. Another taxi pulled up. He got into it, found himself muttering, 'Follow that car.'

They followed it. They followed it at a slow, leisurely pace. Too slow. There was no hurry, the driver said in a strange language he could somehow understand. The city had narrow, clustered streets with steep roofs and innumerable turns and they took one corner, then another and another. They came to a bridge, crossed it at the same leisurely pace. Just as they reached its end, he saw the first taxi coming back the other way. There was a person next to the driver. He recognized the head. His friend. Recognized the driver, too. It was a woman with the regal carriage of Simone. And then car and friend and baggage and baby vanished, swallowed up by a fog so thick, it obliterated sight.

Stephen woke in a panic of loss. It survived the alarm, the pacing through the empty house, the coffee. Persisted throughout his attempts to reconstruct the dream.

He wasn't sure what loss it was the dream signalled, but that sense was so strong that it hollowed him out. He tried a list of possible losses. His work. The attempt to give it to Jan. Jan himself, the friend who wasn't where he was meant to be at the station. Ariane. His youth. His sense of himself.

And Tessa. Of course. The cases on the taxi trailer. They were hers. Brown canvas. He recognized them now. And the stairs in front of the station. They were like the Capitol stairs in Rome, where they had spent a brief honeymoon. Tessa.

A bitter taste in his mouth, he reached for the telephone.

11

——— * ———

Sites where history has recently been made are not like other places. Their ordinariness is bleaker, crying out for a heroism no longer there, but not quite forgotten.

As she sat by her window in the Grand Hotel Europa overlooking Wenceslas Square, Simone wished she could say that to Stephen. She found herself selfishly irritated by his absence, announced in the note the hotel receptionist had handed her yesterday. After all, she had come here in part for him.

She tried, as she gazed out of the window, to evoke the presence of a crowd which was not simply the gaggle of guitar-strumming tourist youth found in every big city. Antoinette was probably down there, together with that friend she had made at the hostel where she worked. They had both accompanied her – a last-minute whim which she had been pleased to accommodate. The company did her good, particularly now that Stephen was away. It prevented her from disappearing altogether into the past.

Her gaze travelled towards the helmeted head of Good King Wenceslas, the smooth flanks of the horse which, legend had it, would gallop him into action and save the Czechs in their hour of need.

But the good king, Simone reflected, hadn't budged, either for the Nazis or when the Russian tanks rolled in at the end of that summer of 1968 which had buried too many hopes. It had taken another twenty-one furtive, limping years for Dubček to return to the balcony opposite, this time with Havel at his side, to proclaim the birth of a new era. Throughout Eastern Europe in that momentous year of 1989 the cheers of the crowd had been punctuated by the quiet flap of turning coats.

She hadn't come back here in '89, though she had gone to Berlin and Bucharest, to Moscow and Budapest.

She wasn't altogether certain she should have come back now either. Over twenty-five years had passed. Too long a span to allow a graceful encounter. Stephen's absence had dwindled her resolve.

Perhaps she shouldn't have chosen this hotel, brimming with the wrong memories. She had sat in the decaying grandeur of the café yesterday for too many hours and wallowed in them as the orchestra romanced its tunes. Memories which made the disclosure she was set on more difficult and brought her old woman's shredded vanity into play. In the *fin de siècle* elegance of this hotel, she felt as faded as the silk brocade of its upholstery.

Memory was sometimes easier than thought, certainly easier than action. Yet she needed to immerse herself in the grooves of those older memories, the ones she had denied for too long, so that she could meet the imperative she had set herself. The splintered, dead bones of her story called out for the passionate flesh of history. Without it, she would emerge, even in her own eyes, as that pitiable thing – a jealous, guilty woman.

She hadn't rung anybody, neither professional contacts, nor that new breed of politicians with whom it might have been interesting to have an audience. She wasn't here for work. And the few old friends she would have liked to see, Franci foremost amongst them, were dead. In this country one didn't live as long.

With a grimace of exasperation, Simone tugged on her coat. Shielded by its sleek fur, she made her way out into the cold expanse of the square and turned quickly into the narrower streets of the old city.

Coal smoke curled out of chimneys, just as it had done all those years ago. It wrapped the atmosphere in a heavy haze so that the houses loomed out at one, their outlines vaporous, animate. She followed the twisting streets and found herself on the edges of the old Jewish Quarter. As a girl, she had loved the din of hawkers shouting their wares, extolling the virtues of puppets and potato peelers, stuffed birds and cloudy gems in intricate settings. She had liked the reek of the streets less. If she closed her eyes, she could still smell it through the obliterating cold, a musty, acrid smell of sewage and cramped bodies and dank, ancient walls.

At the entrance of the Old Jewish Cemetery, there was a queue of tourists. One had to purchase a ticket now to visit those hundred thousand bodies buried twelve deep beneath their higgledy-piggledy stones.

When she had walked here with Staszek, the cemetery had been empty. Staszek. Stanislaw Mánes, her new tutor, a philosophy student at the university, called in to teach her Czech. Instead he had instilled in her an ardour for social justice. A more personal ardour as well. Had she woken from childhood into a painful secret love for him on that very first meeting when they had strolled amidst these sloping, random headstones, clustered together like decaying teeth in the cavern of an ogre's mouth? Her feet had been more solid on the ground then. Only her emotions stumbled.

It was her thirteenth birthday. September 1938. She was a painfully shy and secretly romantic schoolgirl who had lived in too many countries and read too many books. On Wenceslas Square, they had seen columns of marching, uniformed men and two giant armoured cars, moving with ponderous menace. Staszek had told her that if she didn't understand something or ran out of words, she must speak to him in French or in English. He no longer spoke German.

She had stared up shyly at the dark, proud set of him, the wave of hair which tumbled over deep-set eyes. 'You mean you have forgotten how?' she had queried, and seen those eyes flash contempt.

She was either very young or very stupid, he had said, and she had flared in turn, declaring she was certainly not stupid.

'No good Czech should speak the language of the Nazi enemy. Nor any good French person, for that matter,' he had announced, his handsome face very pale against the jet of his hair.

Simone smiled to herself. She had taken in his imperative and hardly breathed a word of German until after the war, though to his face she had protested and said German did not mean Nazi. It had been there far, far longer.

In the silence of the cemetery, they had hushed their voices. It was in a whisper that he decoded the pictures on the tombs for her, the squawking chickens on either side of a head indicating an adulteress whose eyes had been pecked out, the scissors denoting a tailor, the tweezers a doctor.

Beside Rabbi Loew's imposing baroque sarcophagus, he had told her a story she suddenly remembered afresh.

The great and ancient Loew, it was said, had a secret for keeping death at bay. He had learned it in his wise books. If he could concentrate on life and only on life, death would not touch him. In that way, during the plague, he had clutched hundreds from death and managed to survive himself. But one day, when he was already very old, his pretty little granddaughter gave him a splendid rose for his birthday. Enraptured by the gift, by the beauty of the rose, he bent to sniff it, his attention only on its beauty. And in that moment he fell down dead.

Death had been hiding amidst the fragrant delicacy of its petals.

It was funny how she remembered that story rather better than all the politics and readings from Marx which Staszek had introduced into their tutorials. Remembered it better than the painful moment when he had refused to come to their house any more because the French had signed their name to the Munich Agreement and effectively sold Czechoslovakia to the Germans in the false hope of peace.

Death had hovered over her relationship with him from the very beginning.

Shivering despite her furs, Simone picked up a stone and laid it carefully on the rabbi's tomb. She and Staszek had done that then. They had also discovered that they both had Jewish mothers, though Staszek's was already dead.

With sudden decision, Simone hurried from the cemetery, hailed a taxi, and in clear, precise tones asked the driver whether he might consider taking her to Mělník.

He frowned from beneath the peak of his cap, exclaimed ill-temperedly about the distance. Simone silenced him, told him she would pay the equivalent of his day's takings. The frown transformed itself into a shrewd smile. His eyes fixed on her coat, he ushered her effusively into the back seat.

'You're Czech, but you had the good sense to leave, eh? When? In '68?'

'I am not Czech,' Simone said bluntly.

'Beautiful town, Mělník!' he exclaimed, eyeing her in the rear-view mirror as he pulled away. 'You want to visit the ossuary in the crypt of Saints Peter and Paul?'

'No.' Simone signalled her unwillingness for chit chat and leaned back in the seat with its bright animal covering of fake fur.

She stared at the back of the driver's head, the straggling line where hair met skin and collar. For a moment she found herself wondering, as she did with every encounter in countries of the former Soviet bloc, what the man had done before 1989. Had he worked for the secret police? Been an informer? Betrayed any and every friend?

It did no good to think like that. The regimes had had more eyes and ears than they had citizens. Yet that was her problem. That was why she knew she was too old for this new world. She couldn't wash herself altogether clean of suspicion. She couldn't forget. It was far more expedient to forget. To bury the murky slate with its profusion of major and minor crimes and begin again. They were all, after all, mired in sins, smaller or greater. She was too.

Repressing queasiness, Simone turned her face to the grubby window and looked out. The grace of the city centre, the bridge over the racing river, had given way to the drab decay and grimy tenements of Holešovice. She had come to the exhibition grounds here with Staszek. But that was later. After the war. First there were those blissful snatches of time together in London.

Her father had been posted to the French Embassy there in 1939. Soon he was engaged in clandestine operations for the Free French, so her mother and she saw him only at irregular intervals. When the bombs began, Simone was shunted off to live with a family in Wales. On her sixteenth birthday, she determined she had had enough of school and strangers and of a safety so nervously oppressive that any danger was preferable. She made her way back to the capital. The scars the city wore – the black ash, the heaps of rubble, the devastated shells of buildings – shook her. Yet in an odd way their very reality gave her a strength the laundered reports and gossip had sapped.

She went directly to Bush House, where her mother worked. She hovered round the busy reception area, noticed the difficulty the receptionist had with the babble of foreign tongues she was forced to confront. An idea lodged itself in Simone's mind. At last, she might find a use for all those languages history had inflicted on her.

Two months later, she was standing behind the reception desk. It was there that one afternoon towards mid-summer she found herself gazing into the proud face of a uniformed man with eyes of such an intense darkness that her throat grew instantly dry.

'Staszek?' The name had croaked out of her. 'Don't you recognize me?'

A few hours later they were sitting in the hotel bar opposite and he was staring at her in a way which confirmed what she had only begun to suspect. She was a woman now, a woman men noticed, no longer that inconsequential, ungainly child – a prisoner of longing, confined in a body inappropriate to the emotions it contained.

Now as they talked, his eyes never strayed from her face. She learned that he had left Prague, too late really, after the Nazis had already started their deadly reprisals against the rebellious Czech students. She learned how he had made his way stealthily across the mountains into Slovakia and from there through Hungary to the Balkans and by boat to France, where he had joined a Czech division. He had tried to search her out in Paris, but there was no one in the house in Neuilly. He had worried for her.

By the time he had finished his narrative, her hand lay between two of his, a snug, well-caressed creature which felt it had at last found its home.

Two nights later, when her mother was working an evening shift, he came back with her. They were living then on two floors of a house which gave onto the lower end of Hampstead Heath, all glittering moonlit ponds and the tracery of trees and sprawling thickets. After work, she liked to sit by her window and watch the secret darkness steal upon the park. That night, they watched together, glasses of whisky magically in their hands. Before the shadows disappeared, they were kissing on the bed.

Simone could still taste that first real kiss, the smoothness of his lips, the small gasp of his breath, the surprising echoes of his fingers on her skin, a melody which had found its counterpoint.

The emotion she had hoarded over all those years cloaked everything in wonder, even the initial pain. His discovery of her became her discovery. She revelled in both, was amazed at what now became a mutual intensity, so strong, so avid and tender by turn, that she felt she had both come home and been cast out on dangerous seas. When the blare of a siren interrupted their passion and exhorted them to take refuge, they looked into each other's eyes and simply clasped each other more firmly. The only death which could impinge on them now was the death of separation. They both knew it. There was no need to speak.

The next morning, hand firmly in hand they walked slowly down the street towards the bus which would separate them for the length of the day. At the end of the street they saw it: the burnt-out shell of a house, the firemen dousing the last flames. They gripped each other more tightly to fill the yawning space of horror. They had been spared. Their love had been sanctioned.

As she gazed out of the cab window onto the slight roll of the wintry countryside, the old Simone with her thin old woman's legs neatly sheathed in the best French stockings felt the tremble of the young Simone within her. It was odd, she told herself, that she could now recapture that trembling, smell the faint lemon-clean whiff of Staszek's skin, feel the weight of him – though she no longer had a clear sense of the exact order of things which followed, the run of events which so intractably shaped their small, individual history.

Staszek was working with the Czech government in exile. He was part of an intelligence unit. For long stretches, he would be away and then he would come back for a week or two or three at a time and shower her with love. Once she knew, because of something he let slip in one of their extended nighttime conversations, so perhaps he wanted her to know, that he had been to the Soviet Union. At another time he described to her the elation, the relief which attended the sound of a parachute's snap as it opened to the buffeting of air. But she didn't know what fields the parachute had landed in. And she knew better than to ask.

Each time he came back from or left for one of these expeditions, Staszek gripped her with fierce fingers. 'You musn't worry,' he said, hoarse insistence in his voice. 'I can't allow myself to die with you to come back to. You know that. And there'll be so much to do once this war is over. We can't afford to die.'

She believed him so that he could believe himself. She lived in a taut bubble of pure energy, working, volunteering for this and that, helping out where and whenever she could, as if time did not exist and was marked only by Staszek's comings and goings. Having so recently been corralled in childhood helplessness, she was still young enough to feel omnipotent.

Even her mother's growing despair could do nothing to dent the golden capsule in which she floated. Her mother was worried, worried about everything and everyone, fretting and gnawing away at the fibre of herself as if continuous worry on an epic enough scale might actually alter the course of history. Beneath the worries with their objects clearly named and delineated – black-outs and buses and tubes and food – was a generalized anxiety which she couldn't or wouldn't put a name to, an intimation that the horror was even greater than the sum of her worries.

The war had swallowed up her father. They hadn't seen him since the previous year. Messages came only sporadically, sometimes delivered by an Englishman, sometimes by an old Embassy friend whose face was so devoid of expression, Simone thought he might as well have used a telephone to convey his 'All well.'

'The trouble with men,' her mother said to her after one such visit, 'is that they believe they can be heroes. They really believe heroes exist. They haven't learned that heroism is all in the way you tell the story when you get home.'

Simone had laughed and recounted her mother's version of history to Staszek when she next saw him. His cheek had dimpled, but he had shaken his dark head and said no, no, there really were those who behaved with absolute heroism.

Simone teased, 'At last, I have incontrovertible proof of your manhood.'

She was always laughing and teasing in those days, partly perhaps to balance out her mother. Buried beneath her mother's fears for her father was another set of worries. One day Simone had come across a manila file at the side of her mother's bed. She opened it to find a series of newspaper clippings in a variety of languages. The clippings were mostly small, but each contained news of another horror, another humiliation visited upon the Jews of occupied Europe: yellow stars which had to be worn and paid for out of the family textile ration; cinemas, theatres, restaurants, shops, closed to them; huge round-ups and cattle-like transports to labour camps, where conditions were appalling; an uprising in the Warsaw Ghetto followed by massive reprisals, the mass obliteration of starving men and women and children.

Simone had closed the file before getting to its end and had not looked at it again for the duration of the war, despite the fact that she could see its increasing thickness. Sometimes she thought that the thicker it grew, the more gaunt her mother became.

It was to cheer her mother that she finally mentioned marriage to Staszek. He had told her – it must have been early in 1944 then – that he was going off and that this next expedition might be a long one. When they met again, he hoped the war would be over.

They were walking on the Heath. Massed clouds filled the sky and beneath them the trees were skeletal in their bareness. As he looked out over the ponds to the crest of the incline where the shrubbery was dense, his expression was solemn. There were new lines on his face, she noticed, a deep, tense etching from nose to mouth. She had clutched his hand and simply said it, right out, blatantly: 'Let's get married before you go, Staszek.'

His kiss had a taste of desperation. 'We are married, Simone. In all the ways that count. After the war, when my country has laws and institutions one can live by, we'll have that marriage sanctioned by the State.'

She wasn't upset. She understood how he felt and she trusted him utterly. But when she told her mother what Staszek had said, her mother had murmured, Cassandra-like, 'He is afraid he will die.'

After that, as the months passed with no sign of him, she had begun to be afraid too. Maybe it was because of that fear that she hadn't been able to sustain her mother. When they returned to Paris, the fear grew. Peace had opened the floodgates of the dead and their numbers now came pouring in, named and listed. Grandparents and relatives and friends. Her mother's entire family, lost to the gas chambers of Auschwitz along with too many others.

One evening when she came home from work, she found her mother in the garden of the house in Neuilly. She was surrounded by her paintings which had miraculously survived the occupation. In front of her a huge bonfire leapt and danced, its flames aqua and indigo, amber and scarlet, as they swallowed her life's work – portraits of herself, of Simone as a child, landscapes and oils and water-colours.

Simone's attempts to stay her hand had served no purpose.

'Don't cry.' Her mother had patted her shoulder as if in a trance. 'It is necessary.'

When Simone met her eyes, she realized the necessity. Her mother's haunted gaze was the one she met daily in the agency for missing persons where she worked. It was a look which spoke of an unassuageable guilt. The guilt of having been left alive when so many had died.

Her father's eyes didn't have it. Guilt hadn't taken hold of him in the same way, perhaps because he had spent his war fighting with the Resistance. It was helplessness which bred that seething guilt in survivors.

But her mother didn't survive long. After the episode of the pictures, she refused to leave the house, refused to see the dawning life around her. She spent her days in the pictureless attic, sifting through all the newspapers that could be bought for her.

The file Simone had found by her bedside in England grew until it spilled out over the entire space of the attic, like some vast labyrinth of recorded horror. Trapped in her labyrinth, her mother came downstairs less and less until one evening, she asked that a cot be moved up for her. A week later, she was dead, her body as brittle as the paper which surrounded it.

At the funeral, Simone was dry-eyed. The next day, she stayed home from work. Piece by piece, she read and burnt every scrap of her mother's archive. When she had finished, she lay on her bed and hugged herself. It was time, she thought. Perhaps already too late. Time to seek out Staszek, from whom there had been no word. It was hardly surprising that letters, like people, might not find their destinations. Or was there more to it than that? She had to know now, before despair, kept at bay by that single hope, engulfed her. Unlike her mother, her father could manage without her. He could also help her find some kind of job at the Embassy in Prague.

*   *   *

Bare fields had given way to small hillocks of vine, their branches fettered and coiled into rows as neat as a sewing machine's stitches.

'Ludmila vineyards.' The taxi driver shot Simone a smiling glance, forcing her out of reverie. 'Good wine. Good enough to fuel Mozart while writing *Don Giovanni*.' He broke into a snatch of '*Millee Tre*'. The distance from Prague had visibly freed him into a jovial humour.

'My wife is from near here. Very nice. Me, I come from Nitra in Slovakia. But now I am Czech. Citizen of the Czech Republic.' He grinned.

Simone met his smile for the first time. She was interested in the blithe tone with which he had pronounced that new designation, Czech Republic. Irony or celebration, she couldn't tell.

'And you feel Czech now?' she asked him.

'Czech, Slovak. What does it matter? I tell you something. My mother was Czech, my father, Slovak. I . . . I drive my taxi and only ask that they leave me alone with all their politics.' He turned round to face her, almost forgetting his wheel and grinned again. 'You know that story about the old man from the village they announced was the very centre of Europe?

Simone shook her head.

'A traveller like you asks him where he's from and he says, "Well, I was born in Austria, then lived in Romania, Czechoslovakia, Hungary, Poland, the Soviet Union, again in Czechoslovakia and finally Slovakia." "You've moved around a lot," the traveller says to him. "Oh, no," says the old man. "I've never left this village."'

He let out a barking laugh. Simone joined him.

The floating borders of Eastern Europe. Moved by tanks and arms, by revolutions and wars and dictators and solemn treaties. Out of desire or fear, but always littered with corpses. People dying for nations which had no state or states which were not their nation.

Death again. It wouldn't leave her thoughts now that she had set out on this journey. The tethered vines had begun to look like so many crucifixes strung out on the hillside. She closed her eyes.

It was the autumn of '46 when she arrived back in Prague. Everything was as she remembered it, despite the eight-year gap. The curve of the domes glittering in sunlight, the clatter of the trams, the sweep of the castle hill above the river. As if war had eluded the city.

She learned soon enough how stone could lie.

In the visa office of the French Embassy where she took up her job, there was a Czech woman of about her own age with whom she struck up an instant friendship. Franci Kupkova, a small, pert blonde with fragile limbs and a cutting wit. On her second day in the office, they had lunch together in an arcade restaurant near the looming church of St Nicholas. Simone told her new friend she was looking for an apartment.

Before Franci could answer, a tub of a man with brilliantined hair approached them. 'Franci, my pretty little Franci,' he leered. 'And how are you today? Have you considered my proposition?'

'The answer is still no, Pan Gurek.' Franci plastered an artificial smile on her face which twisted into scorn as soon as the man's back was turned.

'Now that one could get you an apartment if you had the cash to show for it and were willing to deal with scum,' Franci whispered to Simone. 'He nabbed three huge ones from Jewish families who were forced out because of his, shall we call it "intervention", at the beginning of the war and he's been hanging onto them for dear life and money ever since. We need the communists to get rid of the likes of him. Introduce a little justice.'

'How do you know him?'

'I live in the same building. He was a sneaking collaborator. The worst kind, the kind who always pretends to be on the side of who he's talking to, so you never know where you are. Now he's trying to get me to move, offering me a bigger place somewhere else. Probably because he knows I have too much on him. He's afraid I'll report him.' She crossed her arms with an angry shrug. 'But I'll ask around for you.'

It was Simone's first introduction to the hatreds and resentments that simmered beneath the bustling surface of the city. It was like Paris, but somehow more so, the anger and betrayals of occupation lying closer to the surface. Thousands of eyes peering suspiciously at each other.

And there was another difference, she soon learned. Prague had been liberated by the Russians while the Americans stood idly by in Pilsen some fifty miles away. As a result, everything to do with Russia or Communism was in the first instance a good. In France too, the communists had fought boldly in the Resistance, led it in many instances. But this rankling sense that it was the West which had sold the country to Hitler, that it was the Russians who had offered help when everyone else had abandoned it, did not exist. The French post-war battle of words between the Left and the Gaullists, between capitalist and communist factions, was not ever and always settled by the emotional trump card – and who were our friends?

Sometimes, in the midst of all this, Simone longed for England, an unoccupied soil where politics seemed at once simple and irrelevant.

Simone didn't want to be thrust into politics – the flare and anger and zealous passion of it, the loud, battering voices calling for retribution or peace. She felt the only passion she wanted was the quiet personal one of lying in bed of a morning with Staszek and looking out on the fresh green of a tree or capturing the mellow, quivering highnote of a sonata as they had done when they played together in the old days. There had been too much of the other kind of passion.

But the choice wasn't hers. People talked of little else and she needed to talk to people. She was looking for Staszek. There was no sign of him at his old address and the neighbours knew or would say nothing.

Some three weeks after her arrival, she was processing a new pile of visa applications when his name suddenly leapt out at her: Stanislaw Nikolaus Mánes. She clutched at her desk and tried to refocus her eyes. But the name kept its shape. The application gave the place of work as the Ministry of Foreign Affairs. There was a phone number. She lifted the receiver blindly, thinking only that she hadn't known his name was Nikolaus, not allowing herself to imagine the name could belong to anyone else.

When she heard the voice she could barely bring herself to speak.

They met that evening. He had suggested a bar not far from the Embassy, just beneath the Karlův Most, and she arrived far too early and threw the door open on a smoky room filled with the smell of bodies and sour beer. The only seat she could find was at a crowded table. But it gave her a view of the door and she stared at it as if the figure she was looking for might never materialize.

When she spotted him she realized that she had forgotten to breathe and a gasp came out of her, so loud that the people at the table turned to stare. He must have heard it too, for he was beside her a second later, his eyes vast in a face that was too thin.

'Simone.' He took her hand and held it between his. They gazed at each other. She couldn't speak. She couldn't get up. She just sat there staring at him, watching the beauty of his features, watching his tense movements unfurl as he drew a chair close to her, noting how his hair had grown long, how it curled slightly at the nape, how his jacket was shiny from use at the elbow and flapped around him, how he flicked a cigarette from a pack and held it before lighting it, his attention only on her.

'You're here. You're alive,' she mumbled at last. She reached for one of the cigarettes, met his fingers halfway.

'I'm alive.' Irony suddenly played over his features. And something else she couldn't quite read. 'More or less.'

'You . . .' They both said it together and laughed nervously and tried again. 'I . . .'

She waved her hand at him. He caught it and brought it to his lips.

'Let's go upstairs. It's quieter. I need to see you where it's quieter.'

They found a table in a corner from which the river could be glimpsed. Again the words wouldn't come.

'So how do you find Prague?' he asked at last.

'Fine.' The question and answer both seemed to her inane. 'But . . .'

'I was just hoping to get a visa. I wanted to come to Paris and see you.'

'So you knew I was in Paris?'

'I assumed.'

'And you didn't write?'

He shrugged, looked beyond her, towards the small window. 'I didn't know . . . There weren't the words.'

'Know what?'

'About you. About me, perhaps.' He lit another cigarette. 'About what we are now.'

'Oh.' She suddenly felt dizzy. She put her hands to her face.

'You used to do that as a child. I can see you so clearly. The concentration, shutting out the world. A funny, serious little girl.'

'Is that what I was?' She looked at him. It wasn't what she had intended to say. She wanted to talk about what he meant by not knowing, about their love, about the missing years. Why was it so hard? It had never been hard before.

She picked at the food he had ordered for her, watched

him do the same. She emptied her glass too quickly. 'And your father?' she asked.

That blurry expression she had seen in so many came over his features so that she didn't need his lips to confirm the answer.

'He was shot.' Staszek lit another cigarette. 'After Heydrich's assassination, when the Nazis carried out their massive reprisals. Thousands of ours for one of theirs.' A short, dry laugh, more like a cry, erupted from him. 'They probably knew I was with the government in London.' He pushed his plate away.

'You should eat,' she heard herself saying. 'You're too thin.'

That dry laugh again. 'I've been thinner.' He gripped her hand with sudden force. 'Simone, why have you come to Prague?'

'Don't you know?' Her heart was beating so hard, she thought it might burst her chest.

'For me?' he whispered, then turned away. 'I don't think I'm worth it. Not any more.' His face was a dull mask.

'Where do you live, Staszek?' She suddenly made up her mind.

'Not far from here.'

'Are you going to invite me over?'

He looked at her with a seriousness she recognized. 'If you'd like to be invited.'

She nodded.

'But you may not like it. It isn't as nice as Hampstead.'

Simone didn't notice. Didn't notice anything for days – until that first wave of the passion which had carried them off as they walked homeward, ebbed. Then she began to see the cracks in the wall above his head as he rested on the propped pillow, the dirty, peeling paint, the dingy sheets, the newspaper-covered crate which served as a bedside table. Through the window she could see only another wall.

'We should find a place together,' she said as he handed her coffee in a chipped cup.

'It's not so bad.' He curled beside her, stroked her. 'And you make it lovely.'

She realized over the next weeks that he didn't care about the apartment, didn't notice it really except when he thought to see it through her eyes. He had lost all sense of secondary comforts. He was oddly abstracted from everything except the tasks at hand, the building of a future he talked about with daily relish as their present vanished into it. If she brought home some bright object, a poster to cover a damp spot, or a chair with a graceful curve, he would only focus on it if she drew his attention to it. He was pleased enough with its presence, but somehow oblivious. Importance did not reside there. She wondered about this, tried to work out if he had been different before, wasn't sure.

Over the next months, she found them a new flat, a top floor with three rooms overlooking the smooth dome of a church, which pleased her whenever she caught sight of it through the window. She painted the apartment herself in a pale yellow which trapped the sunshine; furnished it with whatever pretty bits and pieces she could find – a porcelain bowl, an ironwork table with delicate deco lines. The prize was an old piano on which they sometimes played duets as they had in the old days when he was her tutor.

Everything was scarce. But she didn't mind, and while she worked or scoured the city, she thought about the changes in Staszek.

There were many, but she was only gradually able to piece them together. First, what she privately called his 'lost time' had to become clearer to her. He never talked about those months directly – he didn't want memory toppling this bridge to the future – but they emerged for her in oblique comments, bits of stories abruptly curtailed, and in those nightmares which occasionally haunted him, so that he shouted in his sleep and woke up crying.

His last expedition had somehow overshot the mark and landed him in Poland, rather than Slovakia where he had instructions to meet up with the Resistance. He had been picked up and arrested. He wasn't in uniform, so there was no question of POW treatment, even if that would have made a difference. He had been sent to a prison camp, done harsh, gruelling, pointless labour, watched disease, exhaustion, starvation decimate the older inmates. But that wasn't the worst of it.

The worst of it was what he could see on the other side of the barbed wire, could hear, could smell – the murder of the innocent which he was helpless to impede. He was young, strong, able, an officer in his country's military, yet he was utterly impotent. It was that impotence which weighed on him and with it came a kind of shame, a guilt not unlike her mother had suffered. Though his sacrifice was different.

For Staszek that guilt could only be kept at bay and transformed by a life dedicated to the common good. On his own, he told her time and again, for this was something he would talk about, the individual was helpless. You couldn't shout 'it is my right to be free' in a concentration camp and find freedom thrust upon you. No, freedom was not a gift; it had to be worked for communally. Earned. Before the war, they had assumed it as a right and it had been frittered away. They must never allow this to happen again. A common front was essential to ensure lasting peace and social reconstruction.

Later, when she was wiser and it was already too late, Simone realized that Staszek's experience of war had put the psychological seal on what had been a youthful set of idealistic dicta. Back then his Communism had been a critical and intellectual stance against the wrongs of his world. Now he needed Communism, because only a martyrdom in the service of a future and greater good could assuage his guilt. And silence the dead who had given their lives for him.

He was not alone, though he was the best of his kind.

Sometimes, for months on end, Simone could share his zeal for the future. Sometimes she couldn't. She had waited for him for so long that somehow he was future enough. She wanted this present with him, not its glorified postponement. Building a world in which there would never again be national or racial or class oppression, where tolerance and equality prevailed was one thing. She could believe in that. Blinding oneself to the chicanery or pettiness or greed of acquaintances, simply because they were Party members or working class, was another. Not, she knew, that Staszek blinded himself wilfully. He simply couldn't see, in the same way that he couldn't see the flowers she brought home with such delight.

Fixed on the horizon, his eyes didn't focus on the daisies or the cowpats at his feet.

Simone saw both with great distinctness. The scepticism her father had so ingrained in her didn't help. She was always arguing this side and that side and maybe and perhaps until Staszek lost patience with her and took out the work he had brought home with him, concentrating on it with such intensity that there was no budging him.

As she watched him, not only at home, but at restaurants and gatherings, she increasingly worried for him. It seemed to her that his very innocence, his very idealism, acted as a reproach, a potential threat to those whose hands were mired in past crimes or in opportunistic greed.

Meanwhile they worked hard and, after three or four or perhaps it was six months when the surprise of their skins next to one another had worn off, made love less and less. Staszek was promoted to head of his section at the Ministry. He often came home late, exhausted by the shifts and about-turns of a foreign policy which, though nominally independent, always had first to pay heed to Soviet plans.

Simone would see him struggling to put the latest Soviet intervention in a good light and not always quite managing to. Though he might admire what had taken place there, his idea of Communism had never included a bowing to Soviet will. Now, as the Russians prevented the Czechs from accepting the American Marshall Plan which would have so greatly helped to restructure the economy, she could feel him bowing, trying to put a gloss on things, murmuring about how others knew better than him, half believing it. He looked so pale in those weeks, she couldn't bring herself to argue with him.

Late in August she went to Paris to visit her father. She returned laden with presents, shirts and socks, tins of pâté and crab meat, a bottle of Grand Marnier, books and her old violin.

As she unpacked and brought out delight after delight, Staszek hovered over her. He seemed nervous.

'Why have you brought all this? For whom is it all?'

'Idiot.' She danced towards him, held out a shirt to his chest. 'It's for you. For us. It's almost our anniversary. The unofficial one.' She kissed him playfully.

They had got married in December, so unostentatiously it felt like the after-thought it was, though she was pleased he had wanted to, doubly pleased at the weekend in the mountains. Yet she thought of the real moment to celebrate as the one when they had first met again.

'You know I can't wear any of this,' he said tensely.

'Why ever not?' She refused to give up her playfulness. 'The blue is perfect for you.'

He tore the shirt from her hands and thrust it on the bed. 'I can't be seen in all these foreign goods. They're bourgeois. They're . . .'

She stepped back as if he had hit her. 'Like your French wife,' she finished for him. 'Nothing has really changed, has it? Before the war you couldn't be seen with me because I was French, a signatory to the Munich Agreement. And now it's just the same.' She pushed him out of the room, fumed, shouted after him as she slammed the door, 'Was it worth all those dead, I wonder?'

Later, when the clock in the hall had already struck midnight, he lay down beside her. He was apologetic, tender, sad, shamed and she cried silent tears as he came into her. But he never wore the shirts. She took to using them as nighties. Whenever she had one on he would laugh. And he always made love to her on those nights. She was pleased about that, she didn't quite know why. It was as if the shirts were some kind of transgression. And they were both secretly delighted that he still had the ability to transgress.

At the beginning of March, just after the elections of '48 had brought the communists to power, Franci said to her, 'I'm leaving, you know. My boyfriend thinks it's not a good idea to be working for an Embassy now.'

'Oh?'

'No.' She lowered her voice, pointed towards the castle. 'They don't like it up there, he says. They don't like us mingling with Westerners. We might pick up bad habits.' She made one of her silly faces. 'Like friendship.' She laughed.

The conversation upset her almost as much as the suicide of the head of Staszek's Ministry – though there were dark rumours that it wasn't suicide, that he had been assisted to the Ministry window by two men in grey suits who didn't believe that the free-thinking son of the first Czech president had the right profile for the new government.

A distraught Staszek told her that Masaryk had long been depressed, that it was an illness with him. But she could feel his uncertainty. A few weeks later, when he came home from work looking particularly fraught, she said to him, 'You know, I've been thinking. What if we went to live in Paris for a change. My father's getting frail. He's all alone in that big house. And . . .'

'No.' He cut her off before she had a chance to elaborate on the picture. He didn't meet her eyes. 'My place is here. There's so much to be done. I'm needed.'

Shortly after that, Staszek was promoted. He told her about it with a touch of pride and also a hesitation. He didn't know whether he was equal to the task – and it would mean even more work. But the job would bring with it a bigger flat, if they wanted one. He stroked her hair softly. 'Perhaps we'll have a child soon.'

There had been no sign of a child, though there had latterly been none of those precautions her mother had once been so worried about. Simone wondered about that, wondered whether there was something wrong with her. But she put the thought out of her mind, consoling herself with the notion that perhaps one really had to want a child to have one. And she wasn't sure she did, though for Staszek's sake she wished it. She reflected that, for all their occasional disagreements, she loved him so much that she couldn't imagine life without him.

Yet increasingly she loved him only when they were alone. When protocol forced her to accompany him to gatherings, she could hear the women's voices around her, lowered in malice, like the sibilant and envious tones of a Paris concierge, pointing to her foreignness, her lack of working-class credentials, her mother's necklaces. And she could never say the right thing. She was always being rebuked for her comments, criticized. She complained of this to Staszek.

'Don't be so sensitive,' he admonished her. 'They're simple women. They still have things to learn. But there are things we could learn from them, as well.'

'What things?' Simone challenged. 'Taste? Greed? Have you seen the way they deck themselves out? Like overblown circus performers. And their apartments? Stuffed with furniture that's obviously been nicked from others. Just because you put a category on something – working class – doesn't make all its individuals perfect, you know.'

Staszek paid no attention. He was caught up with events, the blockade of Berlin, the shifting Soviet attitude to Yugoslavia, a growing hostility between East and West. The day-to-day run of ordinary life was irrelevant in comparison.

'Mělník. We are here.' The taxi driver pulled the car to a halt in a sleepy baroque square with a fountain at its centre. 'The castle is that way.' He directed a stubby finger towards a steep incline. 'Want me to walk with you? It's open for tours.'

Simone looked at him from glazed eyes. 'No. No,' she said too sharply, then, collecting herself, suggested that he might take himself off to lunch. She didn't know quite how long she would be.

A jabbing cold met her as she slid from the overheated car. It forced her into wakefulness. Ahead of her, up the escarpment, was a church tower topped with an onion-shaped cupola. She stared at it for a moment, then turned abruptly and walked in the opposite direction.

Light snow had begun to fall, skirmishing flurries which dampened her cheeks and bit at her eyes. At the fountain, she paused to adjust her collar and glance at the stone figure of a stout peasant woman bearing grapes. Their surface was whitened by snow. From across the square in front of a building with a warm yellow facade, a child shouted, was stilled by her mother who carried a string bag, heavy with vegetables. An old lorry shuddered past. Then, quiet – that small-town quiet of ancient buildings and ordered lives.

The streets looked innocent, Simone thought. Too innocent. She turned a corner and, as if her reflection had been noted, all but collided with a tank. A lumbering, immobilized tank, its sides corroded, but its red star still vibrant.

Odd, that. She had assumed all traces of the Soviet past would have been eradicated. But no. This tank was still here, a monument, the plaque firmly stated, to the liberating Russian soldiers of 1945.

With a shiver, Simone retraced her steps and headed slowly uphill, in the direction of church and castle. She forced her feet and her thoughts where they didn't want to go.

In August of 1948, Staszek had taken her on a brief holiday to the spa at Karlovy Vary. They stayed in the opulence of the Grand Hotel Pupp. The waters tasted foul. Nor did she like the medicinal *becherovka* which was supposed to wash away the flavour, but she sampled both as often as Staszek insisted, and giggled when the look on his face echoed hers. They were happy and for once Staszek seemed relaxed. They behaved like children, walking gaily hand-in-hand down the regal promenade or scurrying noisily up the hillside, icecream melting on their faces, their smiles wide, as innocent as if the war had never happened.

On their second to last day, Staszek told her he needed to work for a few hours and urged her to take the waters without him. She ambled down to the great hall, sipped a little of the liquid and then made her way through the lobby. The day was glorious, begging to be walked in, the hills behind the hotel particularly fragrant.

She had made her way halfway up the incline when a blonde woman of Valkyrie proportions emerged from the shadow of a tree and greeted her. Karolina Dostolova. A friend of Staszek's from way back. She had met her once before the war. It was at the small party her parents had given when she and her mother were leaving Prague. Staszek had brought her and Simone, in the throes of her still-secret love, had loathed her on sight. Latterly, she had bumped into her now and again at official gatherings. Karolina had risen in the Communist Party hierarchy and

Simone preferred to stay out of her way. But she returned her greeting pleasantly enough.

'Fine weather.' The woman said it as if it might be an infringement of celestial duty.

'Mmmn. But the waters are foul, aren't they?'

'Are they? No matter. I have no time for small talk, as you must know. I've come to give you some advice.' The woman's face was sternly impassive. She didn't meet Simone's eyes.

'What advice can you possibly give me?' Alert now to the fact that this meeting wasn't an accident, that the woman had been lying in wait for her, Simone was tempted to make her dislike evident.

'I'm worried for Staszek. You know he and I have been comrades for many years.'

'I don't really see what business Staszek is of yours.' Simone quickened her pace and turned off the path in an attempt to lose her. But the woman was put off neither by her coldness nor her lack of interest. She matched her steps to Simone's strides.

'At this stage of our work, he really can't afford to have an inveterate bourgeoise beside him. You receive too many letters from abroad. The letters you send home carry too many complaints. Then, there are your contacts with your Embassy . . .'

Simone blanched. She had the vertiginous realization that she had been spied on for months.

'The Party needs complete loyalty from its members. Without you, Staszek will rise high.'

Simone turned on her. 'You call this advice? I'd call it a threat. A low and offensive threat.'

The woman shrugged. Beneath the veneer of politeness, she was implacable. 'I have shielded him for months now, ensured his promotion. But he should never have married you. It was a madness. It was because you pressured him. You must know that it was only because of your pressure.

You should return to France. Yes, it would be best if you went back to France.'

'You have no right . . .' Simone began to splutter. 'No right to speak to me like this.'

'If you thought for a moment, you would see that I have every right. Indeed, a duty.' The withering look the woman turned on Simone made her feel she had been transformed into a subspecies of vermin. 'My rights were very well established even before you showed your face in our country. Think about it. But don't think too long. That would be unwise.'

Without a goodbye, she strode off into the woods.

Simone stared after her and then, feeling her legs grow weak, sank onto a stretch of grass. Pain catapulted through her, tearing at the foundations of her existence. Karolina and Staszek. Of course. She should have guessed.

She didn't say anything to Staszek immediately. She felt concussed, a sleepwalker grappling amongst shadows. Only on the drive back to Prague did the words tumble out. She tried to make them light, easy. 'I bumped into Karolina Dostolova in Karlovy Vary. Did I tell you?'

She watched the muscle work in his cheek, the sudden shift in the car's speed. 'Oh? Was she well?' His voice betrayed nothing.

Simone didn't speak.

'I didn't know she was taking a holiday.' He flashed her a look, a pleasant smile, reached for her hand.

It was the touch that had made her burst out. 'She told me she had been your lover. Your lover for years.'

The car lurched abruptly. After a moment, he pulled off to the side of the road, turned to her, murmured her name. 'You don't understand, Simone.'

'I understand too well. I am not a child.' She had stared out on sun-bleached fields and refused to meet his eyes.

'Karolina and I . . . Before I even met you . . .'

'You don't deny it.' Her voice had a bitterness she didn't know was in her.

'It's not like you think. She ... Of late, it was only to protect you.'

Simone cut him off. 'I don't want to know.'

They had driven back to Prague in silence. At the apartment, the snooping concierge, who doubled as a local youth group leader, handed Simone a telegram which had patently already been opened. For some reason, this released the tears she had held back. She rushed up the stairs and locked herself in the bathroom. She wouldn't come out, despite Staszek's pleading. Instead, she stared at the telegram urging her home to her father who had been taken ill. And she wept. The tears wouldn't stop. At last, when the stillness of sleep had descended on the apartment, she emerged to curl up on the sofa alone.

When she woke, Staszek was gazing down at her, the crumpled telegram in his hand. He bent to kiss her, but she turned her face away.

'You must go to him,' he said.

'You can't wait to be rid of me,' she hissed at him and he gripped her hand, too hard, so that she had to struggle from his grasp.

His look had grown cold then. 'I love you, Simone. But love is not the most important thing in the world. Understand that. Please try to understand that.'

Something in her recoiled. In the morning, she nonetheless determined to give him another chance. She purchased a train ticket for the following day, so that she could see him once more that evening. He had come home, looking pale and harassed and she had found herself saying, 'Come with me, Staszek, please. Paris will be good, for both of us.' She had begged, a tone she didn't know she possessed taking her over. Coming with her, it had seemed clear to her, would constitute a choice: her over Karolina.

The tormented look on his face had turned to anger. He

had treated her like a spoiled child of limited intelligence. 'You refuse to understand. There's too much pressure at the moment. The Party couldn't allow it.'

'But you'll come. Soon.' She had held out a dying hope. He had shrugged.

She couldn't bring herself to share his bed that night. The tangled, unspoken emotions lay between them like barbed wire tearing the skin at every move. In the morning he had driven her to the station. He had waved at her for a long time, a dark, receding figure whose very smallness frightened her. She had sat there, worrying over her father. Brooding over her relations with Staszek. Trying not to think of that woman with him. And then thinking that all along she had shadowed their lives. Karolina had been there before the war, perhaps already more than a comrade. Karolina had been there ever since Simone's return to the city, a lover with arms as long as those of the Party which embraced him.

As the train wheezed and chugged its way towards France, Karolina's proportions grew as vast as the distance that separated Simone from Staszek, blended in her mind with the Party which had stolen Staszek from her, became its flesh and blood embodiment – a mistress with a thousand eyes and tentacles, who demanded a loyalty beyond all others.

Yet Karolina was also simply another woman. And Staszek a betrayer who had made his choice.

The snow was falling more thickly now, dense white flakes whirling before her eyes, shrouding her vision. In the graveyard behind the church, the stones wore mantles of filigree, like old women stooped in prayer. Oblivious to the cold, Simone stared down the escarpment. The swathe of the river lay beneath her, that point where the Vltava and the Labe flowed into one.

It was somewhere near here that Staszek's body had been

spotted, its dead, bloated weight carried by the current from Prague, where he had plunged into the swift-moving waters. But that was later.

First, some three months after she had returned to her father in Paris, there had been that call summoning her to the Czech Embassy. Michel had come with her. Her father had already introduced her to Michel by then, his younger colleague and friend from the Quai d'Orsay. Michel had watched her as she scanned the pages of the documents that the taciturn embassy official placed in front of her, his stubby fingers indicating the place where she had to sign. Divorce proceedings. She had signed the papers in an angry black scrawl like a silent howl. Whatever hopes she may have held out for Staszek, it was now patently clear that that foul woman had totally won him over. He had not even bothered to give Simone advance warning. There had been no personal note.

Later, she realized that even if he had written, there was little likelihood of a letter making its way to her. The purges had begun, effectively sealing off the country from the West. It was from a former superior in the French Embassy in Prague that she heard the news both of Staszek's re-marriage and subsequently his arrest.

They had met at the Café Voltaire and she had smoked furiously during the meeting, despite the fact that she suspected she was pregnant with Michel's and her first child. Monsieur Duval had spoken to her in a flat voice.

'As you know, the Party has been engaged in a major job of internal cleansing. It keeps the mind off the failures of the economy. All members are potentially at risk of being purged, but particularly those who've had any links with the West, who spent the war years here, or who show signs of bourgeois deviation – code word for intellectuals. And Jews, of course, who combine all of those.'

'And Staszek?' Simone was trembling.

'He's in jail, which means he's probably been accused

of sabotage, betraying the Party, perhaps spying, taking bribes. It doesn't matter. It's all a pack of lies, trumped up, a way of scaring people so they toe the line. Though some of the accused seem to believe it, the sincere ones. They really believe that if the Party accuses them, they may have done something wrong, something outside their knowledge. Or even if they know they're innocent, they feel their accusation must, in some inexplicable way, be in the best interests of the nation. It's a strange form of self-immolation, a loyalty beyond reason.'

'Yes.' Simone recognized the portrait. 'Can we do anything?'

'Not very much at the moment. We're powerless. We have no right to interfere in the internal workings of their country. All we can hope is that the thing will burn itself out soon. And there are so many arrests that it will have to.' He had tried a smile. 'The joke is making the rounds that on Thursdays and Fridays after the Central Committee has met, it's best to go to the movies so that you're not home to hear the knock on the door.'

Despite repeated attempts to get news, she didn't hear any more of Staszek until after Rudolf Slansky, the Secretary General of the Party, had been arrested at the end of 1951. Then a letter delivered by special courier reached her in the house where she now lived with Michel. The envelope contained a note from Monsieur Duval, saying the enclosed letter had been delivered by hand to the Embassy, addressed to her.

Simone's fingers had shaken so violently that it had taken her three readings to make sense of the letter.

My dearest Simone,

I want you to know that I have thought of you often over these last years. I also want you to know that it has taken me a very long time, but I have at last realized that you were right. Always right. In prison it was the playing and replaying in my mind of every note of the Spring Sonata that saved me from madness and the confessing of lies I had all but begun to believe were truths. A sharp is not a flat and to put F where E should be destroys a sequence. The little things count. They become big things.

Do you remember that turn of the hill on the Heath, that little grassy hump where we used to sit and hold hands? I thought of that far more often over those months than of the opening lines of the Manifesto. So you were right. My darling.

I used to laugh at you for liking the stories of our Prague golem. And now I feel as if I have helped to create one and he has turned his envious vengeance on all of us. He wears no cabbalist's gown, but the plain suit of the Party.

I do not know why and how everything I have believed in has gone so badly awry. I cannot bring myself to think that everything we hoped for was utterly bad. But at the moment I feel I have been an accomplice in a terrible crime and there is only one way for me to stop being that accomplice. I am also afraid that if they take me in again, I will break and sign the inquisitor's piece of paper and you will think that not even at the last did I know the difference between truth and lies.

As for my relations with Karolina, whose name I know you don't want to hear, I can only say that I was wrong. At the last, it was a brief coming together in the vertigo of false hopes and blind lies and not a little arm-twisting.

Forgive me. I wish I had more to leave you than my love.

Staszek

She had wept hot, burning tears. Through them, Staszek's words had etched themselves into her mind, letter by letter.

Some lines of Karl Marx's that Staszek had been in the habit of quoting came to her then. 'Men make their own history, but they do not make it just as they please; they do not make it under circumstances chosen by themselves, but under ones directly encountered, given and transmitted from the past. The tradition of all the dead generations weighs like a nightmare on the brain of the living.'

But perhaps she had thought of that later, after she had already learned of Staszek's death, and rage whipped through her, a hot and terrible desire for revenge propelled by memory and nightmare.

Simone stopped by a lone grave at some distance from the main cemetery. She leaned her hand against it. Her gloved fingers left an imprint in the snow, like the brush of a bird's wing. With tears pricking at her eyes, she found a stick and prodded at the frozen earth until she had excavated a tiny crevice. From her bag she took a plain gold wedding band and placed it in the gap. She covered it as best she could.

When the cold had so stiffened her old limbs that she could barely put one foot in front of the other, she forced herself into movement.

It was too bad she hadn't known about the child.

12

——*——

Ted Knight picked the fax out of the newly installed machine, looked at the brief lines of type from his LA office and felt all his well-tuned muscles tense.

'The lowdown you asked for on Tessa Hughes: most interesting thing is that she's Stephen Caldwell's wife . . .'

He didn't bother with the rest. Without putting on his jacket, he strode from the room and jabbed at the elevator button. Too slow. With a glare of impatience, he made for the stairs, took them two at a time for the length of three floors.

What the woman was playing at, he didn't know. But he didn't like those kinds of games. Didn't like them one little bit.

Room 832. That's what the note had said. He knocked loudly and, without waiting, tried the knob. Locked. He knocked again. In the old days he would have bashed the thin strip of ply in. No problem.

Maybe she was in the bathroom. She. Tessa Hughes. Stephen Caldwell's wife. Unbelievable! He thumped at the door again. She shouldn't have kept that from him. There had been plenty of opportunity to tell him.

Still no answer. He glanced at his watch. Nine thirty. She was playing the early bird today. If she was out, she was up to something, that was for sure. That proper little note, left for him last night when he had got back from the reception. 'Exhausting day. I need some sleep, some time on my own. Got myself a room. 832. See you tomorrow.'

Maybe Jan Martin had mentioned Caldwell and she had taken fright. Didn't want her husband bumping into her. *In flagrante delicto.* Or was there more to it than that? Women. They were always his weakness. He should have checked her out sooner. But she had seemed so clean. So innocent.

Ted Knight vented his anger on the door.

A face peered out from the neighbouring room. He gave the woman a smile of stunning artifice. She smiled back and with a murmured 'Good morning', he retraced his steps.

In his room, he stared again at the fax. It complicated things unnecessarily. He would have to punish her for that.

Tessa stood in the shower and pretended to be oblivious to the muted sounds at her door. She wasn't in the mood for Ted. All she wanted was for the jet stream of water to wash away the image of that baby she had abandoned to the arms of the police. But it wouldn't. The imprint of that small head nestling against her survived the soap, the towel's rubbing, just as it had a night of tossing and turning.

She caught her reflection in the sharp-eyed hotel mirror. Despite the traces of age, the slight sag of bottom, it wasn't a bad body. But it was a maidenly body. The breasts were trim, the nipples small, the aureoles neat. There were no smudges or spreads or stretch marks on bosom or belly. Her sister had pointed that out to her one day when they had been swimming together. They had stood in the changing room in front of the mirror and Pen had groaned, 'It's just not fair. Look at the two of us. You, slender and virginal. And me, the survivor of some volcanic cataclysm.'

Tessa hadn't said anything except a murmured 'Don't

be silly', since there was no contradicting Pen when she decided to engage on a gargantuan orgy of self-hatred which took in the curl of her hair and ended with the calluses on her feet. After which, she would pick up the children and cuddle them and laugh and get on with daily life.

And leave Tessa feeling insubstantial.

Why? Tessa asked herself yet again as she flopped onto the hotel bed. It was not as if she believed women's destiny lay in having children. Could it really be simply the ticking away of the biological clock, the whiff of middle age and mortality that made her so adamant? An animal need, a genetically encoded imperative to reproduce herself? She didn't like that. Didn't like the sense of being reduced to a few simple formulae which determined everything from the start.

Tessa gripped the pillow and felt the little girl nestling against her, clinging, round dark eyes staring into hers. A void opened inside her, deep, crisscrossed with pain, as dark as that gaze. The child had needed her and she had betrayed that need.

And perhaps that was it. She wanted a child because she needed that need. The need grounded her, gave her substance. She had never really been needed. Stephen didn't need her. That was patently obvious. Nor had lovers before, whatever the nature of their attachment. And work – well, at work one was always replaceable.

At home, she had been the middle daughter, the negligible filling between a strong-minded elder sister, apple of her father's eye, and a baby brother, doted on by his mum. And by Tessa. She suddenly remembered that. She had lugged Robbie about, a squirming weight, too big really for her five-year-old limbs, and her father had laughingly urged her on while her mother chastised her. And then, no sooner was Robbie deposited, than everyone promptly forgot about her.

She didn't mind really. She had plenty to get on with. Games, homework, friends and later, books. She wasn't unhappy. But she felt somehow insubstantial, a bit of flotsam floating on the surface of life.

Babies stopped one from floating. She had felt that. Felt it intensely yesterday. Their need gave one ballast. They were an anchor which prevented a drunken careering. Off and over the edge.

With sudden decision, Tessa pulled on clothes, applied a modicum of make-up for Parisian reassurance and made her way down to the lobby. As the lift doors slid open, she held her breath and glanced round swiftly. No sign of Ted. That was a good beginning. She hastened towards the front desk, put her question and, after a moment, was handed a printed list by the assistant, together with a small map on which he painstakingly marked Xs.

Outside, the cold was bitter. A dingy grey sky clothed castle and spires in gloom. Exhaust billowed from cars, furled and hung in the icy air. People hurried, their collars turned up against the wind, their faces obscured beneath hats and muffled scarfs.

Tessa turned her back to the river and followed the map through twisting cobbled streets. The first agency turned her away with a promise that they could accommodate her in one or two days' time. The second suggested she return after lunch. She considered making an appointment, then tested her own disquiet and hurried on.

She was in a street so narrow that the tall, thin houses seemed to bend and meet above her head. The few shop windows were murky with age, their only goods a smattering of frayed posters. She fixed her gaze on these. Amongst them, as she turned the corner, she noticed a sign in several languages announcing personal guided tours. She glanced down at her list, then, impatient with it, pushed open a door whose fresh blue paint put its neighbours' grime to shame. It was a door that invited confidence, though the loud bell which clattered above her as she pushed it open made her jump.

The tiny office was empty but for a large Star of David on the wall, a clock, and a computer, brazenly new, on the desk. Tessa cleared her throat, had not quite finished doing so when a young woman appeared from behind a rustle of beaded curtain. She was younger than Tessa, thirty perhaps. A curtain of straight blonde hair opened on a fresh scrubbed face which was all cheekbones and wide eyes. She was wearing jeans and a lumberjack shirt in bright checks, and she stuck out her hand at Tessa in brusque mannish fashion.

'*Gut' Morgen*. Hi.'

'Hi,' Tessa ventured back.

She grinned. 'English. Good. How can I help you?'

Tessa grinned back. The woman's accent was broad Brooklyn but the gestures seemed to have come from a Western.

'I'm looking for a guide. For today. Straight away if possible.'

'That's a bit hard. I'm all alone in the office. You could join one of the other parties, if you'd like that. There are only two in each.' She glanced at the large classroom clock. 'Probably in the old synagogue by now. I take you over. Okay?'

'No. You don't understand. I'd like a guide for myself. And I don't want to go to the synagogue. I want to go to a police station.'

The woman placed a hand on her hip and rolled comic eyes at her. 'So what are you doing in a Jewish tour agency? We specialize in the Josefov. Jewish Prague. You think that constitutes a special relationship with the police?'

'No, no.' Tessa flushed. 'I ... You see, what I really want is an interpreter. Yesterday ...' Tessa found herself recounting her story in tense detail to that engaging presence.

Eyes of chocolate brown glimmered. A dimple came and went in a downy cheek. 'Boy. You sure know how to see Prague. A baby, eh? And some gypsy. Now I understand. They sent you here because we Jews know all about stealing babies.'

Tessa was about to react when she saw the glint of irony in the woman's face. She found herself giggling, despite the tears that a moment ago had threatened to form. 'Yes, that must be it.'

'But listen. I'm expensive. Really expensive. 'Cause I'm an expert in all this.' She waved her hand effusively in the direction of the window. 'Twenty dollars an hour, I charge. That's ten dollars for the guiding and ten dollars for the PhD in theology, which you don't need. So maybe you should go to another agency. I've got some addresses.'

'No. No. That sounds reasonable to me.'

The woman's direct gaze played over Tessa with brazen curiosity. 'Okay. You got yourself a deal. But I think I can save you some money.' She picked up the telephone. 'Which police station did you say it was?'

Tessa waited, listened to a rush of incomprehensible language, watched the woman put her leg up on the chair and gesture emphatically as if her listener could see her, watched her put the phone down with a bang and mutter, 'Idiots.'

She turned to Tessa. 'We'll have to go down there. I'll pretend I'm your lawyer or something.' She grinned. 'And I'll give you a discount on the theology. I've had too much of it this week anyway.' She stretched out her hand again. 'My name's Rachel Witzmanova, by the way.'

'Tessa Hughes.'

'Hughes. Like your royal poet, eh?'

'Just like. But no relation.'

'Good.' Rachel examined her for another moment, then swiftly penned a note, pressed a button on an answering machine and ushered Tessa out of the office.

It didn't take long for Tessa to decide that Rachel, with her slightly bow-legged stride and her inexhaustible lore, was worth every penny of her fee. Each twist in the streets of the old Jewish Quarter sparked a new wisecracking story, of the medieval guild of Jewish fire-fighters who saved Prague from enemy flames, of the Chevra Kaddisha, an august funeral brotherhood who succoured the dying and performed acts of charity for the living, of the new Chief Rabbi of Prague who, much to the consternation of the reactionary elders, was a convert. By the time they had bundled into the dilapidated old Fiat which would take them to the police station, Tessa had begun to think of her as some Scheherazade with street cred. She also realized Rachel was working hard at cheering her. She hadn't been altogether aware that she needed the cheering.

As they waited in a line of traffic, Rachel dug in her coat pocket and brought out a watch. 'I broke the strap this morning. It reminded me of this great joke.' She winked at Tessa and pulled away with a screech of the gears. 'About an old lady who breaks her watch as she's walking along one of the streets of the Josefov and she sees this store with lots of clocks and watches in the window, so she goes in. There's this old guy behind the counter and she says to him, "Do you fix watches?" and he shakes his head, so she asks, "Do you sell watches?" and he shakes his head again. So she's getting just a little bit exasperated and she says, "So you make clocks?" and he shakes his head one more time and now she shouts, "So tell me, what do you do?" And the old guy says, "We do circumcisions." And she stares at him and asks, "So why do you have all these clocks in the window?" and he says, "Enh. So what do you want we should have in the window, lady?"'

Tessa met Rachel's warm eyes and giggled.

'So, you feel a bit better now?'

Tessa nodded.

'Good. 'Cause we're here. Just act rich and pull out your

wallet when I look at you. Be prepared to open it. We have a healthy respect for money these days. And its circulation.'

The station was as empty as it had been yesterday, but this time a new policeman lounged behind the counter, his legs sprawled atop a desk, his face bent over a newspaper. He sprang up at their footsteps. He was very young, his face pink where he had cut himself shaving.

Rachel approached him with a pronounced swagger, as if she had just parked her horse at the kerb and was bent on outmanning a gang of desperadoes. She let loose a volley of words at which his shoulders visibly tensed. The shake of the head seemed painful. Another barrage followed. During it, Tessa placed her bag emphatically on the counter.

The policeman glanced at her, then back at Rachel. With a shrug he ambled towards a large wooden cabinet and pulled out a tray of files. Out of this he picked a folder. With irritating slowness, he began to look through its contents.

Rachel winked at Tessa and gestured at her bag. Tessa took out some bills and handed them to her. The policeman, she noted, was now scribbling something down on a sheet of paper. He passed this to Rachel who nodded briefly and with a nonchalant gesture shook his hand, leaving the bills behind.

'What did you tell him?' Tessa asked as they climbed back into the car.

'The truth, more or less. He wasn't worth a story. I also told him you wanted to make sure they had done the right thing. And that he needed new shoes.' She laughed and glanced down at the piece of paper. 'This place is miles away.'

'But you'll take me.'

'Sure. Said I would. If I can find it.'

The tiny car lurched into motion, clattered its way across tram lines, zigzagged through bumpy streets, wheezed onto a dual carriageway where the traffic was heavy. Every few minutes, Rachel bent forward to wipe a screen grown misty with their breath. Stately nineteenth-century houses gave way to dingy high-rise apartment blocks surrounded by scrubland. A vast red-brick factory with a towering chimney blew black smoke into the air. And then, for a while, there was nothing but bare fields and an empty stretch of road.

'I think this is the one. I hope.' Rachel veered the car into a narrow country lane.

After a few moments, a drive appeared on their left, at its end an elegant stuccoed house with a dome at its centre and two gracious wings. Tessa stared at it in surprise. It was not at all as her Dickensian forebodings had led her to imagine.

Two men were raking gravel in front of the house. They wore identical caps and khaki-coloured overalls. Rachel stopped the car in front of them and shouted something. One of them turned a blank stare on her. The other started to gesticulate wildly.

'Oops. A mistake.' She backed the car from the drive with a splutter of gravel. 'This is one of our, how do you say it, hospitals, a mental hospital. We have to go a little further.'

The further seemed to bring them back by some detour into Prague itself or at least to some dilapidated outer precinct. They parked beneath a high spiked wall, found a gate which led them, after a ring and a long wait, into a yard filled with rubble. At its far side stood a smallish old stone building with bars on its windows. Around it, there was a cluster of square, ungainly structures which looked as if they had been put up on a bad weekend by some do-it-yourself addict with a military imagination and little talent.

An orphanage, Tessa concluded, was worth less than an asylum.

As they opened the door into the main building, a smell of mingled cabbage and bleach and dank walls attacked their nostrils. A stout woman, greying hair perched in a net, stared out at them from a dim corner cubicle and muttered a greeting. Rachel pounced on her with her usual brightness, only to turn back to Tessa.

'What's the baby's name, by the way?'

Tessa stared at her with bleak apprehension. 'No idea.'

'So they probably don't know either.' Rachel's manner was all reassurance. She started to talk to the woman. Tessa watched suspicion turn to hesitant acquiescence, the glimmer of a smile which never quite reached faded eyes, saw a shrug. And then the woman pointed them back in the direction from which they had come.

'Doesn't she know?' Tessa asked. She felt her heart flutter oddly, as if she had just been told of a death.

'Second building on the left.'

'Oh.' Tears leapt to her eyes.

'Heh, we're there.' Rachel gave her an inquisitive glance. She put a steadying hand on her shoulder.

They walked through the gloom of the courtyard, turned down a narrow path past a teeming rubbish bin. A holly bush stood by its side, rampant berries hanging from leaves glossy with health. Tessa stared at it, took a deep breath, then stepped through the door Rachel held open for her.

A cacophony of wails greeted them, shrill cries, forlorn and demanding. Rachel grimaced, slapped a palm against her forehead.

'I'm sorry. Would you rather wait for me outside?'

'No, no.' She gave Tessa her sardonic face. 'I was just thinking, here I come with you so as not to go to the synagogue and what do I hear? The same thing. Moaning, crying . . .'

'*Co si přejete?* What can I do for you?' A woman in a thick navy blue dress emerged from a side door. She was wearing a bizarre headdress which gave her unadorned face a pale height of brow from which the wrinkles seemed to have been ironed. It took Tessa a few moments to realize that she might be a nun. After an exchange with Rachel, she directed a bland, assessing stare at Tessa then led them through to what Tessa had already named for herself 'the room of the cries'.

It wasn't a large space, but it was grim, bleak with lack of paint and tawdry curtains. And every inch, apart from the narrow aisle down which they walked, was covered in old-fashioned cots with thick metal bars and bare mattresses. From between grey blankets of a thick, military cast, babies' heads poked, dark and blonde, their faces contorted with cries or wheezy in sleep. Tiny fists pawed the air. Toddlers sat in unnatural stillness and gazed towards an invisible space.

Tessa stared at one face after another, her hands clenched tightly to her side. She hadn't foreseen that the sight of these hapless children would so distress her. She wanted to wrap them all in her arms, transport them to bright gaily painted rooms where mobiles twirled from ceilings and friezes walked across walls and stuffed toys cascaded from every nook and cranny.

A pain she didn't recognize tugged at her entrails and blurred her vision, so that she almost failed to spot the little girl she had come to see. Only the sight of flailing stripes alerted her – the blue stripes of the pyjamas she had bought.

She lifted the child into her arms, felt the face that had pursued her nestle against her bosom, snuffle. She stroked the tuft of dark hair, cradled the slight weight. Tessa smiled.

'That's her, is it?' Rachel looked dubiously at Tessa.

Tessa nodded. 'You can leave me here now, if you've got better things to do. I'll be all right.'

'You want me to ask if they've had any news of her mother?'

Tessa hesitated, then nodded. 'Oh, and here.' She fumbled for her bag.

'That's okay. You can settle up with me tomorrow. I'll see if I can find out anything.' Rachel paused uncomfortably. 'You won't go and do anything dumb? You know what I mean . . . They have rules.'

'Nothing dumb, no. Maybe something smart. See you tomorrow. And thanks. Thank you very much.'

'Ya. Okay.' Rachel made a self-deprecating gesture, ambled off with her quick, bow-legged gait. Tessa looked gratefully after her and then turned back to the child.

As the baby's soft hand curled round her fingers and dark, intent eyes met her own, a strange sense took her over. She didn't know quite what words to put to it, but she felt, yes, that was it, claimed. A new power seemed to flow into her from that tiny form and at the same time an odd vulnerability, a dawning knowledge of the fragility of life. Maybe that was what love meant, Tessa thought. She gazed down at the child and in her mind, she gave her a name. Amy. Love.

The lobby, with its array of polished mirrors and false columns, thronged with people sporting plastic badges which bore their names beneath the starred logo of the European Union. Laboratory chiefs who had long given up research for the more arduous business of raising and managing funds consorted with bureaucrats and practising scientists. There were Russians working on the genetic basis of alcoholism who would have their glasses liberally refilled with each genetically determined sentence. There were French working on HIV and British working on memory and Dutch and Germans and Hungarians. There were even a few lawyers and philosophers thrown in to keep a watch on the scientific community and tabs on the ethics of the flourishing biotechnical sphere. And there were journalists bearing microphones or notepads.

Ted Knight skirted an oncoming mike and strode towards the doors of the hotel. It was an excellent congress as congresses went. His notebook was packed with leads and there was one definite triumph. Scholti was prepared to come to California. That had been a good morning's work. But his energy wasn't what it should have been today. First there had been the news about Tessa. Then there hadn't been the news he had expected at lunchtime. On top of it all the lying woman had vanished, had failed to return any of his messages.

He pushed open the hotel doors. Cold air gusted towards him, bringing with it a flurry of powdery snow. He stood on the threshold and breathed deeply, considered a night-time sprint. Then, with a cough and a scowl, he retraced his steps. The air was more polluted than LA on a hot smoggy day.

He peered round the lobby, the lights too bright after the interval in the dark. And then he saw her, all trim and self-contained, her hair slightly windswept and with that unselfconscious prettiness which had drawn him to her in the first place. She was standing off to one side of the crowd and talking to Jan Martin.

That was it. Jan Martin. Maybe she had fallen for him at that lunch he had sent her off to yesterday. Or maybe she already knew him. Of course. Caldwell's wife. Talk of two faces.

With quick strides, Ted marched towards them, only stopping himself in time to adopt a pleasant grin.

'Hi there. Having a good day?' He gripped Tessa's arm so hard she sprang back with a barely concealed wince.

'Ted, hello.' Her voice was cool. She extricated her arm. 'I was just coming to find you.'

'Miss Hughes has had a very interesting day, I believe,' Jan said in his unnervingly even tones. 'She finds Prague to be full of surprises.'

'Does she now?'

'She does.' Tessa gave Ted one of her ironic glances. Her lips looked very pink, as if someone had been biting them.

'Well, I guess she can tell me all about it.' Ted met her irony. 'You'll excuse us, won't you, Dr Martin. I've had quite enough of the leisure of the theoried classes for one day. And Tess and I haven't caught up with each other for a while.'

'Of course.' Jan considered them for a moment, seemed about to say something else when he was dragged off by a journalist bearing a microphone.

'Come on. You and I need to talk. Quietly.' Ted manoeuvred her through the crowd.

She shook off his hand and thrust ahead of him towards the elevators.

'Don't want to be seen with me now. Is that it?' He caught up with her.

She gave him her cool, appraising look as the doors hissed to a close behind them. The look both excited and infuriated him.

'What's the matter, Ted? Bad day?'

'Not great. Where've you been?'

She looked past him. Her expression grew soft, the eyes moist, dreamy. He lifted her chin roughly and made her face him. She wriggled away, slid out of the door as soon as it opened.

'Don't worry,' she murmured. 'I'll pay for my own room.'

'Will you, now?' He clutched at her as they walked down the corridor, wrapped his arm firmly round her waist so that she couldn't evade him as he propelled her into his room. Maybe she had guessed he knew. 'Is that all you have to say to me?'

She took her coat off and went to stand by the windows, stared out at the flickering lights of the distant castle, pressed her face to the glass so that a circle of mist formed.

Headlights shimmered into water. A car hooted, its blare contagious, picked up by its kin.

'Well?' Ted came up behind her.

She turned towards him suddenly, her bosom brushing his hand. 'I don't really want to talk about it.'

'Don't you? Now there's a surprise.'

She shrugged and started to move away. He clasped her wrist hard and brought her back to him, kissed her roughly, prised those resisting lips open. He didn't mind the resistance. No, ma'am. It roused him. He could play different games too. He kneaded her tight little butt, yanked her hair back, forced her to her knees, unzipped his trousers. She was looking up at him, her pupils wide. Suited her, really. Mrs Stephen Caldwell on her knees.

'Take it.' He ordered, jabbed his penis towards her mouth.

With a shiver of fear, Tessa stared up at what had suddenly occurred to her was a brutal face. She forced her gaze to that bulky object, the crisscross of veins, heavy, almost purple. Like something from that butcher's window she had gazed at in Paris.

Funny, how everything had changed. Yesterday, she had thought their bodies were perfectly attuned and now . . .

'Take it,' he repeated, pressing hard on her head.

Tessa closed her eyes, felt that hot, musky penis pushing against her lips, filling her mouth. She would gag, she thought, and tried to get her tongue out of the way as the penis grew slippery with her saliva and moved, too slowly, in and out and round. Above her, she could hear his sharp intake of breath.

Pleasure, she made herself think so as not to think, what an odd thing it was. She tried to wonder at it, tried to think of something pleasant, the soothing scent of warm chocolate, the crisp pages of a newly printed book – anything but the trace of that dangerous face which wasn't the Ted she knew and that vengeful object in her mouth.

From somewhere she heard a bleep and a whirr and a mechanical clack, and for a moment before she could place the sound it seemed to her that the thing in her mouth had become motorized and was about to take off and propel her into a space where she didn't want to go. When she recognized the fax, she also recognized that Ted was at home with all the buzzes and beeps and pings and peals and hums and drones and whines and screeches and bangs, too, which made up the discord of everyday life. She was tempted to see what kind of sound he might produce if she bit down hard on his penis.

He had taken her hands and pressed them against his buttocks, so that she seemed by some absurd unwanted motion to be responsible for the jutting which choked her. She tried now to imagine a tree ripe with autumn apples, the smell of freshly mown grass, the soft scent of Amy's skin. But, for all her attempts, she couldn't obliterate that waxy bulging thing alive inside her mouth. Or the presence of that bullying hand straining against her head. She dug her fingers into his buttocks and hoped they hurt and as she did so, a warm sticky stream invaded her throat, a pungent, gagging taste like the raw egg she had once been forced to swallow as a child.

Above her, she heard a low, guttural laugh. 'Thank you for that. Thank you, Mrs Caldwell. Mrs Stephen Caldwell.'

Tessa sprang up. He was whistling. Nonchalantly zipping up his trousers. She turned away. Her throat felt bruised as she mumbled, 'So you've found out?'

'I have. And it doesn't exactly fill me with joy.'

'No. I'm sorry.' Tessa's hand trembled as she straightened her jumper. 'So you've talked to him? He's here?'

'I would have thought his wife could tell me that. Where were you? Yesterday? Today? And what do you think you're up to? Lying to me like that.'

Her legs felt weak. She wanted to head for the door, but one glance at his face told her she wouldn't make it. She perched at the edge of the bed, clasped her hands together on her knees. 'I . . .' She averted her eyes. 'I want to adopt a baby.'

'Adopt! What! Have you gone crazy?'

She could feel him staring at her. 'Why do you say that?' she asked softly. 'Anyhow. That's where I've been.'

'Tess, no! Not really! I don't believe it. Anyhow, is that a reason to lie to me?'

'I didn't exactly lie. I just omitted. I . . . I liked you and I thought if you knew, you . . . we wouldn't . . .' She shook her hand vaguely, examined her shoes.

'And this adoption business? Christ! I knew you wanted a child. But not this way, Tess. Really. It's mad.'

She shrugged, her face desolate.

From the small icebox hidden inside a cabinet, he pulled out a bottle of whisky and poured them each a glass. On his way back to her, he paused at the fax. She saw his shoulders stiffen, saw consternation cover his features. She could go now, she thought.

'You need to work,' she murmured, hurried towards the door.

'No, Tess, stay. We've gotta talk. What's got into you?' He put a glass into her hand, urged her into an armchair, tidied faxes into a pile. 'You can't do this.' He was smiling at her, his face all sweet concern. 'It's Stephen, isn't it? I never thought he was up to much that way. But look. I showed you how easy it all is. Marriot's clinic. There are lots of good places in England, too. But adoption . . . believe me, Tess. You have to be careful of these things. The genetic mix and all that. You never know what you could be getting into. Some halfwit. Drink up. You're looking pale.'

He refilled her glass.

'You know . . .' He came to sit at her feet, stroked her fingers. 'Look, I'm sorry about just now. I know you didn't like it. I was just, well, jealous, I guess. I thought you and

237

that Dr Martin . . .' He waved his arm. 'Feeling a bit miffed, too, to tell you the truth. I thought you trusted me.' He wrapped his hand softly round hers and gazed at her in silence for a moment, an appeal in his eyes.

'And rather than have you contemplate that – adoption, you know.' He shook his head with an air of apocalyptic gloom. 'Well, you and I, if you like, if that's what you want, if Stephen can't. We could have a go. My track record for babies is pretty good. Though you'll have to make yourself small and secret for the next few days. Stephen isn't here yet, as far as I know. But he's due any minute. I gather you don't want to be found out.'

That rugged face met hers in soft persuasion as she shook her head, though she didn't quite know why she did so.

'Jan Martin doesn't know who you are, does he?'

'No.'

He pulled her gently down beside him on the carpet, held her. 'What do you say, Tess? Now that everything's open between us.' He touched her breast, brought her hand to his trousers and for a shiver of a second she almost forgot Amy.

13

'Madame Lalande Debray? One moment, sir. I will check.'
The stiff-lipped receptionist behind the desk at the Europa
Hotel picked up the telephone, waited for a moment, then
shook his head. 'No, sir. It is as I thought. She has not yet
returned. You wish to leave a message?'

Stephen penned a quick note. He had hoped to find
Simone in time for dinner. He needed to find out whether
she had heard anything of Ariane. But he was evidently
too late. His plane, not unusually, had been delayed.

He looked round the lobby and wondered whether he
might still have time to walk down river and just catch Jan
at the congress venue. Jan would be eager to hear about
the meeting with Franklin at Camgene that morning. It
had not gone too badly, despite Stephen's tension. He had
minimized his fears about the possible leak, concentrated
instead on the miracle of Chrombindin, on the need for
a quick patent application, on collaboration with Jan's
Institute. Franklin had bought it all with a rare display of
enthusiasm.

The downside was that when he had rung the Cambridge
travel agency to get Tessa's hotel number, they had told
him she had cancelled her trip to the Caribbean at the
very last minute. He had considered ringing her sister, but
hadn't wanted to set off alarm bells. Tessa would have her
reasons. He didn't think he was going to like them.

Glancing at his watch, Stephen concluded that he would

probably just miss Jan. He would try him at home later. The door to the restaurant caught his eye. Simone might be in there.

The crooning voice of a latter-day Frank Sinatra made its way to him through billows of cigarette smoke. He peered through gloom, wound his way slowly amidst tables and quick-paced waiters and their mirrored reflections. From the cacophony of voices, he suddenly distinguished his name. He turned to see a waving arm. It wasn't Simone's. For a moment, he wasn't certain to whom it belonged. Then, beneath a swirl of blonde hair, he distinguished the face of her granddaughter, Antoinette.

'Come and join us, Dr Caldwell. No, I'm not a phantom. Grand-mère invited me along, though I don't know where she's got herself to. And I've brought along a new friend. I think you know each other.'

The friend, who had had her back to Stephen, turned and stared up at him with a slightly fearful smile. 'Hello, Stephen. I told Antoinette you had helped me when all my things were stolen.'

Antoinette clapped her hands, laughed gleefully. 'And since Cary had taken such a dislike to Paris, I suggested she come along with me.' She gestured Stephen towards the empty chair.

Stephen felt a flush creeping up his face. He raked his mind for an escape route and, unable to think of one, sank into the proffered chair with as much dignity as he could muster.

'Your money came through, then?' He risked meeting Cary's eyes.

She fidgeted, matched his discomfort. 'As promised.'

'So I took her mind off Paris and asked her to come along with us. Grand-mère is not a great one for clubs. She prefers this.' The girls looked at each other and burst into giggles as Antoinette raised a hand to hail a waiter, who arrived with smitten alacrity.

Watching them, listening to their patter about the clubs they had visited the previous evening, Stephen suddenly felt like some invisible ancient. He downed the tiny glass of *becherovka* that had been placed in front of him and cleared his throat. 'Are you expecting Simone?'

Antoinette hoicked up the sleeve of her leather jacket, glanced at her watch. 'She's over an hour late already. She told us to meet her here. Maybe the snow's held her up.'

'You'll tell her I came by.' Stephen signalled for the waiter. 'And that I'll try and get hold of her later.'

Antoinette nodded. 'You do that. She's in a foul temper and needs cheering. I don't know why she's bothered to come here if it puts her into such a bad mood. And despite the fact that I told her I was going to break up with Jean-Michel.'

'I think she's terrific,' Cary offered. 'On the plane, she gave me a lecture on Communism and Capitalism. No one at college taught me that much.'

'Mmnn. That's what I tell her.' Antoinette flicked her hair back to reveal a stretch of smooth skin. 'Between her and my parents, university's a waste of time.'

'I don't know about that,' Stephen heard himself saying. He stood up abruptly. 'I had really better be off.'

'We'll see you around, then.' Antoinette flashed him her languid look.

Cary raised her eyes to his. 'And thanks. Thanks for rescuing me. It's great to see you again.'

'Yes.' Stephen's smile felt like a grimace. He turned away with an attempt at a breezy wave and made his way out into the cold.

The extended rectangle of Wenceslas Square was shadowy with artificial light. Neon tinged sky and snowflakes a ghostly pink. The pavements teemed with the youth of all nations. Like exotic birds, they spilled out of the new fast-food spots, sprawled against the facades of buildings, sat around the fountain buttressed with an assortment of

241

rucksacks. To his side, Stephen could hear the strumming of a guitar and in the air he smelled the slightly fetid odour of marijuana riding high above petrol fumes. In the distance two women's voices, hoarse with the night, merged in the mournful strains of some American folk song.

As he crossed the street, the raucous blast of a rock band assaulted his eardrums, music with a beat that was like speed itself. Leather-clad men, drunk on night and youth and equally short-lived substances, heaved past him, their assortment of chains clinking as they strode from the door of a club. One of them loomed against him, a leer on his face. He was mumbling something Stephen couldn't make out and before he had understood it, he felt an arm through his, the rub of a hip.

Roughly Stephen disentangled himself, tried to disappear into the crowd, but the man was right there in front of him as he turned the corner into an arcade. In the light, Stephen saw he was a mere boy, the down on his upper lip as smooth as a child's, his pupils vastly dark against pale eyes. He was muttering something again. Stephen stilled his nervousness, shook his head, then took some bills out of his pocket and handed them to the boy. He gave him a single wild stare and disappeared into the throng.

Money, the universal panacea. Stephen tried to calm himself, glanced at the blare of movie posters arguing with each other for space and attention, saw the straggly queue leading into the decaying grandeur of the picture palace, unchanged over all the years he remembered it, like the Secession curves of the arcade itself. The young had always gathered in the grand public arena of Wenceslas Square to manifest their pleasure or displeasure, to welcome in republics or rebel against dictatorial regimes. Or simply to while away their youth.

He had never been young like that, Stephen reflected. Somewhere between the deaths of his parents and the austere excitements of the lab, the youth of all-night revels and tightly knit bands and blatant excess had passed him by and not bothered to look back.

He walked on, past the entrance of the metro, into the quieter arm of the arcade with its down-at-heel emporia, as grey and faded as the communist regime whose traces it still bore. As he turned the corner that brought him out into the cooler air of the street, a woman detached herself from a threesome and came towards him. Her skirt was so short and tight, her heels so high, that for a moment he was mesmerized by the length of her legs and didn't understand the lewdness of her expression.

'Want love-y love-y?' She passed her tongue over carmine lips. 'Very good.'

Stephen blushed through darkness. He shook his head, tried to move past her, but she blocked his way, pressed herself against him.

'No, no, thank you,' he mumbled.

'Very cheap.' She scurried alongside him as he quickened his pace, tottering a little as if she were unpractised on her heels. 'Have place. Not far.'

He had a sudden image of a dank room, a single stark light-bulb, long legs curled on a tousled bed, carmine lips closing over his penis which was dishearteningly hard. He forced another 'no' from his parched throat and tried not to break into an undignified run. From behind him, he heard the woman curse. He wanted to reach into his pocket and extract more bills, but he didn't know how to without prolonging the encounter, so he hastily turned a corner and then more quickly another and another and only then slowed his pace and caught his breath.

The lamp post cast a murky yellow light on a fraying poster. Harrison Ford, he read, and then the unrecognizable name of a film in translation. He stopped to look at the man's bronzed face. Cary had remarked at some point in that night they had spent together that he looked like Harrison Ford, but one who had been left out in the rain for too long and would find adventure a strain. The gym would do him good.

She had said it kindly and since the name Harrison Ford brought no particular image to his mind, he had laughed and teased her about being a card-carrying member of the Health Police and told her, give or take a few years, the gym wouldn't make any difference. It was all there, encoded in his genes. She had come right back at him, sounding more like himself than he did at that point, and told him that within pretty broad limits, you could make what you wanted of your genes and there was a difference between a well-toned gene and a sagging one.

And now here she was in Prague. Stephen stared at the tattered poster, felt his heart still pounding too loudly and acknowledged that, even though this Harrison Ford had evidently been out in rain and snow for a long time, she was right.

When he looked up and around him, he realized that in his flurry he had lost his bearings. He crossed the street and walked down a narrow lane in the hope that it might return him to a recognizable area.

How did these people choose whom to approach, he wondered? Was there a particular look on his face tonight which made him open to advances? A depressed echo to his footsteps? Hardly surprising if there were, he reminded himself. First Ariane. Then Tessa. He didn't want to think about that.

Stephen shivered, forced himself into a brisk pace. He avoided the eyes of passers-by. Coming on top of the meeting with Cary, those two separate advances had unsettled him. Seeing her with Antoinette had underlined for him how inappropriate the whole thing had been. She was just a girl. Yet he had wanted her. He had to come to grips with that. Not now, though. He didn't want to think about it now.

His street suddenly appeared at an odd angle, when he

least expected it. He made his way gratefully towards the hotel. He had stayed here on his last two visits, drawn to the place because it had once been a dilapidated barracks of a house which had served as a dropping point for manuscripts. It was also conveniently near the Institute and he liked the fact that it was too modest to sport a name. It went only by its street number.

He liked chatting to the owner too, who had a distant, barely polite smile and who seemed to spend her life behind the reception desk. The hotel was in fact her childhood home, taken away by the State in '48 and recently returned to her. A bank loan had been used for refurbishment and she would be paying it back for many years to come. Meanwhile Pani Stasna worked and worked and sometimes chatted in order to complain about how only she and none of her employees worked and worked. It was the state of the State, she mourned, as it had always been.

Tonight she was in her customary place behind the mahogany veneer of the new bar, which doubled as reception counter. She greeted him benignly and handed him a number of folded messages along with his key.

Stephen didn't stop to chat. He couldn't have brought out anything sensible now. Instead he made his way quickly up the stairs which curved round one side of the atrium and shook the snow from his hat on the way. When he reached the third floor, the lights came to the end of their timed cycle. He fumbled unsuccessfully for the switch and ended up by groping towards his room at the far end of the corridor. His key when he tried it failed to fit the lock. With a flare of impatience, Stephen prodded the latch. The door swung open.

A scent of lavender mingled with a whiff of mothballs caught at his nostrils. He found a light switch. He was in some kind of linen store. Blankets and sheets lay neatly folded on shelves along the walls, but beneath them on the floor there was a scramble of odds and ends – lamp bases without shades, white candles in stubby holders, a tangle of loose wire, an old wooden chest, creamy lace peeping from its interior. Stephen stared, then hurriedly closed the door and tried the one beside it. It opened smoothly to his key.

The scent of mingled lavender and mothballs followed him. He pushed open the window with its new casing and watched the gauzy curtains billow. But the smell wouldn't leave him. It made his head swirl. Dizzy, he stretched out on the bed and closed his eyes.

He was at the door of some dark, musty room. His legs ached. He had walked too quickly, climbed too high, and the stairs seemed hugely big, too tall. Perhaps it was because he was so small, his legs too short for the stairs' height. A little boy standing by an attic door which squeaked. He was clutching something in his hand and as the door opened wider, that smell was there, dust and mothballs and a lingering scent of crushed lavender. His mother picked it from the garden and crushed it into a bowl. She must have brought it up here into the dark.

There were a lot of boxes here and a lamp base and a stack of old blankets. But they would find him if he lay on those. They were rough and damp anyway. There was a box, though, a big chest, just big enough for him. He opened it and smelled the lavender again. There was something white and satiny inside. He climbed in on top of it and made a soft nest for himself. He was excited and a little frightened. He took the tiny torch from his pocket and shone it on the object in his hand. It was beautiful. A pale yellow stone. A crystal tear. An elephant's tear. It glowed softly. And inside, the shapes glinted and changed, tiny threads of them like the cat's eyes. The tear was warm from his hand as he pressed it against his cheek. It had been warm when the woman had taken it off her neck and given it to him. Because he had been staring at it. Because it had perched there, skirting the V of her dress and catching the light like a giant eye. And it was warm with her skin.

Stephen snuggled more deeply into the creamy satin, let the lid of the chest fall over him. They would never find him here. He could bury the tear here if he liked and come back to see it when he wanted. But his father would be angry. They hadn't seen him sneak away. His mother was making tea and his father was too busy talking to the lady who had given him the stone from her neck. She was sweet. Had smiled at him sweetly and had talked in a funny accent. The satin was as soft as her smile. He put the tear on it and stared into it for a long time.

He woke to the sound of footsteps, heavy and light, the creak of a door, his mother's voice, soft. 'Perhaps he came up here.' He didn't quite know where he was, but the satin told him. It was damp, snug. He hid further into it, making a swish of a sound like the long-tailed lizards in the glass cage. Then the lid of the box opened and he saw his father's face, stern. Behind him the glare of a single bulb.

'What on earth are you doing here, Stephen?' His father heaved him out, held him up towards the light, shook him and the tear tumbled from his hand onto the floorboards with a clatter.

'You gave us such a fright, Stephen,' his mother was murmuring, but his father's voice was louder. 'Trying to steal it away, were you? Bad boy.'

'On my wedding dress. Oh dear. He's wet it.'

He couldn't see his mother's face for the shaking and the bad, bad boy, but then his father put him down and he saw his mother looked sad. She had taken out the satin and was smoothing it around her, rubbing where the wet patch was.

'Say "sorry" to your mother.' His father looked very big and angry.

'Don't punish him.' His mother had put her hand on his father's arm. 'Look, he's crying. He is sorry.'

247

His father picked up the tear and held it to the light. 'And all for this. I don't believe it. I can't believe it of you, Stephen. A bauble. It's not what you see and touch that counts. It's what you can't see. What's important is what happens in your heart and mind. The invisible. Goodness. Do you understand?'

Stephen didn't know whether he understood. What he understood through his tears was that his father placed the jewel in his pocket and he never saw or touched it again.

Stephen lay on the narrow hotel bed and watched the billowing curtains. Funny how that memory had come upon him, uncalled for. Unnecessary. How old could he have been? Four, maybe. Or five. A silly little boy, spoiled by his mother and lectured to by his father. Had his father really said all that about the importance of what one couldn't see? Like some puritan preacher. Or was his memory playing tricks on him?

He shifted restlessly on the bed. It was probably why he'd gone off to stare into microscopes at things too small to see. Or, more likely, done a little perverse misinterpretation and collided the invisible with the secret. The secret as a site of meaning, like that old chest with its body-warmed satin. Or furtive ferryings to the East. The puritan hatred for the material and visible leaving its secular legacy in the English hankering after spies and secrecy.

With a grimace, Stephen turned his face into the pillow. There was a crackle of paper beneath him. He had left his messages unread on the bed. He switched on the light and looked at them now. There were four of them. Two from old friends wanting to meet up. One from a conference delegate. The last from Hanka, who said she wanted to see him urgently.

He glanced at his watch and picked up the telephone.

Twenty minutes later he was standing in front of the Martin apartment. Hanka opened the door. She was a tall, slender woman with wide grey eyes, her hair gathered up in a loose, sleek knot from which strands always descended. She had a penchant for wearing silky scarfs which she knotted around her throat in a variety of elaborate styles. It was the one thing Stephen always remembered about her attire. He had even on occasion brought her a scarf himself. He thought he recognized the one she was wearing this evening.

'Stephen. It's so good of you to come.' She gestured him into the room he had last visited some two years ago and he looked round him covertly to see what changes had taken place with Jan's departure. Everything seemed the same, the greying walls, crowded with posters and pictures, the tables covered with drooping cloths. Even the old portable typewriter sat on the tiny corner desk by the window. It was on this machine that Hanka had spent long hours typing the various clandestine books and articles which for so many years had helped to supplement the country's official reading.

'No, nothing has changed. Jan left everything behind him.' Her tone was waspish and he couldn't for a moment bring himself to meet her eyes. When he did, he saw that she had an ironic tilt to her lips.

'Don't be so embarrassed, Stephen. You'll remember, some American wit said marriage for a woman was the exchange of the attention of many men for the inattention of one. Well, I have decided on the attention of many. It is not so bad. Now, it is not so bad.' She glanced up at him flirtatiously.

He cleared his throat. 'And Eva?'

She poured him a glass of wine as he sank into the worn brown sofa.

'Eva is okay, beginning to work harder at school. She will come and say hello. Eva . . .' She turned to call down the small corridor. 'It is because of Eva I particularly wanted to see you. I knew Jan wouldn't ask you.'

A tall, slim girl Stephen didn't recognize walked into the room. She had milky skin and pale hair and shy grey eyes and a coltish gait emphasized by the way she swung her hair.

Hanka laughed. 'You are amazed. You do not know our Eva. She is a young lady now.'

'Hello, Dr Stephen.' The young lady lifted her cheek to him.

He brushed it with his lips.

'I do not think Dr Stephen is used to kissing young ladies,' Hanka said, adding to his discomfort.

Eva perched on the sofa beside him. He had a distant memory of another girl with just that mixture of musing reticence coming to sit beside him in a room crowded with old furniture. Sonya. Of course. His breathing suddenly felt constricted. He fought for something to say, felt the clichés forming in his throat.

'It's true that I wouldn't have known you. You've grown so much.' He groped for another topic. 'What are your favourite subjects in school?'

'Science and English,' Eva smiled at him shyly.

'Yes,' Hanka intervened. 'That is why I thought it would be good for Eva to go to England. And we wished to ask you whether she could stay with you for a few weeks. Perhaps over Christmas. If you're here for another few days, she could even go back with you. Or next summer, when she can attend a language course. She will not be much trouble. She is good at tidying up.'

Stephen was intensely aware of the girl's uncomfortable flush. He was also aware that he would have a lot of explaining to do to Tessa.

Hanka seemed to read his mind. 'You will have to check with your wife, of course. But you must tell her that Eva has always been a very good daughter. Quiet, not wild.' She sought out Stephen's gaze as if she needed its confirmation. 'And I have told Eva that you will be like a father to her, a kind father. You will give her enough freedom, but not too much.'

Stephen was transfixed by the word 'father', as if its context gave it an altogether different charge. He turned to Eva and struggled for what he hoped was a reassuring and fatherly look. Funny. When Tessa talked of children in his mind's eye he pictured only squawling babies. But the babies grew up into Evas.

'I think you might like Cambridge,' he said. 'It's very small, though. Not like Prague.'

'I will like it. I will like to punt.' She shaped her lips hesitantly over the last word, then smiled sweetly. 'Do you have a piano?'

Stephen nodded.

'Eva is a good pianist,' Hanka commented proudly, then rushed on. 'But perhaps if your wife is not for it, you could find us another family? With children, maybe. For the summer.'

'I'm sure. I'm sure it will be fine.' Stephen stole another glance at the girl. Sonya and not Sonya. Bolder, stronger, her own person. Yet with that trace. 'Absolutely fine,' he said with conviction in his voice.

'Thank you. Thank you very much.' Eva was all excitement tempered by politeness as Hanka shooed her off to bed.

'She has been a great help to me these last months,' Hanka remarked when they heard the bedroom door close. 'It would have been much harder for me without her. And lonely, too.'

'Yes.' Stephen suddenly had an uncomfortable inkling of the things he hoped she wouldn't talk about. He reached for his glass.

'I am almost unhappy to send her away, even for a little while. But it will be good for her, a special treat as you say.'

'Yes,' he said more emphatically.

'Do you think your wife will agree?'

Stephen stared towards the shadowy darkened window with its half-drawn curtains. It came to him that he didn't know what Tessa would think. He hadn't the slightest idea. It was odd to acknowledge that. Odd and more than a little uncomfortable.

14

———— * ————

'Not this morning, Stephen.' Simone pushed away the breakfast plate of sweet cheese *palacinky* and took a last sip of thick Turkish coffee. 'I'll drop in on the congress at the end of the day. We can have dinner together, if that suits. Right now, my taxi driver is waiting for me.' She laughed girlishly, her eyes glowing with humour. 'We've become great friends, Pan Hrdlicka and I. He's told me his darkest secrets. He once took a trip to Moscow and enjoyed it. Not a fashionable opinion.'

Stephen met her smile. 'I'm glad you're having a good time.'

'That wasn't quite what I said.' She studied him. 'On the other hand, you're looking distinctly unwell. You aren't still worrying about Ariane, are you?'

He grimaced. 'That, too.' For a moment, he considered telling her about the suspected theft, but he didn't want to burden her with problems that were altogether of his own making. He contented himself with saying, 'I really do need to locate her. It's urgent. For my peace of mind. You didn't hear anything in Paris, did you?'

Simone smoothed some crumbs from the cloth. 'I have been making inquiries, Stephen. By the time I get back to Paris, there may be some news. If I could, you know, I would bring her here for you this very moment.' She covered his hand with hers, gave him a reassuring squeeze. For a moment, she looked abstracted. She tapped her lighter abruptly on the table, then, with a determined air, put it into her bag. 'But we should carry on with our day. It's a rare thing for me to say, but this is one I want to get through quickly.'

'Oh?' He looked at her curiously as, with a sigh, she got to her feet. He rushed to help her with her coat. Something about her demeanour worried him.

'Perhaps Antoinette . . . the girls,' he stumbled, 'should keep you company.'

'No, no, Stephen. This is something I need to do alone. Until later, then.'

At the entrance of the hotel, she waved him away and disappeared into the open door of a cab.

As the taxi crossed the river into the Malá Strana, Simone felt she was embarking on the second stage of a pilgrimage – one that did not necessarily promise a healing relic at its destination. But then, she told herself sternly, she had never held out any hopes of salvation. The only promise at her journey's end was that of a little lightness, a little surplus of truth which might indirectly, though only indirectly, be of use. Though not necessarily to its principal player. She considered that for a moment, didn't like her thoughts and put them away. One step at a time. She had only ever done things one step at a time.

The immense dome and bell tower of the church of St Nicholas loomed before them, as forbidding in its Counter-Reformation vastness as the castle itself. Between and around the two, the streets climbed and clustered, abutting on the palaces with their famous names, Buquoy and Thun-Hohenstein and Lobkowicz and Lichtenstein and Morzinsky. Stately portals and grand gardens, baroque statuary and blind cherubs. The streets of her childhood – now overlaid, like some palimpsest, with darker, more devious scratchings.

Simone signalled the driver to a halt. 'I'll walk from here. It will do me good.'

'But the cold!' The man shivered. 'You must take care. It is slippery.'

So are my memories, Simone wanted to say, but she merely smiled and asked him to wait.

She walked slowly, her feet inching their way along pavements made icy by their thin crust of snow. The slowness suited her. She strolled into the icy church and wondered what chinks and crevices had been used as dropping points in the dark days when the only truth was that ordained by the Party. She stopped at a bookshop to see what other truths or stories were now in circulation. Their cheapness or difficulty, rightness or wrongness, didn't matter, she told herself. The importance lay in the multiplicity. Like nature. One rampant, dominant weed which killed off all other strains of vegetation did not make for a healthy eco-system. Multiplicity was necessary to life.

She paused to stare into the windows of boutiques and cafés, their simple pine furniture so patently new that she felt sure if she looked more closely she would spot the IKEA label. The marks of transition, a love affair with the other which had been forbidden. That too was necessary.

She peered through scaffolding to examine how masons were handling the renovation of facades rich in leaf and tracery and festoons. She was in no hurry to arrive at her destination. No one was waiting for her, only a cluster of buried experiences she had long denied – herself in another, more vicious guise, hidden in a remote room in one of these buildings. Simone forced herself to remember.

It was spring of 1953. Stalin was already dead, but the slow haemorrhaging of Eastern Europe continued. Through friends – she was no longer certain if it was through a contact in the French Communist Party or an Embassy official – she had had certain confirmation of Staszek's death. The confirmation was no surprise. Since 1948 the Czech Party had already rid itself of over 100,000 of its members, charged them with spying or sabotage, condemned them to death or to labour camps which often meant the same thing. The specificity of the crimes was immaterial. The mere fact of being Jewish or intellectual, landowner or army officer, unrepentant peasant or unrepentant believer, was more than enough. So was drinking or working, too much or too little. Scapegoats were needed on whom to pin the dire state of the economy. Informers were everywhere. No amount of purging seemed to satisfy the Party's voracity.

Yet Karolina Dostolova remained unscathed, impassively survived everything, remained loyal to the workings of a Party that eliminated her closest comrades. The woman Simone held responsible for Staszek's death, the woman who had stolen him from her, the woman for whom he had refused to accompany her to France, carried on rising through the Party hierarchy as bodies fell around her. Around this single fact all Simone's rage over the crimes of Eastern Europe coalesced.

It was hard for her to recapture that rage now as she inched her way along the streets which lay below the castle. But then, she had woken with the acrid taste of anger on her tongue, felt its fierceness throughout the day, had fallen asleep with the sensation that she would choke on it in the night. Even the sturdy limbs of her two small girls couldn't eradicate the fury she carried everywhere with her.

Simone knew that she had to confront Karolina or go mad. She had no plan, no words that she could put to the meeting. But she knew she had to see her.

For months, she had tried to obtain a visa and in April it had finally come through. Her ostensible purpose was to accompany a small group of French Communist Party delegates on a tour of industrial sites. This she had done. She had done little else. To see old friends would cast suspicion on them. But towards the end of her visit, she had wrapped herself in an old raincoat which made her one of a muted crowd, and had slipped away to stalk Karolina.

As stealthily as if she had been born to it and without attracting the attention of the uniformed guard, Simone had for the length of a rainy afternoon paced the precincts of the Ministry of Transport building where she had found out Karolina worked, and waited for her to appear. On the second afternoon she had been rewarded by the sight of a woman in a brown coat and a soft brown felt hat. As soon as she saw the tilt of the square jaw, the determined heave of briefcase and arms, she knew that she had found Karolina. She was walking with a man, slightly shorter than her, in a drab belted raincoat.

Simone shadowed the couple for several blocks. Near Nerudova Street, the man headed off to the left and Karolina increased her pace. With a perverse flash of satisfaction as she hastened to her side, Simone noted that Karolina had thickened, that her bottom beneath her coat had an ungainly amplitude, that her cheeks were flushed with the exertion of her walk.

'Karolina Dostolova,' she called, so loudly that she saw the woman stiffen in fear as curious passers-by turned.

'Yes. That's me.'

'I know it's you. Who else could it be? One doesn't forget the face of the woman who's murdered one's husband.'

Simone hadn't known she was going to say that. She hadn't known she would shout it, so that not only Karolina, but people all around her stared. The hush in the street was tangible, as if a curtain had suddenly been raised before an audience waiting for a drama to unfurl. On that stage, she saw the momentary shock of recognition on Karolina's face, then a shuttered look, a tensing of shoulders.

'I don't know what you're talking about. You must be mad. Who are you?' Karolina's voice was low, steady. 'I will report you to the police.'

At that word, people round them turned on their heels,

hurried away. Karolina did the same. Simone pursued her, put a rough, staying hand on her arm. 'You know very well who I am,' she said in the same abrasive voice.

Karolina shrugged her off. Her face was very pale, the pupils dark with apprehension. 'Madwoman,' she muttered and raced off towards the square, leapt onto a tram.

Simone didn't follow. She didn't need to. As the tram clattered away, she met Karolina's eyes with the full force of her long-nurtured fury. The woman was frightened. She could almost smell her fear. It was good for Karolina to taste fear, to have it hover over her at night as it must for so long have hovered over Staszek.

As she walked towards her hotel, Simone felt she had grown vast wings and, like Nemesis, could pursue her prey with deadly force wherever she might run. But the dream of power vanished all too quickly. Towards the centre of town, she found her path blocked by a procession. Young communists, bright red scarfs round their necks, waved banners. Song poured from them. Their faces radiated inane smiles of communal optimism. As surely as if she had been there, she could see Karolina beatific in their midst, immune to the individual human price of that unthinking collective joy.

That night, amidst the rattling water pipes and musty smells of her hotel, Simone lay in bed and wept hot, impotent tears. A bloated Karolina paraded through her dreams, as vast and many-tentacled as the Party itself, an icon painted in primary colours, with arm thrust heroically upward and innocent smile veiling venomous intrigue. She woke feeling paralysed. The realization that there was nothing she could do had crept icily over her limbs and rendered her numb. Karolina was shielded from any individual sense of responsibility by her total identification with the Party.

With movement came the vague notion that she would somehow have to isolate Karolina from the protection of the group. Disgrace her in some way. And perhaps in that isolation, she could rupture her stolid immunity, impel her to some acknowledgement of her guilt.

As if in a dream, she dressed herself in her best Western clothes, a new single-breasted woollen suit in deepest brick which Michel had chosen for her, a perky matching hat. Without thinking about it, she armed herself with what might be presents – two brightly wrapped boxes containing a scarf, a bottle of Chanel, those suspicious foreign goods the regime considered anathema. Bearing these, she marched to Karolina's office, demanded in a loud, heavily accented voice to be allowed to see her, claimed she was an old friend, had brought her presents. She made a fuss, insisted.

Either because he was cowed or simply because he wanted to get rid of this potentially contagious alien virus, the man at the front desk directed her towards a room where Karolina was addressing a group about the goals of the latest railway plan.

Simone made her entry as conspicuous as possible, not that in her present attire she could have done anything else. Karolina's eyes rested on her for a moment. Effusively Simone waved a gloved hand, beamed, put down her boxes with maximum display. She was rewarded with a stumble in Karolina's speech, a fluttering nervousness in the hand she raised to turn her sheet of paper.

The lecture was soon finished. Simone positioned herself at the door. No sooner had Karolina approached it, than Simone flung her arms around her and started speaking rapidly and noisily in French and then in that heavily accented Czech she had found somewhere.

'I'm so happy to see you. I've brought you such lovely things. How well they'll suit you.'

Karolina squirmed, said nothing, nodded at members of the group, turned to walk brusquely towards the stairs. Simone was right beside her.

'It's so good of you to make a little time for me. I know how busy you must be.' Simone kept her voice loud, chattered inanely all the way to Karolina's office, slipped in before her.

Karolina closed the door and leaned heavily against it. Her breath was audible. 'What do you want? What on earth do you want?'

'Just a little of your time,' Simone said sweetly. She deposited her packages with a thump on the laden desk.

'I don't have any time.'

'You'll make some.' Simone started to pace from desk to window to filing cabinet. Above the desk, she noticed, there was a picture of a dour President Gottwald. She stopped and stared at it, then turned on Karolina.

'You remember you told me I would be Staszek's ruin? You remember, don't you? So I left. Left him to your mercies, your marriage bed.' A strangled laugh rose to her throat. 'And then what? Arrest, torture. And now he's dead. Dead, do you hear?' She was shaking Karolina by the shoulders. She hadn't known she was shaking her and she stopped now. There were odd red blotches on the woman's face. Simone stared at her, lowered her voice from its scream. 'I want to know exactly what happened to Staszek. I want to know when you started sleeping with him. I want to know how you coerced him to get rid of me. You denounced him, didn't you? To save your own thick, ugly skin. Your old comrade. Your husband.'

The woman slapped her hard across the face, looked at her as if she were a dog in need of discipline, some stubborn peasant ripe for re-education.

'Someone should have done that to you long ago,' she hissed. 'Now get out of here. You're demented. And Staszek . . . Staszek was a coward. And a traitor. Yes.' Her eyes reached for some distant horizon that could provide confirmation of her words. 'A traitor. A saboteur.' She looked back at Simone, her face contorted with hatred. 'I should have known it was too late for him after you had got your selfish, sticky paws on him. Now, out.'

Karolina opened the door and with an imperious gesture pointed Simone towards it.

'Not that easy.' Simone moved in the opposite direction, slid into the chair behind the desk.

'Right. If you won't go of your own accord, I'll get someone to make you. You won't like that.' She laughed harshly as she turned, strode heavily down the corridor, each of her angry steps clearly audible.

Simone looked at the empty space where Karolina had been and then down at the desk in front of her. There was some kind of map there, photographs of fields and railway lines and wooden cabins taken from the air, an assortment of papers. In a trance which seemed to float above her rage, she picked these up and folded them into her bag, tucked the larger ones beneath her coat. For good measure she pulled open one of the cabinets and randomly picked out some files. With the calm gestures of a sleepwalker, she walked out of the door and down the stairs, a smile plastered on her face for the benefit of passers-by. Outside she quickened her pace, leapt onto a tram which took her back to the hotel. She packed hastily, addressed some letters. There was a night train she could catch. Better that than the morning train she was scheduled to be on. She didn't want to spend another minute in the city.

The building where Simone had last seen Karolina was now covered in scaffolding and plastic sheets. A tasteful sign in blue and yellow announced the soon-to-be-opened offices of a Japanese computer firm. Simone took a deep breath and peered through the open doors. Tins of paint lined the lobby. A man in overalls stood atop a rickety ladder and wielded a dripping brush. He shouted something at her. As she turned away a flash startled her. She slipped on the step, fell to the ground.

'Sorry, sorry.' A man was standing beside her, helping her up. A camera drooped from his neck. 'Very sorry,' he said, his Rs lilting into Ls. 'You okay, now?'

Simone leaned heavily on his arm, felt pain whip through creaking limbs. 'Yes. Thank you. I lost my balance.' She tried to turn her wince into a smile.

He smiled back, bowed. 'I help you. You have car?' He walked down the hill with her until, feeling her legs grow steadier, she urged him away. Beneath the cover of her coat, she rubbed her thighs and flinched. Coffee. That was what she needed. Across the street she spied one of those new pine and whitewashed cafés.

Gratefully she sank into a pink-bolstered chair, treated herself to apple cake and milky coffee.

She had needed to fall, Simone told herself. To feel something of the pain that had impelled her towards her next act of treachery. Unplanned, yet somehow inevitable.

She had got on the train that night, had dozed fitfully while it clattered and clanked its way through darkened countryside. At the German border, she had been woken by guards. They scrutinized her passport, examined her face with steely eyes. Then they had gestured towards her suitcase. She had unlocked it for them.

Right at the top lay the files and photos and maps she had taken from Karolina's desk. These they scanned with darkening faces.

'What are these?' the taller one asked.

'I have no idea,' Simone said truthfully. She found herself batting her eyelashes, behaving like a flighty, flirtatious girl. 'A friend asked me to take them to Paris. So, of course, I said yes.'

'Who was the friend?' the smaller one quizzed her. He had thick, ruddy eyelashes which met above his nose.

'I don't want to get her into trouble,' Simone demurred.

'You're in trouble,' the taller one said. He poked his

finger at the stamp of the Ministry of Transport and exchanged glances with his partner. Within a second, they had all but lifted her from her seat and marched her and her suitcase off the train.

'But . . .' She allowed herself an astonished laugh. 'You don't think I'm a spy, do you? Would a spy be so stupid as to carry papers at the very top of a suitcase?'

They didn't answer. They simply tightened their grip on her arms and half carried her towards the end of the station platform. Here she was unceremoniously thrust into a cell, with bare stone walls and a recess which served for a bench. The heavy bars of the door clanged and shook as they shut. Her suitcase went with the guards. She could see them walking off with it, could see the train chug away moments later. And then there was only night and cold and a single station lamp illuminating an abandoned cattle car.

She shivered in the damp cold, but she didn't allow herself to be afraid. She thought of Staszek, whose cell wouldn't have allowed a view, and gripped the bars and shook them and waited. Some forty minutes passed and then a small man in a thick grey coat appeared beside the taller guard. He had a thin, pointed face, stubbled with that morning's beard. Rounded specs sat astride his nose, half masking watery blue eyes. His hands moved continuously as he talked.

'Simone Lalande Debray?'

'Yes.' Simone stood to attention, examined the scrapes and scratches on the stone floor.

'Born Paris, 1926. Married Prague, 1947, to Stanislaw Mánes. Divorced 1950. Remarried Paris, 1951. Husband, Michel François Debray, Head of Division, French Ministry of Foreign Affairs. Two children.'

'Correct.' Simone hid her sudden desire to laugh.

'Purpose of visit to Prague?'

'I was part of a delegation from the French Communist Party.'

The man grunted. 'And these papers found in your case? Who gave them to you?'

Simone hesitated, met the eyes of the uniformed guard, cleared her throat. 'Karolina Dostolova,' she murmured.

The guard noted the name.

'Address?'

She eyed the ground. 'I saw her at the Ministry of Transport. But . . . She's an old acquaintance.'

The men exchanged glances.

'I don't want . . .'

'We are not interested in what you want,' the man barked. 'Destination of the papers?'

'Karolina asked that I give them to . . .' she paused, 'what was his name, now? I wrote it down somewhere, maybe in my case. Oh, yes. Dr Osustky. Stefan Osustky.' She named the man who had headed up a Czech exile government. 'I don't know him, but she said he was a friend.'

With a sudden expression of greed, the small man passed his tongue over his lips.

'But, look,' Simone hurried on. 'You can keep it all. I don't care. I was just doing Karolina a favour. And I have to get home to my children. I have to get on the next train. You can phone the French Embassy in Prague. Monsieur Roland. He'll vouch for me. Or the ambassador himself, though it would be silly to disturb Yves on such a minor matter.'

The two men walked away without a word.

Simone sat in the cell and waited. She told herself that these were minor officials, that they would be impressed by the names she had dropped. That she herself was not worth starting an international incident over. That they had what they wanted. That it might even earn them a promotion. She allowed herself a moment's tingle of delight over the trouble she would cause Karolina. She could sniff the fear gathering in Karolina's armpits as she noticed the missing papers, as her superior called her in. She didn't want to think any further than that. But as the long night merged into a grey dawn and the birds began their song and still no one had come to unlock her cell door, Simone began to think that she had perhaps over-reached herself.

It was only when the distant roar of a morning train had already begun to make itself felt in the rattling door of her cell that two new guards appeared and released her. She was handed her passport and her suitcase and without a word bundled onto the train. By the time she reached Paris, she was calm. The desire for vengeance that had obsessed her for so long had burnt itself out in the action of those last days.

Simone took a long puff of her cigarette and sipped the coffee in its white Swedish mug. Over the next years, she reflected, she had buried the Staszek of life and limb and kisses and gesture, buried her first love, deep in the recesses of her mind. He grew diffuse, depersonalized, became a kind of fuelling energy for the entirety of her life's work, as if she had to live for two, but the other, the lost one, could never be named.

She also buried Karolina, though it was not until later that she learned she had helped to bury her in fact as well as mind. Of this she was deeply ashamed. Infuriated by Karolina's stolid condemnation of Staszek, her lack of grief, her denial of any ordinary emotion, Simone had ended up by using the tactics of the regime itself. Trapped in the logic of vengeance, her own messy bundle of jealousy and spite had translated itself into an act which was equivalent to that of the everyday informer or Party hack. She didn't altogether forgive herself, but she forgot. Forgot conveniently until her nose was rubbed in the mud and she herself was threatened with disgrace.

It was an exemplary tale, Simone told herself with grim self-derision as she stubbed out her cigarette. A very modern tale which had countless parallels in Eastern

Europe, though hers had in part played itself out in the West. It was too bad that she was one of its actors and now felt impelled to tell it and suffer its shame.

At five o'clock, as promised, Simone made her way to the mezzanine of the hotel where the congress delegates were gathering for drinks. She had taken a rest that afternoon to gather her strength. A long soak in a fragrant bath had eased some of the pain of her fall. And she had dressed carefully, cast aside a grey dress for the emphatic bottle green of her favourite Chanel suit. She didn't want to shock him with the signs of her age.

The room was bright with low shafts of late afternoon sun. They slanted across the burgundy carpet, lit faces with an inquisitorial beam, bounced off the silver trays and sparkling glass of the long buffet table. In a far corner, the harsher glare of television spots created a makeshift studio.

Pausing at the door, Simone reflected that she would have preferred a kinder setting. She walked slowly into the crowd and looked for Stephen.

Before she could find him, a voice accosted her.

'Simone. Well, what about that!'

Simone turned to find Ted Knight striding towards her. He was wearing his charming, inane smile above a fashionably collarless shirt and a roomy suit.

'I didn't expect to see you in Prague.'

'I was hardly expecting to see you either.'

'Oh?' His eyes glinted. A muscle played in his cheek. 'I'd hoped that just maybe . . .'

'Don't flatter yourself, Edward.' Simone muted the spikiness in her tone with a soft laugh. 'I haven't come for you.'

He kissed her cheek familiarly, his large hand resting on her shoulder. 'What, then? I didn't know you were interested in this lot.' He waved towards the room.

'Stephen Caldwell invited me.' She watched his face carefully. The muscle had started its work again.

'I didn't realize you two knew each other.'

'You can't know everything, Ted. For all your sharp eyes. Now I really must find Stephen.' She pulled away from him, but he was right at her heels.

'Anything else you want to tell me? You're not going to do anything foolish, Simone?' His voice was low in her ear, a tense whisper with a hint of menace.

She steadied her eyes and met his with a challenge. 'Not by my reckoning, no. But, look, there's Stephen now.'

Stephen waved her towards his little group, introduced her. She half caught a mixture of German, Italian and Slav names, scientists, journalists, a philosopher.

A man with a double chin and red striped braces was enthusing about the breeding of superplants which contained all necessary proteins and amino acids – a vital food supplement to indigenous crops for the poorer nations. A woman with an Italian accent protested. This was simply colonialism by another name – a genetic colonialism which would make the poorer nations dependent on the rich in a new way.

'Living beings are not merely survival machines,' a bearded man intervened. 'Life cannot be transformed into a mechanical order, a question of arithmetic in which low-priced fodder is converted into high-priced flesh. Cows are . . .'

A second woman interrupted, a teasing expression on her face. 'You Germans are so sensitive. You worry so much. Not all science is Nazi science. What do you say, Dr Caldwell?' She turned towards Stephen. 'You know Gino Salvatore here is doing a piece for *La Repubblica* on ethics. How heavily should we scientists be regulated? Do we need restraints?'

'I don't like talking to journalists,' Stephen grinned, but his eyes were serious. 'It's curious. But no matter how boring and ordinarily sensible real scientists in fact are, the media somehow manages to transform us into holy saviours or dangerous Dr Frankensteins poised to unleash terror on the world. Or, at best, uncontrollable boys toying with powerful chemistry sets.' He laughed. 'I'm afraid I've just intimated that to the cameras, amongst more important matters.'

'You're not gonna tell me you guys are just like everyone else!' Ted exclaimed.

'I'm afraid so. We're just as exposed to social forces as anyone else and we're shaped by them. With very few exceptions, we function within the usual moral, political and financial constraints. At my end of the scientific wood, as you know too well, Ted, the financial usually dominates. Governments or private companies decide what research is to be invested in. At best, social need with a sprinkling of fashion combines with market interest. But that's enough of that.'

He took Simone by the arm and led her away. Ted was right beside them. 'Simone has just told me you're old friends.'

Stephen looked in surprise from Ted to Simone. 'We are that. But I didn't realize you two knew each other.'

'Simone knows everyone.' Ted draped his arm familiarly over her shoulder and chuckled.

She shrugged him off. 'That is praise from you, Ted. I gather you're here to do some of your high-powered shopping, the kind that leaves our poorer countries bereft of their best.'

Stephen caught the note of tension beneath the lightness in her voice. 'Shall we find Jan, Simone? And Ted, I really should introduce you to Slava Aronovitch.'

'Not now, thanks.'

'Look, there's Jan over by the buffet.'

'Leave us, Ted.' Simone steadied herself, tried to shake off Ted's eyes which seared and followed her. She walked slowly at Stephen's side, letting him manoeuvre her round clusters of people. Only when she could see the white of the tablecloth, and against it a pair of grey trousers, did she let her gaze rise slowly. She noted a jacket, a lean, long-fingered hand, a yellow print tie, obviously chosen by a woman, and then his face. He was half turned towards the table and examining parcels of salami and heaped crudités as if they were intruders from a foreign planet. The freshness had gone from his skin, but the wry intelligence was still there, more pronounced now, etched in lines round eyes and lips, the nose somehow bolder, the hair strewn with grey here and there.

She took a deep breath as he turned towards her. The eyes. She had forgotten the wonderful clarity of the eyes.

'Simone.' He grasped her hand in both of his, lifted it to his lips. 'You'll permit me,' he said in Czech. 'It's been so long.'

'Better not to dwell on the years,' Simone murmured.

'Let me look at you.' He held her shoulders and scrutinized her and smiled. 'Beautiful. Still as gloriously beautiful as our long-ago spring. It must be the Paris air. The air of liberty. Or your particular genius,' he added in French.

Ted leapt in, understanding this last. 'Now, Jan, you mustn't go falling in love with Simone. Her particular genius is to treat men as a superior form of entertainment. Am I right, Simone?'

'I do not find you very entertaining at the moment, Ted. I would really rather you left us. Jan and I have a lot of catching up to do.'

Ted's face darkened. Before he could protest, Stephen intervened. 'There's Professor Aronovitch. Let me introduce you to him now.' He drew Ted away.

Simone watched them for a moment. 'That man is dangerous, Jan. Don't let yourself be charmed by him. I was once and I have regretted it ever since.'

'Oh?'

'But let's not talk of that now.' She gave herself a little

shake. 'I want to know everything about you. I have neglected you for too long.'

'I think so, too.' He wrapped her arm through his.

'For very bad reasons.' She met his eyes, wondered at the fact that she was here. With him.

'No, no. For very good reasons. I was so stupidly young. So gauche, as you say.'

'Not that, Jan. Never that. I'll explain it to you. But perhaps not tonight. Tonight I want to get to know you all over again.'

PART THREE

15

———*———

Change in a relationship is a peculiar process. You can never quite chart all the big and little things, all the external circumstances and subliminal impulses that bring it about.

If anyone had said to Tessa three days ago that on this grey Thursday morning she would wish for nothing more than that Ted's attention should momentarily find another object, she would adamantly have denied it. Yet as she stood at the arched doors of St Agnes's Convent and felt the full force of his eyes on her back, she wished just that.

With a flinch of irritation, she turned to wave a second goodbye and hurried into the cavernous quiet of the building.

Timing. The two parts of a couple rarely seemed to want or need the same things at the same time. Then, too, she didn't understand this new jealous vigilance of Ted's. It had become the tenor of their relations ever since he had found out she was Mrs Stephen Caldwell. Yesterday morning, he had decided they had to move hotels and now they were ensconced between spires and domes at the Pariz, their breakfast lit by beautiful chandeliers. Later, despite her protests, he had insisted on personally depositing her at the National Museum and had more or less demanded a detailed itinerary from her. She hadn't followed it, of course. What she did with her days was her own business.

The process had been repeated this morning for St Agnes's Convent.

Maybe, Tessa thought as she purchased a museum ticket, now that Ted knew her husband was someone he admired, his combative instincts had simply come to the fore. He was afraid she would give him up for Stephen before he was quite ready to give her up. Certainly his passion for her seemed to have trebled. Today she felt exhausted by the adventures of the night, her legs shaky as she pretended to look at pictures. It was odd, too, that this should make her plaintive.

There were men like that, she supposed. Men whose passion was competitive and inspired by the near presence of another man. But somehow she didn't feel Ted was altogether like that. There were other things. She still hadn't discovered how he had found out about Stephen. The whole business made her uneasy. And Ted was so much moodier now, as if the fact that they had made unprotected love rattled him. It rattled her too, if she was honest with herself.

It was odd, given that she had so much wanted it, had dreamt of little else since she had met him. But no sooner had her dream come true than she found herself trying to imagine an ordinary daily life with Ted. She realized she couldn't. And what of Stephen? Everything had grown so confusing. The bubble she had climbed and soared in had suddenly burst in mid-air.

Tessa clenched her fist and forced herself to look at the painting in front of her. It showed a peasant family in a dark interior. A white-kerchiefed mother ladled something out of a copper pot on an open hearth. A fat toddler played at her feet. A tabby cat curled beneath a rickety chair. At the door, a thick-set man was removing his jacket. Tessa stared at the child.

That was it, of course. Amy had displaced all her more nebulous wishes. A real child, whose presence in her mind was far sharper, more precise than the notion of any seed that might germinate inside her. She didn't dare say that to Ted. He was so against the idea of adoption.

Yesterday, after he had dropped her off at the museum, she had waited ten minutes and then taken a taxi to the British Embassy. She wanted to investigate the mechanics of adoption and she needed to talk to someone about that. They had told her she needed an appointment, but she had insisted there wasn't time. So she had waited. One hour, two, three, before she was at last allowed to see some minor official.

He was a young man with a thin face and neatly parted hair, and she knew from the public-school reek of him, the slight disdain of the lips, that he would hardly make things easy. No sooner had she breathed the word 'adoption' than he began to treat her like a menopausal biddy whose grey matter had gone decidedly soft and slightly rancid. It was as if the very notion of adopting a foreign child was tantamount to opening the flood gates and inviting in a sea of alien invaders. Definitely something to be frowned upon, something unclean and to be avoided at all costs. Despite the difference of tone and gesture, he had reminded her of Ted.

He had told her in no uncertain terms that nothing could be done from this end. She must return to Britain and put in her application with her local council. They would investigate her. The social workers would investigate her. It would take, oh, at least six months before a report came through. She would also need medical certificates and marriage certificates – she was married, he presumed? He said it as if that notion, too, filled him with distaste, then hastened to add that all this applied to her husband as well as herself. Criminal records, bank accounts, financial status, would have to be checked. And character references supplied.

All that before one confronted a single nappy, Tessa had thought to herself. She wanted to say it aloud, wanted to ask that singularly self-important young man whether a mother had ever changed his, but she kept her mouth shut, nodded politely and left. Only after she had done so did it come to her that he had not once met her eyes.

She felt slightly battered, as if he had whipped her with words and behind each one stood the weight of a mountain of official forms and procedures. She wandered through the narrow streets beneath the castle, knowing that she was probably lost and not particularly caring. She wished for a moment that Stephen was with her, Stephen who knew how to talk to bumptious officials, whoever it was he cared to sleep with. Then the careful parting in the young man's hair appeared before her again, the hint of a stubborn slick. She couldn't allow herself to be beaten by that, she thought ruefully. She straightened her shoulders, found the Charles Bridge and walked emphatically across into more familiar territory.

It had been too late to go to the orphanage, so instead she had dropped in on Rachel Witzmanova. She was sitting with her feet up on her desk and she grinned and didn't bother to put them down when she saw Tessa.

'Come to pay your debts?'

Tessa nodded. 'And to get your advice.' She realized as she said it that something about Rachel made her feel safe, imbued her with confidence.

By the time she had finished telling Rachel about her experience with the Embassy official, they were sitting in a dilapidated bar and Rachel had flung back a tiny glass of some potent concoction and ordered her to do the same.

'Pah! All alike, these red-tapers. You should go and talk to a friend of mine. A lawyer. He's relatively honest, but he knows how to fix things. And I know he's not one of those who would snatch a baby from its mother's womb.' She stuck her stomach into the air and made a snipping gesture.

'What! What do you mean?' Tessa was shocked.

'You know. Like those baby thieves in Paraguay. They make millions. Everyone except the mamas.'

'Oh.' Guilt hovered over her. She urged it away. 'But if the mothers want to give the children up for adoption?'

Rachel shrugged. 'Okay then. Why not? A better life.'

'Will you come with me to see your friend?'

'You can't afford me, I told you already.' Rachel winked. 'And at this rate, I can't afford you. I'll phone him for you. Tomorrow.'

Tessa stood at the doors of the convent and scoured grounds and street just in case Ted was still lurking. No sign. She walked quickly through the gates. Later today she would go and see Rachel, but first she must visit Amy. Her heart started up a rapid patter.

The orphanage looked more propitious today. Pale sunshine glinted over snow. Dirt and rubble wore a feathery cloak. In the courtyard a group of children played, their voices muted, but not unfriendly. They all wore blue, the boys overalls and the girls knee-length skirts above thick woollen socks. Their jackets had seen better days. As she walked past them, they stopped their play to watch her. One of the boys put out a begging hand and retracted it quickly when a woman wearing a nun's wimple approached. Beneath its white, she was black and she smiled sweetly at Tessa. Tessa smiled back, didn't attempt language.

She made her way past the holly bush and into the little building where Amy was housed. She had brought something with her today, a wooden rattle with a shiny red bead at its centre, and she dug it out of her bag and showed it proudly to the nun who came to greet her.

The woman looked at her askance and started to chatter away incomprehensibly. She shook her head, made odd gestures. It took Tessa a few minutes to understand what she didn't want to know. Amy was gone. Where? Tears sprang into her eyes. She tried to make herself understood, said 'where' in all the languages she could summon, '*où?*', '*dove?*', '*wohin?*', finally remembered her phrase book and brought out, '*kde je?*'

Again the woman shook her head. Either she didn't know or wouldn't tell her. She pointed her towards the main building. Tessa didn't go. There was no point. If she was to find out anything, she would have to come back with Rachel. But there was probably no point to that either. Amy had been returned to her mother. Her real mother.

By the time she reached the street, Tessa's vision was blurred with loss. She felt emptied out, desolate, as hollow as if she had suffered a death. Amy's little face rose up before her with its dark-eyed trust, and obliterated houses and people and traffic. She saw only that steady, sorrowful gaze; those tiny hands with their surprising grip.

She didn't quite know how she arrived at the hotel, but suddenly she was there amidst marble and mosaic and she heard her voice asking for her room key.

'Ah yes, Madame Hughes. There is an urgent message for you.' The receptionist placed a piece of paper in her hand. 'The police. I'm afraid it is the police.' The woman gave her a look of avid curiosity.

Tessa scanned the note. 'Attend Vyšehradská Police Station. Two o'clock.' She glanced at her watch. She had five minutes to get there. Her heart lifted. Amy. Perhaps they had Amy.

The station clock showed fifteen minutes past the hour. Tessa steadied her voice as she addressed the young policeman she had met two days before with Rachel. He made no sign of recognizing her. Instead, after she had pronounced her name slowly three times, his face lit up. '*Ano, ano.* Yes, yes.' He picked up the telephone and blurted something down the line, then led her into a back room.

Seated on a long wooden bench was Jan Martin. He rose as she came in, an ironical lilt to his features. 'Your interpreter has preceded you, Miss Hughes.' He stretched out his hand. 'I have spent more time with the police in these last few days than I have for over a decade.' He smiled. 'In the interim, I have worked hard to stay out of their way.'

'I'm so sorry. So sorry to have put you to all this trouble.'

'No, no. It is an experience for me. I have rarely been in a station as a helper before.' He winked at her, then studied her face more seriously. 'You are not well. You are troubled.'

She didn't have time to answer. The officer she recognized from her first visit had just come into the room together with the policewoman. They were both in uniform today. He nodded at them and gestured them out of the room. They followed him through a dank, airless corridor, through a vast, bolted door, down a series of narrow concrete steps. The walls here were made of large stone which crumbled moistly to the touch.

Tessa was suddenly filled with foreboding. No place for a baby here. She gripped her bag and held it to her like a talisman.

At the bottom of the steps, the man unlocked a second heavy door and ushered them in ahead of him. Cells bordered one side of the long rectangular room, their bars as heavy and forbidding as those of a medieval dungeon. There was a persistent sound of rustling, like rats, Tessa thought nervously, and the drip, drip, drip of water.

From one of the cells on the left a lone prisoner stared out at them. His face was a mass of bloated veins and jagged teeth. Gnarled hands gripped bars. He called out something. Tessa jumped, turned towards Jan. He shook his head, put a steadying hand on her shoulder.

In the last of the series of cells, two women sat on scruffy, uncovered mattresses. One of them rose as the officer called a name. It was the woman from the church. She was wearing the same faded, flowery dress. A tangle of long electric hair spilled over her face. Seeing Tessa, she started to shriek, hurl what could only be imprecations. She spat, pointed, as if Tessa were the accused in an identity parade.

Tessa began to tremble. The woman's rage seemed to swallow her balance. She leaned against Jan for support.

'What is she saying?' she murmured, her voice echoing oddly against stone walls.

Jan didn't answer immediately. Instead he addressed the officer and as he did so the woman stopped her diatribe. She followed their movements warily with slate-dark eyes. As the men walked out of her line of vision, a new nervousness invaded her face, a tiny tremor at the lip. With a furtive motion, she wiped beads of perspiration from her brow and rubbed her palms on her skirt.

Tessa was suddenly engulfed by a wave of compassion. If she had known how, she would have tried to console her.

Perhaps the woman sensed it, for she suddenly threw a rough woollen sweater over her shoulders with such regal aplomb that it called forth a rich floral shawl. She began to pace, her shoulders and colour high, her demeanour so dramatic that the sordid cell took on an operatic aura. The woman had a strong vital beauty, Tessa thought, a physical pride which made her feel shadowy, somehow ashamed.

'Apparently they picked her up at the orphanage, who phoned the police station.' Jan was addressing her in muted tones. 'Somehow she found out the baby was there. Now she claims that you stole her, walked off with the baby when she had only asked you to hold her for a moment.'

Tessa gazed at him in incomprehension. 'But that's not true. I waited for her to come back. Waited for over an hour. It's not true. Not true.'

Tears bit at her eyes and for a moment, as she glanced from Jan to the suspicious face of the officer to the woman, she felt that perhaps it was she who wasn't telling the truth, that she had indeed walked off with Amy, whatever her protests. Her thoughts were askew. Could she have acted on her fantasies? Had this woman unearthed them? She did want Amy. That one thing was clear to her. But so it now seemed did her mother. A sob escaped her.

She felt Jan's arm round her shoulders again, calming her. She had to hold onto the facts, cross the tightrope which separated the real from the imaginary. 'It's not true,' she protested again. 'I didn't steal. I came to the police. I . . .'

'It's all right.' Jan was speaking. 'The police do not believe her. She had more money on her than she ought to have had in the normal course of things. And she has no papers. That is serious. But the police have to make certain. That is why we are here.'

'How will they make certain? I have no proof. There was an old man. But no one understands me. It was all a misunderstanding.'

The woman was screaming again, pointing at her, skewing her thoughts, saying horrible things. She knew they were horrible.

'I don't want anything bad to happen to the baby. That poor mite.' Tessa was blubbering. She reached in her bag for a tissue and her passport fell out. Small, red, insignificant, but for a moment everyone in the room stared at it in silence. She picked it up hastily, aware of the flicker of envy in the woman's eyes.

'Don't worry. We will sort it out.' Jan patted her on the shoulder, drew the officer off to the side again.

Tessa stood there, wishing she could sit down, wishing she could speak logically, coolly, for herself. For the first time in her life she had the distinct knowledge of what it might mean to be robbed of the power of language. She felt the woman's eyes on her bag again. Yes, that too. What if, on top of everything, she didn't possess that small document which gave one a place in the world, a status and identity which went far beyond any individual attributes or even wealth?

'Do you want to press charges?' Jan was at her side again.

'Charges? For what?'

He shrugged. 'For ... how do you say ... bearing false witness. Accusing you wrongly. Her name, by the way, is Prohasky.'

'No. No. Of course not. I just ... I just want Amy, the baby I mean, to be safe.'

He nodded. 'I think you will need to sign some forms. Upstairs.' He left her again, and despite herself she looked up to meet the woman's eyes.

She was silent now, her expression dejected. Perhaps she knew she had lost, Tessa thought. She wanted to tell her it wasn't a loss. She wanted to take her aside and say that her little girl was beautiful, precious. But she already knew that. She had come for Amy, after all. Maybe she really had convinced herself that Tessa had stolen the child away. Maybe she had wilfully forgotten her own act, just as Tessa had begun for a moment to believe that she had no clear grasp of where the truth lay.

'Come.' Jan led her towards the door. 'They only want you to sign some papers saying this was the woman you saw in the church and who handed you the baby.'

Tessa looked back one more time. She wished there was a way of communicating what she felt to the woman. A way of telling her that the loss was all Tessa's. But she had begun to shriek at her again, her voice so resonant against the stone walls that for a long time after the door of the room had closed behind them, Tessa could hear her curses.

They sat in a nearby café, all white tablecloths and women curling amongst ferns in pastel posters.

'I'm sorry to have put you through all this. To be taking so much of your time,' Tessa was apologizing.

'It is not a problem. You are distressed.'

'I really didn't steal the child, you know. I think, well,

maybe her mother changed her mind. She couldn't bear giving her away.'

'Or perhaps she changed her mind for the sake of the police. We buy and sell most things now. But we have not yet reached the point of buying and selling babies. That is still illegal.'

Tessa looked at him askance. 'I'm so worried. What will happen to her? And the baby? I feel responsible somehow.'

'Why?' Jan examined her with his intent clarity. 'You think you provoked her into doing something stupid? By the very fact that you happened to be in the church at that time? And because you are rich and fortunate.'

'I'm not . . .'

'In her eyes.'

'Perhaps. But what will they do to her? They won't keep her under arrest, will they?'

'I do not think so. It is too complicated and these days we prefer fewer complications. You have not pressed charges. They will probably just let her go. Or send her back to her country.'

'How terrible!' Tessa scrunched up her paper napkin. 'I would have happily adopted that baby, you know.' She paused. 'Do you think the woman will do the same thing again? Try to get rid of her?'

'You would adopt her?' Jan repeated inanely. 'Why? Because you feel responsible?'

'Yes. No. I don't know.' She looked up at the window. There was a man gazing in. He had a pale, slightly crooked face with vast eyes. He looked hungry.

'You English. You have such a complicated sense of morality. I told you before. I do not understand it. Myself, I don't think this woman is your responsibility.'

'No. Perhaps not. But the child . . .'

'You know, Tessa,' he suddenly turned a fatherly air on her, 'it is not nothing to adopt a child. It is not a matter of impulse. Or even perhaps morality.'

'I know.' Her smile wavered, uncertain of itself. 'It is something I have thought about before.'

'I see.' Jan was gazing at her in a way that made her uncomfortable.

Tessa began to gather her things, thanked him again for his kindness. She left quickly. She had the distinct impression that if she said any more, he would soon reach the certain decision that she had indeed tried to steal poor little Amy.

It was growing dark, the sky a low charcoal mass. People bustled homeward. She would go home, too, Tessa thought, if she had a home to go to here. She didn't want to see Ted. Not now. She didn't have the energy for him.

Suddenly she missed Stephen, the Stephen of the old days, to whom she could have recounted her story and who would have trusted her implicitly. And comforted her. He might not be good at other things, Stephen. But he was good at comforting.

Yet what would he have done if she had come home with Amy? That's what she ought to have done, of course. On that very first day. Straight from the church where Amy had been handed to her. For that was indeed what had happened. Amy had been abandoned and paid for. She should have taken the child back to the hotel, found a large hamper, given her a sleeping pill and caught the first train home. They didn't have those screening machines on trains, did they?

But she could no sooner have done that than she could have handed her own child over the way that wild woman had done, Tessa acknowledged. She didn't know how to break the law. It wasn't a question of rules particularly, she had simply never been driven to it. Nor was she any good at the irrational, the turbulent, unthinking gesture. Never had been. Maybe she was just too English, too middle-class, too scared for that.

Once, though, after her miscarriage, she had felt it, everything slipping out of control, her life flowing away with her blood, her baby. She had wept unstoppably. Terrible visions had taken her over: her own body floating Ophelia-like in a stream, trailing a dead baby by an umbilical cord. She didn't like to think of it any more. She could easily then have slipped under the surface of the bath water or taken the kitchen knife to her wrists. Stephen must have known that. He hadn't let her out of his sight. He had comforted her. He had been sweet then, had even eventually rung her mother to have her come and stay, had brought home that large and clumsy-footed bundle whom they had named Paws.

But his explanation for everything was hormones. It was the hormones, he said, their disappearance, which were responsible for her state. Yet the knowledge that there was some secret invisible substance to blame for things made them none the easier to bear.

Tessa looked up from the slush on the pavement and stopped her steps. The windowless bulk of St Cyril's loomed before her. Had she intended to come here? Her feet must have, she conceded. With a shiver, she walked up the short flight of stairs and pushed open the heavy door.

Incense wafted into her nostrils, more intense than it had been on that first visit. An elderly man with a long, full beard and a cassock nodded at her, then returned to his arranging of chairs. Perhaps there had been a service. But now everyone was gone and once again she had the impression of a vast echoing chamber where she could hear her own breathing returned to her from the distant dome. On tiptoe she walked down the nave and found a chair half-hidden behind columns. She perched on it and gazed towards the sanctuary.

This is where she had been sitting when Amy had been thrust into her arms. Tessa relived the scene: the voice hailing her from behind, the money handed over and then the child passed in return, left there in Tessa's arms. A sob shook her. She hastened to muffle it with her hand, caught the patriarch looking at her. She tried to give him an even glance. He nodded and disappeared through one of the openings in the iconostasis.

Tessa would have liked to pray but she didn't know quite how to any more. It had been so long since she had imagined a god. Then he had resembled Santa Claus with a slightly less ruddy face. She could address some invisible force, perhaps, some universal fixer who might so arrange chance as to bring Amy back to her. Or, if not that, at least make her well and sound and not too terribly unhappy.

A loud creak at the door obliterated her thoughts. She sat up straighter. A man had come into the church. He looked round furtively, then walked in her direction. Tessa averted her eyes, heard only the echo of footsteps on stone. They stopped beside her. A chair scraped. A halting voice began to murmur. English. Broken. Ungrammatical. Addressing her.

'Lady. You good lady. I watch. Watch today. Watch other day.'

Tessa looked up into a bony dark face, the eyes too large beneath the straggle of overlong hair. She had seen that face somewhere. But it was the voice that mesmerized her.

'You want baby, lady. My cousin, she no want baby. Want baby have good home. West home. She talk lie for police. We give baby you, good lady. For money.' He held up five long, skinny fingers. 'Five thousand. Dollar. Okay, lady? Need money.'

Tessa stared at him speechlessly, sniffed stale breath, sweat, felt her arm gripped. She pulled back, suddenly afraid of that skeletal face with its long slash of a mouth.

'Okay, lady?' He gripped her harder. 'You want baby. You bring money. Cash money. When?'

Suddenly he veered round, his face as alert as a startled night creature's. He dropped her arm. From the front of the church, Tessa saw the priest emerge.

'Okay, address,' he muttered. He thrust a piece of grubby paper at her. 'You come.'

Before she could say anything, he was at the front of the church, crossing himself, nodding at the priest. And then she heard the creak of the door.

The piece of paper lay crumpled in her hand. It was warm. She smoothed it out and gazed at large, childlike printing.

'Amy,' she thought. 'Amy.'

16

——✽——

'Stephen. My apologies. I am so late.' Jan Martin closed the door of his office behind him and strode over to embrace Stephen.

'Have you been with Simone?'

'No, no, nothing quite so amusing. I have been with the police. But I'll tell you about that later. We have so much to get through.' He gestured towards his desk which was covered in sheets of paper bearing his small, neat writing. 'And so little time. I promised to help Eva with her maths this evening and later, there is Simone . . .' He raked his hand through his hair and didn't offer his customary smile.

Stephen was struck by how fraught his friend looked. His face was peaked, his eyes red-rimmed as if he hadn't slept for days. His shirt needed a wash. It occurred to him that Jan might not have gone home last night after their dinner with Simone, indeed perhaps no longer had a home worth going to. He hadn't yet seen where Jan now lived. He wondered whether there was a new woman in his life.

'Should we give it a miss, Jan? We can take some time off from the congress in the morning. Turn up only for the round table.'

'Play truant, as you say. Is that permitted, for the convener? Yes. Why not, just after the opening words. An excellent idea.' His face lit. 'But we could make a start. You have given me a whole banquetful of new problems. No, no, don't look unhappy. They are exciting problems.'

'I'll postpone my departure for a day or two.'

'Wonderful.'

'By the way, I took the liberty of using your phone for a few calls abroad. I had to speak to the lawyers, the office.'

Stephen rifled through his case for some papers and looked out of the window for a moment. He could feel Jan's eyes on his back.

'Any news about our beautiful Russian thief?' he asked softly.

'I got hold of her friend, Natalya, at last. She claims she was away on holiday and was as surprised as I was to find Ariane gone on her return. She's worried. She thinks Ariane is trying to keep one step ahead of her brother's Mafia pursuers.' Stephen straightened his tie nervously. 'I don't know any more, Jan. Maybe I've just imagined the whole thing.'

'I've never known you to be a fantasist.' Jan looked at him shrewdly.

'But Ariane . . . It's not like her.'

'Except perhaps about women.' Jan's smile teased. 'Ariane, from my short encounter with her, struck me as above all what we now call an excellent business woman.'

'Maybe.' Stephen felt the gloom, which in these last days seemed to wait for him around every corner, descend on him again. 'The trouble is, only time will tell.'

'And that is what we have least of. So we had better make ourselves busy. Come, I have made a schedule. Today we can concentrate on the basic equipment the Institute will need even to begin to replicate your research so far. Then tomorrow we can work on the technical side, look into the specific chromium compounds your protein can mop up. Which will only leave the plans for the trials. Luckily we have no shortage of rats. Or of cancer patients.' A frown creased his brow. He shook it away with an effort. 'I guess we'll want to wrap the protein in a liposome to inject it?'

Stephen nodded. 'And we'll have to monitor the level of chromium toxicity in the rats carefully.'

Work took them over, pages of lists, until Stephen, glancing at his watch, protested that it really was time for Eva.

'Yes, yes.' Jan leapt up guiltily. 'Now let me see. Somewhere here I have a fresh shirt, even perhaps a tie.' He pulled open a cabinet drawer and gave Stephen a wry glance. 'The joys of bachelor life, eh, Stephen. Simone, who remembers me as a glowing youth, will not be too pleased if I appear as an old tramp. Perhaps a shave is necessary, too.' He brought a razor out of his desk.

Stephen watched him change. 'And Simone, how do you find her?'

'Simone is a pleasure. A special woman. A great lady.'

Something in his tone made Stephen look at him queerly. 'Were you and she ever . . . ?' he faltered, flushed. 'I knew you'd met her in '68, but I didn't suspect . . .'

'Briefly. Too briefly. No, don't be embarrassed, Stephen. It's so long ago now. A different life. And it was a good moment, I think for both of us. Though for a long time I had no idea that Simone had kept her eye on me for all those years in between, or indeed originally mentioned me to you. Ah, the Byzantine complexity of those old secret networks!'

They were silent for a moment, musing over the past. Jan shaved. When he finished, he looked at Stephen with a plea on his face. 'You will come home with me now, Stephen, yes? To keep Hanka company while I see to Eva.'

'Of course, if you like.'

They walked up the dimly lit hill, past the old TB hospital with its tree-lined garden, past what had once been their favourite tavern. Jan was quiet. Stephen knew these brooding moments in him and waited for them to pass. He thought instead of the times they had met in that shabby, but cosy, bare-tabled bar over the years, times when it would probably have been better for Jan not to be seen with a foreigner, others when it didn't matter. Now, the front part of the place had been subjected to an overhaul and looked like a ghastly replica of some early '60s Scandinavian bar. He knew this modernization should please him. At home, he hardly belonged to the heritage buffs. But he wasn't sure.

Jan's thoughts seemed to be following a similar track. 'You can help me with a problem, Stephen. A problem of transitions. There is a scientist I wish to invite on the new team. Josef Teige. He is a very good biochemist. The problem is he was a Party member and he was demoted after '89, just as I was promoted. I do not think that to be a communist makes you necessarily a bad scientist. Nor was he a particularly bad communist, just an old one. Though, as you know, we also had a lot of bad scientists who were really apparatchiks dressed as scientists. Anyhow, the problem is that if I invite Teige, the other members of the team may object. So what should I do?'

'If he's really good, have him.'

'This is what I think, too. Otherwise we just perpetuate endlessly the crime of recrimination.' He laughed suddenly. The sound echoed through the empty streets. 'Change is so difficult, Stephen. We think we must replace everything. But not everything can be replaced. Men's hands are always just a little bit dirty. There are no clean sweeps.'

Stephen smiled.

'I am mixing up your language. To tell you the truth, I am a little tired. Seeing Simone both excited and distressed me. All those years. Wasted. But I must not say that. There is my Eva. She is turning into a beautiful woman, my daughter, no? Soon I will have to become a jealous father.'

'Very beautiful,' Stephen murmured. He wanted to say that she had reminded him of Sonya, but he bit his lip at the inappropriateness of it.

A car drove past, its tyres squelching through slush. They skirted the Dvořák house, lit up more brightly than its neighbours, its garden trimmed and tidied for tourist eyes.

'It is the ultimate irony in a man's life.' Jan's voice was suddenly strained. 'To have to face the fact that men like yourself, rogues, will seduce your daughter. Maybe that is one of biology's little acts of vengeance. Just wait. You will see.'

Stephen mused uncomfortably over the fact that he might never see and wondered again where Tessa had taken herself.

As they climbed the stairs to the apartment, Jan gripped Stephen's arm and turned a taut face to him.

'You must help me, Stephen. The atmosphere here is not easy. Hanka, she . . .' He didn't finish, for no sooner had they rung the bell than Eva opened the door and threw herself into her father's arms. Hanka was standing behind her, wiping her hands regally on a dishcloth, and scowling. She collected herself when she saw Stephen.

'I'm sorry, I wasn't expected.'

'Neither of you was expected,' she said with emphasis as she took Stephen's coat. 'Eva only told me five minutes ago her father was coming.'

'I'm sorry,' Stephen mumbled.

'There is nothing to be sorry for. He is allowed to see his daughter.'

'But not his wife of fifteen years.' Jan shook his head in a mock sadness which had too much of the real thing in it.

'No longer his wife. And not without an appointment.' In her vehemence Stephen noted that Hanka looked altogether beautiful.

They broke into Czech and Stephen, not wanting to hear, took Eva aside, talked to her a little.

After a moment, Jan joined them. 'So, Eva and I will go next door and solve these maths problems.'

Eva jumped up with a happy smile.

Hanka let out an abrupt laugh which seemed to hide tears. 'Now that you are here, you had better have a drink. Otherwise Stephen and Eva will tell me I am impolite.' She handed Jan a glass.

He thanked her with stiff politeness and left the room with Eva at his side.

'You should tell him not to do this, Stephen. He will listen to you.'

'Do what?' Stephen fidgeted in his chair.

'Drop in whenever he pleases. As if this were still his home. Either he has to come or to go. He cannot have it two ways.'

'How long has it been going on for?'

'Six months.'

'And do you want him to come back?'

'No.' She said it proudly, then added, 'Not on his terms.'

Stephen had a sudden desire for the pipe he hadn't smoked in years.

'You don't have to turn away. I will tell you the terms. It is not so great a thing to ask. In your country it would not be a great thing. I wish him to stop running around with his mistresses. That is all. For years, I allowed it. I said to myself, he has a hard time at work. It is always us two against the world and he needs a little relaxation. I pretend not to notice. Now I notice. I am, as you say, fed up.'

'I see.'

'Maybe you see. Maybe you don't. In any case, now it is probably too late. I do not want him back. I want to travel.' She looked at Stephen with an air of vehemence, then turned away. Her voice when it came again was light. 'And I want new friends. Can I get you some supper, Stephen. Something quick. Some bread and ham and salad. With me. Eva has eaten and Jan is not my business.'

She seemed to want to move, so he nodded, helped her

lift books and papers from the table and cover it with a cloth.

'Did you speak to your wife about Eva?' she asked, as she sliced a thick dark loaf.

'Couldn't yet.' Stephen looked out of the window and saw nothing but a puddle of grimy light. A dog barked. 'She's away on holiday. When she gets back. Then I'll ring you. I'm sure it will be fine.' He put more confidence in his voice than he felt.

'Okay.' She smiled at him with a touch of coyness. 'It would be nice one day to meet your wife.'

'Yes, you'll have to.' He nibbled at the food, found it suddenly indigestible. Hanka hadn't touched hers. She looked sad. Stephen cleared his throat.

'You know that Jan is quite brilliant, Hanka. That he is not an ordinary man.'

Her laugh sounded like a nail scraping sandpaper. 'I know you think he is brilliant. Other people think he is brilliant. I have not asked him to give up his brain. And if it happens to live between his legs, well, that is his problem.'

Stephen coloured.

'I am sorry. I have embarrassed you. I always think that you are so much more open about these things than we are that I am allowed to speak frankly.'

'Yes, yes.'

Eva bounded into the room and saved him the need of saying anything further. Stephen took a deep breath and nursed his beer. He heard Eva announce in great excitement that her father had said that perhaps she could go to Paris with him one day soon.

Hanka stood up with sudden rage and threw her napkin across the room. It landed at Jan's feet. Her teeth were clenched. 'If there is suddenly money for so many trips abroad, then by rights some of it should come to me, who has never been out of the country. Not Eva, who will soon be going to England.' She burst into tears and rushed from the room.

Jan looked shamed and very pale. He put his arm around Eva and told her that of course her mother was right. He hadn't been thinking clearly. He was tired. She should go and tell her mother that he would pay for them both to go to Paris. Yes, he would find the money somewhere.

Eva followed obediently after her mother.

'I am an old fool, Stephen. I think I had better leave. You stay if you wish.' He moved towards the door then turned back. 'No, I must say goodbye.'

He re-emerged after a moment, his face bleak. 'Hanka says it is better if we both go. She is tired. She will phone you before you leave Prague.'

They walked slowly from the house. A pale sliver of a moon emerged from scudding clouds and threw shadows on the street. Wind gusted round corners. They both drew their coats more tightly round them. It was Jan who first broke the silence.

'My life seems to have become much too complicated, Stephen.' He shook his head sadly. 'The problem, you see, is this. Maybe you have an answer. How does one, after the passage of years, eroticize one's wife? Tell me.'

Stephen was glad of the shadows which permitted a mere grunt in response.

'If I could solve this, maybe it would be as important as your Chrombindin.' He laughed with a touch of bitterness. 'So, do they have an answer in England?'

'Not in my bit.'

'No.' Jan studied his profile for a moment. 'But come, we mustn't be gloomy. Look. There's our old tavern. Let's stop for a drink. I still have a little time before meeting Simone. And I will tell you a funny story. To cheer us up. One of our Russian delegates told it to me.'

They found a small corner table at the back of the sparsely peopled bar. The wallpaper here still curled with ungainly blooms and dusty beer mugs adorned the mantel. A pot-bellied stove gave off a muggy heat. They warmed their hands over it and downed some *becherovka*, while Jan told him his story.

Its setting was an unlikely one: Moscow's first infertility clinic. A woman from the Caucasus had travelled the two thousand or so kilometres from her native mountain village to the clinic to be inseminated. How she had heard of the clinic was a mystery. What had led her there was a more profound one. She had told the doctor that she had come because her husband was dead. He had died due to her own failure of duty. A road leading down from their village was known to contain a bend so fatal that it could only be safely navigated if a lamb was sacrificed before the journey was begun. She had failed to carry out the necessary sacrifice before her husband set out and he had been killed. So now it was essential that she make good her dereliction by having a child which would bear his name. Speed was of the essence, since her fellow villagers had to believe the baby was indeed her husband's; though her brother-in-law had given her his blessing and urged her to go ahead and have a donor baby.

It was the way the incident brought two disparate worlds crashing together which had struck Jan with the force of an epiphany, as it now struck Stephen. On the one hand, the remote village moving in its age-old patterns, maintaining hoary rituals. On the other, the high-tech world of infertility clinics and frozen sperm samples. And in the midst of them, straddling the two, this woman with her desire.

'But perhaps it isn't so strange,' Jan said when the second small glass had arrived. 'After all, fertility has always been a question of magic rites and potions. Dances round maypoles, leaps over bonfires, witches' brews. Eh, Stephen, maybe we only delude ourselves with the special rationality of our science?'

Stephen didn't answer. He stared at the glass window in the pot-bellied stove, saw the leap of flame and, for the first time in active memory, found himself more intent on pondering the woman with her desire than the place of science. Like Tessa, he thought to himself. Like Tessa. He struggled to change the subject.

'You still haven't told me what you were doing with the police this afternoon?'

Jan laughed. 'That is almost as strange as the Caucasus story. There is this woman I met through your Edward Knight. An interesting woman. Attractive. But she has been making me run in circles for her. An English woman. You should meet her. From Cambridge. Tessa Hughes.'

Stephen felt his stomach turn. He put down his glass too hard, so that the colourless liquid tipped over the edge and made a small puddle on the dark wood. 'Tessa Hughes?' he repeated inanely.

'Yes. She is from Cambridge. But not the university. She managed to get herself into a predicament and I came to her rescue. Linguistically, that is. A baby was thrust into her arms in the Orthodox church. She brought it to the police, who eventually located the mother, but were also suspicious of Miss Hughes, who feels an inordinate responsibility for the child.' He told Stephen a complicated story at the end of which Stephen burst out:

'But this is very odd, Jan. Tessa Hughes is my wife's name.'

Jan stared at him. 'Tessa, you have told me. But . . .' He scrutinized Stephen's face. 'Your wife wears a different name? Your wife is here and you do not know?'

'Maybe it's a different Tessa Hughes,' Stephen said with not quite the right amount of conviction.

'So I see you have problems, too, Stephen. I believe she is travelling with Edward Knight.'

'It can't be Tessa.'

'No. I shall introduce you.' He chuckled. 'You know, it

is a good thing you tell me now. I was beginning to find her quite attractive. A woman with a mind that is not always stubbornly her own.'

'You should get going,' Stephen said with more moroseness than he intended. He rose to his feet, pushing back his chair with such vehemence that it tipped over and he had to rush to right it.

Once outside, he said goodbye to Jan and headed off in the direction of his hotel.

Tessa here. Tessa with Ted Knight. He couldn't believe it. Not Ted. Yet why not? For all the attention Stephen himself paid her, she might as well be with Ted as with anyone else. He kicked a chocolate-bar wrapper into the gutter and hastened his steps.

At the corner of his street, a woman emerged from the shadow of an arch and put her hand on his shoulder, rubbed against him. He looked into a fragile, heart-shaped face, a lipstick-smudged mouth. She couldn't be much older than Eva, he thought with a pang. He put his hand into his pocket and brought out some bills, thrust them in her direction and hurried into the safety of his hotel.

'Prosím.' He heard her call her thanks in Russian from behind him.

He didn't look back. He bounded up the stairs and made determinedly for the telephone. The shock of Tessa's name on Jan's lips was still with him. It couldn't be the same Tessa, he told himself now as he dialled their home number. His Tessa was certainly safely back in Cambridge. But after a few rings, all he heard was a click and then her cool, clear voice soliciting a message. He looked at the receiver as if it might be deceiving him, then found himself speaking.

'Tessa, it's Stephen. If you're there, if you're back, please ring me in Prague on 29 53 28. Please.' He wanted to say something else, but he didn't quite know how to phrase an endearment.

For a moment he sat at the edge of the bed. But he

couldn't sit. He had to know. He grabbed his coat and rushed out. There were no taxis in sight, so he hastened towards the river, then remembered, too late, that the one-way system led in the wrong direction. The wind whipped at his coat with Siberian fervour, bit fiercely at his ears. With a curse, he headed into it.

By the time he reached the congress delegates' hotel, his rage was as hot as his feet were cold. He felt if he bumped into Ted now, he could easily plant a fist in his smoothly handsome face, without asking any prior questions. He was certain Jan's story was about his Tessa. The baby confirmed it.

At the desk, he huddled in his coat, tried to make himself invisible and stammered out Tessa's name as clumsily as if it were a complex series of foreign syllables.

With a clack of pointed nails, the assistant punched out the name on a keyboard. He saw her shake her head.

Stephen felt a rope had been loosened from his neck. He took a deep, unhampered breath.

The clacking at the keyboard went on. The woman turned towards him, pushed a stray strand of hair neatly behind her ear.

'No. She and Mr Edward Knight checked out yesterday morning. I have a forwarding telephone number for Mr Knight, if you wish.'

Stephen shook his head, couldn't quite bring out the necessary thank you. He wanted to ask the woman if she knew what this Tessa Hughes looked like. He gave her his back instead, then with a change of mind turned round again and asked for Ted Knight's number. He dragged his feet towards the telephone. The receiver felt as precarious in his hand as a beaker of acid. A voice at the other end would unstop the plug. He waited, four rings, eight, then a voice announced the Hotel Pariz. He heard himself mumbling Ted's name, heard the 'no answer'. With a sense of exhausted relief, he put down the receiver. His eyes glued to marble tiles, he hurried from the hotel.

By the time he had arrived back at his own street, he had half-convinced himself that Tessa would be better off with Ted. He would give her the child she so wanted, whisk her off to California.

He imagined them walking towards him side by side. Ted with his brisk, athletic strides, a beam of possession on his face; Tessa, slightly shy, uncomfortable, removing her arm from Ted's grip. Or perhaps not. Perhaps she would be cold, distant, disdainful, her life shuttered against him.

He tried to see through the shutters, but everything was slashed by their presence, fragments of figures and objects and life that wouldn't coalesce into a whole. He picked up a snowball that some child had packed hard and placed on a window ledge, and flung it towards a lamp post. Its splayed fragments were white and fragile against the dark ooze of the pavement. He bent to pick them up, tried to shape them into a smooth white ball again. It was icy hard, but the grit clung. He found himself looking up at the sky, wondering if fresh snow would fall. Carefully, he replaced the ball on the ledge.

What was it Jan had said to him? How did one, after the passage of years, eroticize one's wife? The trouble was, he was no longer sure he had a wife any more. He could no longer recognize the figure he imagined on Ted's arm. She had grown taller, her face shone with a strange glow. There was a provocative smile on her lips directed at something tantalizing and bright, beyond his shoulder. In its light, she had grown mysterious, like some complex foreign code he couldn't crack.

He had walked past his hotel without noticing. With a scowl, he retraced his steps. In the sudden heat of the small lobby, his glasses grew misty. As he took them off to give them a wipe, a voice accosted him.

'Hi. I hoped you wouldn't be too late.'

A figure he couldn't immediately identify came towards him. He pushed his glasses back onto his nose and saw the girl with the copper hair.

'I thought we might have a drink together. I . . . I wanted to thank you properly.' She gave him a tentative smile.

Stephen looked at her in confusion, then towards the bar where he half-expected to see Antoinette.

She read his glance. 'Antoinette met this guy at a club and . . .' She waved her hand awkwardly, studied the carpet. 'So I came to see you. But if you're busy . . .'

'No, no,' Stephen said, grappling for a little relief from thoughts of Tessa. 'Have you eaten? Bit late by Czech standards, I know, but I haven't got round to a proper dinner and there's a little place near here which isn't too bad.'

'That would be great.' She zipped up her padded jacket with a swish and a crackle. 'I'm permanently hungry.' She patted her stomach and bounded towards the door ahead of him. 'Antoinette keeps forgetting about food.'

They sat across a chequered tablecloth in the warm, smoky restaurant and ate schnitzel and boiled potatoes dotted with parsley while everyone around them tucked into creamy desserts. Stephen tried not to ask himself what he thought he was doing here, listening to this young woman's chatter. But he listened, desperate for the distraction, and was soon, despite himself, altogether distracted.

Cary provided him with meaty chunks of ready and bizarre knowledge, straight out of courses he imagined, great eclectic heaps of facts and figures that she trotted out at random intervals. None of it altogether assimilated and all of it mixed with equal bits of ignorance or innocence, but it was a heady mixture all the same, and he had to run to keep up.

As he had already sensed on the night they spent together, she had a great many decided views on a great many subjects, few of which tallied with her actions. But he found himself charmed by the unselfconsciousness of the disparities. As she dug into her schnitzel, she told him, her blue eyes altogether candid, that it was wrong to eat meat. It made one into a murderer. Animals had feelings, just like humans. At home, she was a vegetarian. Here, of course, it was impossible. She had tried for a day. No way, unless one was intent on OD-ing on potatoes. But they would learn here, too. Soon. Apart from that, it was a pretty nice place.

Except for the prostitutes. There were thousands of them. Everywhere. He had seen them, hadn't he? Lots younger than her, too. The men forced them, of course. Pimps. She had read how some even pretended to adopt orphan girls only to put them on the game. And hooked them on drugs. Horrible.

Cary's eyebrows shot up suddenly. She peered at him from beneath copper curls, her face wary. 'You don't go with prostitutes, do you?'

Stephen swallowed a mouthful so hard, he could feel the lump sticking in his oesophagus. He took a gulp of beer, shook his head.

'No. I didn't think so. You're nice. I like the English. I even liked Rochester. You know, in *Jane Eyre*. Though all the women in my class thought the only good thing about him was that he was punished by blindness and created by a woman. I'd like to go to England, see some castles in storms.'

'Well, you must come then.' Stephen hoped he wasn't flushing.

She smiled, hopped on to another subject. 'It's not that I believe in marriage. In happily ever after and all that. Not at all. Men and women don't really like each other. Don't really get on. Take my parents. They fought all the time. Were hateful to each other. And they were hardly unique, if divorce rates are anything to go by.' Her laugh rasped. 'I read the other day that about 165,000 people get divorced every year in Britain. So I guess most of you don't like each other very much either.'

'That's not to do with liking. Not in the way you mean.' Stephen suddenly felt restless. He fiddled with his glasses.

'What's it to do with, then?' She was looking up at him, as if she might etch his answer in stone.

'I don't know.' He shrugged, tried to find an even tone. 'The pitfalls of everyday life. People changing. The difficulty of both sides of a couple feeling they've got everything they want. An idea of happiness. Everything that life's meant to promise.' She didn't look satisfied and he went on. 'A kind of selfish individualism. Or boredom. Poverty. Children or their absence. A hundred and one reasons. I'm really better on proteins and enzymes.'

'Hmmm.' She folded a paper napkin carefully into a triangular hat.

'I'm married, you know.' He said it as if there were still a hot potato in his mouth and he was afraid either the marriage or the girl would dissolve with the eating.

'I thought you were. You have that safe look about you. Oh, I don't mean it like that. It's just . . . well, I don't like being afraid and I sort of think, if another woman can vouch for you, well, that makes things better.'

Stephen laughed, despite himself. She laughed too, then, her eyes round, she went on to catalogue her fears. She was afraid of men, most men that is. Two friends of hers had been raped. In the US, there was a rape every 1.3 minutes, she told him with a catch in her voice. That was why she worked out all the time. And she was strong now, really strong. He could feel her muscles, if he wanted. She flexed her arm, but Stephen held back from touch and she grinned and rushed on. She was afraid of going out alone at night, too, but she forced herself. She wouldn't be beaten by all that. And she was afraid of AIDS, felt terrible about the pain people suffered.

Her face grew so downcast as she said this, that Stephen found himself patting her hand in consolation.

There was more, too. At night, she was afraid of the sound of footsteps and the sound of quiet. The bustle of the city where men jumped out at you made her nervous with apprehension, but so too did the isolation of the country where they might. She was anxious about the possible poisons in food and the known pollutants in air.

It seemed to Stephen that she lived in a world of imminent violence and in a state of near panic. The peculiar thing was that she carried on taking risks, as if the greater the catalogue of her fears, the greater the dazzle of everyday life.

Over coffee, he found himself saying, 'You're excited by fear, aren't you? You get high on it.' He hesitated on the word 'high', which felt odd on his lips, then rushed on. 'I can understand that. But it must be hard to live with all the time. Especially when you find it where it might not be.'

She gave him a look of disbelief. 'Boy, you sure haven't been a woman,' she said after a moment. 'Especially a woman in a country where one of us is assaulted and beaten every fifteen seconds!'

'That's true,' Stephen mumbled. 'But . . .'

'Shall we go?' She leapt up, her face bright. 'I've got a present for you.' She patted a dainty new rucksack.

'Go where?'

'I thought we might . . . I thought . . .' She was suddenly downcast. 'You don't want to be with me.'

'It's not that, Cary.' He paid the bill, draped his arm round her shoulder as they walked through the doors.

'I bought you a bottle of whisky. We could just have a drink. Antoinette won't be back for ages,' she added mournfully.

'All right, a drink. A single drink.'

She snuggled close to him as they walked down the cold,

empty street, raced ahead of him up the stairs, so all that he could see was the flick of long, jeaned legs. When they got to his room, she flung off her coat, passed him the bottle of whisky and stretched out on his bed, her chin resting on her elbow, her haunches high. In imitation of that picture she had supposedly so hated in the Paris flat, Stephen found himself thinking with a little inner smile.

He sat on a chair and looked at her and sipped the whisky he didn't want. She stretched out her hand to him, patted the space beside her. When he didn't move, she touched his knee. In confusion, Stephen suddenly saw Tessa's face where Cary's had been. Her lips had their wry curve. She stroked his leg with arched fingers, flung her hair back, touched her throat, and as she did so, his penis grew painfully hard against the seam of his trousers. He stood up with an abrupt gesture.

'Look, Cary. I'm not like this.' He gestured feebly. 'My wife . . . you're too young. It's not right. We can be friends.' He didn't dare look at her for fear that Tessa would appear again.

She leapt up behind him. 'Okay, if that's how you feel,' she said with a morose note in her voice.

'That's how I feel. I'll see you home if you like. Or ring for a taxi.'

'Sure. Whatever . . .'

'You're being very understanding.'

She laughed with a funny pitch in her voice.

Later, he lay on the bed where Cary had lain and wondered sleepily whether desire was as random as it seemed and whether with assiduous probings that particular biochemistry might reveal any immutable laws. He imagined strings of complex linkages and bindings shifting and coiling, secrets waiting to be plumbed and exposed. Then he thought of Tessa and uncomfortably saw her with Ted. She looked very young, her hair bound unusually in an innocent plait which Ted unwound with greedy fingers before he obscured her from Stephen's view, his buttocks moving in unseemly frenzy.

With savage distaste, as if he were master of life's kaleidoscope, Stephen forced the image to fragment into a thousand coloured segments before it could work its perverse magic on his dumbly stirring nether parts. A statistic with reassuring properties bounced helpfully into his mind. He couldn't remember its source. Nor could he vouch for its accuracy, but it claimed that eighty per cent of sudden deaths during sex were related to extramarital activity, whereas sex with a long-standing partner made no more claims on heart and blood than a brisk climb up and down two flights of stairs.

He buried his head in the pillow which smelled of an unfamiliar body and imagined Ted Knight happily dead.

17

——— * ———

U Mecenáse lay tucked in a half-renovated arcade on the east side of the central Malostranské Square dominated by the baroque bulge of the church of St Nicholas.

As he crossed the Karlův Most and picked his way through crowds of foreigners, old and young, Jan Martin wondered at the residual dislike he still harboured for the side of Prague on which the castle was situated. Like the glimpse of a hairy spider for an adolescent who thinks he has long mastered his fear, the proximity to the site of State power always triggered in him first the desire to avert his eyes and run, and then the need to challenge and confront. Even though now everything had changed and a stealthy bureaucracy no longer injected its daily dose of poison into the social order.

He had been happy to see the last of that police station, too, this afternoon, pleased with himself for not allowing the old discomfort to show. How long would it take for all the traces the old order had so deeply imprinted on nerve and bone to vanish? Five more years? Ten? A generation?

He watched a young couple kissing in the shadow of a stone saint and smiled. Eva would be free of it all. That was certain. Though perhaps he would never be.

With something like relief, he pushed open the heavy, leather-embossed door of the restaurant and let it fall completely shut behind him. Only then did he walk through the second door into the richly appointed medieval interior with its medley of Gothic arches and crystal chandeliers. He spied Simone almost instantly. She was sitting at an alcove table studying a menu, and he allowed himself the pleasure of looking at her for a moment before moving to greet her. The sheen of her hair, the concentrated drama of her features, even with her eyes lowered, the regal set of shoulders and neck in the high-collared blouse, all gave him pause. She had aged well, not like those women who had the faces of young girls in an advanced stage of withering. Hers bore all the traces of experience, an accumulation of riches, like one of those Rembrandt portraits which drew the eye and fixed it in contemplation.

When he had met her in 1968, during those short, intense weeks of their affair, she had seemed to him not only finer and wiser than any woman of his acquaintance, but, yes, also far older, a creature from a different world. Now, strangely, it was as if the distance between them had receded. He had hurtled over the barrier into middle age and she, like some friend embued with greater vitality, had waited for him there.

He had been so young at the time of their first encounter, as fresh and full of hope as a child. A time it was now almost impossible to recapture, before Hanka, before fatherhood, before the long, grim years of quasi-occupation. Simone had taught him so much, not only about passion, though here she had taught him everything, but about time itself. She had shown him how to take his time and how to appreciate the particular textures that time took in that intimacy which was as vast as the world itself. Time's swiftness and its slowness, its capacious intensity, its miraculous distance from history.

She had taught him so well that, after her departure, he wanted to immerse himself in it time and again. Wanted to recreate that magical world away from the world – a sphere both of minutiae and grand tectonic movement. Here, like a naturalist, he could study the miracle of sameness and difference, the down on skin, the arch of ankle or toe, the sweep of a brow or the curve of a breast, the ripple of laughter as it worked its way down from a woman's throat. And bathe in that small eternity of pleasure. It had everything and nothing to do with love. Hanka didn't understand that. Wouldn't understand the relief of it after the blanket generalizations which had made up the fodder of their stifled intellectual lives. Or maybe she had understood.

Jan gave himself a mental shake and focused on Simone again. What she wanted with him today, he didn't know, but she had made it clear that she wanted him alone. He suspected she might broach the subject of why she had abandoned him so abruptly all those years ago, why she had never come back or written to him directly. He had never believed her 'trouble at home' story. After the initial shock, the inevitable depression, he had flattered himself with the notion that perhaps she had upped and gone so quickly because she had taken him more seriously than he assumed. At least that was what he had told himself during that long month in prison in '69, when there had been all too little else to flatter himself with.

Yesterday their talk had all been external, about politics and the state of the nation and the progress of the congress. Today, he sensed, the agenda would be of a more intimate nature.

'Jan!' Her grave smile was on him. 'You see how eager I am to see you. I got here very early. And I've already started on the wine.'

'I hope I won't disappoint your eagerness.' He sat down opposite her, found himself suddenly nervous at the intent examination of her eyes. She was nervous too, he thought as he listened to her chatter about the old-style delicacies of the menu, the hare and wild boar and stuffed duck.

'As long as they're not cooked according to our *Recipes for Warm Meals*. Our new government has been too busy to abolish the law intended to ensure quality in our State-run restaurants. And you can imagine what kind of quality that meant!'

She joined him in laughter. It didn't altogether ease the atmosphere, so they ordered quickly from the new-style, pony-tailed waiter who hovered assiduously over their table. Then, like fencers who had forgotten the art of thrust and parry, they danced round each other, commenting on the irrelevant, waiting for the first serious pass.

It was she who made it, once the thick mushroom soup they had ordered as a first course stood in front of them.

'Contrary to appearance, Jan, I did keep up with you over the years. Messages came, through Stephen, of course, but also through others. I know things were not altogether easy. Sometimes very hard. I admired your courage.'

He shrugged.

'I know it doesn't excuse my abrupt departure at the time or the fact that I never communicated with you directly.'

'You don't need to make excuses to me, Simone.' He met the intentness of her eyes for a moment, then looked away. 'You came like a present out of the blue. It was only natural that you should go that way.'

'You never questioned it, then?' She sounded a little disappointed.

'You mean, did it hurt? Of course it hurt. You were everything and I was nothing. But I understood what we had to be an interlude. And I was resilient, have had to be.' He put his hand on hers to bridge that distance and to ease her mounting tension. 'It is a long time ago.'

'I am glad you are resilient.'

Her face surprised him. He was suddenly aware that this little dance of emotions and nostalgia was not what was at issue. The thrust he had intuited was yet to come.

She pushed her plate to one side. 'I have never been a great one for confessions, Jan. Pre-scripted purges or the more personal kind.' She gave him a hint of a smile, then rushed on. 'What I have to tell you now is something that I have kept back for many years. Its telling may do neither of us much good, even if it is the truth. The truth is sometimes too much for flawed beings, like myself, to bear.'

Her voice had taken on a density which threatened to submerge the individual words. She paused, forced herself into irony. 'Luckily, yesterday you told me you believed in the aegis of truth. I understood you to mean not the single big capitalized Truth of the sort which inevitably needs guns and terror to keep it alive and well-fed – but lots of smaller everyday truths, including unpalatable ones.'

'Go on, Simone.' He found himself reaching for one of her cigarettes, emptying his glass of wine too quickly. The waiter scurried to refill it. She waited. Her eyes lowered to the white tablecloth, she slowly traced its embossed pattern of flowers.

'I knew your father, Jan.'

'You knew Josef?' He looked at her in confusion. It was hardly an announcement which necessitated such tension. 'You didn't tell me back then. Embarrassing for you, I guess.' He grinned, imagining his own embarrassment at the age of eighteen, if he had known he was making love to a friend of his father's.

'Not Josef Martin. But Stanislaw Mánes, your biological father.'

'Oh?'

'Yes. He was my first husband.'

He tasted the flavour of that, found that like a hot, untried spice, it burnt his tongue. He hadn't known about the existence of Stanislaw Mánes until Josef had taken him aside during the excitements of that long-ago Cambridge summer of 1967 and told him that now, given the way the political wind was blowing, it was time Jan took on board the fact that he had a hero for a real father, not just dull, steady Josef Martin. He had no memory of Stanislaw Mánes, but the revelation, its attendant story, had acted as an electric charge, stimulated him into a political awareness, a concern for the history and present and future of his country he had never before had.

'So are you trying to tell me that I'm . . . ?'

Her eyes had never left his face and now she shook her head vigorously, let out a sharp, abrupt laugh, so that the people at the next table turned and stared. She lowered her voice to a murmur.

'No, Jan. I am not your mother. Not quite Jocasta. Staszek and I were divorced and he married your mother, Karolina Dostolova. After, or perhaps it was even before his death, she married Josef Martin.'

'I see.' Jan's voice had a peculiar pitch and he tried to alter it. 'And it was when I told you about what to me was a new and exciting family history that you upped and ran. Of course.' He smiled, tried a joke. 'Like father, like son. A familial attraction. Or perhaps you unknowingly recognized something in me.'

'If it were only that, I think I might never have mentioned it.' Simone gave him her woman of the world face, all shadowy delight at the impishness of fate. 'No, Jan, I'm afraid there's more. And it's the more that makes the difference.'

She told him then slowly and in great detail, so that his mind began to reel, about her vengeful hatred for his mother, about her sense that Karolina had helped to destroy Staszek, about the retributive justice she had blindly sought, about its unhoped for success, his mother's imprisonment, her eventual death. She spared neither herself nor him. When he asked her questions, she answered fully, coolly, like a judicial archivist who had no vested interest in the documents on display. She gave him new insight into his father and his history. As well as into herself.

'So you see,' she said, after his questions had given way to extended silence, 'it is not a pretty story. Not one I wanted to tell you when you were eighteen and full of hope in humanity. And, though I flatter myself, a little enamoured of me.'

'You loved my father very much,' he murmured. He didn't meet her eyes which were too full of fire.

'That is to put a very kind light on it. Thank you, Jan. You could have said, instead, that my antipathy for your mother was of an unforgivable pettiness. I suspected you might hate me. You may still, yet.'

'If you're afraid that I may want to avenge myself in my mother's name . . .' He paused, picked a crumb off the table. 'No, what I need to do now is come to terms with the fact that my mother was so distinctly on the other side.'

'That too.'

'Josef rarely talked about her. I think I assumed, I was so little, that she had simply been taken ill and died. And later, when he told me about my real father, about Staszek, either he led me to believe, or I took it for granted, that their fate had been the same. That they had shared shall we call it a disenchantment with communist power.' He found another crumb, stared at it. 'I think I am really rather grateful to you for not having come out with the facts about Karolina until now. During the '70s and '80s, it gave me strength to think I was carrying on an honourable tradition of dissidence.'

He met her eyes, saw that tears had gathered there.

'I hoped that might be the case,' she said softly.

'I remember neither of them, you know. Though I have a photograph of her. Only of her. She looks very large and very stiff in it. She is standing in front of a building made of large stone slabs. But maybe that is the child in me talking. I haven't looked at the picture in years.'

'I shall send you one of him. In uniform. From our London days. You'll see. He was very handsome.'

'Pictures instead of memory.'

'Better, perhaps.' She took a deep breath and stared at the untouched plate in front of her. With a little shiver, she poked at meat and vegetables. 'I feel oddly empty now. Maybe that is the true point of confession. Emptiness, a purging of too many memories, so that one can fill up on life again. But I'm not hungry.'

'No.' He refilled her glass, gestured for the waiter to take away their plates. Everyone around them had left. Only across the room was there still a single couple. But he didn't want to leave yet.

Simone read his mind, wondered a little at the closeness she felt for him, despite the passage of years, despite everything, despite what might still be a damning verdict – as if he had really all along inhabited a sunny corner of herself which needed no dusting away of cobwebs, and which was only accidentally linked by a grimy corridor to that older history.

'We might have some dessert. Something sweet to wash away those bitter tastes.'

He didn't smile. He was studying the salt cellar intently. Only after they had ordered, did he meet her eyes.

'Tell me, Simone. Why now? Why not have rushed back here in '89? Or have bothered at all? I am no longer a child deeply concerned about parental histories.'

She swallowed hard, found herself coughing, grappled with her shame.

'Before '89 . . .'

'Yes, I understand. Then it was difficult. But since?'

She didn't answer that inquisitorial gaze and suddenly it softened.

'You're not ill, Simone? Setting the record straight before it's too . . .' He cut himself off.

'I'm a coward, Jan. Vain. I didn't want you to hate me. To spoil something that in itself was good. But that's enough of that for one evening.'

'Yes.' He was immediately all concern. 'You must be

tired. I will ask them to order a taxi for us and I will see you back. And we will talk only about the present. I would like you to meet my daughter. Then you will know all the generations of my family.'

'I would like that very much.'

In the dark of the taxi, Jan suddenly covered her fingers tensely with his. 'Have you confided all this to Stephen? I know how close you are.'

'No. No, of course not.'

He relaxed his hand.

Simone laughed. 'You know, I gave Stephen your name. It was his second trip to Czechoslovakia, if I remember rightly. I thought you might like each other, given the shared Cambridge experience, not to mention other things. And then there was your sister ... A great sadness, that.'

'Yes. I had no idea you were involved in the network until much later. And then Stephen and I talked about you now and again. But only when we became very good friends.' His face in the shadows took on a musing expression. 'Not because we saw each other so much. That was rare enough. But the very passage of time gives things depth.'

'Like us,' Simone said softly and, hoping he hadn't heard the sudden rush of emotion in her voice, hurried on. 'Stephen is very secretive.'

'Yes. He doesn't give very much away.' He looked out of the window at the curve of lights along the river. 'I am concerned about him, you know. First there is the matter of this possible plundering of his work – work he so generously wants to share with our Institute. Then ...'

'What plundering?' Simone veered round towards him so abruptly that her bag fell from her lap.

He retrieved it. 'He hasn't told you? As we said, he is very secretive. It could be serious.'

They had arrived at the Europa and Simone gripped his arm. 'Come in with me for a last drink. Or a coffee. You must tell me about this. I suspected something.'

At the door, Jan hesitated, stamped cold from his feet like a small boy. 'You know I never come here. Has it changed very much?'

Her voice was rueful. 'Not as much as we have.'

The bar was crowded with bodies and a cacophony of voices in an assortment of tongues. Beneath them, above them, a saxophone strained pouring out a melody which was halfway to speech.

A couple rose from a window-side table and Simone and Jan made their way quickly towards it.

Sitting with her back to the room, Simone blotted out all sounds but his voice.

'Tell me about Stephen.'

'He is a little like a son to you, isn't he?'

She avoided the choice of words, yet remembered how her liking for Stephen had intensified into a sudden sense of kinship ever since, all those years ago, he had blurted out his passion for Jan's half-sister. 'I care for him. What is this theft?'

Jan hesitated. 'I don't know that it's for me to tell you. I . . .'

She cut him off, sensing their complicity, their brotherhood of secrets. 'It's not a moment for tact, Jan, believe me.'

He looked up at the ceiling where the smoke curled against dim light. 'It's not certain, but it seems that his computer was broken into. There is the question of a woman. It's a little complicated.'

'In Paris? Ariane Mikhailova?' she prodded him.

He nodded.

'I see.' Her face grew grave. 'It's potentially valuable, I presume.'

He nodded again. 'Very. To both of us. Then on top of it all there is perhaps a problem with his wife . . .'

Simone was no longer listening. 'Look, Jan, it's very rude I know, but having invited you in here, I think I will have to leave you. There are some things I have to see to. You'll forgive me. Forgive me for everything, I hope. Eventually.'

She rose and he rose with her, brought her hand to his lips.

'Are you going or coming?' A waiter approached them, surliness in his manner. Right beside him was a woman, fair, with candid eyes and a graceful turn of neck.

'Jan, how very nice. I insisted that Ted bring me here and now we find you. May we join you?' She spoke in English and turned a wide smile on Simone. 'If we're not interrupting, of course.'

'I was just leaving,' Simone murmured. She flung her capacious fur over her shoulders before Jan could rise to help.

'But I must introduce you.' Jan held her back. 'Simone Lalande Debray, Tessa Hughes.'

Simone nodded, extricated herself, felt Jan scrutinizing her. 'Please excuse me. There's something urgent . . .' She waved at them, walked briskly round tables towards the side door which led to the hotel, almost collided with Ted Knight.

'Simone!' In the smoky half-light, his eyes glinted like a large cat's. He blocked her way. 'We need to talk, I think.'

'Yes.' She gave him her impassive face. 'Tomorrow. I'm tired now. Around ten or ten thirty if you like. Here.' She gestured stiffly towards the bar and before he could stop her, walked off.

'Simone Lalande Debray, did you say?' Tessa interrogated Jan with something like disbelief.

He nodded.

'Order a whisky for me, will you, Jan? I think I need it.'

'Still suffering from the ill effects of our encounter with the police?' he asked kindly.

'That too.' Tessa didn't meet his eyes. She was staring in the direction in which Simone had gone. 'You're sure that's her name?'

He laughed whimsically. 'More certain of that than I am of many other things tonight.'

'Do you know where Stephen Caldwell is staying, Jan?' she asked suddenly.

'Of course.' He looked at her in curiosity, but she had averted her face.

'Tell me later.' She lowered her voice to a whisper as Ted Knight approached them.

'Jan, a pleasure to find you here.' He pulled up a chair from a neighbouring table and squeezed in close to Tessa, gesturing to the waiter at the same time.

Watching the muscle work in his face, Tessa didn't quite believe in the pleasure. She edged away slightly, felt his arm coil possessively round her shoulder.

'You've been with Simone? Lucky man.' He winked as Jan nodded.

'Who is she?' Tessa asked.

Jan studied her. 'You really haven't met before!'

'Tessa's not much interested in our congress.' Ted spoke for her. 'She's been keeping her distance, doing a bit of sightseeing.'

With a sullen clink and clatter, the waiter deposited glasses on their table.

'He still hasn't mastered the virtue of good service,' Ted mumbled. 'But apart from that, this is a pretty good place. Very *belle époque*, eh, Tess?' He raised his glass to them. 'The singer's not bad either.'

They listened to the throaty strains of a blues number, watched a woman in slinky silver lamé make love to a bulbous microphone. Tessa felt Jan's eyes on her. There was a peculiar expression in them. Had he found her out, she wondered. If only Ted would go to the loo and leave them for a moment, but he had been so assiduous in his attentions that it seemed unlikely. Odd and exhausting to find oneself so jealously desired, Tessa reflected.

'You were going to tell me about Simone Lalande Debray,' she murmured in Jan's direction when applause at the song had died down. The name stammered through her lips. She realized that though its owner had so obsessively preoccupied her for days, she had never said it aloud. How different her fantasy Simone had looked from this rather grandly dignified and well-preserved older woman. 'I've heard her name . . .' Tessa urged Jan on.

Again Ted intervened. 'You may have come across her books. I think one of them has been translated into English. Well, into American, in any case.' He laughed his generous laugh, bent towards Jan. 'I've been trying to convince Tess here to come back to California with me. I could use a sharp new assistant. Cool, unruffled and with a plush English voice to woo the contacts with.'

'Are you tempted?' Jan gave her his whimsical smile.

Tessa examined the buttons on her jacket, was saved the need to answer by a shout from behind her, closely followed by a man's bulk careening into her chair.

'Heh! What's going on?' Ted leapt to his feet with all the aplomb of a trained fighter. He picked the man up by the collar, scowled at him, shoved him back towards the bar, so that he fell against a stool and looked at them with dazed eyes. A tussle had broken out. Fists flailed. Bodies tumbled to the floor and bounced up again. Someone rushed through the door. A woman screamed.

Only their waiter was peaceful. He was leaning against the neighbouring table and shaking his head. There was a big smile on his face, the first of the evening. 'Capitalism,' he announced and beamed.

* * *

Simone paced the length and breadth of her room and waited impatiently for the telephone to ring. While she waited, she thought how well Jan had responded to her words. She sighed and sank into a chair. She needn't have put it all off for so long, needn't have boarded up this tawdry part of her past with such thick planks. Needn't have been so fearful. She was a coward, a sentimental coward afraid to despoil a memory which meant far more to her than to him. At least, it was done now. The information had come from her. That was important. And soon she might be able to confront her mirror with a little more ease.

With relief she heard the phone ring. She picked it up quickly, heard the operator, then a deep baritone.

'Ivan. Good. Hello. Have you found her?'

'My friends have tracked her to Nice. Found her two days ago. I tried to ring you in Paris. Our pretty friend was taking the sea air and waiting for a visa to the States. She'd given a poste restante number to Sacha, paid him to keep it secret. But there's money and money...' He chuckled. 'Once we knew the town ... well, it's hard for someone like Ariane to be invisible, even with dark glasses.'

'Excellent. Who's with her?'

'Dmitri Burov. You don't know him.'

Simone noted the name and tapped her pencil impatiently on the cabinet. 'He's reliable, I take it?'

'He hasn't let her out of his sight. As ordered.'

'Good. Tell him he can communicate to her that if she doesn't sit tight, she'll be marched straight to the police. And I'll testify. There won't be any visas.'

'What's she done?'

'She's a greedy, thieving fool. And, Ivan, for good measure, get him to go through all her things. Take away computer disks, cassettes, any papers he can find. Be thorough. Don't let her get her hands on them. Better still, have him post them to me in Paris.'

'Done.'

'And, Ivan. Warn him. Don't let her seduce him.'

'Simonka,' Ivan chortled. 'You haven't seen Dmitri! Maybe if she had a gun.'

'She may.' Simone was grim. 'Get him to check and get rid of it. The silly girl doesn't really understand the size of the trouble she's dealing with.'

He was silent for a moment, then cleared his throat. 'After this, we're quits, right?'

'Altogether quits,' Simone said. 'I just hope it isn't too late.' She hung up with a sigh and went to draw the curtains, shut out the lights and movement of the square.

How right she had been to be suspicious of Ariane's sudden disappearance. How right to bully Ivan into having her tailed. Her instincts were still intact, even if her energy left a great deal to be desired. Slowly she took off her boots, rubbed her ankles. So thin, now. Almost too thin to carry the weight of the years.

With a sudden gesture of exasperation, she flung a boot across the room, watched it land in the centre of the carpet. Odd how that single discordant object made havoc of the room's arrangement. She went to pick it up, tidied it into the wardrobe.

Yes, there was one more element to be dealt with before she could taste harmony. Nothing obviously painful, nothing that tugged and pulled and twisted at the deepest emotions of her life. It was something minor. Minor, but corrosive, like a single speck of rust that had dug beneath the patina of her days and slowly eaten away at them so that only recently had she realized that the entire structure of her being was at stake.

18

———✳———

Something woke Tessa, some faint, irregular sound that jarred her from the depths of dream and edged her over the surface.

The room was dark and at first seemed strange. A plump coverlet with a satiny stripe, ornate bedposts, a secretaire with spindly legs like a ballerina performing a pas de chat.

The glimmer of light from the corner of elaborately assembled curtains reassured her. A new hotel room. She turned, stretched out a limb, realized in the doing that Ted was not there, realized too that there was a second light at the far end of the room, a dim beam from a torch, focusing on something. Her bag. Someone was rifling through it. Her muscles tensed. Fearfully she lifted her gaze, then with a start fumbled for the light.

'Ted, what are you doing?'

'Shh. Go back to sleep.'

'But . . .'

'I'm just looking for an aspirin. Don't trouble yourself.' He switched the light off and bent to brush her forehead with his lips.

Tessa stared at the luminous face of the clock. Ten past five. From the bathroom, she heard water running. What was Ted doing going through her bag when he had a cabinetful of pills in there? She heard the soft fall of his bare feet, the rustle of sheets next to her.

'I ran out,' he whispered softly and wrapped his arm round her.

The arm was heavy and she slipped away from under it, murmured a conciliatory 'G'night'. She lay there unable to sleep and not daring to move, lest he should take her movement as some kind of overture. When she heard the regular rise and fall of his breath, she allowed herself to find a more comfortable position. Only one more night, she told herself, then Ted would be gone and she would be free to do exactly as she wished.

He had invited her to go to Budapest with him tomorrow, the last lap of his European trip. She had said neither yes nor no. She owed him these last days and would prefer them to pass pleasantly. After all, he had been very good to her. He had also talked about California, said she must come and visit him there. She had listened and smiled. Her thoughts were not on California. He knew that. That was probably why he was so insistent.

Tessa sighed. Feelings were so unpredictable. And hers were all with Amy these days. And Stephen. Yes, suddenly with Stephen.

Seeing Simone Lalande Debray last night at the Europa had given her something of a shock. That subtly draped and expensive burgundy dress, the swathe of fur, the statuesque agelessness of her features, the grand gestures. This was hardly the coy mistress or blank-eyed bimbo of her imaginings. Not Stephen's mistress at all. She felt that with a certainty.

Tessa turned over restlessly in her bed and tried to recapture the emotions which had first spurred her on her journey. They now seemed lost in a dusty distance. A woman's seductive voice on the answering machine. A jealous suspicion about a husband for whom she felt only hostility, a need for confrontation, a sense that everything must end between her and Stephen or somehow change radically – Stephen, who had been reduced in her mind to that one-dimensional creature who refused to give her a child.

In the interim everything had changed. The being she recognized as Stephen had been metamorphosed as surely as butterfly from caterpillar, though more surprisingly. It was the shimmering Stephen displaying his hidden colours on a conference platform who had inadvertently led her to Ted and then to Jan who spoke of him with such warmth and then to Amy. Amy who called to her from some small, dank room where parents didn't want her.

She too felt different, she realized. Less plaintive, more assured, less constricted, as if the crossing of physical borders had opened up equivalent frontiers in herself. And Amy had given her a purpose which wasn't just amorphous wish.

She really ought to thank Simone for impelling her out of the limbo of inactivity in which she had been trapped.

But what if there was another woman of Stephen's who wasn't Simone? Tessa slowly tasted the thought. Funny how it no longer tasted so bitter. That was Ted's doing. Maybe it was occasionally better to have two women in any case. Or two men. It didn't feel wrong about her and Ted. Maybe, too, it was better not to know the other woman. It stopped one having to wish for the other's life.

Yet this newly found equanimity about lovers was hardly the point, Tessa told herself. Amy and Stephen were the point. She had decided, even before she had met Simone last night, that it was imperative that she talk to Stephen. She needed him, wanted him beside her too. It had come to her over these last few days that the Stephen who wasn't the Stephen of her resentment would be good with children once they were there. He would teach them to see strange life forms in a microscopic world. He would collect things with them, bugs and beetles and those bits of fossil stone one found on beaches, whorls of shell encrusted in their depths. Funny. She suddenly had a sense that it would be nice to be old with Stephen. It was all those years in between that posed a problem.

Yes, Stephen would help her rescue Amy. Of course he would.

Ted wouldn't. Ted had to know the exact provenance of his children's DNA, have it catalogued before him in a detailed print-out. And Ted was the rub. What if his seed had taken root in her? She would have to tell Stephen that. She would have to tell him in any case, to explain her presence here. Perhaps he would understand, if she underlined what had made her come to France in the first place. Their marriage, after all, had had nothing to do with all that for an eternity. Her fault, too, she would tell him, now that she could see it better, see the burdened, unappealing, trapped self she had been.

And if he didn't understand?

Tessa pushed the thought away as last night she had pushed Ted away. They hadn't made love. It hadn't been so difficult. They were both tired and Ted had been preoccupied.

He was still breathing evenly. Tessa listened for a moment, then glanced at the luminous clock. Six thirty. With smooth, quiet gestures, she rose from the bed and crept towards the bathroom. She would wash and dress softly and head off. There was so much to do.

In the marbled bathroom, she closed the door quietly and switched on the light. Her face in the sudden brightness looked distraught, her features blurry. The confidence of darkness, in which the world could be shaped according to one's dreams, faltered. In this pitiless glare, she felt far less certain that Stephen would want anything to do with her.

And then? A single woman of rising age could no more scale the Himalayas of adoption than a mangy dog could run the Derby. Adoption was difficult enough with two. A colleague at work had told her stories which if they hadn't been so horrific could only have been humorous. A bad joke. Endless interviews by an investigating social worker. Questions which asked one to foresee an unimaginable future. Foresee everything. As if biological parents did that every time they embarked on the sexual act! Questions which nudged and winked and presumed common assumptions.

'And how will you feel when you meet other parents and they comment on how different you look from your child?'

'And what if your husband ups and leaves you and you're left alone with some stranger's offspring?'

'You do know, dear, that in the first months, even a year, after a baby comes into the family, men get a little hesitant about sex. How will you manage about that?'

Well, at least she could answer that one. Tessa frowned and scrubbed her face. But the problem remained. How would she put it all to Stephen? Explain? At the best of times, it was laborious enough to get him to focus on her for more than two minutes.

Now if she could get Ted to act as her ambassador, with all his force and suasiveness . . .

Tessa stopped the hysterical laugh that rose to her throat. I'm not mad, she told her reflection. Or maybe just a little. For a moment. We all are sometimes.

Hurriedly, she applied some make-up to disguise the madness. Switching off the light, she made her way soundlessly into the bedroom. The mirrored wardrobe slid open with a slight whoosh. Softly she took out tights and knickers and bra and lifted trousers and jacket from a hanger. Morning gleamed faintly round the edges of the window. In the room above someone scraped a chair along the floor. She glanced at Ted, then dropped her clothes on the armchair and started to dress with swift, stealthy movements.

'Planning to steal away?' Ted's voice leapt out at her just as she was pulling on her tights.

'No. I . . . I fancied an early breakfast.'

'Only that?' He stretched out his hand to her.

She hesitated, then walked reluctantly towards him. 'There's so much I want to do today.'

He pulled her down beside him. Beneath the covers, his body was warm with sleep and he moved against her with the drowsy languor of a big cat, rubbing his head against her belly, burrowing into her bosom.

'Not now, Ted,' she murmured, as he brought her hand towards his penis. She started to edge away, but his arm imprisoned her. Against her back she could feel the effects of her resistance in his tautness.

'Not now.' He imitated her primness. 'Now is good,' he rumbled in his own voice. 'We can welcome the dawn.'

He turned her round and she could feel how her coolness roused him. The drowsiness was gone and now he was all strength, strength that pressed her down so hard that she could feel the coils of the mattress digging into her back.

She wouldn't respond, Tessa told herself, wouldn't respond even now as his tongue did intricate things with her nether parts. She thought of Amy. And Stephen. Imagined the three of them walking along the Cam, stopping to throw dry bread to the squawking, warring ducks, shiny in their spring plumage. Imagined them in Madingley, the sky winsome in its pale clarity, Amy perched on Stephen's shoulders, gazing up at the flutter of birds and cloud.

She stifled the moan which came to her lips as Ted pushed inside her and despite herself, the pleasure of him worked its way through her body.

And what if she was wrong? The thought wormed its way into her. What if her destiny lay, however briefly, with this robust man, who would structure her days and ways with unflagging energy? She tried to imagine herself in the California he had portrayed, a world of big skies and unshadowed light and futures in which the word 'old' had never been invented.

No. Tessa clenched her legs, hoping he would hurry. It wouldn't be right.

She opened her eyes and saw him gazing down at her, his lips tensed, his eyes slits of glinting anger. She sensed the slap before it came. It didn't obliterate the surprising force of it, the loosening and shuddering and moan which followed in its wake.

When he finally rolled away from her with a grunt, there was a triumphant look on his face which told her in no uncertain terms who had won the last round in this particular bout.

It made her angry, but she gave him a loser's shaky smile and hurried for the shower. She didn't want to think any more. She just wanted to get out. His pervasive presence sucked the oxygen from the air, so that she could only breathe in shallow gasps. It had been like that with Jonathan at the end, her body responding against her better will. And with Stephen, these last years, it had been the other way round, her will zeroing in on the idea of sex, her body poised in some distant, bloodless void. How did one ever get it right?

Tessa let the rush of water wash her clean, then wrapped the heavy towelling robe the hotel provided round herself. When she emerged from the bathroom, Ted ruffled her hair and without a word made his way past her. She dressed quickly, stopped to glance at herself in the walnut-framed mirror. She needed to look composed, Tessa told herself, and reflected that instead her eyes looked feverishly bright, her mouth indecisively lax. She brushed her hair to a vigorous sheen, applied the peach-brown tinge of her French lipstick.

As she puckered her lips, she heard the clack and whizz of the omnipresent fax machine. Ten past eight, her watch told her. Ted's business started early. While she put on her coat, she paused to look at the unfurling message.

'URGENT!!' it screamed. 'What's up? Third instalment on promised program still not here. Client impatient. Double or nothing. Is this a technical hitch or worse? Am pacifying but urgent reply needed. With schedule.'

'Heh! That's private business.' Ted glowered above her, gripped her arm.

He didn't reply to her mumbled, 'Sorry'. Nor did he release her as he scanned the letter. It only etched the glare more firmly on his face.

Tessa shook herself free. 'Bad news? I'm sorry. I'll leave you to work now.' She made her way to the door, murmured a goodbye under her breath.

Her fingers were already on the knob when she felt his hand clutching her shoulder.

He turned her round. 'You're not planning on running back to Stephen just yet, are you, Tess? 'Cause we need to talk. Gifts of one's DNA don't come altogether free of sub-clauses, you know.' He patted her stomach.

Tessa shivered, not quite sure why. His handsome face had an odd look on it, half menace, half desperation.

'Lots of talk. Later.' She forced playfulness. 'And a special candlelit dinner tonight. Hope your headache's better.'

'Where you off to?'

Tessa faltered. 'I thought I'd have a stroll up to the castle. Go into St Vitus's. Haven't been there yet.' She slipped out of the door, didn't let the weight of his eyes on her back slow her steps. He could hardly pursue her in his dressing gown. Just in case, she decided to forgo breakfast in the hotel and made her way out into chill streets.

The hum of workaday life had begun. Muffled in hats and scarfs, people walked quickly towards shops and offices. A rubbish disposal van, with the all the heaviness of a converted tank, lumbered past, then stopped, blocking impatient traffic. In its wake, a single street cleaner made vague sweeping motions with a large broom. A child scurried to keep pace with his mother, stooped to pick something off the pavement, and was rewarded with a yank.

In the market square, stall holders had begun to put out their wares. Clumps of bananas, wrinkled apples and tiny oranges lay next to tourist bric-a-brac. Small bundles of parsley and dill spread their greenery from chipped mugs. Single carnations were proudly displayed amidst embroidered Indian waistcoats and brightly crumpled skirts. Puppets with grotesque leers and bulbous noses drooped from rails, their stage a crate of potatoes still bound by dank soil. Short stocky cucumbers gleamed green next to jars of plum jam. The assortment of articles in any stall obeyed no law but that of availability.

Tessa stopped to purchase a banana and two apples from a stocky, kerchiefed woman who lingered so disconsolately over her change that she abandoned it. Across the square she spied an Espresso bar, its sign as new and shiny as its flowered plastic tablecloths were marked with yesterday's stains. Despite the cold, she positioned herself at one of two outdoor tables and ordered coffee from a lanky waiter.

She had walked in this very market with Jan on her second day in Prague. How long ago it now seemed. So much life had passed in so brief a space. She stirred restlessly and glanced at her watch. Yes. The office might just be open by now. She popped the last bit of banana into her mouth and downed the coffee, then made her way towards the narrow, still-quiet streets of the old Jewish Quarter.

When she reached the office, there was a bearded and hatted man sitting in Rachel's customary place. The eyes he turned on her were surprisingly blue and youthful above the ageing tangle of his traditional beard.

'I'm looking for Rachel.' Tessa hesitated.

'Not here, I'm afraid.'

'Do you know when she'll be in?'

He shrugged. 'I'm not a regular. Sometime this afternoon, I guess. Not for long though.' His accent was unmistakably American. 'It's the Sabbath tonight and she's got some kind of event on,' he offered by way of explanation. 'Can I help? We cover some of the same ground.'

Tessa shook her head dismally. 'You don't by any chance know where I might find her?'

'She could be anywhere today. Maybe one of our regular tours. Maybe not. I can sign you in.' He looked at her curiously. 'Or give her a message when she arrives.'

'Just tell her Tessa Hughes came by. I'm staying at the Pariz now.'

She made dispiritedly for the door, opened it, then turned back. She scrabbled in her bag, brought out a crumpled piece of paper. 'You couldn't by any chance point out this address for me on the map.'

He stared at the paper as if it were a piece of encrypted code. 'You've got me there. Wait a minute.' From behind the counter he brought out a map and carefully unfolded it. 'I haven't lived here all that long,' he muttered. 'Ya . . . somewhere around here.' He jabbed a stubby finger at the eastern corner of the map. 'Past Žižkov, which is already pretty insalubrious. Past all those concrete heaps which it will take an explosion to pull down. You don't really want to go out there, ma'am. There isn't much to see. Unless you're a sociologist.' He gave her that curious look again.

'Do you have any idea how to get there?'

'Well, if I had a small fortune, I'd probably opt for a taxi. Otherwise . . .' He rubbed his beard, started on a long and complicated inventory of trams and tubes. Tessa diligently took notes, sensed that, for all his willingness, they would lead her nowhere.

Outside she looked around her with something like desperation. She had a feeling that if Jan had managed to give her Stephen's address, she might go running to him now.

But it was better not. Better to face him with a *fait accompli.*

If only she could hold Amy in her arms for a few moments, it would give her strength. She had wanted to talk to Rachel's lawyer friend before heading off. But maybe ... She glanced at the complicated set of instructions she had noted, and put them in her pocket. She would go to the American Express office which her guide book told her would cash cheques quickly, then find an appropriate bank and initiate a transfer. Then she would check back again for Rachel and if she wasn't there, she would risk it on her own.

With a determined set to her shoulders Tessa made her way towards Wenceslas Square. By the time she reached the American Express office, there were already several long, straggly queues. She settled herself for an extended wait.

A story Jan had told her popped into her mind. A very Eastern European story, it was about a man who, just before the fall of the Berlin Wall, had been interviewed on the free Western side of a frontier and asked why he had chosen to cross the border. He had admitted, a little shamefacedly, that there had been no prior intention. He didn't even know where he was. He had simply seen a long queue and joined it. There was always something interesting at the end of a queue.

Maybe the English felt the same way, Tessa thought as she edged patiently forward. She could still remember enjoying queues when she was small. The people next to you always chatted. You made friends. And at the end, there was usually something nice: a ride on the bus, a movie, an ice-cream cone or candy floss, pink and sticky so that it got all over your face and hair.

Ted didn't like queues. She knew that. He would already somehow have been at the front of this one and made his business blatantly plain. That was probably why she knew it could never be more between them than an affair, however delicious that at first had been. Now, she had to admit to herself, it was no longer delicious. She felt . . . what was it exactly she felt?

A loud voice intruded on her thoughts. A large-bellied man was shouting something at the slight woman by his side. His fierce brows moved in time to his mouth. The woman cowered, turned away, unwilling to be seen to be associated with him. He grabbed her arm. 'I've had enough for today.' Tessa heard the strident rise of his voice. He manoeuvred the woman towards the door. Her tremulous smile was a vain attempt to save face.

That was it, Tessa thought. With Ted, she had begun to feel a little like a prisoner, however soft and velvety the chains with which he bound her.

Ted Knight strode into the café of the Hotel Europa, looked around him for a moment and then made his way to the front desk.

'Madame Lalande Debray. Tell her Ted Knight is here.' He tapped his fingers impatiently on the wooden counter and watched the movements of the receptionist as she bent towards the register. Not bad. She had a soft, small butt and her nose turned up and quivered like a greedy little rabbit's as she talked into the phone.

'You're to go up to her room in twenty minutes, please, sir.' The snout looked up to him.

'Twenty minutes!' Ted exclaimed, scandalized.

'That is what madame said, sir. She is running a little bit late.'

'Hope she's got some coffee waiting,' Ted mumbled. He brought out a copy of yesterday's *Wall Street Journal* from his pocket, found a chair, and forced himself to concentrate, though it wasn't easy amidst the fray of gawking tourists.

He didn't like the feeling he had at the base of his spine.

An irritation, as if the nerves had decided to gang up on the central column. This had all the makings of a black day, his luck at a low ebb. Good thing he still had those last few chips in his pocket, though he had been forced to let one of them out on a string this morning. Couldn't very well bring her up to Simone. Still, at least her purse had been clean, except for that suspiciously scrappy address. He had memorized it, just in case.

He counted the odds against him and decided that it was just about time for a big gamble. Ted liked gambling, liked pitting his instincts against the odds. Like that first time he had gone to see Simone. That had been a risk that paid off, until now at least. Or when he had fished Torriano out from under Melzer's nose and brought him to San Diego. And these last weeks had added a few pretty smart heads to his list.

But this current and potentially lucrative venture wasn't going smoothly. And he had staked a lot on it. Too much.

He gave his newspaper a violent shake, then turned to scan the market listings. Chiron was going up. That meant White Jnr had a lot of loose change in those deep pockets of his. He could afford to dangle him just a little longer before bringing him in. With a little bit of luck. And Genentech was doing pretty well. That meant the new division would be going ahead and a little more headhunting would have to be done. As for Biotech Enterprises, his eyes moved to the opposite page, well, just look at that, they were branching out to the Czech Republic. If he had to stay on a few more days, he might just do a little sniffing while he was here.

Ted folded his newspaper and buried it in his coat pocket. He felt a little better now. Almost able to face the old sphinx, who was bound to give him bad news. He would need his wits about him. And that poker face which usually served him so well. He didn't want to fall into any traps or find himself dashed against a stony cliff. Maybe he had better bring her a box of chocolates or some flowers. He looked around the lobby. Nothing much here. He just about had time to find something in the square.

As he wrapped his camel-hair coat round himself, he saw Stephen Caldwell walking in his direction. Not only Stephen, but Stephen with two extremely young and extremely attractive women. Especially the leggy blonde. Well, well, well. Fancy that. He had to give it to Caldwell. He had brains and taste. Though maybe his wits weren't altogether what they might be.

Ted chuckled, made himself visible. But Stephen hurried right past him. Cut him.

A veritable cut, Ted reflected, his good humour vanishing more quickly than it had come.

With a shrug, he steeled himself for his meeting with Simone.

19

---- * ----

The old tiled radiator gave off a sparse, dry heat.

Simone placed her hands on it and gazed out of the window. Snow was coming again. She could almost smell it. The clouds had the dark heaviness of a school of whales. With a sigh, she prodded a cigarette into an alabaster holder and went to sit in the delicate Louis XVI chair which graced her suite.

She needed to rehearse the speech she would make to Ted Knight. But all she could think of here in this city of memory was that fatal meeting they had had in the early '70s. The autumn of '71 it must have been. He was still working in the American Embassy in Paris then, posing as some minor official in the Trade Delegation. And he was strikingly handsome. That had been her weakness in those days, which she now counted as her youth. Soon after that, she had learned better.

For several months, she had bumped into Edward S. Knight here and there in Embassy circles. Then, because her elder daughter was going through some love crisis, she had decided to invite him home for drinks and introduce them. But Paule had stamped out of the house before Ted's arrival, saying she really didn't need her mother's help in that domain. Simone had been left alone to entertain him.

In the event, it was Ted who provided all the entertainment.

He had arrived bearing a bouquet of torch lilies and

dahlias as dazzling as his smile and his suit, and he had sprawled on her white settee, offering compliments and gossip and bonhomie. As talented a charmer as she had ever met, with his dimple and his dramatic sweep of fair hair. He had drawn her out, too, asked her about her work at the International Relations Institute, about Prague before the war. She didn't know how he knew about that, but his manners were impeccable and she had chatted, not with any particular seriousness, but with pleasure.

And then without any change of manner or tone, though perhaps he had sat up a little straighter, he had said, 'I know a little secret of yours. A love affair you had.' He had laughed cheerfully, though her back had stiffened and her nerves were setting off alarm bells.

She had resorted to urbanity. 'If it's a secret, we had better keep it so.' Her laugh had tinkled, alongside his.

'Maybe. But just so long as you know that I know. And one day I may tell.'

The hint of menace was buried beneath a smile, yet she had sensed it as acutely as if a diamond-studded dagger had been poised at her back.

'So what is it that you know?' She had still maintained the mask of lightness.

'All about you and a young man by the name of Jan Martin whom we've been keeping our eyes on.'

She didn't immediately question the 'we', though she noted it. With a wave of the arm, she made light of the whole thing, put on her superior woman of the world face and said, 'Ah, that. We're allowed a little escapade now and again.'

'But perhaps not with the son of a woman we've fed to the Stalinist hounds.' His eyes were on her then, pinning her to the wall, and she knew there was nothing to deny.

'You have age-old sources!'

'Oh, yes.'

'Will you reveal them to me?'

'If it makes you more amenable.'

'To what?'

'A few little favours. Now and again.'

In a language whose innuendo she was well enough versed in to decipher both the level of knowledge and the level of threat, he had told her then about a certain James Redford who had worked at the Embassy in the '50s. He didn't have to do more than drop the name, for she knew it well enough. Redford had been an old friend of her husband, Michel, and it was to him that in her cold trance of vengeful rage she had posted from Prague some of the materials she had lifted from Karolina Dostolova's desk. She had written his name with a prominent flourish on three successive envelopes, assuming, rightly as it transpired, that they would never reach him, that the censors would hold them back and investigate the sender.

But she couldn't be one hundred per cent certain of her assumption, so, on her return to Paris, she had confided in James and confessed her act. At the time, she still felt little compunction about what she had done. Nor did she have much of an inkling about the full extent of the damage it would cause. Or at least, that was what she told herself. She only wanted to give Karolina a taste of her own crippling medicine, have her suffer something of what Staszek had suffered.

Redford, good bureaucrat that he was, had obviously kept a record of their meeting. And this had fallen under Ted Knight's perspicacious eye.

'I see,' Simone had murmured when this piece of history came clear. 'And the rest? About Jan?' At that time, their passion still felt so recent that it was a struggle for her to speak his name aloud.

'Ah. Jan Martin.' Ted had picked a handful of cashews from the crystal bowl on the table and popped them into his mouth with greedy pleasure. 'Our friends across the Channel were interested in him at the time.'

He had given her the quick, assessing glance of the man who enjoys more than cashews. 'Young Mr Martin spent an inordinate number of hours at the Hotel Europa during a certain period which just happened to coincide with your visit.'

It was then that Simone had the certain realization that she was dealing with no run-of-the-mill member of the American Trade Delegation. Years ago, she had left the Congress for Cultural Freedom when she had learned how closely its activities were aligned with those of the CIA. And now, just as the network she had slowly and assiduously begun to build up was beginning to function, here she was confronted by its insidious power once again.

She had dropped the mask of urbanity then and said in a steely voice, 'So what is it exactly that you're telling me?'

Ted Knight had chuckled, ever friendly. 'I'm telling you that young Mr Martin might find it something of a shock to learn about your relations with his mother and father. So too might your daughters, your friends, your contacts . . .'

'I see. And what precisely do you want of me?'

'Oh, nothing much . . .'

He left it for her to hear the unspoken 'yet'.

'The occasional favour. A name. A contact. A parcel. An independent runner. Nothing much. Nothing frequent.'

'You had better go now.'

'Had I? But I'll be back. You know that I'll be back. Thank you for the drink. You serve a fine malt.'

After he had gone, she realized that she was being blackmailed with more subtlety than even she was capable of in her worst moments.

She hadn't slept that night. She had weighed up the damage on either side – to Jan, to her family, her good name and, as importantly, to the network whose success depended not only on her, but on a complete lack of notoriety. On the other side, there was the inevitable if delayed damage of blackmail itself. She told herself that in the extended sphere beyond her own emotions and relations, she could not immediately see what the CIA might ask of her which would run contrary to her own network's covert battle against the monopoly on truth which the Soviet states exercised.

She did nothing. She waited. The tension the waiting produced was detrimental both to work and to family life. She found herself relieved when Ted Knight turned up at her door a month later, again bearing the bouquet which gave his arrival all the outward flavour of a social visit.

'It's time for that little favour,' he drawled after a few minutes of chit chat about a current ballet.

Simone turned her back on him, fiddled with drinks at the corner cabinet.

'Nothing much. We need a tame academic. In Baku. Someone who's familiar with the oil sector. Got a lead for us?'

Simone had hesitated, then mumbled, 'I might.'

'Good. Phone me.' He had jotted down a number on a slip of paper, given her his genial smile. 'Three days. No more.'

She had done as he asked. It had seemed so little.

And so it had gone on, for four years, five. A favour here and there, sometimes simple, sometimes more difficult. And she had bent, not liking it, but finding it easier to bear than the alternative prospect.

Then, some time in the mid-'70s, Ted Knight had vanished. She didn't know where. She suspected Latin America. She hoped, Mars. No other operative turned up in his place. She began to breathe more easily.

Towards the end of 1981 – she remembered quite precisely, for it was soon after Stephen had told her of his encounter with Jan Martin – suddenly, without warning, Ted Knight was back. Fit and bronzed and beaming geniality, he stood at her door as if only a week had passed. In his hands was a resplendent bouquet, odd that she should still remember that, of long-stemmed roses of the palest yellow. She wanted to tell her housekeeper to slam the door in his face, but it was already too late. He was bending to kiss her cheek, embracing her like an old friend, pouring them both drinks.

Lounging on her sofa as if it were a familiar haunt, he told her how he was now based in California, had a wife, children. Told her of a small company he was running which had interests here, there, and everywhere, talked a great deal of expert gibberish about pharmaceuticals, and confided in her in a low, excited voice, that he was now a headhunter.

'Couldn't be more appropriate,' Simone had commented drily. She didn't ask him whether this was a new front or whether he had severed all his CIA links. She knew too well that they could never be severed absolutely. All she wanted was to hustle him out of the house as quickly as possible.

But Ted took his time. And though she waited, he didn't mention anything of their previous business. Only at the door, when he had already donned his coat, did that sabre-sharp glint come into his eyes, that hard little twist of the mouth. 'I hope ... I trust, Simone, that I can still call on you for the occasional favour. No, no, don't look like that. It's not what you think. But when I'm passing through, you never know, it might be nice, it might be useful for me to meet some people, some friends. Get your vote of confidence. You always have the whole world at your fingertips.' He had laughed.

And he had come back.

Sometimes she had the feeling that he was the truly contemporary man, spending his life in airplanes, charging back and forth, bounding in and out so quickly that he was never grounded long enough to learn the difference between good and bad. The seductive smile on his face was almost always in place, except when something he wanted was refused. Like some hyperactive toddler.

What he wanted from her now was mostly introductions and invitations. When she refused them or tried to keep him away from closer friends, he would remind her ingeniously or with overt menace, not only of her increasingly distant crimes, but of the more recent one which he himself had induced – her association with the CIA.

With her *légion d'honneur*, her eminent standing, it would be a terrible scandal, wouldn't it, to expose that long-standing link? To mire her life's work, the entire edifice of her operation – which based itself on openness of information and a lack of affiliation – by pointing to its close relation to its less salubrious but more powerful neighbour.

So more often than not, she had done as he asked. Ted Knight, she had told herself, was the cross she had to bear for her revenge on Karolina. The vindictive pendulum of vengeance. Its razor-sharp edges cut and scarred, back and forth, back and forth. Until someone, somehow, demolished the mechanism.

And now, now it was enough. She had confronted Jan. As for the more public exposure, she could no longer bring herself to care.

Then, too, she was tempted to give Ted Knight a small but deserved taste of his own medicine.

The knock on the door had already sounded three times when Simone stubbed out her cigarette and moved to answer. Her awaited visitor had arrived, his cheeks fresh, his eyes clear and unfathomable beneath the broad brim of his hat.

'Simone. How nice of you not to keep me waiting too long.'

'Was it not quite long enough? Perhaps you'd like to return when you've prepared yourself a little better, Edward.'

342

She would insist on calling him Edward, Ted thought. No one had called him Edward except his mother and his school teachers. And that was aeons ago. He grinned nonetheless.

'Now, now, Simone. No need for the acid. I've brought you a second breakfast. To sweeten our encounter.' He thrust a cardboard box into her hand. 'I was not altogether polite with you on our last meeting.'

'I wonder that you can still gauge such things,' she muttered and put the box down on the table unopened. 'So.' She turned back to him, watched him take off his coat, drape it neatly over a chair, make himself comfortable on another. 'We meet on the site of one of my several crimes. Appropriate, wouldn't you say?'

'I sure could use some coffee, Simone. It's as cold as a Siberian camp out there.'

'If you want coffee, you shall have to fetch it. Room service is unreliable. And I assumed privacy would be best.'

'Of course.'

'You know why I have agreed to this meeting?'

'To lecture me about our dear friend Ariane. As I lectured you, somewhat abrasively, if I remember.' He chuckled, smoothed the leg of his trousers. 'I don't get enough exercise in Paris. So the old temper flares.'

'Not about Ariane. You misunderstand me.'

'Oh?'

He gave her that look of blue-eyed innocence which made her want to rail.

'What then?'

'I have spoken with Jan. I have told him everything.'

'Oh, that.' He made a disparaging gesture, but she caught the slight clenching of his left fist. 'I'd almost forgotten all that.'

'How convenient. Nonetheless, there are now no longer any demons you can pursue me with.'

'None at all?'

'None at all. I no longer care about the rest. You are free to do your worst.'

'Simone, really!'

He rose, pretending an offended air as if she had just insulted a long-standing friend, then strode round the room, examining the furniture, the silk of the upholstery, the elaborate tiles.

Simone feigned calm, relaxed in her chair, watched only the pattern in the carpet. She tested herself for that hoped-for burst of relief. It hadn't come yet.

He turned back to her with the sudden stealth of a panther. 'You really like this Stephen Caldwell, don't you?'

'There are a great many people I like,' she said warily. 'You know that very well.'

'Very well.' Ted laughed. 'Do you like his wife, too? I hope so. In these last weeks, she has become, shall we be tasteful and say, my companion.'

Simone stopped herself from flinching. 'Your loves are hardly of my concern, Edward.'

'No, of course not. Though in the interest of friendship, ours, yours, I am quite prepared to keep this companion-ship quiet. Even if things so turn out that she is carrying my child.'

Simone watched him preening himself. She stood up with a sudden spurt of impatience. 'I have had enough of your blackmail, Edward. You may leave now.'

She waited until he had donned his coat and hat, then plumped the box of pastries in his hand.

As he reached the door, she called him back. 'Edward, as for the small matter of Ariane, you will understand my meaning when I say she is safely in my protection. There is nothing more to expect from her. Except perhaps a visit from the police. The time for these old games is up, Edward. For me too. I have recognized it. And you, you are distinctly out of date.'

It was her parting shot and she was happy to see his

face fall, less happy to see how quickly it reassumed its customary beam. 'I don't think so, Simone. No, no. Not that. Ariane has, in any case, always been altogether peripheral.' He bowed slightly, then was out of the door.

Simone turned the key in the lock and with a sense of exhaustion went to sit by the window. She had a sudden longing to see the blue of the Mediterranean, to stretch out on a deck chair and watch the sun setting pink over the sea until the lap and thunder of the waves drowned out all other sound, all other voices, her own ghosts as well as the frantic cries of the papers, the countless screams of injustice.

If only one could establish a little order before death.

She had tried. Her will was made, carefully apportioned between her children and the foundation for the Maison de l'Europe de l'Est. Her papers were sorted and sifted. And now Jan. It had been right to set the record straight with him.

Simone had been spurred to Prague, not only by her inner voices, but by a concatenation of events that had made her both suspicious and fearful. First there had been Ted's abrupt appearance at her Paris home. He was in a rage. It was only the second time she had seen the mask slip and it was not a welcome sight. His tone had been openly bullying. He had sworn at that vixen of an Ariane she had introduced him to, told her that she was charging him far too much for a little job he had given her, told her she had better take the woman in hand. Or else, he was prepared at long last to do the dirty.

The open threat had jarred her slumbering conscience in a way that the gilded menace had never done. However unwilling she was, however difficult, it was time to shake off the hold Ted Knight had on her.

Stephen's announcement the following day that Ariane had vanished had made her aware of an unsuspected link, though she had no clear sense what it might be. The last person in the world she wanted inadvertently to hurt was Stephen. Whatever his self-estimation, Stephen was good. He had always been a staunch, a generous friend. And a man of considerable scientific talent, to boot. She cursed herself for having helped to bring Ariane to France.

And now? Now she was still not certain she had acted in time.

Simone took a deep, shuddering breath. Her hand, she noticed, was trembling. With an effort which seemed to defy gravity itself, she rose to her feet and, walking at a pace she would never have allowed anyone to see, she made her way step by weary step towards the telephone.

The coffee was black and bitter and scalded his throat.

Barely containing a curse, Ted Knight set the cup back on its saucer and drummed his fingers against the table. With the vehemence of a large trapped animal hunting out modes of escape, his eyes flitted from corner to corner of the gilded café.

It was all that bitch of an Ariane's fault. She might be good in bed – even though she didn't mean a minute of it – but as for anything else . . . Worthless! Oh, yes, she had got the material adroitly enough. He could swear Caldwell suspected nothing. But then, she wouldn't hand it over for the agreed fee. Had sniffed its importance. It was pure extortion, what she had asked of him, a series of instalments and payment points as complicated as a Hollywood contract. Fifteen grand here and fifteen grand as soon as he had a nibble and then more and more to be paid in advance into an American account, all details provided. And now the stupid bitch had got herself into Simone's clutches and the old sphinx wasn't playing. Was threatening *him*! But she wouldn't bring in the law. No. That wasn't her style. Unless she had suffered a sea change.

Out of date, indeed! What did the old crow know about the world?

Ted Knight clenched his fist and slammed it against the table so that cup and saucer and spoon jumped and neighbours turned.

No. He didn't like being thwarted like this. Not one little bit. Nor did he like being some thirty grand out of pocket. His own pocket! Though he wouldn't so much mind sinking it if the bankroll at the end came through. A pretty hefty bankroll it was promising to be, too.

So he would somehow have to draw on his insurance policy. He would have preferred not. But that was the way the wind was blowing. The question was, how to go about it? He needed an inspiration. It would do no good to implicate himself. As things stood, there was no proof of anything.

With a surge of impatience, Ted flung a couple of wrinkled bills on the table and strode out into the square. Wind gusted at his hat. He jammed it more firmly on his head, noticed the box of pastries he was still carrying and tossed it towards an old geezer who was leaning against a wall and looking hungry.

Where to now? He had better check in at the hotel and see whether any better news was coming in on the scroll. One never knew. Simone might have been bluffing. Yes. Or that hungry Ms Ariane Mikhailova might have flown the coop. She had enough cunning wiles to wing her way round most, that one, if the rewards were good enough.

Ted Knight thrust his way north through the busy square. As he crossed over Havelská, he heard his name called and turned to see Gustav Hauser, one of the conference delegates. He walked with the man for a stretch, fobbed him off with the promise of a cocktail-hour meeting, then turned in the opposite direction. He wasn't interested in that particular hunt now. And Hauser was old hat. It was always the ones you didn't want who chased you. That was one of the troubles with this town, particularly the historic bit. You bumped into people at every turn. Not like LA, where you could disappear for weeks.

He turned the corner and was suddenly aware of another familiar figure, this time in front of him. Neat, quick steps, a mushroom of a hat. Well, well, well. So little Miss Tess hadn't hopped and skipped over the bridge and carried her basket to the castle. He didn't think she was headed that way now either. Maybe she was on her way back to the hotel. Maybe not. A little sleuthing wouldn't go amiss.

He slowed down, matched his pace to hers, keeping well behind, but with her hat always in view amidst the flurry of passers-by. She was walking quickly, not at a tourist's pace, even an ardent one's. No, she had a destination and it wasn't the hotel. She had skirted that turn, was making her way into a cramped street all but devoid of people. He slowed his steps, didn't want the crunch of feet on snow to alert her to his presence. Too late. She turned to look behind her with a furtive expression. He leapt into the recess of a doorway and made himself small, held his breath for a moment. When he peered out again, she had vanished.

Briskly, he walked to the street corner, looked in all directions. There was no sign of her. He swore beneath his breath. How had she managed to elude him? He retraced his steps, scanned the ground for the imprint of her boots. Their rubber soles had a semi-circular marking of wedges with three Vs down the centre. He had noted that. But the snow's crust was too hard to show any clear indentation.

Ted had almost reached the far corner when he heard steps behind him. He skulked into the arch of a portal, peered out when the footsteps grew more distant. There she was, walking in the opposite direction. A small bolt of triumph shot through him. He waited until he saw her turn right, then hastened after her, wondering where she had popped in and out of. He passed a grimy window displaying cut leather and a pair of boots – a shoemaker's tiny establishment. Maybe that was it. Or this agency announcing tours of the Josefov. Harmless enough. He glanced at his watch. Still a little time before that lunch meeting with Otto Schluss.

A taxi trundled past him and he saw her try to flag it down. Luckily it didn't stop. She was hurrying now and he matched her steps into the tourist-crowded Staré Město Square. She wasn't looking at sights, that was for sure, didn't swivel her head up at the old astronomical clock or the wedding cake of a church. She was making a beeline for the taxi rank.

He paused in the shadow of an ironwork stall and poised himself for the leap into a second taxi. But she wasn't getting in. The driver was shaking a disgruntled head, pointing her towards another car, where the response was the same. Maybe they didn't understand her. And now she was making determinedly for the metro.

From the top of the stairs, Ted watched her looking around in confusion, heading towards an empty ticket booth. The Czechs hadn't got that together yet. Anyone could just leap onto a train and whizz off. Chances were, they wouldn't meet up with an inspector checking for stamped tickets. Maybe she had worked that out as well, for she was walking towards the platform now. He waited until he heard the train, then plunged down the stairs and into an adjacent car.

The train rattled and jolted. It wasn't exactly dirty, but it looked tired and tawdry and what dirt it had, showed. Because it wasn't old, encrusted dirt like in New York or London, but a mere twenty years new. Modern dirt – a Russian present to make up for the debacle of the '68 occupation.

Ted smiled at his reflection in the door. He was enjoying himself. This was better than sifting through e-mail or waiting by the fax.

As the train screeched to a halt, he looked out, ready to jump if he saw her emerge from the next car. But there was no sign of her. Where on earth was she heading? Two more stops and he saw her get out. He waited until the buzzer warned him of the door's imminent close and squeezed through.

At the base of the escalator there was a platform-wide huddle of noisy kids coming in the opposite direction. She was edging her way through them with obvious difficulty. They wouldn't give ground. Quick as a flash he saw it. A little one, lifting her bag from her shoulder, butting through the group like an experienced player, his friends making way, then forming a block round Tess and forcing her towards the steps.

He couldn't allow that. No way, man. He darted and caught the little runt full front, shoved him to the ground and grabbed Tess's bag, gave him a kick for good measure, shouted one of his few words of Czech, just for the hell of it, at full blast. '*Pomoc! Pomoc! Help!*'

The entire platform turned and stared. Ted pointed at the youth on the ground and strode off, holding the bag high, rattling away in English. 'Heh, he nabbed this. I saw him do it. Does it belong to someone here?' He burst through the dispersing group of kids. 'I've got this purse.'

'Ted.' Tessa was looking up at him, her face pale. 'That's mine. What a relief.' She leaned against him, as if she might faint.

'Easy now.' He put his arm around her. 'What's up? What are you doing here?'

'I . . . I was just . . .' She started to cry, great, fat silent tears.

'Heh . . . It can't be that bad. Come on. I've got your handbag. All's well.' He ushered her up the escalator. 'You look worn out. Let's grab a cab and I'll take you back to the hotel. You can join me for lunch with Otto Schluss. Okay? And tell me all about it.'

In the taxi, she took her bag from him and with a deep, halting breath opened it. He saw her finger a large envelope.

'Thank goodness.' She slumped back into the seat.

'Got something important in there?'

'An awful lot of money. Fifteen hundred dollars.' The eyes she turned on him were large and round.

'Lucky Tess.' He wrapped his arm firmly round her. 'Lucky I came along.'

20

——— * ———

Stephen put down the office telephone with a bang and went to stand by the window which looked onto the courtyard.

The little girl was there again, skipping rope on a bit of concrete from which the snow had melted. The bobble on her hat kept time to her jumps. Up, down, up, down, until the rope got tangled in her boots. She glanced up in his direction and after a moment, waved. Stephen waved back.

He watched her for another minute then turned abruptly back to Jan.

'Look, Jan. I'm not sure there's much point in going on.' He took off his glasses and rubbed the bridge of his nose.

'Is that what your lawyer said?'

'No. The patent application is coming along. But . . .' He jammed the glasses back on his nose. 'Her assistant was doing a little web surfing and she clicked into a new medical news site and lo and behold, right there was an announcement about a possible new breakthrough in cancer therapies which sounded remarkably like Chrombindin.'

'I'm not sure I understand.'

Stephen paced. 'It means one of two things. Either someone,' he swallowed, 'Ariane, has sold on my material with amazing speed. Or someone has come up with the same research. In either case . . .' He made a despairing gesture.

'In either case, time is of the essence.'

'You sound just like Katherine,' Stephen said bleakly. He slumped into the chair opposite Jan.

'Was there any detail in the announcement?'

Stephen shook his head.

'So from what you, yourself, explained to me, it could simply be the American way of signalling a "We got there first".'

'That's right. A little signpost for a future patent battle.'

'But it is your research, Stephen. So you must be way ahead.'

'Maybe. Maybe not.'

'Listen, Stephen. You're a little depressed now. In a few days everything will look different.'

The look on Jan's face told him he was set for a lecture. Happily the ring of the telephone deflected him.

Stephen looked away, drawn to the window again. Yes, he was depressed. He hadn't slept enough. The thought of Tessa with Ted Knight clawed at him. At daybreak he had marched towards the Pariz, needing to confront the reality of his dread, and then turned back. What would he say, what would he do, if he found them together? And what if this was another Tessa Hughes? In either case, he was both superfluous and ridiculous, like a character out of a Russian novelette.

Finding himself on Wenceslas Square, he had had the notion of calling in on Simone, confiding in her. And then he had bumped into Cary and Antoinette, who had told him that Simone wanted to see no one until lunch.

'It's for you, Stephen. Simone.' Jan interrupted his thoughts.

'Hello, Simone.'

'Stephen, I'm glad I've found you. Look, this would be better said face to face, but you're tied up, so . . .' She paused, the pause as sombre as her tone. 'I've tracked down Ariane.'

'Oh?'

353

'Yes, she's in Nice. I suspect she's taken something of yours. You'll have it back soon.'

'It may be too late.'

'Yes.' She hesitated. 'You may want to press charges, Stephen, but you should know that Ted Knight is more than likely behind it all.'

'Ted Knight!' Stephen felt himself choking.

'My conjecture is that he's instigated all this, yes.'

'How do you know?'

'Don't ask me that, Stephen. Just be careful. When he's desperate, his kid gloves come off and what's underneath isn't pretty.'

There was another pause, longer this time, in which Stephen tried to collect his thoughts.

'And, Stephen, your wife is with him. So, if you mind, be doubly careful.'

'But Tessa wouldn't . . . not even if . . .' He had started to stammer and Simone cut him off.

'Ted is clever, Stephen. She may know nothing. It is probable that she knows nothing. On the other hand, he knows how to be attractive. He may have told her about your relations with Ariane. He may . . . well, he is capable of a great deal. So. I have warned you. We will meet later.'

She rang off. Stephen stared at the receiver. Across an immense distance, he heard Jan's voice, its tones muffled by the buzzing in his head.

'Tell me, Stephen. We will work it out. We have been through worse.'

Stephen wasn't listening. He already had his coat on. 'Later, Jan. The talking is for later.'

It had started to snow, great, fat, moist flakes whitening the world and his vision. Stephen took off his glasses as he rushed towards the corner. There were no taxis in sight. He hurried on, unaware of the cold, alert only to the urgency which now drove him.

'Tell me, Stephen.' Jan had caught up with him, was panting at his side.

He told him bluntly, didn't spell out the apprehension Simone had communicated to him, the fear that made his throat as raw as the wind.

'But if that's the case, we must expose him. He is dangerous. All those trusting people at the congress. You leave that to me, Stephen.' Jan's voice was taut. He thrust out his hand, hailed a passing cab. 'None of them will speak to him again,' he muttered as they climbed in.

Stephen wasn't listening. He implored the taxi to drive quickly, paid no attention to the disgruntled face the driver turned on them, sat clench-fisted as they huddled in growing traffic, almost leapt out when Jan held him back and pointed out it would nonetheless be faster in the cab.

'I will leave you at the Pariz and go onto the congress. You will prefer to be alone, yes?'

Stephen nodded abruptly.

As they were approaching the hotel, he saw them, right there in front of him, Ted bending over to talk to a taxi driver, Tessa standing behind him. He stared. Tessa looked ... well, she looked different, beautiful, yes. And composed. Very still. With a peculiar light in her eyes. Maybe she was in on it. With Ted. That clandestine visit to his office. The change of holiday plans.

The thought took him unawares, made his mind reel. He saw Ted's hand on her shoulder, saw too the vulnerability in the face she turned up at him, the uncertain smile. He pushed the nefarious thought away, was about to leap out of their finally stationary cab, when the one in front pulled off.

'I'm going to follow them, Jan,' he murmured.

'I'll have to leave you here, then. We will catch up with each other later. Don't do anything rash.'

Stephen didn't turn. He was gazing at the taxi in front of them as if his eyes were charged with the opposite magnetic force. As it twisted and turned through the narrow streets, he urged his driver on with directions – '*doleva, doprava*' – and when they emerged onto the ring road and the old town with its whitened domes and spires was to their side and the man complained that they were going far, '*daleko*', and the snow was falling too thickly for his single windscreen wiper, Stephen spurred him on with the promise that he would pay double.

They were crawling along now, keeping pace with the yellow cab in front of them, driving into a distant Prague of tower blocks and scrubby hills, brightened by their cloak of snow. The snow silenced things, muffled and distanced. Like his dream, Stephen suddenly thought. That terrible dream in which he had followed and lost his friend. He sat up stiffly in his seat, gripped the upholstery in front of him.

The taxi in front had overtaken a car and turned abruptly left. He saw it skid, then right itself and proceed out of sight down the curving ramp. His driver followed at a snail's pace. When they reached the bottom of the endless ramp, a proliferation of small roads opened up in front of them. On none of them could Stephen see Tessa's cab.

'Left, *doleva*,' he muttered.

The driver did as he was ordered, carried on for a few dozen metres then pulled up short. He looked back at Stephen, shrugged, then declared, 'That's it. I'm not going any further. No customers in there.' He gestured at dubious streets. 'And I wanna get back home tonight.' He pointed in the opposite direction. 'Before we get snowed in.'

'But . . .' Stephen protested.

'But nothing. You can get out here and look for another cab and freeze. Or I can take you back to the centre.'

Stephen made for the door.

'You're gonna wait for a long time. And I'd take care of my money.' His voice carried a snigger.

Stephen peered around him through flurries of snow. He

was in a street of numbered blocks which had no place on maps. Where was Ted taking Tessa? He forced himself out of the panic of his dream into sobriety. He would never find them here on foot, never find them at all without an address.

With a grunt of impatience, he got into the cab again. Ted was bound to turn up for the last session of the congress. He wouldn't know Simone had warned him. And he had asked to be on the platform for the plenary – so he could inject a little 'hard sense' into the proceedings. With a shudder that had nothing to do with the cold, Stephen wondered just how hard that sense actually was.

Tessa looked around her with a feeling of growing unease. They had left tower blocks behind them and were now heading past a car graveyard, ramshackle warehouses. Scraps of metal and tyres adorned with white caps littered the roadside.

'Not anyone's favourite part of town,' Ted murmured, but when she turned to him, he had that good-natured smile on his face. It had been there, offering degrees of consolation, ever since he had saved her from those thieving little villains.

She had explained to him then, told him where she was heading and with a shake of the head, he had offered to accompany her. 'Poor little Tess,' he had sympathized as, somewhat incoherently, she gave him the gist of the story. 'In love with a baby and not with me.' And then he had said to her that since she was so intent, since he was leaving tomorrow, the least he could do was to help her. He had even cancelled his lunch appointment in order to do so.

Tessa reclined back into the seat, felt his arm resting behind her head. Perhaps she had been wrong about him. She had underestimated him. He was so willing to help now.

But she didn't really want to think about Ted. All she wanted was to see Amy, make sure she was safe, make sure that the man's offer had been as real as she hoped. Then she would convince him that the whole adoption procedure had to be embarked upon legally. Yes, legally. Convince him with money, if need be. She didn't like to think that Amy's mother, Mrs Prohasky, would not so easily be convinced.

They had pulled up now, in front of what looked like a series of abandoned warehouses. The driver was shaking his head, explaining in broken English that he had no idea if they were in the right place, but he couldn't take the car any further.

Ted asked him to wait for them.

Even though it was only mid-afternoon, it felt oddly dark, the sky a deep slate grey, obscured by flying snow. She hadn't known snow could cover the world so fast. Tessa put the tip of her tongue out and tasted it. Like soft sorbet. Beyond the dilapidated buildings with their corrugated roofs, there were trees, the underside of their branches sombre against the stark whiteness. Amy would like the snow when she was bigger.

Tessa felt Ted's arm fall protectively over her shoulder. They trudged along what might have been a path, between derelict buildings. There were no numbers or names, no markings of any kind except the scrape and scrawl of age. Like barns, Tessa now thought, not warehouses at all. In the distance one of them emitted a thin streak of smoke. Tessa pointed and they trudged in its direction.

Two pint-sized children suddenly appeared from behind a building. Like jesters, they wore raggedy clothes in a bizarre mix of colours. Above their trainers, she could see a sockless stretch of skin. But they seemed oblivious to the cold. They paused to look at them only for a moment before scurrying off to a distant field.

The presence of the children reassured her. She took a

deep, icy breath and watched the mist form around her face as she exhaled.

At the building from which they had seen the smoke curl, Ted knocked, then pounded at the door. After a few moments, the top half of it creaked open an inch, then a second. An old woman, her face a mass of wrinkles, peered out at them, her eyes sullen with suspicion.

Quickly, Tessa took the crumpled address from her pocket and passed it through to her, murmuring her request in an English she knew would not be understood, repeating the name Prohasky.

The woman opened the door a little further and stared blankly at the piece of paper.

'She can't read,' Ted muttered. He linked his arms in a cradling gesture, rocked an invisible baby back and forth, shouted the single word, '*Pan*', 'man', as if she were hard of hearing.

The woman didn't move, but from the depths of the house, they heard a response, a baby's long, feeble wail, like a cat mewling.

'Amy, Amy.' Tessa felt herself begin to tremble. 'Let us in, please, please,' she pleaded to deaf ears. The woman had already begun to shake her head, shut the door, when Ted pushed it ajar, showed her the colour of his money.

The woman's eyes narrowed. A tentative hand reached towards the bill. Ted gestured, pushed at the door. '*Pan. English ... Anglicky pan*,' he reiterated.

There was the slip of a bolt and the black-clad woman opened the door to them.

The windowless room smelled of smoke and onions and poverty. By the faint light of a lantern, Tessa saw a largish space which seemed to be subdivided by tattered grey blankets hanging from rope. A toddler sat on the floor beside a small coal fire and played with a slightly older child. They were piling hand-hewn blocks one on top of the other in a precarious tower. On a formica-topped table

359

stood an old iron pot, three potatoes, one of them half-peeled. Two rickety chairs and some wooden crates were the sum of the furniture. The sound of a child whimpering came from one of these crates.

Tessa stooped. She couldn't help herself. Cradled amidst rough wool, she saw a small dark head. 'Amy,' she crooned. 'Amy.' She picked up the child and held her to her bosom, saw the eyes flutter open, imagined recognition. 'It's her,' she murmured to Ted. 'Look how sweet she is. Look.'

'Mmmm,' Ted grunted. 'Seems a bit feeble. I'd have her checked out before I paid any money over.'

Tessa wasn't listening. She stroked the fuzz of hair on Amy's brow, held her close.

'What d'you want to do then, Tess? Your man's evidently not here.'

'Write, or rather print, a note to him. Say I'll meet him at the church tomorrow. At noon.'

The old woman was looking at them suspiciously again. Suddenly she started to rattle away in a thin, high voice. Tessa smiled at her, attempted serenity. She hummed to Amy, made a hundred wishes as she gazed into that little puckered face. It was just as the eyes closed that she heard the slam of the door behind her. She turned to see Amy's mother standing in front of it. The brightly coloured dress that had imprinted itself on her mind peeked out from beneath an old black coat. Her eyes in the lantern's glow looked round and beady. They moved warily round the room.

In a moment, the younger woman had taken the situation in. She marched towards Tessa, lifted Amy abruptly from her arms. The child started to whimper. Ted began to speak, short, authoritative pidgin sentences which made no impression on Amy's mother. She interrupted, gesticulated wildly, stamped her foot. Ted stamped back so hard that wobbly boards rebounded.

The toddler had crawled over to pull at the woman's skirt. She brushed him away and with a fierce gesture pointed Tessa and Ted towards the door.

'What do you want me to do, Tess? I feel like Solomon here.'

'If only I could make myself understood,' Tessa murmured. 'I'll have to come back with Rachel.'

'Who?'

'It doesn't matter.' Tessa cast a lingering look at Amy, met her mother's set face. Maybe she had been wrong. Maybe the man in the church hadn't understood his cousin's intentions. Tears filled her eyes. Through them, she rifled in her purse, brought out some notes. 'For the baby,' she gestured, pointed to the food on the table.

The old black-clad woman took the money from her hand before the younger one could move. Her lips curled to show a single jagged tooth. In a stern voice, she muttered something to what Tessa supposed was her daughter. The younger woman barked back, pointed at Ted with an emphatic finger.

'Come on, Tess. You don't want this kid anyhow. It's probably sick. You have to have it checked out.' He cast an appraising glance at Amy's mother, watched her angry fierceness. 'Though that one would probably make a good donor mother. I should mention it to Marriot.'

Tessa looked at him askance, didn't have time to snap at him, for the door had just opened wide, letting in a whiteness which dazzled in the dark, confined space. In its light stood two men almost identical in their sombre, narrow features. Tessa could feel Ted's fist clenching in readiness.

'That's him,' she whispered. She stretched out her hand to the man from the church. 'I've come. As you said.' She tried to smile.

'Good lady.' His jagged face twisted into a grin which

looked oddly boyish, then settled into suspicion as he looked at Ted. 'Who is?' he muttered.

'A friend.' Tessa put her arm through Ted's.

'Not police?'

'No, no, not police,' Tessa confirmed as Ted let out a boisterous laugh.

The man stared at them for a moment, then ushered them towards the table, pulled out the two chairs, righted some crates, all the time barking something at the women.

The old woman brought out a bottle of wine, four tiny glasses. Ted hovered, unwilling to sit.

'You come. Good.' The young man addressed Tessa. 'You bring money?'

'No money, yet,' Ted boomed.

All eyes turned towards him.

'You see, your cousin doesn't want . . .' Tessa began.

'Course she want.' The young man stared at Amy's mother. There was a rapid incomprehensible exchange between them in which Tessa took in only the word '*policie*'. When it was over, the woman suddenly smiled at her, a wide, toothy smile, which illuminated her face. Slowly she walked towards Tessa and with a flourish placed Amy in her arms.

'Cousin think police come,' the man explained.

Tessa looked down into Amy's face. She stroked soft skin, smoothed her hair, bent to touch her forehead with her lips, curled her finger into that tight little grasp, sheltered her slight form.

She could feel the mother's eyes on her. She looked up and met them for a long, silent moment. A wordless understanding passed between them. The woman nodded and with a rustle of skirts moved towards Tessa and placed a kiss on her cheek. Then, as if in embarrassment, she rushed to pick up the toddler and hold him firmly. Of course, Tessa thought, she already had two children.

The man's voice invaded her consciousness. 'Good. Now you give money. Take baby.'

Tessa struggled with her instincts. How wonderful it would be just to walk through that door with Amy in her arms. But that was the path of madness. She knew that, she told herself.

She shook her head sadly at the man. 'Not yet. I haven't got all the money yet. And we need to go to a lawyer. Make it official.'

'No police. I say no police.' He glared at her.

Amy's mother interrupted. There was a quick, vehement exchange between them.

Tessa addressed her. 'No police. You don't understand. A lawyer. Advocate. To sign adoption papers.' She scribbled in the air.

'And a doctor,' Ted muttered.

'Advocate?' The young man paid no attention to Ted.

Tessa nodded. 'To sign papers. Write. Adopt. Make English,' she added in frustration.

The man raked narrow fingers through long hair, looked at her with a mixture of anger and incomprehension.

'Look, tomorrow. Twelve o'clock. Come to the church. I'll bring a friend. To explain. Translate.' She gestured her sense, then with a sigh went to tuck Amy into her makeshift bed. There was straw at its base. An old sweater served as a blanket. She drew it round the child. Silence had fallen on the room. In it she could feel the others' eyes on her. I am not wrong, she told herself. It will be better for everyone this way. Amy cannot grow up in stealth.

She reached for her bag.

'Remember what I told you,' Ted murmured. 'Only a hundred dollars.'

Tessa took the prepared envelope and handed it to Amy's mother, who passed it to her cousin.

He counted the money. 'No good. Need more.'

'More tomorrow. At the church. St Cyril's. *Kostel Sv*

Cyrila. Twelve o'clock. *Dvanáct.*' She remembered her phrase book. 'And more at the lawyer's. Much more.'

'*Kostel*? Church? Twelve o'clock? Okay. No police.'

'No police,' Tessa repeated and, to emphasize the point, suddenly crossed herself, like a schoolgirl – cross my heart and hope to die. She raised her glass to the assembled group, smiled at everyone in turn. Like a benediction, she thought, her smile lingering on Amy's mother, who now had her older son by the hand as well.

Amy's first mother, she corrected herself silently, and felt her heart race. Almost.

The taxi inched its way through what had become a veritable blizzard. But for the gleam of snow, it had grown dark. The headlights of oncoming cars beamed small pools of blurred light. Windscreen wipers moved with heavy slowness. In the muggy heat of the car, Tessa was aware of Ted's silent scrutiny. She turned to him.

'Thank you for coming with me, Ted. It was kind of you. And very helpful. I might not have got there on my own.'

'Sure. No problem.' He was quiet for another moment, then murmured, 'Now you've got your heart's desire. Which isn't me.'

She was about to protest, to explain, but he stopped her. 'I'm not dumb, Tess. I can sense these things.'

He looked out of the window, his head a little sunken. They had just turned off the dual carriageway into more familiar streets of pale nineteenth-century houses.

'No. You don't want me. You want to go straight back to your old man. Play happy families.'

It was true, Tessa thought. There was nothing she could say. She bent her head, gestured an apology.

'And what about this, eh, Tess?' He turned towards her suddenly and placed his large hand, palm down, beneath her coat, covered her stomach. 'What will Stephen say about this, if it happens? What will I say?'

She shrank away from him. 'I don't know, Ted. One step at a time.'

'Well, I know. I wouldn't exactly welcome little wifey home with another man's child tucked in her womb. On top of an adopted brat.'

The heavy cynicism in his voice grated on her ears. She turned away from him, tears pricking at her eyes.

'It's okay, Tess.' Ted's arm made its way round her shoulder, drawing her close. 'I'll stay out of the way. Clear off and stay out of the way. If that's what you want, I'll do you that favour.'

She made a soft sound, squeezed his hand.

'But I think I should extract a favour from you in return. A little favour of some kind.'

'Of course, anything. Just ask.' Tessa felt guilt beginning to lessen. She smiled at him. 'Anything within reason.'

'Well, let me think.' He gazed out of the window, his face whimsical in the shadow of passing streetlights.

'I know. I know just the thing. Stephen's got this big fat address book tucked away inside his computer. Filled with the whole of the European scientific establishment. It could be enormously useful to me.'

'Oh?' Tessa balked. 'I don't see how . . .'

'Sure, it's easy. I'll just give you a couple of disks.' He reached down for his briefcase, opened it. 'And you can copy it for me. Copy everything. Stop off and do it right now. His hotel's not all that far from here.' He glanced at his watch. 'He might still be at the congress.'

'I couldn't do that, Ted. Anyhow, I don't even know his code, don't know how to go about it.'

He laughed. 'I'd forgotten what an old-fashioned girl you are.' He drew her closer. 'Tell you what. You just bring me his PC. The whole machine. I can do it in a jiffy. Now. Tonight. Whenever.'

Tessa stiffened, shook her head. 'It wouldn't be right, Ted.'

As he rifled through the briefcase, she saw the glint of silver. Her breath caught. A gun. Why would he have a gun? She moved to the far end of the seat.

'And you think this is right?' His hand clawed at her stomach.

'If you want those addresses so badly, you could ask Stephen. I'm sure he'd give them to you.' Her voice choked through her throat. She tried to control it.

'Hey, what do you take me for? You think I could face him now? Ask him for favours?'

'It wouldn't be right,' Tessa repeated.

'Well, then, I'll just have to come back and haunt you. We wouldn't be quits.'

Tessa stared at him.

'And I have been good to you, haven't I?'

She nodded, unable to deny that.

'But you won't do anything for me. It's because you think that husband of yours is so honourable, isn't it. Pure as the driven snow.'

His chuckle echoed coldly along Tessa's spine.

'Well, I could tell you a thing or two about Stephen Caldwell. Like all about a finger-lickin little Russian number he's been keeping in Paris on and off over the years.'

She felt him gauging her reaction, but she couldn't help the shudder that had gone through her. So she had been right about Stephen, only wrong in her choice of object.

'But I guess that's for the two of you to sort out. You're gonna have quite a lot to sort out, from the looks of it.' He sprawled against the seat in a semblance of good humour. 'The last thing you'll want is sweet ol' me knocking at the door. So I really think you should do this thing for me, Tess. I really do. And then you'll be rid of me.'

Tessa wanted nothing more than to be rid of him right

now. It had come to her with a sensation as chill as metal on skin that he wasn't just asking her, he was telling. Demanding. Coercing. A whiff of fear attacked her nostrils. That gun. It had been a gun. She calmed herself. All Americans had guns, didn't they?

'Look, why don't you just drop me at his hotel and I'll ask him right now.'

'Good girl. But I don't want you fobbing me off with just a couple of names or I'll have to ask for more. I've given you something precious and I don't want peanuts in return. So maybe you had better bring me the whole kit and caboodle.'

'I'll try,' Tessa murmured.

He instructed the driver and turned back to her. 'You just talk to Stephen sweetly and when he's otherwise engaged, you march right down to the taxi here and hand it to me. The PC itself. I'll wait for as long as it takes.'

'And if he's not there?' Tessa found herself weirdly fascinated by this precise series of instructions.

'Well, you just get them to let you into his room. You are Mrs Caldwell, aren't you? Tell them you've just arrived.'

They were on a wide, hilly street. Katerinská, a sign announced. On one side a row of buildings which could only be official stretched in a sameness of facade. On the other, past a dip, shielded by iron rails, there seemed to be a secondary street level. Here there was a series of large but dilapidated family houses. Only one stood out by the brightness of paint and twin lanterns.

'That's it.'

Tessa reached for the door as soon as the taxi had stopped, but Ted's arm was on her shoulder, holding her back, digging through her coat, indenting her skin. 'And, Tess, I don't want you reneging on me. We understand each other. I want to see that at least you've tried for me.'

She looked at that handsome face for a moment, nodded, and hastened from the car. Did they understand each other, she wondered, and shivered, drew her coat more closely round her. She had no intention of doing what Ted asked. Or of coming back. Certainly not. She would tell Stephen everything. Everything. She was hopeless at lying in any case.

Tessa tried to find some steps to lead her from one street level to the next. The snow slipped and crunched beneath her feet. She held onto the rail. No, she wasn't coming back. Ted could just pack up and leave her clothes at the Pariz. She certainly wasn't going back there tonight. She pushed open the door of the hotel with a sense of relief.

The hall was narrow and freshly painted. An umbrella rack stood beneath a wood-framed mirror. Trust Stephen to find this modest establishment, even if Camgene was paying. She smiled to herself and brushed the snow from her shoulders. What would she say to him? How to begin? She rushed to the desk before she lost her nerve.

'Dr Stephen Caldwell,' she said to the rather severe-looking woman who greeted her.

'He has just gone up. Who shall I say is calling?'

'No, no. I'll go straight to his room. Number . . . ?'

'Thirty-seven.' The woman gave her a queer look.

Tessa hurried from her gaze, quickly clambered up and round the curving staircase to the first floor, then slowed her steps. From above her on the stairs, she could hear voices. A woman's first.

'Stupid of me to leave my scarf. Really dumb. It's so cold now.'

'Yes. Though the snow is fine, don't you think? We get so little in England.'

Stephen's voice.

Tessa walked softly, saw a pair of long jean-clad legs, a fall of copper hair. And Stephen, a broadish-brimmed hat on his head.

As insidiously as a tapeworm, Ted's words slithered into

her mind and ate up her courage. She stopped in her tracks, listened to the receding voices.

'We get too much. I thought I was going to be rid of it. It just makes me want to curl into bed and sleep.'

She waited for Stephen's reply, but there wasn't one. Instead she heard a door open. And shut. She waited some more. She didn't quite know what she was waiting for, but she perched on the step and put her face in her hands and waited.

After a few minutes, she got up and walked down the stairs. She didn't stop at the reception desk, where the sleek-haired woman with the tight face looked up at her queerly again. She nodded and murmured a thank you and slunk towards the door, hoped she could slink out of it invisibly and disappear along the darkened lane into the snow.

21

————*————

The street was deserted, hushed under its white blanket like a drowsy child. Where its upper and lower levels met, houses gave way to a secluded stretch of park. In the distance, along a sloping path, Tessa could see a boy romping with his dog. Barking burst upon the stillness, a child's happy call. Tessa looked for a gate in the stretch of iron rail.

Before she could reach one, she felt a staying hand on her shoulder.

'And where do you think you're off to?' Ted turned her towards him. She didn't like the shadowy look on his face.

'I couldn't see the cab. I thought you'd gone.'

'Any luck?' He pressed her towards the taxi which was crawling down the hill in their direction.

'He wasn't there.' Tessa watched her feet make tracks in the fresh snow. 'And the woman at the desk wouldn't give me the key. She wouldn't believe I was his wife.' The sound of her laugh echoed uncannily through the night.

Ted joined her with a cheerful guffaw. 'Oh, well. Guess we can try later. Or in the morning.'

She glanced at his profile. 'Ted, I don't ... We can't really spend the night together. It wouldn't ...'

'Be right,' he finished for her and slammed the door of the taxi behind them. 'No, maybe not.' He smiled a smile so cheerful that she was left with the odd sensation that she had hallucinated all those earlier alarm bells.

'But you're not just going to up and leave me without a farewell dinner. Really, Tess. That wouldn't be kind.'

'No, no. Dinner, of course.'

'Good, good. I'm famished. We managed to forget lunch, if you remember.' He leaned back in the seat and took her hand, played with her fingers.

She waited for him to say something more about Stephen's computer, but nothing came. Instead, after a moment, he slapped his head.

'I'm an idiot. There's something I've gotta do before dinner. A friend of mine in New York asked me to go and have a look at the apartment he's bought here. To see how the work's coming on. We can do that first of all. Okay?' He gave her an endearing look.

'Of course.'

'It's on the other side of the river. Near the castle.'

'That will be nice. We can eat on that side. My guide book tells me there are some great places.' She kept her voice as light as his.

As they crossed the curve of the river, its banks white now, Tessa wondered again if she had imagined the tone and tenor of their previous conversation, let alone its content. Maybe he had just wanted some proof of her affection. Men were so bizarre. Men. She kept her mind assiduously away from Stephen. No, she wouldn't let herself think of that. She would focus on Amy. On practical things. Tomorrow, she would find Rachel, talk to the lawyer, find him at home if necessary, go to the church. But first she had somehow to get through this evening. If only she didn't feel so distinctly uneasy. Tessa took a deep breath, forced back her shoulders.

The taxi driver was saying something now, pulling up by the side of the road.

'Much, much snow.' He pointed up a narrow, twisting road. 'Better you walk.'

'Sure.' Ted paid him, made effusive thanks. 'It's up there, right?'

In the distance above them, Tessa could see a pool of light, hazy against the dark sky. Fat flakes danced in it like polka dots on a swirling skirt. But the street itself was sombre and sparsely lit. A lone man struggled downhill, his steps slowed by snow and the large white object in his arms. When he came closer she saw he was carrying a refrigerator. She pointed, laughed. The sound echoed against stone and came back to her as a muffled cry.

They walked slowly up the incline, their feet scrunching untrammelled snow. Only an occasional illuminated window signalled habitation. For the rest, the houses displayed their ornate facades to the night as quietly as if they were film sets without an interior. Ted paused every few steps to peer for numbers buried in encrusted portals or behind intermittent scaffolding.

At a corner, they passed a tiny tavern, its wooden door inviting between two old-fashioned lamps.

'Shall we stop? I could use a drink. Maybe even two.' She kept her voice light.

'Let's wait. It's not much further now,' he encouraged her, draped his arm round her shoulder.

What would he do if she insisted, if she dodged him now and simply walked into that cosy, peopled interior?

Tessa shook off his arm, stepped aside. 'I'd really much rather . . .' she began, but his arm was already round her more securely, holding her in a vice, propelling her as if she were as light and insignificant as a marionette, though his voice continued in its persuasive softness. 'Tess, come on. A few more steps. Look, two more buildings.'

The wide double doors were hidden between scaffolding. Ted brought out a key ring. 'Fine-looking place.'

'Mmm. Shall I wait down here?'

'No, come on up. It'll be interesting. You haven't been in a Prague apartment before.'

He found a timed light switch, pressed it to reveal an arched, newly painted hall, plaster cherubs floating from twinned recesses.

'Grand. Look at this.' He pulled back a leaf-strewn ironwork grill to reveal an old-fashioned open lift. 'Don't get this in California.'

As they climbed smoothly to the third floor, Tessa wondered at his mood, tried to still her niggling fears. The building had a preternatural quiet about it. Perhaps no one had yet moved in or the walls were extraordinarily thick. The lift slid open with a resonant clatter.

The apartment was at the end of the hall to the right. Only a single door opposite signalled a second flat.

'You can give me your opinion on the paintwork and the fireplace. I'm supposed to report on that. And check if the satellite dish has been installed.' Ted's voice reverberated through quiet as he fiddled with the door's numerous locks. 'There.' He pushed it open, found a switch.

Mellow light arced from three corners of a large high-ceilinged room. At either side of the far wall there were rounded arches. Between them a lavishly decorated fireplace displayed art nouveau tiles of curling vines and brightly pink tulips. A gilt-framed Mucha poster hung above the mantel: sitting in a draped chair, a young cream-gowned woman with golden tresses beneath a star- and leaf-studded tiara beckoned to them seductively.

'Princezna Hyacinta.' Tessa read the curlicue script. 'Pretty.'

'More than pretty. Lucky old Jake.' Ted prowled behind her, prodding a vast rose sofa, smoothing the lacquer of a corner table, turning a deep blue vase upside down to read the signature.

Tessa was examining the intricate moulding in the centre of the ceiling when she heard his voice from the adjacent room. 'Come in here.'

She followed the tumult of sound and found herself in

an office, complete with desk, an assortment of armchairs and a slim-backed television of gigantic proportions. With a boyish grin on his face, Ted was zapping at it.

'There.' He paused. 'CNN news. Good stuff.' A reporter's face, larger than life, looked out at them from the corner of a screen. In the near distance, tanks lumbered.

Tessa stared, transfixed by the sheer size of the image.

'What do you say I get us a bottle of something and we catch up with the world?' He was out of the room before she could answer him.

With a sigh, Tessa perched on a chair and watched grim upheavals in Bosnia, a report on whale fishing, a congressional committee. She remembered that on her return to Cambridge, there would be a manuscript on the history of the South Slavs waiting for her, perhaps another on nineteenth-century vice squads. On her return to Cambridge.

She got up restlessly and surveyed the room, walked through an arch into a pristine kitchen, its cabinets and breakfast counter a highly polished black. Wondering about the Jake who only occasionally stopped off here, she pushed open a door and found herself in a bedroom which contained a vast unsheeted bed. She closed the door quickly. Well, Jake must be big. That at least was certain. She returned to the study and watched the television some more, then glanced at her watch.

Ted had been gone far longer than it would take to get to the tavern down the road. Perhaps he had had to go further afield.

With sudden decision, she dug into her bag, tore a sheet from a small pad and brought out a pen. She scribbled a hasty note. 'Goodbyes are a struggle, don't you think? It's been good. Thanks. For everything.'

She left the sheet on top of the desk and hastened to the door. The locks were stiff and new and she fumbled and prodded. Turned and twisted. The fact crept up on her and struck with sudden foreboding. She was locked in. Ted had locked her in. She looked at the door in disbelief, pounded at it. But the sturdy wood made no sound as her fist struck. A chill went through her. Why would he lock her in? Why?

Panic clawed at her. She wasn't part of this story. It wasn't her story. She looked round for a telephone. There it was. On the desk. She clutched for her guide book, scrambled through it, found an emergency number, tried to remember the address of the house, remembered instead the name of the bar. Legenda. She picked up the phone. Nothing. There was no signal. She clicked at the catch in disbelief.

Tessa stilled herself. There was no reason to be afraid. Of course not. Of course the phone hadn't yet been connected. And Ted would be back soon. She perched on the edge of a chair. Watched the pictures flickering on the screen. Mountains. Rugged. Ice-capped. Children singing. Coca Cola.

Nice Ted. Bringing a bottle of champagne. To celebrate their last night. Kind Ted. Who had transported her in whirlwind fashion through sights and sounds and sensations. She tried to focus on their first days together. The pleasure of him. The pleasure of his attention. After all those arid years. Grateful to Ted.

But the images wouldn't gel. Tessa clasped her hands together and forced them into calm. There were too many other things, jarring notes. When had they come? Back then, way back, at the pharmaceuticals fair in Paris. Yes. And then here in Prague. The bad temper. Over who she was. And the fax, that message. What had she read?

She tried to remember and as she did so Ted's voice, back there, in the taxi, insinuated itself on her, seducing, cajoling, no. Menacing. The grip of his arm. Taut, brutal. Poised to crush. Why? Something Stephen had. She must alert Stephen. Why hadn't she approached him before? What did it matter whom he was with? Stephen, whom she trusted, despite everything. Stephen, who would never do any harm. Stephen, whom she loved, despite of, with, all his secrets. Yes.

Tessa leapt up, paced, looked out of the window. It was dark out there. No lights opposite, the windows as blank as concrete. Only scaffolding. And snow.

A captive in a gilded cage. That's what she was. Kidnapped. Abducted. The irony of it didn't make her laugh. She turned her back on the window, switched off the television, listened to the quiet and then hastily switched it on again. In the kitchen she found a glass. The water from the tap spluttered yellow. She let it run, moistened dry lips.

She couldn't just wait here. She looked at her watch. An hour. Maybe an hour and a half. Not even a book to hand. Sit and wait. Waiting. She hated waiting. Like waiting for a period to come. Bad or good. Mostly bad. Waiting for her parents to come home to that ominously quiet house with its creaking floorboards when she had been left alone to tend to her sleeping younger brother. Waiting for the phone to ring when it never did when one waited. She hated waiting. The seconds on the clock moving with stubborn slowness.

No. She had to act. She had to warn Stephen. Abductions served a purpose. Entailed violence.

Tessa scraped the chair back on newly varnished wood. She pulled on her coat and walked to the front room, peered out of first one tall window, then the next, and the next. Still no lights opposite. If she saw a car, she could shout. She found a latch. The window moved slowly outwards on new hinges. A flurry of snowflakes blew towards her, fresh, light, free.

Suddenly it came to her. She knew exactly what to do. Deftly she tucked her trousers into the rim of her boots, strapped her bag across her chest and heaved herself onto the window ledge. She sat there a moment, her legs poised in the cold. Only a small leap and she would be out on the planks.

Averting her eyes, she leapt. The scaffolding shook slightly below and above and then was still. Everything was still.

Snow covered the further edges of the walkway, lay in irregular mounds here and there where the wind had blown it. It was sticky and soft and squelched underfoot with a slippery sound. Above her the sky was charcoal dark, but in the distance a sliver of a moon hinted at its presence beneath a lightening of cloud.

Tessa walked slowly, clinging to the intermittent metal poles for balance, forcing her eyes away from the road which yawned too far beneath her. There would be the window of another flat she could hoist herself into, a ladder where she could clamber down from one level to the next. Taking a deep breath, she turned the corner of the building. By the time Ted came back she would be far away.

Ted Knight retraced the evening's route and arrived on Katerinská rather more slowly than he had hoped. Taxis were few and far between. No matter. Time was on his side. All the chips in his pocket. But he had to play his cards well. No point giving out more than the situation merited. He rubbed the snow from his shoulders and straightened his coat.

A couple sat at the tiny bar at the far end of the hall and nursed tall glasses of beer. As he approached the woman positioned herself hastily to the side of the counter which doubled as reception. Her 'good evening' didn't bear even the glimmer of a smile.

He gave her a large one. 'Dr Stephen Caldwell, please.'

As she shook her head, her sleek bob moved from side to side. Her features were pointed. A little ratface. 'Not in.'

'Don't you think you should check?'

'I don't need to check,' she said crossly. 'I know.' For good measure she pointed towards a pigeon hole in which he could see the stubby end of a key ring. He looked at it hungrily.

'Maybe I could wait for him. I'm kinda tired. A bed would be nice.' He smiled his lazy smile. To no avail. She turned cold grey eyes on him.

'We have no free rooms. If you want to wait . . .' She gestured towards a grim little stool which would hardly take the brunt of his bottom.

'You couldn't just let me into his room. He wouldn't mind.'

'I have no instructions.'

No. No instructions. No instructions from the Party boss. He felt like giving her a good tidy slap, but a glance at the burly man at the edge of the bar put paid to the desire. No point.

'Did he say when he would be back?'

She shook the bob again.

'Okay. Why don't you tell him Ted Knight called.' He looked at his watch. 'Tell him I'll be back in an hour. Tell him it's important. He's to wait.'

She put a notepad on the counter, handed him a pen. 'Leave a message. That way, no mistakes.'

'Okay . . .' Ted drawled, scribbled a message.

Outside, the snow was still coming down. Never mind. He'd grab a taxi as soon as one showed its face. He trudged through the snow, his feet heavier and colder by the minute. Christ, he could use a drink. He would have had one there, if the place hadn't looked so godforsaken. As cheerful as the underbelly of a cemetery.

If only that fool of a woman had done her work before. She probably could have too. The sleek little rat might have bent for a wife, under a little pressure. But she didn't know what pressure was, that one. Wrong messenger. Now that bitch of an Ariane would have been up there slithering in his bed in two seconds flat and getting anything she asked for. Correction. Anything she wanted.

There was a shabby-looking bar at the corner. Why not? He stepped in, smelled sweet, muggy heat. He stamped his feet to chip the ice inside and out, and ordered a whisky. A double. Slung it down and set off again. The business had to be finished tonight. He would pack his bags in preparation. Ready for take-off.

Lady Luck was on his side. A taxi was crawling down the road. He hailed it and watched it skid to a halt. In ten minutes he was in front of the Pariz and the doorman in his trim duck-egg blue uniform waved him in with a flourish. Yes, money made a difference. A good difference, he thought as he adjusted his eyes to the light of crystal chandeliers. Jake must have made a killing on his last deal to buy himself that little hideaway.

Ted Knight strode across the lobby, had almost reached the desk, when he saw Caldwell coming towards him. His face was tight, devoid of any expression. His eyes scanned the area behind Ted, so that until he stopped in front of him, Ted wasn't altogether certain of his direction.

'Stephen.' Ted made sure the smile was firmly curled on his lips. There was no answering nicety.

'Where's my wife?'

The words were a growl and the man looked as if he was about to sock him. That wouldn't get him very far. Ted hardened himself in readiness. Nor would it do. Not here, in front of all these people. Not now. Not unless he had that damned computer with him. Which he didn't. Shame. Though it was a good thing he knew about Tess and wanted her back. That would save time, make things a whole lot easier.

'Your wife, of course. Tess.' Ted paused to ask reception for his key. 'We should discuss this in private, don't you think?' He dangled the key in front of Stephen, marched

379

towards the elevator. 'Actually, I'm glad you've come. I've been to your hotel, been looking for you.'

Stephen's face gave nothing away. 'Where's Tessa?' he repeated.

'We'll get to that in a moment.' He gestured round him, pointing out the people clustering into the elevator, urged Stephen into the group. They rode up in silence, but no sooner had Ted closed the door of his room softly behind them, than Stephen reiterated, 'Where have you taken her?'

'A drink, Stephen. We can talk more calmly over a drink.'

Stephen looked warily round the pristine hotel room, watched Ted bring out a bottle of whisky from a corner cabinet. Was it possible that Tessa had left? If only she had. He paced back towards the passage which led into the main room, quietly slid open a mirrored door. Her case. He took a deep, uneven breath.

'Oh, yes, she's still with me. In a manner of speaking,' Ted chuckled, as he handed him a glass. The man missed nothing.

'I want to see her.'

'Of course you do. In due course. All in due course.' Ted waved him towards a chair.

'Where have you taken her?'

'Don't worry. She's quite safe. I wouldn't like to see her come to any harm, but . . .'

Stephen flinched, read the veiled menace though it was nowhere in the man's face. He imitated his casual tone. 'Well, let's go, then.'

'Not so fast, Stephen. There's a little business we need to transact first. You do want Tessa back? Yes, I can see that. Well, I'm not surprised. She's a fine woman.'

'I hardly need your recommendation,' Stephen muttered. He fixed his gaze on his glass, stopped himself from bodily removing Ted's leer.

'No, no, of course not. But let's just get this straight.

You want Tessa. I imagine she wants to see you, too.' Ted dangled it, like a soft, feathery bait. 'But, well, you see, I have Tessa. And there's a little something I want in exchange.'

Stephen kept himself very still, tried to gauge exactly how dangerous Ted might be. If he needed to, would he resort to more than guile?

'Aren't you going to ask me what it is?'

'You're going to tell me, aren't you.'

Ted laughed. 'Yes, I guess I am.' He straightened the crease in his trousers. 'Let's just say I have this little hankering for that PC of yours. Too bad you haven't got it with you, or we could settle all this straight away.'

'My PC?' Stephen played dumb and thought quickly. If Ted wanted his PC, that meant Ariane hadn't handed the Chrombindin program over. Not all of it, in any case. How much did Ted have? Not enough. So Tessa was being used. He had somehow to make certain that she wasn't harmed either before or after Ted got what he wanted.

'But you have your own machine.' Stephen gestured towards the desk.

'Don't act the fool with me, Stephen. An exchange. Fair and square. A little black box in return for a loving . . . very loving wife, safe and sound. Not really much of a bargain on my side.'

Stephen leapt up, turned his back on the man. In a moment, he felt his shoulder in a steely grip.

'You're not planning to use the telephone, are you, Stephen? Because I've just thought of something to make the bargain a little fairer. No police. That goes without saying. And no publicity. No one has to know about this. It's quite common for two teams to be working in the same direction. A little scientific race. Commonplace. Happens all the time.'

With a surge of effort, Stephen shook off his arm. 'How do I know Tessa is safe?'

'You'll have to take my word for it. Would I hurt such a sweet woman?'

'And how do I know she's not in on this with you?' Stephen veered towards him.

'Stephen, really! Your own wife. You've gotta trust her.'

'But I don't trust you, do I? I need to see her first. Hear it from her own lips. See that she's safe. See that she's really with you and this isn't just a ploy. We don't need the masks any more, Ted. Just drop it. I know what you put Ariane up to.'

'Now, now. You really shouldn't talk about those two in the same breath.'

Stephen looked at him coldly. 'You're the expert.'

'Maybe I am,' Ted grinned. 'And I'm telling you. Tess wants to come back to you.' He gave Stephen an assessing glance, as if the choice were a mystery to him, then added, relishing his malice, 'If I let her, that is. Despite Ariane.'

'I need to hear that from her. Otherwise there's not much point in what you call the exchange, is there?'

'Guess not.' Ted scratched his ear. 'But, Stephen, you wouldn't want to see her hurt, would you?' he drawled. The threat was on the surface now, the face suddenly brutal. 'That would be too terrible. Too bad. Really too bad. You couldn't live with that.'

Stephen didn't want to look at that face. He studied his glass. 'My PC is locked up at Jan's Institute. Needless to say, I haven't got the key. You take me to Tessa and if everything is all right, I'll ring him and have him meet us there.'

'Oh, no. I don't want him in on this. No one is to know.'

'We'll just pick up the key, then. Tessa willing, she and I will walk off and you can let yourself in.'

'Okay. A deal. But no funny business.' Ted put out his hand and, unwillingly, Stephen took it, felt the grasp tighten painfully round his fingers. He couldn't shake it off, felt himself career forwards at the bigger man's savage tug. 'No funny business,' Ted repeated, a cruel twist to his lips. 'And you can phone now.' He released Stephen's hand, pointed him to the telephone.

Massaging his fingers, Stephen prayed that Jan might be at home. But the phone rang ten, twelve, fifteen times into the void. 'Not there,' Stephen mumbled.

'We'll just have to wait then. Poor Tess.'

'I'll try his wife's number. He might be there.'

'No funny business, remember.' Ted was standing right beside him.

Stephen dialled Jan's direct line at the Institute, tried to conjure up the appropriate sentences in Czech which would allow Jan to hand him the key at a little distance from the building. With a moment's relief, he heard the answering machine click on. He started to talk, hoped Ted could neither hear the beep at the other end nor understand his words.

He looked at his watch. 'In about an hour?' he asked Ted.

'Make it an hour and a half. This damned snow slows everything down.'

Stephen switched to English. 'Yes, Jan. I need to go up to the office. Can you lend me the key? In front of Hanka's. Yes, downstairs. In an hour and a half. No, no. I need some working time, alone.'

'Good.' Ted smiled at him. He was already throwing clothes into a case. 'And I'll disappear straight afterwards. If you have any second thoughts about pursuing me, you just ask your sweet wife why it may not be a good idea.'

Beneath the looming bulk of St Nicholas, a lumbering plough made a neat sluice through snow and turned slowly up an incline. The taxi followed its path and came to a halt against a freshly piled mound halfway up the street.

'Guess it's time to greet dear Tess and hear her sing your praises.' Ted broke the barbed silence.

Stephen was tempted to land a punch on his face, for the sheer delight of it. Soon. He jammed his fists in his pockets, followed Ted into the building. The buzzer that opened the front door from the inside was on the right, he memorized, the door that led to the staircase about ten paces to the left. At a run, they could be inside the vast expanse of the church in under four minutes. He knew it as well as he knew his lab, could get them through the door that led to the tower and block it in seconds. But the church might be closed. The bar he had seen down the road was probably a better bet. Ted wouldn't resort to any violence in public. That wasn't his style. His successes depended on stealth and secrecy. Yes.

Stephen stole a glance at him as they stood in the lift to gauge the truth of his intuitions. The smug smile had settled on Ted's face again, as if he had just ousted a competitor in some brilliantly devious transaction.

'I think she'll be glad to see us. All this has taken somewhat longer than I imagined.' Ted chuckled.

The chuckle brought beads of perspiration to Stephen's brow. He had a vision of Tessa tied to a chair, a gag stifling her breath. He bounded out of the lift door as soon as it stopped.

'No. She'll be fine. Dreaming about that gypsy child she wants to saddle you with. I wouldn't stand for it if I were you.'

Stephen stiffened at the tone of male complicity. 'But you're not me, are you. Luckily for me.'

'Take it easy, now.' Ted's voice as he unlocked the door with a parcel of keys was low. 'I don't only have my fists at my disposal. Though I'd prefer not to have to resort to anything harder.' He glanced meaningfully at his pocket.

So he was armed. Stephen had suspected as much. No matter. As long as Tessa was all right, they would find a way.

'Tess . . .' Ted's voice boomed through the brightly lit

apartment, with all the good cheer of a man coming home for dinner. 'Look who I've brought you.'

From a nether room, there was the sound of voices. So Tessa wasn't alone. Perhaps she didn't know anything of Ted's more nefarious doings. He had enough guile even for that. To whom did this luxurious flat belong?

A burst of music altered the train of Stephen's scurrying thoughts. A television.

'Tess,' Ted called again as he urged Stephen across the room, into a second. 'Tess.' His eyes bolted into corners. 'Now where has she got herself to?' He picked up the zapper and aimed it at the television with a violent gesture. 'Tess.' He was booming now, racing round the flat, opening doors, slamming them, illuminating darkened spaces.

'Maybe she went for a walk,' Stephen murmured. He felt a dawning relief.

'You crazy? No way she could unlock that door unless she's spent years in the pen. Stupid bitch.'

Ted was angry now, the smiling mask gone along with his self-control, expletives pouring from him as he pulled open closet doors, kitchen cupboards, banged them shut, darted back the way they had come. The gun suddenly emerged from his pocket. Stephen kept himself very still.

And then the noise stopped. Ted was looking towards a window, poised half-open against the night. It swayed slightly on its hinges. 'Well, I'll be damned.' With a single leap, he was up and over the ledge.

Stephen peered out at scaffolding and shadowy darkness. 'Tess. Tess, get yourself back here. Now.' Ted's voice ruptured the stillness of the night. Planks reverberated and clattered with the weight of his steps.

Stephen levered himself softly over the ledge. Tessa would be terrified if she was out there. She had no head for heights. Could he get to her first? He scoured the darkness. Ted had gone to the left, so he looked to the right, searching the shadows. The scaffolding seemed to come to an abrupt end further along the building. No, Ted's instincts were right.

He stilled his fears and, as quietly as he could, edged along the scaffolding, keeping close to the wall, away from the glimmer of streetlights four floors below. It would be better to be invisible, he schooled himself as he neared the corner.

A gust of wind took him by surprise, a skirmish of blown snow. He darted his head round. An eerie silence had replaced the sound of Ted's voice and rebounding planks.

With mounting alarm Stephen crept round the corner and along the building's side. Nothing. He looked for illuminated windows, but within there was only darkness. He hurried now, righted himself as he slipped, pressed on. The wind was heavy here, like that on the narrow ridge of a canyon banked by sheer black escarpment on either side. Only the snow gleamed with a frail light as it raced towards him. And the spire-studded sky was flushed with a faint pink.

As Stephen neared the second corner, the wind brought with it an eerie peal of high-pitched sound. It took him a split second to make out the two shadowy figures. A slight form being dragged from some recess in the wall, a fist flailing without reaching its target. A larger figure, in profile, pulling, slapping. He could hear the sound on the wind's wings, a soft thud, like a shot bird plummeting from the sky and hitting the ground.

Stephen raced, kept close to the wall, his head forward, body braced, like in those hateful school football games when he had averted his eyes from players and ball and simply dashed forward, his father's voice clear to him from the sidelines. 'Run, Stephen, barge, head it. Run.' Stephen ran, tensed for the collision of body or ball, felt it after an eternity, the butt of hard flesh, throwing him backwards, like in a dream.

'Heh?' Ted's voice was loud, shocked. There was a

scrabble of arms. A fist landed on his jaw with a crack and echoed through his head. The planks clattered. Tessa screamed. Stephen regained his balance, saw a flash of teeth, the sudden surprise in Ted's face, a flap of arms. Heard more screams. And then there was only the body falling, more a vision, a sense of emptiness, than a sight.

22

——— * ———

White curtains billowed and flapped against the window-sill, sending flitting shadows across the room. A pale globe of a lamp cast the ghostly shape of a head onto an unindented pillow. From the radio came the limpid sound of a single flute, high, crystalline, evoking forests after rain, the cavorting of antique creatures.

Huddled beneath a blanket, Tessa steadied her shaking hand round the glass and forced some more brandy down her throat. The shaking would have to stop soon, though it had been with her for so long now that it seemed to have taken permanent possession of her limbs. It wasn't only a question of cold, though that had started it. How long ago now? She glanced at her watch, held her wrist still so that she could read the time. Four, five hours. Clock time had become meaningless.

She replayed the skirmish and tumble of scenes, tried to steady them in her mind, but like her hands they shook and trembled and collided, refusing steadiness. She had perched in that boarded-up recess of a window, shielding herself from wind, learning the symmetry of roofs and spires and dense sky, denying thought, and growing colder and colder. Over and over, she told herself that if she stayed quiet until dawn, everything would be all right. The workmen would come with their ladders. People would fill the streets. What she couldn't do was go back into that flat and find herself at Ted's mercy.

The noise had come suddenly, startling stillness: her name distorted on the wind, funnelling round corners, like a hiss. There was a tramping and pounding of boards so that they quivered beneath her feet and threatened to give way. Announcing him. She crouched in her corner, held her breath. But he found her, hoisted her out, shouting, cursing, labelling her at his kindest, 'dumb bitch', slapping her, hitting her hard, so that she was no longer a frozen statue, a gargoyle poised on an eave, but someone who screamed, struggled, resisted.

If only she hadn't. Tessa swallowed more brandy, felt her throat burn, her stomach heave.

And then suddenly there had been that second form, glimpsed in the distance, lurching, then racing, butting. Startled, Ted had let go of her arm and she had kneed him, kneed him hard in the groin and he had staggered, swayed.

And then he was gone.

Tessa hid her head in her hands, felt the stupid wetness of her face.

Gone. There was another arm round her shoulders, shielding her, urging her forwards, step by step, lifting her onto the ledge, through the open window, settling her into the sofa in front of that nubile princess with her rosy-white robes, lifting the dead telephone, murmuring something to her, going through the door.

Stephen. She had chased after him. Not to be left alone there in that flat. Stephen, though she wasn't sure she recognized him, so certain, sure, decisive, his arm round her in that lift, out of that building, down the street. His hand pounding on the door of the bar, still lit from within. The raised voices, chatter. And then the sirens, police, an ambulance, Stephen insisting that she stay there, indoors, a hot mug in her hand.

But she couldn't stay. Had to face it. It. Whatever it was. Now. Not later in dream.

Jan had appeared from nowhere, his kind doctor's face

calming and that woman, Simone, her voice gravelly, assessing her, frowning, taking Tessa's coat, draping her fur round Tessa's shoulders, securing it round her neck, saying, 'yes, they would all go,' saying, 'terrible accident', putting her arm securely through Tessa's, nodding to Jan, walking with her slowly through the snow, back, back up the street.

The men were ahead, uniforms greeny brown and white, crowded in the hall. And Stephen, distant, a confident stranger who had happened to her rescue.

There was no way round, no way out to the yard, save through the barrage of a door. Or keys. Bells pushed, buzzers ringing, pounding. A stout grey-haired man, eyes pouchy from sleep, coming in through the front door, dressing gown over trousers under coat. Shouting. The babble of police. A ring of keys emerging from a pocket. A queue straggling through a door into the dark night of a yard broken by torches. Herself at the threshold, neither out nor in, when she was jostled out of the way. The ambulance men were coming through, the laden stretcher between them. No face. No Ted. Just a grey blanket smooth over a shape.

Tessa screamed. She didn't know she was screaming, but the sound reached her from somewhere else, filling the room with shrill sound. Eyes on her. Stephen's too, his face in front of her, his lips moving, making noises she couldn't altogether grasp, because of the ringing in her ears. Not at first. Except for the word 'dead'.

And then they were outside, Stephen manoeuvring her carefully amidst builder's rubble cloaked by snow, trampled now, crushed, still holding the blurred shape of a body, the fling of an arm. But already snow was filling the crevices, blotting out presence.

'He might have survived, but you see, here. He hit here.' He brought her hand to the hard, jagged edge of a stone slab. Then another and another. 'Jan reckons it was instantaneous.'

She was sobbing, though she couldn't feel the tears on her face. Just cold. 'Tessa, look.' Stephen dabbed at her cheeks, held her, but his voice was terse. 'It's awful, I know. But think of it this way.' He met her eyes once, then looked away. 'It could have been you.'

'Or you.' Her throat hurt as she said it.

He shrugged, pressed her shoulder. Then he was gone, Simone at her side instead, explaining that Stephen had to ride with the police. Jan as well. She would go with her. She had a taxi here. A nice man. She babbled, babbled in the cab too, Tessa half-listening. She moved from French to English as if she couldn't remember what Tessa spoke. Told her it was a shame. *Affreux*. But he was a cad. Edward Knight was a cad. Charming, *ça va sans dire*, she thrust Tessa a sidelong glance. But a cad. A blackmailer and a thief. Still, she felt responsible. Partly responsible.

'No. I am responsible,' Tessa interrupted her. 'I was struggling and I made him fall.'

Simone stared at her for a moment through the gloom. '*Ah, ma fille*. But he put you in the situation. Sometimes one has to hit out. Yes, sometimes it is necessary to hit out. It was an accident. *Affreux*. But you are not at fault.'

After a moment of silence, she started to talk again, something about the dreadful symmetry of things, about tragedy and farce, but Tessa couldn't focus on her words, didn't focus, not even when the taxi had stopped here, at this hotel where she had already come once this evening. Stephen's hotel.

Simone had rung and rung at the door, had reeled out an authoritative stream of language at the man who had opened it so that his expression changed from irritation to obedience. A key was handed over, a tray brought, tea and brandy, a plate of sandwiches, biscuits. And then Simone had filled the bath, water so hot it should have warmed her when she had been ordered into it.

But when she emerged, too aware of the other woman's

presence to soak, she was still trembling. Simone had pointed to the bed and at her refusal, had wrapped a blanket round her, sat her in the armchair, told her she was to stay put until Stephen arrived. She was off to the police station. She didn't altogether trust the men to see to things adequately. She had winked at Tessa then and planted a kiss on her cheek.

'Thank you,' Tessa had said. 'Thank you for being so kind.'

She had thought Simone would leave then, but the woman had hesitated. Her coat already on her shoulders, she had surveyed Tessa for a moment. 'You know, my dear,' she had said, 'your husband and I have been friends for a long time. Good friends, even before he met you. He is a little like a son to me. I have chosen him,' she laughed, 'because there is something very fine about him, even if . . . even if sometimes he prefers his invisibility to his successes. If he were French, he might even know how to handle women. As it is . . .' She had waved her fingers gracefully in a little trilling gesture. 'As it is, we must help him.'

Pausing, she had perched on the bed opposite Tessa. 'And something else. I have lived a long time, you know, and learned not very much. But one thing I have learned is that we spend our lives searching for ways of making good our incompleteness. Sometimes we are ruined by our insufficiencies. That is tragedy. Comedy comes when we learn to bear them. Even relish them.'

Her eyes had twinkled and she had laughed again and leapt up and told Tessa that, despite all that, she mustn't think too much. She should eat something instead, even if it tasted foul. It would warm her.

Tessa looked at the residual tremble of her hands and took another dutiful bite. The food did taste foul, like variations on sawdust which spilled between her fingers. She stared at the billowing curtains and shivered. But she needed the air. It helped her breathe.

Why should she have breath and not Ted? Even if she had wished him gone? Even if he had so frightened her that she saw her own death looming inches away at the brink of that scaffolding? And then Stephen had rushed to her rescue and Ted had released his grip and then ... An accident, Simone had said. A terrible accident.

If only she could obliterate these last hours. But she knew they would haunt her for the rest of her life.

And what of that life? What now? What would she and Stephen say to each other when he came back into the room?

There was the click of the knob now. Tessa stiffened on the armchair, lowered the huddle of the blanket. She must compose herself.

'Tessa. I'm sorry it took so long. I . . . Are you all right?'

He was staring at her from the arch of the entrance hall, his face haggard. As he moved slowly towards her, she nodded. Words wouldn't come. All she could murmur was, 'And Ted?'

Stephen froze in position. 'Of course. You must be mourning.' He ran his fingers through his hair, buttoned his coat again slowly, averted his eyes. 'Look, Tessa, I thought you'd want company. But if you'd rather be alone, I'll stay over at Jan's. I'll leave you the number. If you need anything, just ring.' He searched in his pocket for a pen, bent to the desk.

'Stephen.' Her voice was a croak. 'I didn't mean . . .' She rose on unsteady legs, touched his shoulder. 'I want you to stay. Please.'

He turned back to her. His eyes beneath the glasses glimmered yellow for a moment, then he moved round her, rubbed his chin where she could now see the blue of a welt, a bruise.

'I didn't like Ted much, Tessa. You must realize that. I had two rather major things against him. You know one of them. So though I hardly wanted him dead, I . . . my grief isn't as acute as it might be.'

She stood very still. 'You knew. About us?'

He shrugged. 'I could hardly help but know. Jan. Simone.'

She nodded.

He had taken off his glasses and moved to stand by the window, his coat still on, as if he was poised to go. 'I don't blame you, Tessa. It's not that. We were hardly . . .'

'And the second thing?' She cut him off.

'Oh, the second thing.' He hesitated.

She poured him a brandy, placed the glass in his hand. 'The second thing?'

He met her eyes for a flicker of a moment, then started to pace. 'The second thing was that Ted was committing the cardinal crime in the scientific world. No, not cheating or fudging results. But spying. Stealing. I'd come up with something pretty good.' He gestured into vagueness. 'Chrombindin. A protein that mops up certain cancer cells.'

'And?' Tessa urged him on.

'Well, he paid this woman, this friend of mine, to copy it for him.' He turned towards the window again.

'Ariane?'

'He told you?'

'Not quite like that.' A smile edged onto her face, rueful, musing. 'But he told me.'

'So you know?' He was staring at her now, looking at her as he had never quite looked at her before. 'I'm . . .'

Tessa put a finger to her lips.

They were standing at opposite ends of the room, their eyes locked. The silence between them was thick with the unspoken, swift currents of meaning unframed by words. A mutual fear of the rapids of spoken honesty. At last he plunged.

'You've become unpredictable, Tessa.'

'I could say the same.' She could feel him struggling, so she added, 'The question is, is it a good?'

She wasn't sure who took the first step, but suddenly his arms were around her and she was burrowing against his chest.

'I suppose it all depends what we make of it.' Stephen searched her face, touched her cheek, as if looking didn't tell him enough. It came to him that he was afraid he might lose the enigma she had become. 'Do you really want me to stay, Tessa?'

She nodded. 'I tried to find you. Before. Earlier today, yesterday, I mean. And tried before that.' She floundered. 'I came to Paris to try to find you. You were so grand up there on the platform. So distant. And then, well, everything happened so quickly.'

The stirring took him by surprise. He kissed her, her hair, her eyes, her mouth. He didn't remember the texture of her mouth, the conversation of the senses it elicited from him, the cool smoothness of her skin. Maybe he had never fathomed it.

With a passionate ferocity he didn't know he possessed, Stephen pulled her onto the bed, hunted down Ted's shadow, chased away his sperm, held her eyes so that they would both understand.

Tessa understood. She clutched at him with a dense knowledge of that other slipping away, that ultimate disappearance which made triviality of everyday plaints. She tasted skin and tears and tenderness, rediscovered the familiar in its unfamiliarity, kept mortality at bay.

Afterwards, they lay in a silence which had a little awe in it. It had been so long. He was pleased that she posed no questions and he stroked her hair gently, wondering if she had fallen asleep there on that nestling place she had found on his chest. But when some moments had passed, she looked up with her clear gaze. 'You've led me a consummate masquerade all these years, Stephen Caldwell. Admirable, really.'

He didn't mistake her irony. Yet she felt hospitable. Even to his secrets. Maybe, he thought, it was because he recognized she had her own. Somehow that fact didn't make him afraid.

He found himself telling her then, he didn't know quite why, about Sonya, all those years ago, before her. About her death. And in a rambling, jumbled way about those days of a more necessary secrecy. About Jan, and what he felt for him. The debt. About Chrombindin, which was in part an answer to it, but which Jan refused to have attributed to him. About Eva, too, who reminded him just a little of Sonya, and who wanted to visit them in England.

He stopped then, realizing it was a question which asked far more than it seemed. He sought out her eyes. They were sparkling, but he couldn't quite read them.

'A consummate masquerade,' she repeated. She snuggled against him, closed her eyes. 'The things we do for love,' she murmured.

They slept then, curled round each other, and for some reason he dreamt the shape of a double helix, shifting, multiple, its bases still enigmatic, an excitement of regions to be discovered.

When he opened his eyes, pale sunlight glinted through the mesh of curtains. She was standing, already fully dressed, at the small mirror and pulling her hat down over her hair. He watched her sleepily for a moment. In the mirror he could see a lazy half-smile on her lips. The smile roused him into wakefulness.

'Tessa!' He leapt up, forgetting his nakedness. 'You're not planning on going without me, are you?' His tongue tasted grit and ashes.

She looked at him with a look that made him flush. 'I don't know. I really don't know, Stephen.'

'I know.' He reached for his trousers. 'I'll be ready in a jiffy.'

She didn't move or speak as she watched him. Only when he had finished tucking his shirt into his trousers and turned back to her, did she begin.

'You see, Stephen,' she said softly, her tone as unemphatic as it was certain, 'I have this obsession. It hasn't done us any good. I know that now. It may even have wrecked things. But it needs to be spoken. Again. Afresh. I want a child, Stephen. I've even found one whom I will adopt, if things work out. A little girl.' She paused. 'I would prefer if it were with you.'

Her eyes moved away from him, wandered to her hands. She was lacing some invisible thread. 'But there's something else.' She touched her stomach lightly. 'There might be another. Ted's perhaps. Yours. Though given my record, all that's highly unlikely. Nonetheless, you should be aware. I couldn't guarantee the genes.'

She laughed oddly and he gripped her hand. His voice felt gruff. 'Tessa, I . . . That's not how . . .'

'No, wait, let me finish. You see, we've left everything so late. So very late. Years of asides. And I feel time running out on me.' She met his eyes again. 'I think you would make a good father, Stephen. But if that's not what you want, much as I care for you . . .' She shrugged, waved her arm, gently unfurled her hand from his.

He didn't abandon her gaze. He couldn't have, even if he had tried. And he found himself thinking not of cells dividing or the regulation of chromosomes or genetic hazards, but of the child playing in the puddle beneath the lab and Eva and Jan and Simone and his father, whose stern distance needed to be made good. And Tessa. This new, composed Tessa.

'I do, Tessa. I do.' He took off his glasses so her face grew mysterious and secret and kissed her so hard that they found themselves on the bed again. Her smile was radiant. He wondered he hadn't given both of them the present of it before.

But after a moment, she pushed him gently aside. 'Much as I want to, Stephen, I have to go to church.' She laughed that new enigmatic laugh.

'Church?'

'Yes.'

'But we're already married.'

'A different kind of rendezvous.'

She got up, smoothed her shirt, stretched out her hand to him. 'You can come with me, if you like. You see, there was this child who was handed to me in a church. A gift. Like magic. A little like your Chrombindin, really. I'll explain on the way.'

PART FOUR

23

———— * ————

Thick bands of white foam rose in the ship's wake, separating the murky grey of the waters. Above, the gulls hovered, their wings motionless, until with a shriek they swooped to savour an invisible morsel. Beyond the foam and the gulls, the world vanished into mist.

Stephen stood on the deck, enveloped in a dampness which was only part drizzle, his legs firmly planted against the boat's roll.

Last night they had dined with Simone in Paris. Simone, who had embraced Tessa as if she had always known her. And Tessa, who, in that stunning black sheath of a dress he had never seen, had been almost as grand as Simone and somehow provocative, so different from the woman he had left behind in England that he had wiped his glasses to take a better look.

Stephen laughed at his own foolishness. It had been a good evening. A pre-Christmas Christmas, Simone had called it. Simone, who was lighter and merrier than she had been for weeks. To celebrate this new child, this Amy, who would soon be in their midst. If not quite a Messiah, she had quipped, then at least ardently wanted. And she knew how ardently, for Tessa must have told her. The two women had become fast friends.

He had wished Jan could be with them. They had drunk a toast to him in his absence. Jan had said he would watch over the whole adoption procedure, make sure it went smoothly, hurry it along. Early in the new year, the lawyer whom Tessa had located through that droll go-between of hers had promised. Rachel. He had liked Rachel, had reflected, too, that Tessa had been so busy during her days in Prague that he wondered she had ever had time for Ted. But she had. He forced himself to acknowledge that. Didn't want to ponder the effects of it just yet, though as he had stood in front of the equivalent of the coroner at the inquest and heard the verdict of accidental death, it had come to him that there would be some kind of primal justice in his fathering a child of Ted's.

He had never been an absolutist about genes or believed in their wholesale determination of things. Oh, yes, a few physical characteristics, a few diseases, a general shape and propensity. But these were just letters in a vast and still-mysterious alphabet. The words formed, the language spoken, the meanings garnered were as unpredictable as life itself.

On Sunday, they had traipsed to Prague's outermost edge to visit Amy. With Jan, who had given the little girl a thorough examination. Stephen had held the child for a moment and marvelled at how so certain a presence could be contained in such lightness. Like magic, Tessa had said. He could feel it begin to creep over him. Watching Tessa gently embrace the child, he told himself he had been a fool for too long. He would make it up to her somehow.

Later that evening Jan had taken him aside and said, 'Stephen. I am glad you have brought your wife out of the closet at last.'

His smile had told Stephen he was fully aware of the ironies of his choice of words, and Stephen had laughed and looked at his feet and noted that Tessa had come at least halfway all on her own. The door had never been locked and bolted.

Jan had grown serious then and said, 'You remember,

Stephen, in the old days, before the Wall came down, we used to say in our countries that personal secrets were not bad things. We lived in a world where we were under continual observation, a surveillance aimed at killing off our autonomy, our sense of ourselves. Like laboratory rats with brain implants. And secrets – private dreams, doubts, thoughts – were a way of preserving our sense of identity, of distinguishing ourselves from others. Those same secrets shared nudged one into a sense of alliance.'

'Why are you telling me this now, Jan?' Stephen had asked, and Jan had shrugged.

'Maybe because now I am no longer so sure. Secrets can also leave gashes in the order of things, destroy as well as create bonds.' Jan's voice had hidden a tremor.

'You mean because of you and Hanka? Or Tessa and I?'

Jan had murmured something inaudible and out of his newly and only uncertainly grasped wisdom, Stephen had added, 'Accommodation is possible, Jan. We are no longer so very young or hot-headed.'

'Maybe.' Jan had grinned. 'Maybe I am only talking politics. You see, I am happy that in my country, whatever the occasional injustice, we have opened up the files on the past. It allows us to judge it and forget about it. To breathe more freely. In Poland, for example, where they have buried their files, the aura of secrets, of unnamed past crimes, still poisons public life.'

Last night at Simone's the conversation with Jan had come back to him. While they were sitting over coffee in the salon, Antoinette had traipsed in. With Cary. He had felt the blush creep over his neck as Simone made introductions. He hadn't dared to look at Tessa, but he had felt her stiffening slightly at his side.

Later, when they had returned to the flat where he had lain so briefly with the girl, he had wanted to say something, but Tessa had seemed so happy, so contained, that the moment passed. But he would do it, Stephen told himself.

In the distance, a second ferry ploughed through the waters, sailing the opposite course. Their twin. Stephen followed its progress, imagined himself on its deck such a short time ago. Funny how glad he had been to be leaving then. Leaving Tessa, too. Stealth in his steps. A childish excitement. And now? He straightened his shoulders, took a deep, moist lungful of breath. Now he felt somehow bigger. Expansive. As if an internal border had been crossed and, in the crossing, obliterated.

Tessa had come up beside him. Above the whiff of salt, he could smell the new scent as her hair whipped in the wind and brushed his face. She mouthed something at him, her words disappearing into the roar of engine and elements and she laughed, her look as daring as the arm she wound round him, fingers prying under the warmth of his jacket. The excitement of it still surprised him.

Stephen brought her into the shelter of his coat. They watched a young woman thrusting chunks of bread into the air, saw the gulls dive and wing upwards. The girl reminded him.

'Tessa.' He lowered his lips to her ear, forced himself into speech. 'There's one more thing. About Cary.'

Tessa raised her newly enigmatic face to him, assessed him for a moment. Slowly, she put a finger to his mouth.

'I know.' Her voice reached him with a lilt.

Could she know, he wondered and then stopped wondering, tasted instead the light and salty kiss she had planted on his lips.

What Tessa knew, as they turned to make their way towards the bow of the boat, was that her travels seemed to have made her unfamiliar, even to herself. An audacious stranger who was oddly attuned to this different, rather prepossessing Stephen. A stranger who felt not in the least reproachful. Who, on the contrary, felt only a delicious sense of wonder. She knew that she had in some way transgressed, that he had too. They had both gambled on uncertainty, and now, now there was a kind of mellowness about them as if they had crossed into a kinder, less hostile, place.

What was it Simone had said to her on that dreadful night? Comedy came when one could relish one's insufficiencies. Give up blame. Laugh at the creases and sags and lacks. Or Stephen's occasional myopia. Or his endless hours in the lab. Or his perennial shying away from speech.

And now the house would be full for Christmas. Not with Amy yet, but that was just as well. Stephen and she needed a little time to get to know each other. There was so much more of him than she had imagined to know. It tickled her. And they needed to prepare.

But Eva was flying over with Hanka. Tessa had insisted on that, had said privately to Jan that he should really come too. A surprise for Stephen. Maybe she should have invited that girl, Cary, as well. Tessa laughed, tasting her own naughtiness. A full house. But he wouldn't have liked that.

The things we do for love.

'Look.' Tessa pointed, winding her arm more tightly round Stephen.

The cliffs rose before them, a single ray of pale sunlight glimmering over their white expanse.

'We're home.'